THE DARK PRINCE'S PRIZE

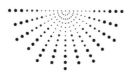

S.E. SMITH

MONTANA
PUBLISHING

ACKNOWLEDGMENTS

I would like to thank my husband Steve for believing in me and being proud enough of me to give me the courage to follow my dream. I would also like to give a special thank you to my sister and best friend, Linda, who not only encouraged me to write, but who also read the manuscript. Also to my other friends who believe in me: Julie, Jackie, Christel, Sally, Jolanda, Lisa, Laurelle, Debbie, and Narelle. The girls that keep me going!

And a special thanks to Paul Heitsch, David Brenin, Samantha Cook, Suzanne Elise Freeman, PJ Ochlan, Vincent Fallow, L. Sophie Helbig, and Hope Newhouse—the outstanding voices behind my audiobooks!

—S.E. Smith

Summary: A woman determined to break a family curse meets an alien
prince determined to capture her heart.

ISBN: 9781952021688 (paperback)
ISBN: 9781952021671 (eBook)

Romance (love, explicit sexual content) | Science Fiction (Aliens) |
Paranormal (Magic) | Contemporary | Royal | Fantasy

Published by Montana Publishing, LLC
& SE Smith of Florida Inc. www.sesmithfl.com

CONTENTS

SYNOPSIS

Royal Flush.... Prince Adalard Ha'darra's mission is simple—stay out of trouble while on Earth. His plans to enjoy his time with a few pleasurable distractions change when his transport is sabotaged, forcing him to land miles from Paul Grove's remote ranch. When a stranger stops to give him a lift to his destination, he sees the colors of her aura and is stunned to discover his mate!

Samara Lee-Stephens has lived with the Lee-Stephens curse her entire life. Determined to break it, she focuses on earning enough money to one day leave her family's reputation behind. She is furious when her stupid brothers drag her into their messed up lives—by losing her in a poker game! As if her life wasn't complicated enough, she soon finds herself fascinated by the Grove ranch's newest client who claims to be an alien prince!

Adalard and Samara discover that time may change them, but not their enemies. Can Adalard and Samara survive the challenges that threaten to tear them apart, or will their enemies succeed despite the precautions and sacrifices they've taken?

**If you love romance in the style of Nalini Singh, Christine Feehan, J.R. Ward, Ilona Andrews, Patricia Briggs, Dianne Duvall, Grace Goodwin, and Laurell K. Hamilton and you're a fan of out-of-this world space adventures like Starman, Star Trek, Star Wars, Stargate, and all the exciting SciFi Romance movies out there, be sure to read internationally acclaimed, NYT and USAT Bestselling Author S.E. Smith's book series! Adventure and hot romance all in one place! Over TWO MILLION books sold!

CAST OF CHARACTERS

The Curizan

Energy-wielding species. Their powers have been disguised as technology prowess. Most non-Curizans are unaware that the Curizans possess innate magical abilities.

The Ha'darra Family

There are many royal families, but the Ha'darras are the most powerful ruling house of the Curizans.

The oldest generation of the Ha'darra Family:

- **Hermon** – the first-born of the Ha'darra royal house. He is the father of Ben'qumain, whose lower-class mother was unsuitable for marriage. Instead, he married Narissa and fell in love with her. He believed that Ha'ven was his son by Narissa. King Hermon was killed by Ben'qumain in a staged hunting accident

- **Melek** – the second born of the Ha'darra royal house. He loved Narissa, but accepted his brother's marriage to her to strengthen their political ties. Melek is Ha'ven's sire. Out of respect for his brother's rule, he chose assignments that kept him away from the palace, and eventually commanded a unit in the Great War, where he served alongside Ha'ven.

- **Narissa** – conceived Ha'ven with Melek just before she married Hermon. Over time she became very fond of Hermon, but she always loved Melek.

The next generation of the Ha'darra Family:

- **Ha'ven mated to Emma Watson** – son of Narissa and Melek. Ha'ven believed that Hermon was his father until after Hermon died. Ha'ven forged friendships with the Valdier and Sarafin and was instrumental in ending the Great War. His mate is a human woman named Emma. Their daughter, Alice, was born with Curizan powers.

- **Ben'qumain** – born just days after Ha'ven. The newborn was sent to his father, Hermon, in an attempt to undermine the new alliance between Narissa's Royal house and that of Hermon. Narissa chose to raise the infant as her own. Ben'qumain was one of the rare Curizans royals born with limited powers.

- **Adalard** – born 6 years after Ha'ven. Son of Narissa and Hermon.

- **Jazar aka 'Arrow'** – Adalard's twin brother.

- **Aria** – Ha'darra cousin. She allied with Raffvin and Ben'qumain to orchestrate the Great War between the Curizan, Valdier, and the Sarafin, hoping to divide the strongest ruling houses long enough for someone new to rise to power. She was responsible for the capture and torture of Zoran and Ha'ven. She seduced Creon for information.

General Rimier Tiruss – Curizan General

Adur Jalar – Adalard's First Officer

First Lieutenant Terac Farma – Pilot and Navigation Officer aboard the *Rayon I*

First Medical Officer Jaron d'Camp – Healer aboard the *Rayon I*

Ensign First Class Quill Umbridge – Engineer Specialist

Kejon Dos – Curizan assassin and traitor

General Hamade Dos – Curizan traitor

Lesher Comoros – Hamade Dos's First Lieutenant

Empress – Curizan power behind the Great War who answers to the Supreme Power

Niria, Traya, and Doray – Adalard's Curizan lovers

The Valdier

Dragon-shifting species

The oldest generation of the ruling **Reykill Family:**

- **Raffvin** – first-born. Raffvin mutated his symbiot with negative energy and waged war on the Hive, the sacred cavern where symbiots are born and the Goddesses reside. He was defeated by Morian, her human mate Paul, the Dragon Lords, and the Goddesses. Raffvin was confined within a crystal, condemned to exist neither dead nor alive for eternity.

- **Jalo** – second oldest. First mate of Morian, the priestess of the Hive. Together, they had five sons. Jalo was killed by Raffvin.

The next generation of the Reykill Family:

- **Zoran mated to Abby Tanner** – first-born of Jalo and Morian. Currently King of the Valdier.
- **Mandra Reykill mated to Ariel Hamm**
- **Kelan Reykill mated to Trisha Grove**
- **Trelon Reykill mated to Cara Truman**
- **Creon mated to Carmen Walker** – Best friends with Ha'ven and Vox.

The Sarafin

Cat-shifting species

- **Vox d'Rojah mated to Riley St. Claire** – King of the Sarafin

- **Blaze** – Vox's brother and a spy embedded in the rebel group trying to overthrow the royal houses.

Humans

- **Samara Lee-Stephens mated to Adalard**
- **Rob Lee-Stephens** – 30; Samara's oldest brother
- **Wilson Lee-Stephens** – 27; left home years ago
- **Jerry Lee-Stephens** – 26; Samara's brother
- **Gary Lee-Stephens** – 24; Samara's brother
- **Brit Lee-Stephens** – 21; Samara's brother
- **Annalisa Hollins** – Detective for Casper Police Department
- **Mason Andrews** – Ranch Manager and friend of Paul Grove
- **Ann Marie Andrews** – Wife of Mason
- **Chad Morrison** – Attorney and friend of Paul Grove
- **Bear Running Wolf** – Assistant Ranch Foreman
- **Alberto Frank Armeni Campeau** – Wealthy businessman and gambler
- **Jack DeSimone** – Campeau's Head of Security

Goddesses/Gods

A highly advance species that has been around since the creation of the universe

Aikaterina – an ancient of her species and one of the most powerful

Arilla – younger than Aikaterina; created by her during in the early formation of the universe

Pallas – younger than Aikaterina; created by another ancient in the early formation of the universe

PROLOGUE

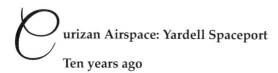

urizan Airspace: Yardell Spaceport

Ten years ago

"You made the wrong choice," Adalard Ha'darra said in a low voice as he shoved the reptilian man away from him.

The Bovdean assassin stumbled back and gripped the dagger protruding from his chest.

"The Ha'darra family's rule is over," the man asserted in a guttural voice. "The new order will be more powerful. So powerful that not even the Ha'darra family can… stop… us." The assassin's voice faded on his last breath.

Adalard dispassionately listened to the man's final words. "Unfortunately, you won't be around to see our supposed demise," he replied. The dark green man's eyes rolled back into his head and his body limply slid down the wall.

Adalard pulled his attention away from the assassin and half-heartedly scanned the dark corridor for the informant he had been following. He uttered a low curse when he confirmed that the spooked Tiliqua had run off.

He gingerly touched his throbbing left cheek and grimaced when his fingers came away wet with blood. The Bovdean had been aiming for Adalard's informant but ended up slicing Adalard's face.

He sent an impatient wave of healing energy to his wound, just enough to stop the bleeding, while he knelt and searched the assassin. As he had suspected, the man carried no identification.

Retrieving his dagger, he wiped the blade on the man's clothing, stood, and surveyed the alley. Yardell Spaceport was home to mostly criminals because it was on the outer rim of the Curizan-maintained shipping channels.

As long as Adalard was here, he wouldn't be able to lower his guard. It was likely that a few of the groups he had angered over the years were around here somewhere. They certainly wouldn't mind finishing what the Bovdean had started.

He turned and set off in the direction the Tiliqua had fled, then slowed when he saw his General, along with two additional warriors from the *Rayon I*, enter the alley. His rueful smile pulled at the deep cut on his cheek. He twirled his dagger and slid it into the sheath at his waist.

"Prince Adalard," General Tiruss greeted.

"Did you find the other two rebels?" Adalard responded.

Rimier Tiruss shook his head. "Not yet. They escaped through the underground maintenance tunnels," he replied. "Do you need a medic?"

Adalard raised an eyebrow. "No. I need the other two assassins. This one died too quickly," he said with an annoyed glance over his shoulder at the dead man.

"We'll locate them. I've ordered a search of all ships before they depart. Any who try to leave without permission will be boarded—or blown out of space," Tiruss replied.

"Good. I want to know who is working with my half-brother. I will meet you back on the ship later. I need to find the informant," he said.

"Be careful. I'm almost certain I saw a wanted poster with your image on it in one of the shops," Tiruss jested.

Adalard raised an eyebrow. "Only one? I must be losing my touch," he replied with a sardonic smirk.

Several hours later, Adalard sat outside one of the station's many drinking establishments. He moodily took a sip of his drink. He knew Ben'qumain, his half-brother, was behind the attempts to assassinate the rest of his family. The attacks began when Ben'qumain murdered their father.

Ben'qumain was hungry for power, but he was stupid and weak. Adalard grimaced in disgust when he thought of their cousin Aria. Under Ben'qumain's orders, the bitch had captured his older brother, Ha'ven, and tortured him. Adalard was still worried about the lasting effects of Ha'ven's time on Hell, the asteroid mine where he had been imprisoned.

The faint beep of an incoming communication broke through his dark musings. He placed his drink on the table and tapped the communicator near his ear. The server hurried toward him. Adalard shook his head and covered his drink with his hand. He didn't want to be distracted while being served. Poison was not as easy to heal as the wound to his face.

"Adalard," he announced.

"Did you find anything?" Ha'ven asked.

"Not yet, although a Bovdean assassin added to my good looks. The Tiliqua who might have had information is dead. Tiruss is searching for the two men who were seen with the assassin," Adalard replied.

He touched the faint line of his new scar. The appreciative glances from some of the women walking by amused him. He might keep the scar as a memento.

"Zoran Reykill has disappeared," Ha'ven abruptly announced.

Adalard stilled—The King of the Valdier missing. *"Tilkmos,"* he cursed, softly muttering the Curizan word for damn. "Do they have any leads?"

"Not yet. Keep searching," Ha'ven growled. "Once these bastards go to ground, it will be difficult to get them to surface."

"Keep me informed," he said.

"I will. Oh, and you might want to check in with Arrow. He was attacked," Ha'ven added.

"How bad?" Adalard urgently asked.

"He said he was in better shape than the assassin who attacked him," Ha'ven responded with pride and amusement.

"I'll contact him," Adalard replied before disconnecting the link.

He detached the vidcom from his belt and cradled it between his hands as he rested his elbows on the small, circular table. Worry for his twin caused his brow to furrow. Arrow had the heart of a warrior, but he was better suited for a lab than out in the field.

"Open communications to Arrow Ha'darra, secure line 183," he requested in a terse tone.

He studied the crowd passing by as he waited for the link to connect. It was impossible to miss the speculative looks sent his way by some of the transient residents. He lowered his hand to the personal defense shield at his waist and switched it on. It was a prototype designed by Arrow to absorb laser blasts and give a nasty shock to anyone who came too close.

"I'm fine, Adalard," Arrow growled in greeting.

"You don't sound it," he replied, picking up on the strained tone in his twin's voice. "What happened?"

"Do you want me to start with the ambush or the explosion that followed? *Dragon's balls!* That hurts! Aren't you supposed to numb the area first? I could do surgery on myself with less pain," Arrow snapped at the unseen healer.

Adalard frowned. "Ha'ven didn't tell me what your injuries were, he only said the assassin who attacked you was in worse shape."

Arrow's low groan filtered through the communicator. "Yeah, well, being dead *is* worse, though at the moment I'm tempted to think otherwise. I'll be fine once this savage who calls himself a healer finishes torturing me," he retorted.

"Who is with you?" Adalard demanded.

"First Medical Officer Jaron d'Camp, sir," the healer replied.

"How bad is my brother?" Adalard demanded.

Arrow's curse-filled orders telling Jaron not to say anything came through the communicator. Adalard listened with a mixture of amusement and concern until the vidcom Arrow had forgotten in his tirade slipped far enough for him to see the scorched material covering Arrow's right side and leg.

"I'm fine. Once Jaron is finished with me, I'll send you a report—not that I found out very much," Arrow finally replied.

"*Tilkmos,* Arrow! You should have stayed in the lab. You look like you've been roasted by a dragon," he growled with a shake of his head. "Jaron, make sure you take good care of my brother," he ordered.

"I will, sir. But, to do that, he needs to cooperate," Jaron said with a stern expression.

Arrow lifted the vidcom to block out Jaron and scowled at Adalard. "I hate healers. I'll send my report in a few hours. This wound might take longer to heal," he ruefully admitted.

"Take your time. I have a feeling I will be here for a while," Adalard said before disconnecting the communication.

He sat back in his chair, lifted his drink, and swallowed the remaining contents. Who would be brazen enough to capture the King of the Valdier and attack the Ha'darra family at the same time? Ben'qumain might attempt one, but both? It wouldn't be entirely out of character for his half-brother, but he would need a massive amount of help— which meant the network of traitors was much larger, more organized, and better funded than Adalard and his brothers had originally thought.

Not to mention that successfully capturing Zoran was no small feat. The dragon-shifters were dangerous. Adalard should know; having fought against them in the Great War.

He moodily thought about the war that had ravaged Heron Prime for over a century. The Curizan, Valdier, and Sarafin warriors were some of the most lethal beings in the universe thanks to the unique abilities given to each of their three species by the Goddess Aikaterina. They would still be at war if not for Vox d'Rojah, King of the Sarafin, and Creon Reykill, Prince of the Valdier, becoming trapped together as they tried to kill each other. Eventually, they discovered that the war had been started and perpetuated by a traitorous alliance determined to eliminate the ruling Houses on all three worlds.

In the end, a strong friendship developed between Vox, Creon, and Ha'ven that became unbreakable. Since then, Adalard and his brothers had been working tirelessly to uncover everyone involved in this subversion and bring peace back to their peoples. With Zoran Reykill's disappearance, the fires of war were sure to be fanned again.

"I hope to Goddess that it doesn't," Adalard murmured to himself. "I really hate fighting those armored, dragon-shifting bastards." He sighed, placing his empty glass on the table. He turned off his shield and motioned to the server for a refill.

～

Hamade Dos stood in the shadows, watching the Ha'darra Prince. His eyes glittered with rage, and he tightened his grasp on the grip of his blaster. The Curizan had easily eliminated the Bovdean assassin. It was the fool's own fault for underestimating the skills of a Curizan prince.

"Do you want me to draw him out?" Lesher Comoros asked in a hushed voice from behind him.

"No. The Curizan already will have ordered each vessel searched. It is best for us to wait," he instructed.

"But why?" Lesher protested with a disgruntled frown. "He is right there! A single blast between his eyes would be one step closer to ending the Ha'darra family. Ben'qumain—" His voice faded when he saw the chilling gleam in his superior's eyes.

"Ben'qumain is an idiot who will get himself killed. If you want to sacrifice yourself for the cause, that is fine, but not when it will compromise *my* escape—besides, he is shielded somehow, probably with a device his twin created. I cautioned Ben'qumain that his half-brothers would not fall easily. He should have let me deal with the three of them years ago," Hamade said.

"What about the d'Rojahs? Can they be blamed if you kill Ha'darra?" Lesher suggested, referring to the Sarafin Royals.

Irritation coursed through him. "Ha'ven Ha'darra and Vox d'Rojah have formed too close a bond to fall for that ruse again. I have someone on the inside who will deal with the d'Rojahs. Now that the royal families have united, a different approach must be taken," Hamade replied.

Lesher frowned and stared at Adalard Ha'darra with a grim expression. Hamade ignored his lieutenant and stepped into the stream of merchants and shoppers. Lesher followed a minute later.

It wasn't that Hamade didn't trust Lesher with his plans; he didn't trust anyone. His allegiance was to a higher power than that of the jealous Curizan or the power-hungry Valdier. It was time for a new power to rule the star systems. One created by a God.

No matter how long it takes, he vowed before he entered a shop to avoid the Curizan General and a group of Curizan warriors walking in his direction.

CHAPTER ONE

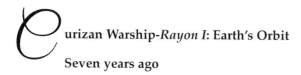

urizan Warship-*Rayon I*: Earth's Orbit

Seven years ago

The lift arrived at the shuttle bay, the doors opened, and Adalard almost walked into Ha'ven. Restless energy filled the entire ship and it was feeding into Adalard's power. He urgently needed to release some of it.

Every unmated warrior was looking forward to meeting a few beautiful females on the planet below. Adalard had impressed on all of them, however, that they must be very discreet. Nothing caused trouble like fraternizing with the locals who weren't aware aliens existed. Adalard had seen firsthand the disaster that could ensue. Given Ha'ven's expression, he must have been thinking the same thing.

"Where are you going?" Ha'ven demanded.

Adalard grinned at his older brother and adjusted the bag he was carrying.

"Exploring. Are you and Emma ready to leave?" he replied, trying to sidestep around Ha'ven.

His brother didn't let him pass. If anything, the scowl on Ha'ven's face deepened. It looked like he wasn't going to escape as quickly as he had hoped.

"Exploring? What kind of exploring? Where? How long will you be gone?" Ha'ven absentmindedly demanded.

Adalard raised an eyebrow. "Yes, exploring—down on the planet, and if I have to tell you what *kind* of exploring, you've been mated too long. You don't have to worry. I'll be back long before the ship is scheduled to depart," he replied.

Ha'ven opened his mouth to protest, but instead, he sighed and gave Adalard a wry grin. "Of course. Still, I *am* worrying. Trouble always seems to find you, brother, no matter where we go. The closer we get to the planet, the more I wonder if this is a mistake. I keep telling myself that everything will be fine."

"It *will* be fine," Adalard reassured.

Ha'ven grimaced. "I know—I'm just distracted. I'm worried about Emma. If you insist on going to the planet, will you do me a favor? Trisha asked me to meet with Mason Andrews and Chad Morrison on Paul's ranch to make sure everything is alright. If *you* can do that, it will save me some time. Be sure to tell them that Paul and the women are safe and happy."

"Yes, I can check in with them. Is there anything else?" he dryly inquired.

"No. There is only one mission for this trip as far as I'm concerned, and it isn't for you or anyone else on this ship to break some poor human's heart," Ha'ven warned.

Adalard shook his head in wry amusement. "My men need a break, Ha'ven. They have been in space too long. Give them credit for knowing how to behave."

Ha'ven scowled. "It isn't your crew I'm worried about. Need I remind you of the barrage of messages the ship's communications officer received in the past month alone from your many avid admirers wanting to know when you'll return?"

"What can I say? I'm good in bed," he declared.

Adalard chuckled at the uncomfortable expression on his brother's face until Ha'ven suddenly paused and turned, his face lighting up as his blonde, petite mate walked toward them. It still amazed Adalard how far his brother had fallen—and how thankful he was that Ha'ven had found Emma. She had literally saved Ha'ven's life—more than once.

Adalard smiled at her. She gave him a shy smile in return, her gaze hesitantly sliding over the long scar on his cheek.

"I hope you have a pleasant trip, Emma," he said when she came to a stop next to his brother.

He fought to hide a smile when he saw Ha'ven fondly wrap his arm around Emma's waist. Ha'ven sent Adalard a grateful nod. Emma and Ha'ven were intending to pick up her mother from the nursing home where she lived. He had to hand it to his brother for embracing the role of a family man. Personally, he would rather face a dozen assassins than deal with a mate, or worse—younglings. A shudder of distaste ran through him. He would leave the breeding to Ha'ven, the Valdier, and poor Vox. Besides, it wasn't essential that he produce a Ha'darra heir with Ha'ven around.

"Thank you. Are you going somewhere?" she politely inquired.

He readjusted the bag on his shoulder and shrugged. "I thought I would explore a little of your planet. You never know when the information will come in handy," he said with a grin.

"Oh. I'm afraid I can't give you any recommendations. My parents didn't travel much when I was young and I... the only time—" Her voice faltered.

"Adalard can find his way around," Ha'ven quickly interjected. "He is going to Paul's ranch. A human there can help him."

Adalard nodded. "Part of the fun is getting lost. Who knows? I might find a female who will offer to be my guide," he teased with a wink.

Emma's eyes widened and she blushed. "Yes, well… uh… good luck," she stuttered.

"Shut up. You're embarrassing her," Ha'ven groused.

With an affectionate smile, Adalard gave her a slight bow. "My apologies, Emma. I'd better take my leave before your mate challenges me," he teased.

Emma giggled. "I've seen his bruises after he returns from the training room with you. Have fun and be careful," she said with a grin.

"Always on the first, never on the second," he replied with a wave of his hand.

He grinned as he walked away. It would feel good to get off the ship for a bit. He studied the shuttle bay. The *Rayon I* wasn't a large ship. His twin brother, Arrow, had designed the warship for speed, maneuverability, and stealth.

"Commander Ha'darra," a warrior called, hurrying toward him.

Adalard bit back an annoyed groan. "What is it, Quill?" he impatiently asked.

"I wanted to let you know I found a bad module on your shuttle—and this," Quill responded, holding out a small silver cylinder.

Adalard narrowed his eyes on the tracking device. "Where did you find it?" he demanded.

"Inside the outer burner casing. Whoever installed it did a poor job. When the module burned, it shorted out the tracking device. The logs show that the module burned out on your return trip from Kardosa Spaceport last month," Quill replied.

Adalard rolled the device in his hand before he held it out to Quill. "Keep this between us. Review the vidcom logs and run a scan to find the manufacturer of the device. I want to know who put it on my shuttle," he instructed.

Quill bowed his head. "Yes, sir," he replied.

"And Quill—run a scan on the *Rayon I*," he added.

Quill smiled. "I've already started one, sir. If there are any other devices, I'll find them," he promised.

Adalard nodded. Quill reminded him a lot of Arrow. His younger brother by a few minutes loved his toys. So did he, the difference was his toys were usually of the soft, alive, and sexy variety while Arrow's tended to be mechanical, hard, cold, and deadly.

"I wouldn't be surprised if Arrow hasn't invented a new PVC with as much time as he spends in his laboratory," he chuckled.

The thought of the Valdier's Personal Virtual Companion software, or PVC as they called it, made him laugh. He confessed, thinking of his immense pleasure in viewing Trelon Reykill's PVC after Trelon's human mate, Cara, used it to test a new communication booster she was working on. Half the known galaxy had the privilege of enjoying it as well after Cara sent it out to test her newest invention-in-progress.

"Perhaps I should reclassify human women as extremely dangerous," he mused before dismissing the idea.

The women were crazy, annoying, and cute but not really dangerous— except for Trisha, Carmen, and Riley. Hell, even Abby Tanner-Reykill had torched his traitorous half-brother, Ben'qumain, and most human women didn't come much gentler than Abby! Then there was Emma— sweet, delicate Emma. He paused on the platform leading into his personal shuttle and shook his head.

"Who am I kidding? They are all as dangerous as hell," he chuckled. He couldn't wait to meet more of them.

CHAPTER TWO

utside Casper, Wyoming

"Samara! Samara! Where in the hell are you?"

Rob's loud, angry voice shattered the peaceful morning. The screen door slammed, punctuating his foul mood. A moment later, Samara heard heavy footsteps on the wooden porch.

She grimaced when Rob yelled for her again. Pursing her lips, she tightened the last bolt on the new alternator she had just installed. Closing the hood of the old Ford truck, she grabbed a stained towel from the bench and exited the mechanic's garage.

The truck was the only thing of value Pa left her when he died three years ago. Everything else—the house, the auto repair shop on the same lot, along with their contents, and the ten acres of land surrounding them had gone to her brothers. Well, all of them except for Wilson.

Wilson didn't get a damn thing but his freedom. He had disappeared one afternoon four years ago after a fight with their father. Personally, she thought he got the best deal of the entire family. They hadn't heard from him since. Samara didn't blame Wilson for wanting to escape the hellhole they called home.

As for her, she focused all of her energy on saving every penny she made working at Paul Grove's ranch. She started working there when she was sixteen, after she got her driver's license. Fortunately, she didn't live too far from the ranch—twelve miles as the crow flies, but longer on the winding roads of Casper Mountain. Paul's ranch covered thousands of acres.

Samara's thoughts grudgingly returned to her home. It was only a matter of time before her remaining four brothers lost this repair shop. None of them had ever held a job for more than a few months before they quit or were fired. They wouldn't even consider working on any kind of engine. They couldn't be bothered to change the oil in their own cars, and they weren't about to do it for someone else's vehicle.

Her Pa, Samuel Lee-Stephens, had inherited the house and the old auto repair shop just outside of town from his dad. Pa had been a hard worker, but his luck was lousy. Every time he had come close to paying it off, he would have to borrow against it again. The last time was to pay for her mom's medical bills.

Pa was too stubborn to sell the family's roots here. He was born and raised in Casper and said he would die here. The sad part was he died not long after making that statement.

Her brothers hadn't sold the property because as long as they made the minimum payment each month, they had a place to hide all the illegal shit they were doing. That was another reason Samara wanted to get out—before the Feds and local law enforcement descended and discovered what true lowlifes most of the Lee-Stephens' men were.

She wiped her dirty hands on the stained rag and walked across the yard. She pursed her lips when she saw Rob's disheveled appearance.

His light brown hair was sticking up, his plaid shirt was hanging open to reveal the beer belly he no longer bothered to hide, and the button on his jeans was undone.

I don't know why I made Mama that promise, she thought as a wave of disgust filled her.

For the hundredth time, she wished her dad had been more like Paul Grove. Maybe then she could really do something with her life. As it was, her biggest fear was ending up like her Ma—pregnant, married to the wrong man, and almost grateful when the doctor told her she had brain cancer.

Even the *thought* of being stuck with a man like her dad made her want to swear off men forever. Some women were destined to make bad choices when it came to men. Her Ma had and so had her grandma. Angelina Lee-Stephens said it was the curse of the women in their family.

Once again, she felt envious of Trisha Grove. Trisha had an awesome dad in the good, attentive, and loving Paul Grove. Samara's father had been so mean that the only ones to show up for his funeral other than herself was Paul Grove—out of respect for her—and the attorney hired by Pa to redo his will after Wilson left. A week after he changed his will, Samuel Lee-Stephens died while working on an old tractor he was hoping to sell.

Her brothers did what they had always done—they played poker, got drunk, and ended up in jail. She had been half-tempted to leave them then and there, but she had promised her Ma that she would watch over them for as long as she could. It didn't matter that they were all older than she was. It looked like that promise was about to come back and bite her in the ass again.

"What do you want?" she called out before Rob opened his mouth to yell again.

Her brother's dark brown eyes still had a slight glaze to them. He also had a whopper of a black eye and a busted lip. She wiggled her nose with distaste when he reached into his pants and scratched his crotch.

"You got any money? Jerry and Brit need bail," he said.

She shook her head. "Nope. My truck needed parts," she answered.

Rob's eyes narrowed at her obvious lie. "If they don't show up at work in an hour, they'll be fired. Where's the title?" he asked.

Anger built inside her. "You aren't pawning my truck to bail them out. I need it. If they don't show up for work, that's not my problem," she retorted.

Rob pulled his hand out of his pants and stepped to the edge of the porch. He had that mean gleam in his eyes that always made her wary. He had never hit her, but he had come close a few times—as evidenced by the holes in the walls throughout the house.

"Without their pay, we can't make the mortgage payment. If we miss the payment, you'll be living in that piece of shit on four wheels," he snapped.

"What happened to Gary? Why don't you ask him if he's got any money?" she demanded.

"He lost it—plus some last night. He was on a winning streak and some two-bit asshole played him like a fiddle," Rob replied.

She shook her head and waved the dirty rag at him. "I'm done with the lot of you. If you guys lose this place, that's not my problem anymore. Mr. Andrews said I could move into the apartment in the barn over at Paul Grove's Ranch," she lied.

"You promised Ma, Samara!" Rob yelled before he cursed. "Damn it, either you bail them out or...."

"Or what, Rob? You and the others have sold everything of value. The little bit of furniture that's left won't get you twenty-five dollars. You've got nothing left and you're sure as hell not getting my truck," she snapped.

Rob looked her up and down. A shiver of unease swept through her when he shoved his hands in his pockets and looked over her head.

She warily waited for him to drop whatever bombshell he thought would force her to help him.

"I told you that Gary lost his paycheck plus some," he said, looking at her again.

She shifted agitatedly from one foot to the other. "Yeah, so," she replied.

"The *plus some* was an IOU," he said.

"So? What's that got to do with me? What'd he promise this time? His first born? The kid would probably be better off," she retorted with a shrug.

Rob shook his head. "Nope—you," he answered.

Samara staggered back and shook her head. There was no way Rob could have just said what he did. Gary—her own brother—wouldn't *sell* her to cover a poker debt.

"You're lying," she finally responded through gritted teeth.

Rob shook his head again. "Nope. If Jerry and Brit work, and we sell your truck, we can pay back part of the debt this month and more each month until it's paid off," he said.

"How much? How much did Gary lose this time?" she demanded, clenching her fists.

For once, Rob had the decency to look ashamed. He bowed his head and scratched the bottom of his bare foot on the edge of the porch. She silently hoped he would get a splinter.

"Ten grand," he mumbled.

She blinked, wishing she had misheard him. "Ten thousand dollars? Gary lost ten thousand dollars in a poker game?" Her head felt light, and she was worried that she might faint. That frightened her more than dealing with the situation. If she fainted, who knew what her freaking brothers might do to her? She shook her head to clear it. "Gary doesn't make that much in six months! Hell, the lot of you combined barely bring that home! How could he be so stupid? Why the hell did you guys *let* him do something that stupid?" she demanded in a faint voice.

Rob angrily waved his hand at her. "I told you, Gary was on a winning streak. Hell, he had already won more than that when the city slicker started buying drinks for everyone. What was he supposed to do, walk away?"

"Uh, yeah," she retorted with a contemptuous glare.

Rob pursed his lips. "None of that matters now. We've got to get our hands on as much cash as possible. There's a guy down at the distribution center who will pay top dollar for your truck. I know you've been stashing the money you've been making. I can ask Teresa for a loan. She'll give me a hundred or two," he said.

"Teresa won't give you shit. You burned your bridges with her a long time ago. The only thing she wants from you is sex, and I know that can't be worth two hundred bucks. Where is Gary? Why isn't he taking care of the mess he made?" she snapped.

Rob glared at her as if all of this was her fault. "He's in no shape to help at the moment. When he couldn't pay up, that's when the fight broke out. How do you think I ended up with a black eye and a busted lip and Jerry and Brit in jail? Turns out the guy Gary owes money to is pretty powerful in Vegas. If we don't pay up, it'll be more than this place and your truck, Samara. It's our lives—and I mean *all* of us," he stated.

Tears of anger and frustration blurred her vision before she blinked them away. She turned her back to Rob and slowly counted to twenty. Ten thousand dollars was more than she had. She had been saving every penny since she was ten years old, hiding it away in the garage where no one could find it. Despite the years of doing anything and everything she could to earn an extra dollar, including the four years of working part-time at the Grove Ranch, she didn't have that kind of cash.

"I won't sell my truck," she said, not looking at him. "Once this is over

—I'm done with you and the others. Wilson was right to get out of here. I don't care if I have to live in the fucking woods, do you understand me?" She turned and faced him again. "I'm through trying to save your asses when you don't give a shit about anyone but yourselves. If you want to waste your life, that's your business. Keep me out of it."

Rob smiled. "How much do you have?" he asked.

Samara stared back at Rob. He was very lucky she wasn't holding the shotgun she kept under her bed for protection. The smug look on his face made her sick to her stomach.

"Twenty-five hundred," she lied. "You, Jerry, and Brit can cough up the rest. You might want to start by selling that fancy new truck you've been hiding over in Teresa's garage."

A savage satisfaction swept through her when Rob's smile turned into a scowl. She walked back to the garage. In minutes, she was holding the box containing every penny to her name. Glancing at her watch, she realized she would have to call Mason and tell him she would be a little late.

Samara would go to town and bail out her brothers. If Gary was lying low, he would be at Pat's place above Teresa's garage. She would never know what Teresa and her sister, Pat, saw in her brothers. She would give the money to help pay Gary's gambling debt to Pat. There was no way in hell she would ever give it to her brothers. They would just gamble or drink it away.

"This is it, Ma. I know I promised you, but I'm never going to let Rob and the others use me again. I've got to make a change, and the only way I can do that is to end the cycle of bad decisions. I'm not carrying the Lee-Stephens baggage anymore," she vowed, resting her hand on the old, rusted metal money box that once belonged to their mom.

She stashed the metal box under the driver's seat of her truck and climbed in. By the time she pulled away, Rob had disappeared back into the clapboard house that desperately needed a coat of paint. The old truck bounced when she hit a pothole in the dirt driveway. She stopped the truck, looked both ways before turning right onto the highway, and headed to town.

CHAPTER THREE

*T*wenty minutes later, Samara pulled into a parking space next to the Hall of Justice. She breathed a sigh of relief and sent a silent prayer of thanks to the cloudless sky when she spotted Annalisa Hollins walking along the sidewalk. She had fixed Annalisa's brakes last week, and the woman told her if she ever needed anything, to let her know.

"Hey, Annalisa," Samara called.

Annalisa turned, smiled, and shook her head in sympathy. Samara's shoulders drooped at the other woman's expression, and she grimaced. She *hated* having to ask for favors or owing anyone anything.

"I noticed that your brothers were spending the night again," Annalisa stated.

"Yeah. Rob just told me. Is there any way you can help me get them out? They've got to be at work in an hour, and I'm already late," she asked with a hopeful expression.

Annalisa nodded. "Yes, but they'll still need to post bail," she said.

Samara held up the box she was carrying. "I figured that," she said with a sigh.

"I just saw Carl Biggie go in. He might give you a discount since he is already here and he'll get two for the price of one," Annalisa said.

Hope blossomed again. "Carl? Cool! I rebuilt the universal joints on his daughter's car a couple of weeks ago. He did say he'd give me a discount the next time one of my brothers was arrested," she replied with a grin.

"Well, today might be your lucky day," Annalisa laughed.

Samara couldn't help rolling her eyes. "That's about as likely as me meeting an alien or discovering that Bigfoot lives outside of town. At this point, I'd almost welcome something like that if it meant getting away from my dumbass brothers," she grudgingly confessed.

Annalisa laughed again. "You know what they say about not being able to pick your family," she said.

"Yeah, but you'd think hoarding all the bad ones in one family should be against the natural order of evolution. I'm totally into spreading the love," Samara dryly retorted.

"Well, let's see if we can get you in and out, so at least you can get them to work," Annalisa replied, opening the door for her.

Forty minutes later, she was back on the road. This time she had Jerry and Brit with her. Jerry was dozing with his mouth open and his head against the door while Brit sat in the middle. Brit, at twenty-one, was two years older than she was.

"Thank you for bailing us out, Samara," Brit mumbled.

"Don't get used to it. I'm not always going to be here to save your ass," she snapped.

"I'll see if I can pull a double to pay you back," he replied.

She turned into the parking lot of the garage, making sure that she hit the pothole near the edge of the road. Jerry was wrenched awake, and he cursed when his head hit the passenger side window with a resounding thud. She hit the brakes a little harder than she should have, sending both men forward into the dash with a satisfying thump.

"You're a real bitch sometimes, Samara," Jerry grumbled.

"Thank you. Now get the hell out of my truck," she retorted with a saccharin smile.

"Thanks again," Brit mumbled as he slid out of the passenger door.

She didn't bother answering. The moment they were clear, she pressed the accelerator. Looking both ways, she turned left onto the highway.

"I am so going to ask Mason about that apartment today," she vowed.

Adalard flexed his hand when he noticed the usual colors of his aura swirling with an ominous dark red. He forced his mind and body to relax. The last thing he wanted to do was take out half of the power grid on this side of the planet.

Instead of thinking about the tracking device and who might have installed it, he surveyed the landscape below. Lush forests, winding streams, and snow-capped mountains greeted him. He could see signs of habitation from the local species, but they appeared to be separated from each other.

If he followed the road, it should lead him to Paul Grove's place. He glanced at the computer readings. Arrow's cloaking device was still shielding his transport's presence from Earth's military and civilian population.

Spikes of red energy surged through him again, causing the transport to shimmer. A warning light flashed on the console. There was something in the transport draining his powers. If he didn't find a place to land soon, he wouldn't be able to.

"Caution, shield instability detected. Shields at twenty percent. Cloaking device instability detected," the computer reported in a calm, male voice.

"*Tilkmos,*" Adalard cursed.

He scanned the detailed holographic map of the terrain. Up ahead, near a river, there was a clearing that was barely large enough for the transport, but it would have to do. It was at the bottom of a ravine and wouldn't be easily accessible, which made it even better. If his readings were correct, he was on Paul Grove's property.

He focused on trying to regulate the energy flowing from him to the transport. By the time he dipped below the treetops, sweat had covered his brow from the effort of keeping the surge that was running through him from shorting out the craft's entire electrical system.

He was livid by the time he landed. An unexpected feeling of weakness coursed through his body, and he frowned at his trembling hands as he shut down the transport.

What the hell just happened? he wondered, clenching his hand into a fist.

Adalard flexed his fingers and made the decision that until he knew what was going on, he wouldn't use the transport. He would take a portable unit and contact the *Rayon I* from Paul's ranch. An irritated sigh slipped from him.

"There goes my relaxation time," he muttered.

He released the straps on his seat and stood. In minutes, he had a bag packed and was striding down the platform. He cursed when he realized that the transport was visible. Without power, the cloaking device wouldn't work.

"Back to the old-fashioned way," he sighed.

He lifted his hand and focused on the surrounding energy. In seconds, a large reflective screen appeared above the transport. He closed his fingers into a fist and the screen floated down, covering the transport. By the time he finished, he was breathing heavily from exhaustion.

He studied his creation while he waited for his body to quit shaking. From the air, his transport would be virtually invisible. On the ground, it was another story.

This must be the work of a saboteur. This person was likely affiliated with Kejon, the Curizan assassin who had targeted Ha'ven and kidnapped Emma several months back. Adalard and his brothers believed Kejon was part of a larger, deadlier group. He thanked the Goddesses that the bastard was dead now, but there were still others out there that remained in the shadows. He couldn't stop until every one of them was captured or killed, preferably the latter.

Looking around, Adalard found it difficult to believe that with so much untapped power in the air, Emma's species didn't know how to harness it. Emma swore that humans couldn't control the surrounding energy, but he knew *she* could. The power Emma interwove with his brother's was a remarkable sight.

He shook his head in disbelief at the thought and refocused on getting out of the ravine and up to the road. He moved the pack on his shoulder to his back and carefully surveyed the area. There didn't appear to be any evidence of human activity.

He looked up and exhaled. Normally he would use his Curizan powers to get out of the ravine. Unfortunately, whatever had happened in his transport left him unwilling to risk it.

"It looks like it will be the old-fashioned way again," he sighed with a shake of his head.

He estimated that it was about eight hundred feet to the top of the ravine. He felt lightheaded already.

He broke the climb into three parts, stopping to breathe through the weakness that made his limbs feel like a pile of gelatinous mush, but it slowly faded the farther away he was from his ship. The rugged cliff face provided plenty of hand and footholds that allowed him to pace himself. Even so, the climb to the top left him exhausted.

"Son of a two-headed Tiliqua," he groaned as he pulled himself over the edge and rolled onto his back.

He stared up at the heavy gray clouds. All thoughts of having a relaxing, fun time looked about as promising as the darkening sky. He muttered another curse, rolled to his feet, and wiped his hands together. Standing there wasn't going to get him to Paul Grove's ranch.

Half an hour later, he emerged from the woods along the roadside. He rolled his shoulders, easing their stiffness. The hike through the woods took longer than he had expected. He paused and looked back and forth. He wished he had brought a hoverboard.

"I'm getting really tired of doing things the old-fashioned way," he sighed as he turned and began walking along the white line at the edge of the road as cold wind pushed against him and the first fluffy dusting of snowflakes began to fall.

Samara glanced at the clock on her phone and muttered under her breath. She *hated* being late. A quick call to Mason before she lost signal helped ease a little of the tension she was feeling. Still, it burned that her family issues had interfered with her job. It reminded her too much of her brothers and they were the last people she wanted to be compared to.

She frowned when she saw someone walking along the edge of the road. They were in the middle of nowhere. It was six miles from town and another six miles to Casper Mountain.

She slowed and crossed the double yellow line as she passed the man. He didn't look like a hiker. His long hair ruled out his being one of Mr. G's military guys that came for training.

"He looks more like a biker who lost his bike," she said with a shake of her head as she thought of the number of city folk who didn't understand Wyoming weather.

Fat snowflakes struck the windshield. She glanced in the mirror again.

The guy wasn't dressed for cold weather. Up at this elevation and especially this time of year, there was always the chance of a sudden snowstorm.

She silently cursed her tender heart. "He better not be a serial killer," she growled as she pulled off the road and waited for him to catch up.

She kept her eyes glued to the rearview mirror and impatiently drummed her fingers on the steering wheel. A moment of self-doubt filled her when she got a closer look at him, and she bit her bottom lip in indecision. She had to force her foot to stay on the brake pedal even though her sense of survival was screaming for her to go.

It would be rude to give the guy hope of a ride then take off like a jackrabbit with a coyote on its tail, she silently admonished.

Yeah, but at least the jackrabbit is smart enough to run, you idiot!

"Shit!" she cursed, pressing the power button to the passenger side window when he reached the back of her truck. "Hey, do you need a ride?"

He walked up to the door. Her finger twitched on the window control. She should have rolled the window down halfway, not all the way. He peered through the open window.

She stared in amazement at the man's unusual violet eyes and the long scar on his cheek. He had the same darker skin tone and silky black hair as some indigenous people who lived nearby, but that was where the resemblance ended. This guy screamed biker, serial killer, movie star, body builder, and a half-dozen other names that streamed through her mind like prairie dogs popping up to see what was going on.

She scowled when he stared back at her as if she were the one with two heads, and she shivered, unsure if it was from the intense look in his violet eyes or the blast of frigid air pouring in through the open window.

"Listen, you're letting all the heat out. Do you need a ride, and if so, where? I'm late for work, and I don't have time for you to decide if you want to freeze your ass off or hitch a ride," she snapped, again regretting her impulse to stop and pick him up.

"Paul Grove," he said.

She blinked at him in surprise before she shook her head and laughed. "Well, isn't it your lucky day. That is exactly where I'm heading. You must be one of his survival guys. That explains everything. Get in," she said, pushing the unlock button.

She pursed her lips when he remained frozen for a moment, but then he nodded. He stepped back and scrutinized the door for a second before he pulled it open. She reached over and cranked the fan to high while he shrugged out of his backpack. He tossed it onto the seat before he slid in and closed the door. She quickly raised the window.

"Seat belt," she automatically instructed before she glanced in the rearview mirror to make sure the road was clear.

He looked around before he reached for the seat belt and pulled it on. She merged onto the highway and sped up. Glancing at him out of her peripheral vision, she noticed he was sitting like he had a rod up his ass. His facial features looked like they had been sculpted from granite. The only thing moving were his fingers as he flexed them and that little vein at his temple. She reached out and adjusted the vent to blow some hot air on him.

"So, what are you?" she casually asked.

"I'm an alien from another world," he said.

She blinked, her mind going blank, before she began to laugh. The sound started low, but the more she thought of his response, the funnier she found it as her conversation earlier with Annalisa came back to her. He shifted in his seat and frowned at her. His expression was priceless and made her snort.

"Oh, man, that was good," she said, wiping at the corner of her eye with her jacket sleeve.

"You find my answer entertaining?" he asked.

She glanced at him and nodded. "Yeah. I was expecting Marine or Navy Seal, or maybe even FBI or CIA with the long hair and jacket outfit, but alien is good. I can go with that," she chuckled. "So, Mr. Alien, do you come with a name and a title?"

He frowned at her. "Prince Adalard Ha'darra of the Curizan," he announced.

She looked at him with amusement. It was hard not to laugh again. His face was so serious, like he honestly thought he was a prince.

Not just a prince—an alien prince from a place called Curizan, she thought, unable to keep from snickering again.

"Well, I guess even a princely rock star needs to know how to survive in the wilderness—especially if his bike breaks down in the middle of an August snowstorm," she replied with a grin.

"Rock star?" he repeated.

She turned on the blinker and grinned at him again. "Yeah, 'cause no soldier in his right mind would be seen wearing that much black leather in the woods. I give you half a day before Mr. G tags you, but only because he'll give you a good head start. It would be even less if Trisha was the one tracking you—" she predicted, "unless she wanted to play with you," she added with a commiserating smile.

"Who are you?" he asked.

She fought a smile. "Samara Lee-Stephens—human, no royal blood," she teased before she nodded her head toward the windshield. "We're here, Mr. Prince Adalard of Curizan."

CHAPTER FOUR

A Few Minutes Ago:

Adalard was lost in thought, wondering what could have caused that drain to his powers, when a white transport passed him on the road. He was a little wary when it pulled over onto the shoulder a short distance ahead of him, but a blast of cold air and the falling snow eliminated his hesitation.

He was bound to meet a human, and this would give him time to test his human language skills. It was hard to tell through the back window if the person was male or female. The human was wearing a heavy brown coat and a dark green cap, and continued to face forward so he couldn't see their face.

An uneasy sensation built inside him the closer he got to the transport. His first thought was that perhaps the enemy tracking his shuttle had followed him to the planet, but he quickly dismissed the idea. He knew the device must have shorted out shortly after he departed Razzine.

He slowed when he noticed the colors of the person's aura flaring inside the cab. Varying shades of blue swirled with such clarity and vividness that he swore he could touch the strands. By the time he reached the back of the vehicle, the waves of color poured out of the open window, eagerly reaching for him.

He couldn't have resisted looking inside if his life depended on it. Never had he seen or experienced the draw of another's aura the way he did now. The bands swirled around him, tightening like steel cables until he was forced to the vehicle's door. It was then that he knew he was in dangerous and completely unknown territory. He found himself staring at his mate, and it scared the hell out of him.

"Hey, this is where you wanted to come, isn't it? You said Paul Grove's place. This is it," she inquired with a raised eyebrow.

Adalard blinked and nodded. He fumbled for the door of the transport, uncharacteristically clumsy. He cursed when he realized he had forgotten to undo his seatbelt. She shook her head, laughed, and reached over to press the release.

"At the rate you're going, you may not make it out of the yard before you're caught," she said with a cheeky grin.

By Ceran-Pax's orbs, this female makes me feel like a teen, he reflected with distaste.

He grabbed his bag and slid out of the transport, slamming the door harder than he meant to in his irritation. The metal bent under the force, leaving a dent the size of his hand. Mouthing a silent curse, he focused a shaft of energy and repaired the damage. He frowned when a wave of fatigue hit him.

"Are you okay?" she asked with concern.

"Yes," he replied in a terse tone. "I am to see a hu—a man called Mason Andrews or Chad Morrison," he replied.

"Follow me," she said with a nod of her head in the direction of a structure.

He fell into step with her as they crossed the wide yard. She had retrieved another hat from the transport. This one had a wide brim around it and protected her head from the falling snow. She pushed her hands into the pockets of her thick coat, then paused a few feet from the steps leading up to a long porch and gripped his arm, gently forcing him to face her.

"Listen, I hope you aren't doing any drugs. No one here will tolerate it, plus it will just get you killed if you go out into the wilderness stoned out of your mind," she said.

"I have no need for drugs," he replied laconically.

She gave him a look that said she didn't believe him before she released his arm and shoved her hand back into her pocket. He was about to argue his point when the back door opened and a man stepped out. Samara greeted the man with a warm smile.

"Hi, Mason. I picked up one of Mr. G's guys walking along the high- way." She grinned over her shoulder at him before she looked back at Mason. "May I introduce Prince Adalard Ha'darra from the planet Curizan. He's an alien," she said with a wink.

She climbed the steps and passed Mason, disappearing inside the house. Adalard shrugged when Mason glared at him. He climbed the steps, pausing with a raised eyebrow when Mason put his hand out.

"Are you really one of them?" Mason asked as he looked up at the sky and gave a short jerk of his head.

"What do you think? By the way, my planet is Ceran-Pax. My *species* is called Curizan," Adalard clarified with a slight grin.

Mason dropped his arm to his side and shook his head. "I wish you guys would give us some notice before you show up. It sounds like Samara didn't believe you. Keep it that way," Mason instructed.

Adalard's eyes glowed with suppressed power at the stern warning. He was not used to being told what to do. He stepped inside the warm house and looked around. They entered through the rear of the house into a large kitchen area.

He immediately focused on Samara. She was chatting with a woman next to a large stove. Her aura filled the large area and wrapped around him. The woman's eyes widened when she noticed him. She looked at the man beside him with a concerned expression. Mason briefly bowed his head in acknowledgment before looking at Samara.

"Well, I'd better get to work. I can make up the extra time today—and Mason, if possible, I'd like to talk to you in private before I leave," Samara said.

"That'll be fine. I'll be here all day. I have paperwork I need to work on. Keep an eye on the weather. It looks like we might have more snow later this afternoon," Mason commented.

Samara nodded. "I heard the forecast on the radio. You have to love Wyoming. It's either hot or it's snowing. I'll bring the horses into the upper barn and make sure they are taken care of," she said. She held up a steaming cup between her hands and smiled at Ann Marie. "Thanks for the coffee. I missed my cup this morning."

"Are you sure you don't want some breakfast? It will only take a couple of minutes to make you something," Ann Marie replied.

Samara shook her head. "No, I'm good," she said, and nodded to Mason before she exited through the door they had just entered.

Adalard jerked when the door closed behind her. The snap of her aura away from his made him think of a rope stretched too taut before breaking. He was—bereft at the loss of her power. The emotion was so strong that he took a step to follow her, stopping only when Mason put his arm out to block him.

"I think we need to have a talk," Mason stated.

Samara paused at the bottom of the steps and took several deep breaths of the icy air. The snow flurries had stopped, but from the look of the heavy, gray clouds, it was only a matter of time before it began to fall again. What was crazy was that it had been almost eighty degrees a few days ago.

A shiver ran through her body. She balanced the coffee in the crook of her arm and pulled her heavy, insulated leather gloves out of her coat pocket, slipping them on. She took a sip of her coffee, her thoughts on the good-looking man, and began walking toward the barn.

The guy's accent ruled him out as a local. She wondered if he was Hispanic. She spoke a little Spanish thanks to taking four years of it in high school and working with the ranch hands who came by the garage, but that didn't feel right either. He seemed more European— not that she had much experience with people from overseas.

"He's got an aristocratic air about him," she mused.

She unlatched the barn door with one hand and pulled it open. As she stepped into the brightly lit interior, she sighed with appreciation for the neatly parked row of UTV vehicles in a range of models. Her favorite was the Can-Am Defender Max. The thing had more bells and whistles on it than her old truck.

"Oh, yes, you sweet driving machine, I'm here," she said with a grin.

One thing about Paul Grove—the man ran a class act when it came to equipment. The compact UTV had heated seats, a hardtop, and could go practically anywhere on the ranch. She walked over to the vehicle, opened the door, and placed her coffee in the cup holder.

Minutes later, she was pulling away from the Ranch Manager's house where Mason and Ann Marie lived. She would pass the main home-stead a little farther up the road, and close by was a state-of-the-art barn and paddocks. Besides offering survival training for military, survivalists, and rich people, the Grove ranch also raised and sold prime cattle and horses.

Her job was the care and training of the horses used by the ranch hands. Fortunately, her love for horses as a child had led to her taking the Future Farmers of America courses at school and volunteering at local stables, giving her the background she needed to qualify for the position. Even then, Red, the previous supervisor for the horses, had spent six months training her.

A good horse, trained to work as the rider's partner, could make the difference between a good or bad day when out in the country. It was a shame she couldn't train her brothers to understand that. Just the idea made her snort.

"I bet Mr. Rock Star Prince wouldn't understand the importance of being a team player. He probably thinks the world revolves around him—or the universe in this case," she scoffed.

She tightened her grip on the steering wheel as she considered the 'alien' prince. She shook her head in wry amusement at the image. Some guys never grew up.

"What kind of guy his age claims to be an alien? I know! He is probably some rich, trust-fund baby who still lives at home and is looking for a good time. He should have started out by buying a more dependable vehicle," she chuckled and ended it on a sigh. "He's just another loser like your brothers, Samara, with a capital L. Let him play his games and leave. It isn't like you'll see him again—or that he was even interested. Hell, he barely said two words. He probably decided that you're some backwoods, uneducated chick—which you are. He would be a love-'em and leave-'em kind of guy," she cautioned.

Properly self-admonished for thinking about the sexy alien prince wannabe, she focused on the road in front of her. Horses were her passion. She was good at training them. A good trainer could make a decent living. That was going to be her way out of here, not on a spaceship.

CHAPTER FIVE

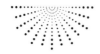

*A*dalard gripped the strap of his bag and followed Mason down a narrow hallway to a room with a large window, polished dark wood floors, and bright white walls with a high ceiling. Paintings depicting different mountain landscapes hung in strategic places, adding color to the room. There was a large fireplace with several logs in place, ready to be lit.

"I guess the first thing I should do is properly introduce myself. I'm Mason Andrews, Paul's ranch manager. The woman in the kitchen is my wife, Ann Marie. You've already met Samara. Ann Marie knows about you and others like you. Samara doesn't, and we'd like to keep it that way despite the fact that you already appear to have broken that rule. Speaking of rules, I need to go over a few of them with you, Mr. Ha'darra," Mason said, speaking as he motioned to a comfortable chair in front of the fireplace.

"Prince Ha'darra or Adalard," he corrected.

Mason paused in the motion of picking up a rectangular remote from the narrow table between the chairs. Mason clicked a button and the fireplace flared to life before he sat down.

Adalard studied Mason. He was about the same age as Paul. His hair was gray with streaks of brown, and his brown eyes were serious.

"I think it might be best to call you Adalard. Calling you a Prince or your Royal Majesty might create more questions to answer. The key is to keep a low profile. Ann Marie and I have two teenage daughters, Marie and Vicki. I'll ask that you stay away from them and Samara," Mason began.

"No," he replied, sitting back.

Mason frowned. "This isn't open for discussion. My daughters have no idea that aliens exist, and they aren't going to," he said.

Adalard waved his hand. "Your daughters are safe. I am no threat to your children. It is your request that I stay away from Samara that I cannot agree to," he replied.

A knock at the door prevented Mason from answering right away. Mason rose to his feet when Ann Marie came in with a tray. She gave him a nervous smile before she placed the tray on a side table.

"I thought you might like some refreshments while Mason goes over the rules with you," she stated, giving her husband a pointed look.

"I've told him to stay away from the girls," Mason said.

"Good," Ann Marie replied with a relieved smile.

Clearly the man didn't want his wife to know that he had only agreed in part. That was good because as far as Adalard was concerned, the subject was closed. There was no way he could stay away from his mate—even if he wanted to. The moment she left, the restless pull of his energy searched for hers, and it was only going to get worse.

Ann Marie handed him a cup of hot liquid.

"Thank you," he said with a bow of his head.

She handed another cup to her husband and placed a plate of freshly baked pastries on the table between them. Adalard sipped the hot beverage and recognized it as some kind of tea. He scanned the room, giving the couple privacy when Ann Marie kissed her mate before exiting the room, and closing the door behind her.

Mason sat down in the chair across from him and sighed. "I hope you don't mind tea. Ann Marie is worried I've been drinking too much coffee lately and has cut back on my caffeine. The pastries help make it manageable," he said.

Adalard tapped his fingers on the arm of the chair. "I did not come to your planet for tea and pastries," he dryly replied.

Mason sighed and sat back in his chair. "Why did you come?" he asked.

"My brother and his mate have come to retrieve her mother. Trisha asked that one of us check in with you and tell you she, Paul, and the other women who were taken off your world are happy," he replied.

"That is good to know. It would have been nice to see Paul again. I take it he has settled in to living among dragon-shifters and golden creatures. By the way, that's another rule—no shifting. Dragons aren't indigenous here on Earth," Mason said.

Adalard shook his head. "I am a Curizan. We do not shift into dragons," he answered.

Mason stared at him in silence for a minute before he spoke. "If you are different from Trisha's guy, then what do you change into?"

Adalard debated on whether to share the differences between the Curizan and the Valdier with the human. Mason moved in his seat as he waited for Adalard to respond. The man's aura was strong. Adalard did not detect any hostility or darkness surrounding Mason. He did detect pain, though.

"What have you learned about us?" he asked.

Mason chuckled. "In other words, you don't want to divulge any information until you know what we know."

Adalard bowed his head in acknowledgement. "Yes."

Mason silently studied him. "How do I know you are one of the good aliens? You can't blame me for having some reservations. You mentioned Paul and Trisha, but I need something a little more substantial to go on," he said.

"The fact that you aren't dead should speak for itself. I could kill you before you draw the laser pistol your mate handed you when she kissed you."

Adalard ignored Mason's surprised expression and continued. "Paul has found his mate with Morian Reykill, Priestess to the golden symbiots that are the dragon-shifters' constant companions. The Curizan need no such companions. We have our own… talents," he said, holding up the laser pistol he had taken from Mason.

"What the hell!" Mason cursed.

Adalard tried to keep his amusement contained when Mason lurched in his seat and slid his hand behind his back. The laser pistol Ann Marie had tucked into the man's pants was gone.

"The Curizan have no interest in taking over your world, human," he wryly said, rising to his feet and holding the pistol out to Mason.

"Then why are you refusing to stay away from Samara?" Mason demanded, taking the pistol and holding it between his palms.

"That is no concern of yours," he replied. "What other questions do you wish answered?"

Mason frowned. "Why did you need a lift? I mean, couldn't you have just beamed down or whatever you guys do?" he asked.

Adalard walked over to the window. His eyes followed a smaller, boxier version of the vehicle Samara had picked him up in as it traveled along a road leading away from the house. He focused on the blue wisps trailing behind the vehicle.

"Yes, I could have beamed down, but it has its limitations. My transport is secure for the moment. I landed a few miles from this location.

Samara came along and offered me a ride. I could hardly refuse," he said with a smile in his voice.

"Trelon and Paul came up with this list of rules. They said it was only a matter of time before more of you guys showed up. That's why Paul set up the ranch in a trust the way he did," Mason said.

Adalard turned and looked at Mason with a raised eyebrow. "Did they also tell you that Curizan warriors don't like to follow the rules?" he inquired.

Mason chuckled and pulled out his reading glasses. "Actually, I believe Trelon said we'd be lucky if any of you guys followed directions. Paul insisted that they at least be given to everyone so that when he kicks their butts, they can't say they didn't know it was coming," he replied, scrolling through the notes on his phone. "Okay, rule number one: No fraternizing with any of the women on the ranch. Rule number two: No killing anybody," Mason read out loud.

Adalard shrugged, turned toward the window again and looked back at the road where Samara had disappeared. He dismissed all the rules Mason was listing. He suspected that most had already been broken if Trelon was involved in the creation of the list.

"I will need lodgings," he announced.

"I'll set you up at the homestead. How many of you can we expect?" Mason asked.

"One, just myself," he replied.

"I'll get my coat," Mason said.

Adalard absently nodded. "I'll meet you outside."

"Is everything alright?" Ann Marie asked with concern.

Mason shrugged and caressed her cheek. "This one is different from the last—but I think so. Why don't you and the girls go stay in town with your sister for a bit?" he suggested.

"Mason Caldwell Andrews, what aren't you telling me?" she demanded, placing her hands on her hips.

Mason gazed into her eyes before he wrapped his arms around her and tightly held her. She relaxed against him and hugged him back. He rubbed his chin along her temple.

"He's an alien. I want to make sure you and the girls are safe until I know for sure that he is harmless. You three are everything to me. We've talked about this before. It's just a precaution. Besides, the girls leave to go back to school in Boston on Monday and this will make it easier on you," he said, loosening his hold on her and looking into her eyes. "I promise."

"You'd better. Stella is going to have a ton of questions thinking that we are fighting—or that you've gone back to the military," she grumbled.

"It will only be for a few days. Tell her you've been worried about her since Harry took off," he teased.

"Oh, God! Now you're just being cruel. I'll tell her you have a squadron of Navy Seals you're training. That will work," she chided before kissing him. "I love you, Mason. Please be careful."

"Everything will be fine, love," he promised. "I'd better go before the alien prince thinks I'm planning something evil."

Adalard adjusted his bag and walked across the yard. He scanned the tracks left behind by the transport Samara was driving. He flexed his fingers and called on his powers within to mark the tracks.

He breathed deeply, thankful when the unusual fatigue didn't reappear as it had on his transport. Whatever had caused the drain and the lingering effects must be confined to his vessel. Until he discovered what it was, he didn't want to return to the *Rayon I.* If he was affected, then potentially everyone on board—at least every Curizan on board—could also be in danger.

The sound of the door closing alerted him that Mason was coming. The man had pulled on a thick, dark brown coat and gloves. He brushed snowflakes off a black hat that was almost identical to the one Samara wore before he placed it on his head.

"I'm not sure if you brought any clothing that looks less like a City Slicker Rock Star. If not, I can get your measurements and Ann Marie can pick up some clothes for you so you don't stand out quite as much. We don't get a lot of guys that look like you around here," Mason said.

"You have no need to worry. I'm very good at blending in when necessary," he responded in a dry tone.

Mason shot him a look of disbelief before shaking his head. Adalard fell into step when the man began walking. They crossed over to the barn where Samara had gone earlier. Mason pushed open one of the large sliding doors. Adalard frowned when he saw the man wince.

"Are you not well?" he asked.

Mason narrowed his eyes in annoyance. "I'm fine. An old injury that plays up when the weather changes," he answered in a curt tone.

"Have you known Paul Grove for long?" Adalard asked.

"A while. Paul is a good man. He took on the responsibilities of this ranch, growing it from a few thousand acres to several hundred thousand. All while raising Trisha. His first wife died from a brain aneurysm. It was a shock to everyone. Paul trained me about fifteen years or so ago. I can tell you this—I wouldn't be here today if not for what I learned from him," Mason said, sliding into one of the boxy transports. "I'll show you how to work one of these. I'm sure it'll be like a toy compared to what you normally drive."

He smiled at Mason. "I'm always up to trying new methods of transportation. Especially when they aren't trying to eat me," he confessed.

Mason paused and stared at him before shaking his head. "That sounds like a good tale to go with a glass of bourbon," he chuckled.

Adalard nodded. He silently listened as Mason shared the history of the area. It didn't take him long to understand how the transport worked. It was amazing in its simplicity, and he had to admit that the heated seat felt good. The snow from earlier had melted. Once he was alone, he would contact the *Rayon I*, warn the officers he had left in charge, and then see exactly how far he was from his transport and the best way to get there.

"Now Trisha…. That girl was amazing. Paul would train the guys and once they were full of themselves thinking they were invincible; he'd send Trisha in after them. Sometimes she'd toy with them. Other times she'd tag them with a kill shot before they made it a mile. Not a one of them ever saw her coming, either," Mason said.

Adalard looked around the rugged terrain. Thick patches of trees opened onto wide, dry plains littered with boulders of varying sizes. It reminded him of different regions on Ceran-Pax, his home world.

"She is a remarkable huntress," Adalard agreed.

The silence that followed his comment made him look at Mason. The hard expression on the other man's face and the way he gripped the steering wheel told Adalard that the comment upset Mason. He should have realized that as protective as Mason was about women on the ranch, his feelings would extend to Trisha.

"I'm not sure I want to know the details of how you know how good Trisha is," he warily stated.

Adalard chuckled. "Trust me when I say that she took care of the situation. She and her youngling are safe. Trelon Reykill is a deadly adversary, and the Ha'darra and d'Rojah families have offered additional protection. If the Great War between our people showed us one thing, it is that the bond between friends can be stronger than those of family," he said.

"Amen to that," Mason agreed before he nodded to the building ahead. "There's the main house. You should be comfortable here. There is another UTV in the garage you can use. We keep Paul's truck here, but since you don't have a driver's license, it might be best if you need anything in town to let me or Chad know and we can drive you. I'll give Chad a call to let him know you're here. Oh, before I forget, I've got a cellphone for you to use. I'll show you how to work it before I leave. Signal here can be twitchy, especially if the weather is bad. There's one of those fancy replicators in the kitchen for food. Trelon installed it the last time he was here. He said you aliens didn't all eat the same thing. If you want to cook, let me know, and I'll ask Ann Marie to pick up a few things for you from the grocery store. She banned me from going after I spent a month's allowance on the processed shit that isn't good for me," he confessed with a wry smile.

Adalard laughed but his focus was on the empty UTV that Samara had been driving. It was parked next to a beautifully crafted, long, wood-and-stone building a short distance away.

"I will be fine," he replied in a distracted voice.

Mason's sharp gaze followed his, and he shook his head. "I'll tell you once more—stay away from Samara. She's too young for you, and she has enough troubles with the men in her life. She doesn't need to add an alien to the mix," he warned.

Adalard's eyes narrowed. "What men? Who is giving her trouble? Is she in danger?" he demanded.

"Only from you, I suspect. Let me show you the house. I've got things to do," Mason replied, pulling the UTV to a stop by the front steps.

CHAPTER SIX

*S*amara softly sang along with a song playing on her cellphone as she swept out each stall. The music helped keep the boredom of mucking out stalls to a tolerable level. The barn was state-of-the-art and contained thirty stalls. It was just one of the many barns scattered throughout the ranch. Fortunately, she was only responsible for keeping this one clean along with her other duties.

There were seldom more than a dozen horses at a time here. They were mostly used for Mr. G's survival training business. Since Mr. G had gone on an extended trip, Mason had taken over the training part of the business.

Mason said Mr. G was spending more time with Trisha now that she had been found safe and sound. A shiver ran through her at the thought of the serial killer the police originally thought was responsible for the disappearance of Trisha and several other women. She was glad they were all safe now.

The thought of a serial killer brought another face to her mind, and she quit singing, thinking of Prince Adalard Ha'darra of Curizan. She would have to Google him when she took a break to see what she could find out about him. Maybe she could ask Annalisa to do a background check.

"Just to make sure he isn't crazy." She chuckled before she let out a squeak of surprise when she turned and realized she wasn't alone. The man she was thinking about was standing at the opening of the stall staring at her with glowing, purple eyes. "Shit! You startled me."

She pulled her earbuds out of her ears, wound them up and shoved them into her pocket along with her cellphone. She pursed her lips and waited for her heart to slow down. He wasn't helping to make that happen when he stepped into the stall.

"Who might be crazy?" he asked, his voice deep.

"You," she blurted out before she grimaced and continued, "need to be more careful. I could have jabbed you."

He looked at the broom in her hand and raised an eyebrow. "With a broom?" he inquired.

"With horse manure in the bristles," she pointed out.

She lifted the broom between them so he could see the bits of brown mixed with straw. Granted, she did it more to keep him from coming any closer than to emphasize her point. She barely covered her smirk when he wiggled his nose with distaste and stepped back.

"You remind me of Melina and Ariel. They both have an affinity for creatures who poop a lot," he dryly replied.

She lowered the broom and frowned. "Ariel? Do you know Ariel Hamm?" she asked.

He nodded. "Unfortunately. I threatened to start a war if her mate sent me another Tasier," he proclaimed with a shudder. "Those things are the bane of the galaxy. I've never seen a creature that can procreate as quickly as they can."

Her frown deepened to confusion. "A Tasier? Wait, her *mate*?" she repeated.

"Yes. Tasiers are small, furry creatures from the Minor Moon of Leviathan. They can keep them there for all I care," he explained. "Mandra Reykill, Ariel's mate, sent two of them as a gift. Before the end of the week, there were hundreds of them. The creatures have since been declared a protected species—why I have no idea—and thankfully reintroduced to the moon."

With a sudden burst of giggles, Samara said, "Ah, that's right!" she snapped her fingers and gave a sharp nod, trying to keep a straight face but failing. "You're an alien Prince. I forgot. Okay, Mr. Alien. I've got a lot of work to make up for before the end of the day, so if you don't mind, I'd like to get it finished. If you are looking for something to do, there are some tourist places still open in town you might find interesting," she suggested.

"Who has threatened to harm you?" he suddenly demanded.

She gave him a startled look and frowned. "Harm me? I don't know what you're talking about," she responded in a confused voice.

He took a step closer to her and his eyes were glowing that weird purple again. Hell, his whole body had a weird glow to it. She could see varying shades of red interspersed with violet and black.

He looks like a frigging mood ring the way he's changing colors! she thought.

"Mason said there are men in your life giving you trouble," he said.

She took a step back. He stepped closer, and she tightened her grip on the broom handle. It took a moment to comprehend what he was saying. The colors around him were distracting her. So were the colors she saw rising from her body and mingling with his.

"You need to leave—now," she ordered in a strained voice, shaking her head.

"Who is threatening you?" he demanded.

"What are you? You're… you're glowing," she whispered.

"I told you who I am, Samara. Who are the men threatening you?" he growled.

"Hello!" a deep voice called. "Samara, have you seen...? I see you have."

"Chad... I-I-I'm glad you're here," she breathed, using Chad's sudden appearance to scoot away from the livid man who was possessively staring at her.

"Is everything alright?" Chad Morrison inquired.

She nervously glanced at Adalard and nodded. "Yeah. I've got to go get the hay for the stalls. Maybe you can show... the new guy around," she suggested before fleeing.

She practically ran to the store room. Slipping inside, she closed the door and leaned against it. She lifted a hand to her chest. Her heart was beating like she had just run a marathon.

"What the hell was that all about?" she whispered.

She placed the broom back on the hook. Her hand shook, and she pulled it back against her chest where her heart was finally beginning to slow down. She leaned her head back against the door and stared up at the ceiling. Once she felt under control, she held her arm out and rubbed her sleeve. There were no colors.

"Today has been one of those days when I should never have gotten out of bed," she said with a shake of her head.

She took a deep breath and grabbed the pitchfork. There was too much to do, and this job was too important to risk losing either her mind or her only source of income. There was also the matter of asking Mason about the apartment above the barn next door to him. At the moment, it was used for storing extra furniture and equipment. It wouldn't take much to clean up, and she didn't need much room.

"Stay focused, girl. Forget about aliens and glowing colors. Stay focused on your goal—and stay away from the new guy!" she admonished herself.

Fortified, she opened the door and peered out. She heard Chad's deep voice moving away from the barn. Satisfied she was alone, she stepped out of the store room.

"Remember, there are no such things as aliens. They are only real in the movies," she whispered.

Adalard gritted his teeth. Chad's appearance couldn't have happened at a worse time. Samara's confession that she could see his colors confirmed what he already knew—she was his mate. It was the fear and confusion in her eyes and voice that worried him.

Ha'ven had warned him that humans were unaware of the power they held inside themselves. Arrow suspected, from Ha'ven's description of what happened when he met Emma, that a chemical and physical bond, latent inside Emma, had been awakened. Adalard didn't care how it happened, just that it had! He would leave the biology of it to his anal twin to figure out.

"Mason went over the rules with you, didn't he?" Chad asked.

"Yes," he replied in a curt tone.

"Good, good. Is there anything specific you are here for? Anything I can help you with?" Chad continued.

"Yes. You can leave," he answered.

Chad stopped and faced him. Adalard didn't care that he was being rude. He wasn't used to being nice to anyone except Emma—and Jaguin's mate, Sara, and his mother. His irritation grew as the list of people got longer.

I am going soft, he thought, stiffening with dismay.

The mental image of the Twin Dragons throwing knives at him helped relieve a bit of his worry. There were also enemies still trying to kill him.

Reassured that his soft spot towards women was normal and not much else had changed, he focused on what Chad was saying.

"I see that the alien sense of humor is still intact," Chad dryly replied.

"There are a few matters I need to take care of. I do not need your assistance… unless…" he began.

"What is it?" Chad asked.

Adalard glanced back at the barn. Perhaps Chad could give him more information on the men who were a threat to Samara. There was a shrewd look in Chad's eyes, and the man was shaking his head by the time Adalard looked at him again.

"Rule number one: no fraternizing with any of the women on the ranch," Chad reminded in a stern tone.

Adalard shrugged. "At the moment I'm trying to avoid committing rule number two: no killing anybody," he responded with a flash of a smile that didn't quite reach his eyes.

Chad paled. "Shit. You should know we have one of those communicator things for emergencies," he threatened.

Adalard chuckled. "Your intimidation skills are good, but they could use some work," he replied.

"You're about to show me how to do it better, aren't you?" Chad warily asked.

Adalard nodded. "If necessary. Now, I have some questions for you," he stated.

An hour later, Adalard was seriously contemplating breaking rule number two as Mason and Chad drove away. When Chad suggested they take the conversation indoors where it was warmer, he should have suspected the man was up to something. He discovered soon enough that Chad Morrison was an attorney.

There were legal counselors back on Ceran-Pax. They were the bane of his existence at times. The worst part of their powers was the ability to pull the truth out of their victims. Chad hadn't yet displayed that ability because Adalard had nothing to hide, but his sheer doggedness was exhausting.

Mason reappeared ten minutes after they found seats inside, and the next hour consisted of their constant explanations that Samara was off-limits. Adalard wouldn't make the mistake of underestimating these two men again. He had received more information from enemy assassins than from Chad and Mason. Of course, being able to torture them might have helped.

If it wasn't for the buzz of his communicator, he would have been tempted to string both men up by their ankles and apply some good old-fashioned Curizan electro-shocks to their asses, or at least imagine doing it. Of course, he wouldn't. Ha'ven and Paul would have his hide and more if he did, but it didn't hurt to dream.

Instead, he curtly bid the men a good day. If he didn't answer the vidcom this time, he suspected Ha'ven would be requesting an away team to find him. He was greeted with Ha'ven's scowling face.

"You interrupted me," he informed Ha'ven.

"I know you aren't on the ship. Where are you? Why haven't you checked in? I've been trying to contact you for the last hour," Ha'ven snapped.

"Since when did I start reporting to you? In case you've forgotten, the *Rayon I is* under my command," he dryly responded.

"Quill contacted me. After he checked over your transport, he was concerned that there might have been a tracking device placed on mine," Ha'ven replied.

"Did you find anything?" he asked.

"No, I checked it thoroughly."

Adalard studied his brother's tense expression. "What's wrong? I can tell something else is bothering you," he commented.

Ha'ven glanced over his shoulder and sighed. "I worry about Emma," he confessed.

"You are worried she may want to stay on Earth. She loves you, Ha'ven. You have nothing to worry about," he said.

"I know," Ha'ven replied with a grimace. "We are going tomorrow to retrieve her mother. She wishes to gather a few personal things to take back. We should return in a couple of days at most."

"Take your time," he encouraged.

Ha'ven's eyes narrowed. "What is it?" he demanded.

Adalard pursed his lips and debated whether it was safe to share everything that was going on. The frequency they were using should be secure.

"I suspect whoever placed the tracking device on my transport also placed another type of device. I need time to locate it," he explained.

"What kind of device?" Ha'ven asked.

"I don't know yet. Whatever it is, Ha'ven, it is dangerous. It was draining me," he grimly replied.

Ha'ven's expression hardened. "Let me know what you discover. I haven't had any issues. I recommend that the *Rayon 1* and every transport be thoroughly searched," he suggested.

"I was about to brief my officers aboard," he said.

Ha'ven nodded. "Is there anything else?" he asked.

Adalard opened his mouth to reply before he shook his head. "No, I will need longer before I return. I don't want to endanger anyone or the ship," he said.

"If you need my help, let me know," Ha'ven replied.

"I will," he promised. "Stay safe. I'll notify you if there are any issues."

Ha'ven nodded and ended the link. Adalard stood and stared out of the window. Samara had emerged and climbed into the transport while he was talking to Ha'ven. Once again, she had eluded him.

Shaking his head, he decided to take care of business first so he could focus all his attention on his mate. A wry smile curved his lips at the thought that after all his boasting, he was well and truly caught—he had a mate. He sighed.

"I'm never going to live this down," he murmured, thinking of his brothers' reactions.

He pushed the thought away and pressed the vidcom link to the *Rayon I.*

"*Rayon I,*" the communication tech responded.

"This is Commander Ha'darra. Set up a secure link with Adur— Primary Code 1," he ordered.

"Yes, sir," the tech replied.

"Adalard, what is your situation?" Adur Jalar, his First Officer, asked.

"I'm fine, but I want the *Rayon I* searched. Talk to Engineer Tech Quill. He can fill you in on what was found on my transport. It may be an isolated issue, but I would rather be sure. I believe there is a second, more serious threat—a device that drains the energy from our bodies. I want a complete search of the ship to make sure it is clean. I will give you more information when I have it. Until everything is completed, all crew members are to remain onboard," he instructed.

Adur grimaced. "The men aren't going to be happy. Fortunately, there aren't very many who are unattached onboard," he replied.

Adalard grinned. "Give them a copy of Trelon Reykill's PVC. That should keep them happy for a while," he said.

Adur laughed. "I want them happy, not comatose. Let's hope a thorough scan doesn't take too long."

"Agreed. Out," Adalard responded, ending the connection.

First things first, he thought. *I need to look like a local.*

With a wave of his hand, the clothing he was wearing changed to mimic Mason's with a few alterations. His black leather pants became faded denim jeans. He kept his boots, black shirt, and vest. His outer jacket changed to dark brown with an interior thermal lining that would keep him warm.

He held out his hand, and a black hat similar to the ones Chad, Mason, and Samara wore appeared in it. He looked at it with distaste before placing it on his head. A glimpse of his reflection in the window made him laugh. He looked human enough in this outfit.

CHAPTER SEVEN

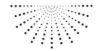

*S*now was falling again by the time Samara guided the horse into the corral next to the barn. Despite promising herself that she wouldn't look, the first place her gaze went was to the main house where the new guy had disappeared with Chad. He had been the only thing she could think about all morning while she worked.

Well, the alien and the strange northern light show coming off of him, she thought.

She dismounted and tied the reins of the mare to one of the posts. Chad's truck was gone. She vaguely wondered if the man had gone with him or if he was still in the house. The thought that he could be inside, watching her, made her nervous.

"Get a grip, Samara," she scolded herself. "You've barely shared six—okay, maybe more—words with him, but that doesn't mean anything. What you think you saw was just static electricity. Maybe whatever he was wearing had wool or polyester in it or whatever in the hell causes your hair to stick up."

She continued lecturing herself as she took care of the horses she had brought down from the upper pasture. She brought them inside the barn one at a time, brushed them, fed them, and made sure they were secure. Bear must have taken a few because there were only five including the mare. She would have to call him later to check.

A movement outside drew her attention. She hurried over to the partially open door and peered out. It took her a few seconds to realize the man striding across the yard was Adalard. He glanced in the direction of the barn and stopped. She quickly pulled back so he couldn't see her.

She heard a low curse, but when she peeked back out, he was gone. Surprised that he could disappear so quickly, she pushed the door open wider and scanned the area, but it was empty.

"What the heck?" she mumbled.

Curious, she stepped out of the barn and closed the door behind her. She walked across the yard, searching the ground for his tracks. They led off into the woods. She bit her bottom lip in indecision, scanning the woods for any sign of him.

"Hey, new guy—Adalard. Are you there?" she called.

She looked at the ground and focused on following the faint traces in the snow. A few yards into the woods the tracks disappeared. For a rock star, he was pretty light on his feet. She turned in a semi-circle, trying to pick up his tracks when the tips of black boots came within her line of vision.

Swallowing, she slowly lifted her eyes to his face. She stumbled back a step and almost fell when she realized how close he was. Her gasp froze in her throat when he wrapped his strong fingers around her wrist and pulled her against him.

"Careful," he cautioned.

"You're pretty good at doing that," she muttered, pulling away from him.

"Good at what?" he asked.

She gave him a rueful grin. "Scaring people," she replied, stuffing her hands in the pockets of her coat. "I wouldn't go too far in the woods without a guide or you may be practicing your survival skills a bit sooner than expected. It's easy to get lost, and there's a storm front moving through in a couple of hours. You definitely don't want to get stuck out here without better clothing."

"You care about what happens to me?" he inquired with a pleased smile.

She laughed and shook her head. "Hell no. I just don't want to have to pull your dead, frozen ass out of the woods. I'm part of the volunteer rescue team. Freezing my ass off to save your dumb butt is not on my list of things to do today," she said.

His smile turned to a scowl. "I can assure you that I can survive very well without assistance," he stiffly answered.

"If I had a dollar for every time some know-it-all said that, I'd be rich. Listen, we're short-handed today. I've still got work to do. Did you at least tell Mason or Chad where you were going?" she inquired.

"No," he replied in a clipped tone.

She pulled her hands out of her pockets. Shaking her head, she bit her tongue against saying anything more caustic. He was a paying client, and she *was* only the hired help. It wasn't her place to babysit those that came here. She was positive Chad and Mason would have gone over the rules with him and had him sign the waiver releasing the ranch and all personnel of any responsibility if he decided to do something stupid—like go off into unfamiliar woods right before a snow storm while dressed inappropriately, and without telling anyone.

"Did Mason and Chad go over the rules with you?" she asked in a brisk tone.

"Yes, and as I explained to them, I don't follow rules," he announced.

She took a step and patted him on the chest. "Well, that is very selfish of you because while you may not give a shit about your own life, what you do can endanger others. I've fulfilled my responsibility by warning you. Now I've got work to do," she snapped.

He wrapped his fingers around her wrist, stopping her from walking away. Her eyes locked with his. There were flecks of gold mixed in his glowing eyes, and it didn't look like he was wearing contacts.

She looked down at his hand. His grip was strong, warm, and there was a tingling feeling through her clothing. Biting her lip, she reached out to touch the colors swirling between them.

"What is going on?" she asked, running her fingers through the colors.

"It is—complicated," he replied in a measured tone.

She gave him a wary look. "Explain 'complicated'," she said.

He opened his mouth but closed it again without saying anything. A truck driving by caught her attention. When she looked back, Adalard was gone. She glanced wildly around, searching for him. She turned back to the road when she heard a truck door slam.

"Hey, Samara, you around here?" an all too familiar voice called out.

"Damn-it-all-to-hell! I swear if any of the others got thrown in jail today, they can rot there 'til next spring," she growled, clenching her fists.

She exited the edge of the woods in time to see Gary wander into the barn. Cursing under her breath, she jogged across the yard. She untethered the mare she had been riding from the post and led her into the barn.

"What are you doing here?" she demanded.

Gary jumped and twisted around, facing her. She sneered and shook her head when she saw his black eyes, along with a busted nose and lip. He also had a bandage on his forehead that was stained with blood.

"No," she said, walking by him.

"I didn't ask for anything," he defended.

She stopped and looked him up and down before turning and leading the mare into a clean stall. Gary stood in the doorway as she removed the mare's saddle, blanket, and bridle. Pushing past him, she placed the saddle and blanket on a sawhorse outside of the door before hanging the bridle on a hook. She retrieved a horse brush from the box attached to the wall next to the stall door and walked past him again. With long soothing strokes, she began brushing down the mare.

"Rob said you were going to help," Gary began.

"I'm not giving you the money. I'll stop by Pat's on the way home. I didn't have time this morning. Unlike some people, I *like* being on time and keeping my job," she said.

"You don't have to—go by Pat's, I mean. You could give the money to Brit. I know you trust him," Gary suggested.

"No. I'm not throwing away half of my savings so that you can bully Brit and lose it," she retorted.

"Half—so you've got more," Gary excitedly commented.

Samara groaned at her slip of the tongue. Her life was going to be a living hell if Mason didn't agree to let her rent the place above the barn. If Gary didn't hound her, Rob would. Brit would give her the poor-pitiful-me look and beg her to give up every last penny to shut them up. Jerry would steal the money and blame her for making him do it. It was Jerry that she worried about the most.

She looked over the mare at Gary. "Be careful what you say, Gary. I have no problem telling you to go to hell for what you did and leaving you and the others to deal with whatever fallout comes from last night," she warned.

"Geez, Sam, I didn't mean it. I was on a winning streak. I've never seen a pot that big before. When that city slicker came in and asked to join, it was like winning the lottery over and over. I was winning—" he explained in an earnest voice.

She paused and shook her head. "You were played, Gary. There is no lottery winning for us. You were set up and you fell for it. Those men played you and *you... fell... for... it.*" She bit out the last four words in a slow, teeth-clenching growl. "The problem is... you made me a part of it without my permission. I said I'd help you as much as I could, and I will, but this is it. I'm done with all of you. Leave me out of your messes," she said.

Gary looked down at his feet. "You don't know what it feels like to always be a failure, Sam. Mom and Dad...," he muttered.

"Freakin' hell! Are you listening to yourself? Didn't you hear a thing I just said? The answer is *NO!* You are not using Mom and Dad as an excuse. I am not going to allow you to use me anymore. You know what... you can get yourself out of this mess on your own. I rescind my offer. One way or another, I will be out of the house tonight even if I have to sleep in my truck. I AM DONE with all of you. Which one put you up to this?" she demanded.

He looked at her with a pleading expression. "Which one?" she demanded.

He swallowed and shifted uncomfortably on his feet. "Jerry," he confessed.

She stared at him in disbelief. That wasn't Jerry's style. Why would he —her eyes widened with rage as a truly horrible suspicion formed in her mind.

"My truck," she breathed out as fear tightened her chest.

She ducked under the mare's head and pushed past her brother. By the time she reached the door of the barn, she was running as fast as she could. She uttered a loud, frustrated cry when she realized that the UTV was still sitting at the upper paddocks. She had ridden the mare here and planned to hike back up or ask Mason for a lift later to retrieve it.

She looked at Gary's truck with narrowed eyes. She ran to it, yanking at the door. Climbing inside, she breathed a silent prayer of thanks when she saw he had left the key in the ignition. Seconds later, the tires of the truck spun on the loose gravel as she gunned the engine.

"Hey! That's my truck," Gary shouted as he ran out of the barn.

Samara was too far gone to care. Her heart was hammering in her chest, and she felt like she was having trouble breathing. If Jerry took her truck, he would find the money box. Those two things were everything that she had.

She wiped the corner of her eye with her sleeve when a tear started to slide down her cheek. She would kill every last one of them. So help her, she would spend the rest of her life in prison, but she would kill every single one of her brothers if they did this to her, starting with Jerry.

She slammed on the brake petal with both feet. The truck slid several feet and fishtailed to a halt in front of the barn. A low, mournful cry of rage filled her until she couldn't contain it. Pushing open the door, she slid out and looked at the spot where she had left her truck earlier.

Broken glass littered the ground where Jerry had broken one of the windows. Samara sank to the ground, her legs no longer able to hold her. Bending forward, she gasped for breath and choked on her sobs.

"NO! Damn you all to hell! NO!" she cried, wrapping her arms around her waist and rocking back and forth as she felt a mental trap of hopelessness closing around her.

CHAPTER EIGHT

*A*dalard was close to a mile into the five-mile trip to his transport when the first wave of uneasiness hit him. He had left to refocus on his mission and put some distance between himself and Samara. The way she had looked at him with a combination of fear, curiosity, and innocence shook him to the core. He didn't want her to be afraid.

The area around him expanded and contracted as if he had unintentionally sent out an energy surge. He stopped walking and slid his hand under his coat to the laser pistol strapped to his hip. He scanned the area, searching for the anomaly. The second wave hit him with more intensity, causing him to swivel and crouch.

Something was wrong. The power inside him was surging uncontrollably. The ground under him shook and several trees groaned and creaked.

"What is it?" he growled, focusing inward.

"NO! Damn you all to hell! NO!"

Samara's heartbreaking cry struck him like a bolt of lightning. The anguish in her voice caused the power surging in and around him to swell until his body bowed with the force of it. She needed him. He must protect her.

He didn't remember giving the command. One second, he was more than a mile from Samara, and in the next, he was wrapping his arms around her.

She briefly struggled against his unexpected touch. He barely tilted his head back in time to miss her fist. Her voice rose, and she released a string of curses that would have made any warrior think twice about challenging her as she twisted around and faced him.

For a moment, everything around them was suspended as she recognized who was holding her and she looked at him with wide, angry, tear-filled eyes. Her body shook as she drew labored breaths. A low, animalistic sound of pain escaped from her throat, and she buried her face against his chest. He tenderly pulled her against his body and soothingly stroked her back.

"I... hate them," she sniffed, shaking her head back and forth.

She hit him with her fist, not hard, just a small thump. His energy wrapped protectively around her, cocooning her in its warmth while his eyes scanned the area for the danger to her.

"Who hurt you?" he demanded in a deceptively calm voice.

She tried to pull away from him, but he kept one arm around her while he cupped her trembling chin, searching her face for any signs of injury. He was shocked to discover his hand was shaking.

"Jerry. He-he stole my truck. It-It's the only thing I have. That and all my money. I'll never get it back. They'll never let me go," she whispered, thumping his chest again with her fist.

"Which way did he go?" he asked.

She shook her head and wiped a gloved hand across her cheek. "I don't know. He's probably headed back to town," she mumbled in a dejected voice.

He looked at the driveway. "Did he go in the direction you came from earlier?" he demanded.

She looked at him in confusion. "Yes." She quickly inhaled a breath and an expression of wild hope crossed her face. "If I take Gary's truck, I might be able to catch him. He can't have been gone long," she said.

He caught her arm when she turned. "I will go with you," he declared.

She hesitated a moment before she nodded. He followed her to a dark blue truck and climbed in. She was pulling away before he shut the door.

"Seat belt," she reminded him.

He waved his hand and the seat belt secured him. She glanced at him with a frown but quickly returned her attention to the road. He reached up and gripped a handle above the door when she slid around a curve.

She slowed when she reached the highway, glanced back and forth, and then pressed the accelerator. Smoke billowed behind them from the rear tires spinning on the hard surface. He gritted his teeth to keep from distracting her.

If they were to catch this Jerry, they would need more speed. He placed his hand on the dash and focused. Energy pulsed through him into the engine.

"What the hell?" she breathed.

"You steer this vessel, and I will make sure we have the speed to catch him," he vowed.

She glanced at him out of the corner of her eye. "We seriously need to talk once I get my truck back," she said through clenched teeth before adding under her breath, "… if we don't die first."

Adalard chuckled. "We will not die, *misha petite lawarrior*," he promised.

"What does *misha* whatever-you-said, mean?" she asked.

"*Misha petite lawarrior.* It means 'my little warrior'," he said.

She scoffed and shook her head. "You are a piece of work. You might want to work on your pickup lines—and your timing. Neither is particularly good," she dryly replied before sitting forward as far as her seat belt would let her. "I see my truck."

Her jaw was beginning to hurt from clenching her teeth. Between the speedometer being pegged out and her nervousness about the upcoming confrontation, she was surprised her teeth had not shattered from the pressure. While she never backed down from a fight, she also didn't go looking for them.

"Pass him," Adalard instructed.

She nodded and made sure there was no oncoming traffic before she swung over into the passing lane. Jerry glanced at them as they passed him. She grimly smiled when he did a double take as he first recognized Gary's truck, then the driver.

The moment she passed her truck, she took her foot off the accelerator. She kept her eyes on the rear-view mirror, making sure that Jerry did not go around. She breathed a sigh of relief when he pulled over onto the shoulder.

"Ok," she said to herself soothingly. She took a deep breath. "I wouldn't be shocked if he tries to take off the minute we get out of the truck. If he does, let him go. The last thing I want is for my dumbass brother to kill you," she warned Adalard, shifting the truck into park before she released her seat belt.

She blinked when she realized Adalard was already outside, and she was talking to herself. A glance out the back window showed he was already opening the driver's door of her stolen truck. Her mouth dropped open when Adalard pulled Jerry out and held him up in the air—by one hand around his neck.

"Geez, I've heard of adrenaline rushes giving people superhuman power but *damn*!" she muttered before she realized she better stop Adalard before he killed her brother.

She opened the door and slid out. Gary's truck was higher off the ground than hers and she had to brace herself when her boots hit the hard pavement. By the time she walked over to her truck, Jerry's eyes were bulging and beginning to roll back in his head.

"Adalard, let him go," she grudgingly ordered.

The look in his eyes when he glanced at her sent a shiver down her spine. She rubbed her hands along her thighs before she reached out and wrapped her fingers around Adalard's bulging bicep.

"Adalard—you really need to let him go," she firmly repeated. "You can't kill him."

"Give me one good reason why I shouldn't," Adalard bit out, staring at Jerry with fire in his eyes.

"Because… he's my brother," she sighed. "I want to kill him, but even I can't give in to that impulse, no matter how much he tries my patience."

Adalard turned his hot glare on her. She wrinkled her nose and gave him a crooked smile while nervously observing Jerry's face. Yep, her brother was definitely turning a Smurf blue.

Jerry's strangled gasping filled the air when Adalard suddenly released him. Her brother's feet hit the ground a second before his butt did. She winced when she heard the impact. Jerry's ass was going to be almost as bruised as his throat.

"Wh-wha-what the fuck?" Jerry groaned, leaning his head back against her truck.

"I could ask the same thing, asshole. You should be thanking me for stopping him," she growled, looming over her brother.

Jerry rubbed his throat and warily glowered up at Adalard. She ignored the irritation on both men's faces. She wasn't in the mood for a pissing contest. She wanted her truck, and she wanted her money.

She stood and bent forward, feeling under the seat. Her fingers grazed the metal money box. She gripped it, pulled it out, and opened it. A low growl of frustration slipped from her and she had to restrain herself from hitting Jerry on the head with the heavy metal box.

"Where is my money?" she demanded.

Jerry glanced up at her with a nasty smile. "I don't know what you're talking about," he retorted.

She raised the box above her head, seriously thinking of clobbering her brother with it, when Adalard reached out and stopped her.

"You said you could not kill him," he reminded her before he continued. "Perhaps I should have a man-to-man discussion with your brother."

She took a breath and nodded. "If you need to add a few more bruises in order to get him to cough up my life's savings, go for it," she stated in a cold, hard voice.

"What the—! Hey!" Jerry yelped when Adalard reached down and yanked him by the arm to his feet. "You're crazy! You can't do this!"

Samara watched as Adalard unceremoniously forced her brother off the road toward the tree line. Once they were out of sight, she focused on the damage done to her truck. Bits and pieces of glass littered the driver's side mat. It looked as if Jerry had brushed most of it off onto the floorboard but there was still some in the seat as well.

She pulled her heavy leather gloves out of her pocket and put them on, grabbed the small trash can she kept behind the seat and a heavy horsehair brush, and swept the glass into it. She kept looking toward the area where the guys had disappeared, but she didn't see or hear anything. She was picking the last pieces of glass out of the seat when the sound of a diesel truck approaching drew her attention.

She scowled when she saw Gary sitting in the passenger seat before she noticed Mason in the driver's seat wearing a grim expression. Her stomach clenched with fear at the thought of him firing her. She couldn't blame him if he did. After everything that had happened today, nothing would surprise her.

Well, almost nothing. Adalard has a lot of explaining to do about the glowing supercharge thing he did to the truck, she warily thought.

"Are you okay, Samara?" Mason asked as he emerged from his truck.

"Yeah, I'm fine," she replied.

Gary looked around with a wary expression. "Where's Jerry? You didn't kill him, did you?" he asked, paling.

She shook her head and had to turn away when Mason stifled his laugh. Her five-foot four inch, one hundred and twenty pounds was no match for Jerry's almost six-foot, two-hundred-pound frame. Oh, she could probably put any of her brothers on the ground. The more difficult chore would be dragging their asses out and burying them deep enough so that they couldn't dig their way back out.

"No, I didn't kill him. He and the Alien Prince Rock Star are having a man-to-man in the woods," she retorted, picking out more glass. "You and Gary owe me a new window."

"Alien Prince Rock Star," Gary repeated in a confused tone.

"Here they come," Mason hastily interjected before Gary could ask any more questions.

Samara looked up. Jerry didn't look any the worse for wear. He was pale and was stumbling a bit, but that could have been the after-effects of almost being strangled. She raised an eyebrow at Adalard when Jerry walked to Gary's truck and climbed in without saying a word.

"Who's that?" Gary asked.

"Why don't you ask Jerry?" she replied with a saccharine-sweet smile.

Gary nodded. "I—okay. Um, about the money you promised...," he began.

"There will be no money to you or to any of your brothers," Adalard coldly stated.

"Uh—alright. Maybe we can talk… later tonight when you get home," he stuttered before hurriedly retreating to his truck when Adalard took a menacing step toward him.

She looked at Mason with a sense of dread. "I'm sorry about the drama. It won't happen again—at least, I hope it doesn't," she apologized.

Mason smiled kindly at her. "You have nothing to apologize for, Samara. Your brothers' reputations are well known. Besides, it added a little excitement to an otherwise—" he paused and looked at Adalard, "… let's just say it added a little more excitement to an already exciting day."

She smiled in relief. "I still have a few things to do. After I finish, I'd like to talk to you about a personal matter, if you don't mind," she said.

"That's fine. Since I'm already halfway to town, I might as well go pick up a few things I need at the hardware store. I should be back in a couple of hours," he replied before he looked at Adalard. "Do you want to ride in with me?"

Adalard shook his head. "There is another matter that I need to take care of near here," he said.

"Oh—alright, then. Nothing too dramatic I hope," Mason replied with a wary expression.

"Nothing that concerns you," Adalard answered.

Mason nodded. "Call me if you need anything, Samara," he instructed.

"I will. Thanks, Mason," she replied, trying to decipher the strange look Mason was giving Adalard.

A minute later she lifted her hand in a wave as Mason pulled away. Lowering her hand to her side, she shivered and looked up at the sky.

The temperature was beginning to drop, and she still had a lot of work to finish back at the ranch.

"Tell me he gave it to you, every cent that he stole from me," she whispered.

Adalard held out a bundle of cash.

"Your brother swore that this was everything. If it is not, I promised him we would have—another talk," Adalard said.

Samara's shuddering breath caused tendrils of steam to rise. She took the money and slowly counted it. It was all there—plus another hundred. That would cover her window repair plus her time.

"You and Jerry must've had one hell of a talk," she breathed, holding the cash to her chest and looking at him with wide eyes.

Adalard smiled. "We came to an agreement," he said.

"Thank you—for this," she said, holding up the money, "and for coming with me and doing whatever you did with the truck."

She swallowed when he stepped close. Standing this close to her, she realized just how tall he was compared to her. She tightened her grip on the cash when he traced his fingers lightly down her chin.

"A kiss—would be a nice thank you," he suggested.

She looked back at him with a skeptical expression before she shook her head and gave him a sassy grin. Far from feeling intimidated by his request, she found it humorous. She had heard that pickup line down at the bar—about once a week. If he wanted to talk payment, it worked both ways.

"Mm, it doesn't quite work that way. You see, if you wanted payment for doing a good deed, you should have negotiated the price *before* you did the job. Besides, in case you've forgotten, I gave you a lift earlier and saved you from hypothermia, so I'd say we're even," she pointed out.

He frowned. "But I want a kiss," he persisted.

She raised an eyebrow at his almost pouty tone. "Well, I want a million dollars. Just because I want it doesn't mean I get it. Besides, I don't know you well enough to kiss you. You still have a few things to explain before we get to first base," she retorted.

Pushing her shoulder into his chest to make him step back, she retrieved her metal box, placed the money inside it, and slid it behind her seat. He was still standing behind her when she finished. She climbed into the truck and gave him a pointed look.

"Time to go. Daylight's burning, your Majesty, and I've got work to do. It's going to be a cold ride home tonight if I don't get some plastic on this window before dark. In the meantime, you can explain the ghostly glow and truck possession thing on the way back to the ranch," she said.

"Are you always this obstinate? Surely one little kiss wouldn't hurt," he stubbornly muttered.

She laughed and gripped the door handle. "What fun is it if I don't make you work for it? So, are you coming or staying?" she inquired, slamming the door.

He gave her a crooked smile and shook his head. "I will catch a ride back with Mason," he said.

She frowned. "Are you serious? It is freezing out here and only going to get colder. I can think of a lot of things more exciting than sitting on the side of the road freezing my ass off and waiting for a ride," she exclaimed.

He stepped up next to the window and gave her an intense look that made her swallow again. There was that spark of danger in his expression that she had noticed before. She also noticed that the colors swirling around him were stretching out to surround her. She felt like she was standing on the edge of a cliff with nowhere to go but down.

"Your kiss would keep me warm," he said, his voice dropping a seductive notch.

"If I give you a kiss, will you get in the truck?" she asked, her focus locked on his lips.

"Yes," he replied.

His short response made her grin. She removed her hat from her head and leaned into him. Her lips barely touched his, yet the spark of heat that hit her felt like she had jumped into the middle of a bonfire. She jerked back before he could take the kiss any further.

"Done, now get in," she ordered, straightening in her seat and pulling her hat back on.

His answer sounded like a muttered curse, only in a language she didn't understand. She started the truck and put on her seat belt as he stomped around the truck to the passenger's side. She tried not to grin as he continued to mutter. He looked like a kid on the playground who had just lost his favorite toy to the class bully. He yanked open the passenger door and climbed in.

"That was not a kiss," he muttered.

She snorted. "Well, it's all you're getting," she retorted.

CHAPTER NINE

*A*dalard was almost thankful that the ride back to the ranch was done in silence. Between the freezing wind blowing in from the busted window and the heat cranked up as far as it would go so they wouldn't freeze, they would have had to yell to be heard. Well, there was another way, but something warned him that Samara wasn't ready to find out that he had been honest about his origins.

He thought about his conversation with Samara's brother. The man was a waste of good oxygen in his opinion. Jerry's disregard for Samara infuriated him, and it had taken considerable self-control not to throttle the man again. Fortunately, he had plenty of experience in retrieving information from those who were reluctant to give it.

"I need to drive the UTV down from the upper paddock. Would you mind dropping me off and driving my truck back to the barn?" she requested. "You can leave it there. I think there is some plastic sheeting I can use in the workroom to seal the window until I can see if the junkyard has one. If they don't, I'll have to order one."

"Yes," he replied.

"Thanks," she said, turning onto the long driveway.

She drove past Mason's house and turned left to follow the road up to the main homestead where he was staying. She continued along the narrow track. Up ahead, the trees grew sparse, and he could see the vast open plains that were visible from the back of the homestead. Snow-capped mountains rose in the distance. Adalard could see a red barn that was smaller than the one near the main house. In front of the barn was the four-wheeled vehicle Samara had used earlier.

She pulled to a stop beside it and shifted the truck into park. They sat in silence, looking out over the valley. He could sense she wanted to say something and was frustrated by his inability to break through the barrier that shielded her mind. He would have to ask Ha'ven about how his connection with Emma had progressed. If Arrow were on board the *Rayon I* he would have asked him, even if it meant getting another lecture about not paying attention to Salvin, their mentor and Keeper of the Archives.

"We still need to talk, but it can wait. You only got here today. It's hard to believe that. It feels like a lot longer." She paused, took a breath, and shook her head as if answering an unspoken question. "Thanks again."

She opened her door and slid out, cringing at the crackle of broken glass. He exited the vehicle at the same time and met her at the front. His expression softened when he saw the metal box that held her life savings in her hands. She held it protectively against her chest like a shield.

He caressed her cheek with his fingers. Her lips parted, and for a moment, she lowered the invisible mental wall between them, allowing him to connect with her for the first time. His chest tightened with emotion when he sensed her confusion, making it hard to breathe.

"We can talk when you are ready," Adalard said.

Samara gave him a brief, uncertain smile before she walked away. He sighed and watched her hurry into the barn. Walking around to the driver's side, he paused and studied the door with the missing window.

With a mischievous smile and a devilish glint in his eyes, he lifted his hand and focused on the door. The small fragments of broken glass rose out of the empty slot in the door, and with a burst of energy, they were expanded and reformed, creating a new window. He tested his repair, pushing and pulling the button on the door to make sure that the window functioned properly.

"Yes, *misha petite lawarrior*, we will have much to talk about later," he murmured with satisfaction.

He climbed into the truck and shut the door. Samara had unwittingly given him a chance to familiarize himself with a human vehicle, which might come in handy over the next few days. He turned down the heat, shifted the truck into reverse, and took his time following the road back to Paul's house.

Five minutes later, he parked the truck outside of the barn. He contemplated what he should do with the keys before an idea formed that made him smile. Lifting his hand, he thought of the painting in the house with the vase of flowers in it.

Adalard relished the feeling of energy flowing through him as a bright red stem formed. It twisted, flowing upward from the palm of his hand. Bright yellow leaves branched out at intervals before delicate, violet petals the color of his eyes took shape.

This flower species only grew along the riverbank near the palace grounds. As a child, he had been fascinated with them. He gently stroked the closed center and it opened. He carefully dropped the keys inside the flower and placed the blossom on the driver's seat. He was confident that none of Samara's brothers would return today, and her truck would be safe.

He shut the door and looked back up the road. Today was without a doubt one of the strangest days of his life. He had started out with the idea of having some fun exploring a new world but discovered his mate instead. Now, he just needed to figure out how to keep from ruining it.

"First things first—find the device on my ship. It is a danger to me and that makes it a danger to Samara," he murmured.

It was too far to phase-jump to his ship. He would have to travel by foot. The journey back would be easier because he could use a hover-board. Within minutes, he was deep in the forest.

It was mid-afternoon when Samara steered the UTV along the road that led to the western section of the ranch. She wanted to check in with Bear, the foreman who oversaw the cattle. It was beginning to snow again, just like the forecaster predicted.

She wished the only things on her mind were the weather and the missing horses, but she was still thinking of Adalard. The scene in the truck and their brief kiss played like a broken record in her thoughts. She muttered a curse when she hit a pothole, and the UTV roughly bounced.

"It wasn't really a kiss. It was more of a peck," she defended, gripping the steering wheel tighter.

She sighed with relief when she saw the bunkhouse, barn, and stables. Bear was talking to one of the cowpokes when she pulled up in front of the barn. She saw a saddled horse out front that she recognized.

Bear grinned and raised a hand in greeting. She responded in kind before grabbing her hat and opening the door of the UTV. Bear murmured something to the man standing beside him and then walked over to her.

"Hey, Samara, what brings you to this side of the ranch?" Bear asked.

Samara nodded toward the mare. "I was missing some horses. I figured this would be a good place to start my search," she responded.

"Damn, I was hoping you'd finally decided to go out with me. I thought Mason would have told you I needed to borrow a few when I didn't see you this morning, but I guess he didn't. He hired some temporary help to look for strays, and I was down a few," Bear said.

"That's okay. I came in a bit late and brought a new guy for the survival training. He probably just forgot with everything going on," she replied.

"A new guy? This should be fun," Bear chuckled.

Samara grinned and nodded. "Yeah. The guy doesn't look military. He's more of a rich European-type, if you ask me. Anyway, Mason will give Adalard his money's worth. How long are you going to need the horses?" she asked.

"I'll need them for a few weeks at least. The recent storms have scattered the herd over half the ranch," he replied with a disgruntled scowl.

"If you need help, I could ask Mason for more hours. I've got a meeting with him later this afternoon," she suggested.

Bear's eyes lit up. "That would be great. Listen, about what I said earlier, I was wondering if you would like to grab a beer and a meal?" he asked.

Almost immediately Adalard's violet eyes flashed through her mind when he suggested a kiss in payment. Panic hit her hard when her body reacted with a strange tingling sensation. She forcibly pushed it down and found herself nodding in agreement. Hell, it wouldn't hurt to go out for a meal. Besides, she justified, she needed to eat, and she liked Bear.

"Sure," she replied before she could change her mind. "When?"

"How about tomorrow night? I can pick you up at your place," he said with a huge grin.

"That sounds great. Well, I guess I'd better go. I still have work," she replied.

She silently groaned as she hurried back to the UTV. She was already regretting her impulsive—or more like defiant—response. She should have told Bear no. He had been hinting around for the past six months about going out with her, but she always brushed him off. This was the first time he had actually come right out and asked.

"One date won't hurt anything," she mumbled as she climbed into the UTV.

She smiled and waved at Bear before backing up and turning around. Her smile faded the moment he couldn't see her face any longer. A rueful chuckle slipped from her.

"Well, if nothing else, I have to admit that today has been an eventful one so far. Hopefully, nothing else will happen—like an alien invasion. At the rate things are going, I wouldn't be surprised," she said with a snort, remembering Adalard's alien shtick. Just *one* of him was quite enough.

At the moment she didn't have time to worry about aliens and dating. She needed to focus on finishing her work and hoping that Mason would let her rent the apartment in the barn. After today's fiasco with her brothers, Wilson was in her thoughts—his decision to escape their family and not look back in particular. If she was to preserve her own peace of mind and future, she needed to get the hell away from them as well.

Adalard's energy began draining the moment he stepped inside the transport. The intensity caused him to stagger. He placed his hand against the hull to steady himself and shook his head. The effect was worse than before.

He slid his hand along the wall, trembling and disoriented until his sense of survival kicked in, and he realized it was imperative that he exit the transport.

By the time he reached the bottom of the platform, he could barely stand. He stumbled over to a nearby boulder and leaned against it. Sweat coated his brow despite the freezing temperature. He shivered as a steady wind cut through the narrow ravine.

This was worse than he realized. The weapon that had been activated could prove deadly to the Curizan race. He pulled the communicator from his belt. His finger hovered over the button before he returned it to his belt and moodily stared at the transport.

His first thought was to connect to Ha'ven, but there was nothing his brother could do. In fact, there was nothing anyone could do—not without developing the disabling weakness that he was experiencing. Because of the mission's location, there was only one non-Curizan personnel member on duty—a Moniker named Crom who had decided he would be Emma and Ha'ven's personal guard. All other members of the crew were Curizans hand-picked to ensure the security of this defenseless planet.

He growled in frustration. He couldn't bring Crom down to the planet. There was no way he would chance the Moniker being seen by a human. There was also no way of knowing if the entity aboard the transport might be dangerous to the Moniker. The species held a latent power similar to that of the Curizan.

If that wasn't bad enough, he couldn't even retrieve the hoverboard. Adalard looked at the sky as thick snowflakes began to fall. This was the second time today that he felt powerless to control the situation.

He must talk to Arrow. His twin could give him some idea of what he could do. Arrow loved mysteries like this. Unfortunately, in order to send a signal that far, he would have to patch into the deployed communication relays or go through the *Rayon I's* communication system—both would take time to install which the weather would not allow. He gritted his teeth in frustration and closed the transport's platform.

"I hope Arrow has some ideas," he murmured, turning in resignation and retracing his steps back to the homestead.

The sound of debris falling from above the ravine caused him to halt and look up. He stiffened when he saw someone standing at the cliff edge. Through the falling snow, he recognized Samara.

"Adalard?" she called out.

She hadn't seen him yet. Using the increased snowfall to his advantage, he focused on a section close to her and phase-jumped. The familiar tingle of energy surrounded him.

The power to teleport was still relatively new to him. When Ha'ven used this ability before in his and Arrow's presence, it had captured their attention. Arrow, using a more scientific approach, had pinpointed the method of controlling the energy in the molecular structure of his body down to the smallest atoms.

Neither of his brothers understood completely how the process worked. He was just thankful for the newfound talent because it had saved his neck more than once in the past few months—including now.

"Samara, what are you doing here?" he demanded.

She sharply turned on her heel, startled. Her lips parted on a gasp, and her eyes widened with surprise when her foot slipped on an ice-covered rock. She reached out to him as she started to fall backwards.

His heart was racing as he wrapped his fingers around her outstretched wrist. He roughly pulled her into his embrace, holding her against his body. She tightly gripped his heavy jacket.

"Th-thank you," she muttered in a shaky breath.

He was lost the moment she tilted her head back and stared up at him. He saw the same remains of fear in her eyes that he felt himself. Leaning down, he captured her lips in a heated kiss.

CHAPTER TEN

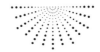

*S*amara parted her lips under Adalard's. It was hard to believe, but her heart was beating more frantically now than when she almost fell to her death after Adalard startled her. She forced her fingers to relax against his jacket and slid her hands up to his shoulders.

The same tingling feeling ran through her that seemed to happen every time she and Adalard touched. She could also see colors swirling around them. Almost like they were threads trying to weave them together in some cosmic way.

Curious, she ran her tongue along his teeth. Images of Little Red Riding Hood and the scene with the Wolf danced through her mind when she noticed that his canines appeared sharper than normal. Instead of being repulsed, she found them sexy.

All the better to bite me with, she mused.

I like the thought of that.

She pulled back, startled again. This time because she could have sworn that she had heard him respond to her thought, except his voice was in her head. He started to bend forward and kiss her again, but she covered his mouth with her gloved hand and gave him a slightly apologetic smile.

"I'll give you that one as thanks. Sorry about the glove on the mouth. At least these aren't the ones I shovel manure with," she said with a wry grin.

His nose wiggled with distaste, and he rubbed his hand across his mouth when she stepped away. She released a strained chuckle and looked back down into the ravine, keeping a healthy distance from the edge. When she turned her focus back to him, she noticed that snow was beginning to accumulate on the brim of his hat.

"We'd better get back. The weather forecast said the storm would be worse than expected," she informed him.

"What are you doing here?" he asked, following her.

She glanced over her shoulder and scowled at him. "Looking for some dumb-ass greenhorn who decided to go where he was told not to go," she stated, turning back to the mare.

"Who—? Ah, you are speaking of me," he dryly realized.

She waved a hand around. "Do you see anyone else? You can explain why you took off without telling anyone on the way back," she retorted, mounting the mare. She waved at the gelding stomping his right hoof against the ground. "I hope you know how to ride a horse."

He studied the gelding. "I believe I can manage," he dryly answered.

She loosely held the reins and waited as he mounted the gelding. Once he was seated, she gently guided the mare back in the direction of the ranch. They rode in silence, single file, for about a quarter of a mile before she turned onto a narrow dirt road that was wide enough to ride side-by-side.

"This would have come in handy earlier," he muttered.

"So, what was so important that it was worth getting caught in a snowstorm?" she curiously asked.

"My transport," he replied.

She looked at him with a raised eyebrow. "Your bike is in the ravine?" she asked with surprise.

"Yes," he answered.

"O-kay. I guess that explains why you were stuck. How the hell you got it down there in the first place amazes me. There is a trail that leads up to the ridge where you can cross the river. Mason had the old bridge replaced last year, so if you get it back up to the top, it won't fall through. The best thing would probably be to take a truck and trailer and pick it up along the highway. I can't imagine why you'd take a street bike off road, but I've seen stranger things," she mused.

"How did you find me?" he asked.

"Bobby, one of the part-time guys, saw you go into the woods. He flagged me down as we passed each other to warn me that he saw someone and wanted to make sure you were authorized to be there. I knew it was you from his description. We'd better get moving. The snow is getting heavier," she replied.

What she didn't tell him was that she had seen fading ribbons of red light leading into the woods. She had quickly saddled the mare and one of the geldings and followed the ribbon trail to the ravine. Her heart nearly dropped to her feet when she noticed the trail of light disappear over the edge. She lost sight of it in the mist rising from the river.

If that wasn't strange enough, there had been the voice in her head. It —Adalard—sounded as if he actually spoke to her. Ever since she had picked him up this morning, weird things were happening—things she didn't understand.

With everything else going on in her life right now, she didn't have time for crazy distractions. She touched her heels to the mare's side, picking up the pace. The snow was steadily falling and beginning to accumulate. She needed to get the horses back to the barn and brush them down, and then tape up the busted window on her truck and speak to Mason before she had the pleasure of trying to get down the mountain to deal with her brothers once and for all.

Besides, picking up the pace also gave her a reprieve to come to terms with their kiss. There was a definite spark between them—one that was going to be hard to ignore.

She accepted the fact that for some weird reason, she was physically attracted to Adalard. It wasn't as if she was oblivious or ignorant about these kinds of things. Hell, with five older brothers, she saw and heard enough to nauseate the strongest of dispositions.

What puzzled her was why. He was everything she tried to avoid. He had that same air of danger—an authority issue—about him that her brothers did. Well, except for Brit. He was just a dumbass that followed the others.

Forty minutes later, they emerged near the barn. She dismounted, and still gripping the mare's reins, walked over to the barn door and opened it. Adalard dismounted and led the gelding in behind her. Once they were inside, she slid the door closed.

"You can put him in any of the empty stalls. I'll take care of them," she stated, leading the mare into an empty stall.

"I will help," he replied.

She was about to argue but one look at his face told her that it would be useless. Instead, she shrugged and focused on removing the mare's saddle, blanket, and reins. She placed the equipment outside of the stall and picked up a brush.

"Thank you—for coming for me," he said.

She looked over the mare's back and chuckled. "You sound like that was difficult to say," she commented.

"What was difficult to say?" he asked.

"Thank you," she replied.

He was silent for a moment before he chuckled. "Yes, I guess it did sound that way," he reflected.

"Why? Don't people do things for you?" she curiously asked.

"Yes, all the time," he replied.

She paused in brushing the mare and gave him a pointed look. "And do you thank them?" she inquired.

He frowned and gazed back at her with a mild expression of confusion. "No, why should I? They are doing what they should be," he responded.

She shook her head and resumed brushing the mare. "Well, that was spoken like a true Prince with a gold spoon shoved up his ass," she muttered, wincing when she realized he had heard her.

Thirty minutes later, she closed the stall door. She waited while Adalard did the same. He was good with the gelding.

"Do you have horses where you live?" she asked in a curious voice.

"The animals we ride are different on Ceran-Pax than they are here. They are larger and have thick, leathery hides instead of soft hair," he said.

She stopped and faced him. "Ceran-Pax? Is that like—a city? What country is it in?" she asked.

Her curiosity changed to confusion when he caressed her cheek, and his expression conveyed that he was torn about telling her something. She remembered Wilson having the same look in his eyes before he told her everything would be alright. By morning, he was gone.

"I find it impossible to lie to you. There are things I want to tell you, but I don't think you are ready to believe me yet," he confessed.

"Adalard, if you are in some kind of trouble...." Her voice faded when he shook his head.

"I have something I must take care of before I tell you more. Until then, I ask that you trust me when I tell you that I mean you no harm," he said.

"Well, that's a relief," she mumbled.

He reached out and gripped her hand when she started to turn away. She blinked in surprise when he bent forward and gave her a hard, brief kiss before he stepped back, opened the door, and disappeared, leaving her staring mutely at the door.

She lifted a hand and touched her lips. That was the third time today that he had kissed her. It had been a while since she had kissed a man this much, especially on the same day!

"Holy moly, but I don't need this right now," she muttered with a shake of her head.

She groaned when she saw that the snow was really beginning to stick. Her truck seat was probably frozen. Even with the heat, she would end up with a wet ass unless she covered it with a horse blanket.

Cursing under her breath, she headed for her truck. She would have to drive it that way down to Mason's place. At least there, she could pull it under the pole barn and work on it.

She pulled her heavy leather gloves out of the pockets of her coat and was in the process of putting them on when she reached the driver's side and looked up. She almost fell when she lurched to a sudden stop. She stared in shock, reached out, and touched the solid piece of glass.

"How the hell—?" she breathed, running her gloved fingers along the smooth glass.

She pulled the door open, examining the other side. The window looked as if it were brand new. A soft glow pulled her attention away from the window to the seat. Her lips parted on a soft gasp when she saw the flower on the worn upholstery. She pulled off her glove and picked up the bloom. Studying the intricate violet petals and bright yellow leaves, she marveled at the colors. The petals reminded her of Adalard's eyes. She had never seen a flower like this in her life.

She switched the flower to her other hand and gently caressed the center bud that was pulsing with light. The petals slowly opened and revealed the truck key. A small puff of fog surrounded it when she gasped again.

"How in the hell did you do this?" she mumbled.

"I'm an alien from another world." Adalard's words suddenly filled her mind. Her cold fingers trembled as she continued to caress the bloom. She had never been into science fiction, but if she had, she suspected that this was what an alien flower might look like. She carefully extracted her truck key from the center of the flower.

I told you that I could not lie to you.

"Holy shit!" she croaked out when Adalard's husky, accented voice filtered through her mind.

She hastily tossed the flower onto the passenger seat, climbed into her truck, and slammed the door shut. Her hand shook as she tried to insert the key into the ignition. It took her three tries before she was successful. Twisting the key, she started the engine.

Cold air blasted her, causing her to shiver uncontrollably. She lifted her hands to her mouth, blowing warm air across her cold fingers before pulling on her glove. Her mind was whirling as she thought about everything that had happened since this morning.

Adalard walking along the highway, the strange swirling colors, the thing he did to Gary's truck, Jerry's pale, shaken complexion after their little talk, and Adalard's insistence on going to the ravine. Her eyes widened with a sudden suspicion.

"Motorcycle, my ass!" she hissed.

CHAPTER ELEVEN

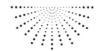

*I*sla Asteroid Base: Heron Prime

Hamade Dos strode along the polished stone floor of the corridor. The lights flickered, casting eerie shadows on the contrasting rough-rock walls. He passed by two technicians repairing an electrical panel before turning left into a small room filled with equipment.

Lesher stood when he entered and silently nodded to him. Hamade glanced at the two-headed Tiliqua, who looked up from where he was soldering a circuit board, and then he studied the slender woman standing in front of a tall cylinder. She was softly speaking to the moving mass of dark matter inside the tank.

He waited for her to finish. The dark mass strained against the glass, trying to burst through it. Hamade could see her shimmering eyes in the glass's reflection.

"What news do you have?" she dispassionately demanded as she turned and faced him.

"None—yet, Empress," he replied.

He kept his expression neutral as she walked over to him and stared into his eyes. Sweat glistened on his brow as intense pain spread throughout his body. It felt as if his blood was beginning to boil. The heat vanished when she looked away.

"What happened?" she asked.

He followed her when she resumed walking. She left the small, contained lab and turned left. He stepped up beside her.

"The tracking device placed on Prince Adalard's transport malfunctioned. There was a visual report of his warship leaving Valdier airspace. The spy we have onboard the *Rayon I* has not reported in," he explained.

She quickly turned around and placed her hand against his chest, over his heart. He clenched his jaw to keep from groaning when the sensation of something crawling along his flesh spread outward from her hand. She studied his expression.

"Failure will not be tolerated this time, Hamade," she stated.

He briefly nodded, breathing a sigh of relief when she removed her hand, turned, and continued walking. He rubbed his chest and followed her into another room. The spartanly decorated room was one of the few containing a window that looked out into space.

"Until our spy reports in, there is no way to know if the other device worked," he said.

"I'm well aware of that. I want a report the moment you locate Adalard Ha'darra," she replied.

Hamade hesitated before he spoke. "What about Ha'ven Ha'darra?" he demanded.

The Empress turned and looked at him with a wintry glare. "Do not let sentiment impede the Order. Kejon was reckless. That is why he is dead," she coldly stated.

Hamade bowed his head. "My apologies, Empress. I will inform you the moment I have more information," he replied.

"See that you do," she answered with a dismissive wave of her hand.

He kept his head bowed as he backed out of the room. The moment he was in the corridor, he breathed deeply and rolled his shoulders to ease his tension. He lifted his hand and sullenly flexed his fingers.

For years, Adalard Ha'darra had evaded every trap set and assassin sent by him. The bastard was as slippery as his two brothers. His brother, Kejon, had implemented a plan that ended in deadly failure. Since Adalard's location was still unknown, he had to put his assassination plans on hold. The Empress also had her own plans for Adalard's twin brother, Arrow.

"General Dos, the ship is ready," Lesher said, pulling him back to the present.

He gave Lesher a sharp nod. "Very well. I want to know the last documented location of the *Rayon I*," he snapped.

"Yes, General," Lesher replied.

~

Paul Grove's Ranch: Earth

"What's wrong?" Arrow demanded, sliding into the chair in front of the vidcom.

Adalard scowled at his twin. "What makes you think there is something wrong?" he tersely responded.

Arrow raised an eyebrow and stared at him in silence. Adalard muttered a curse and sighed. His mind was not on his brother or the issue with his transport, but on Samara.

Arrow waved his hand at the screen then pointed at himself. "Twins—remember? Besides, you only get that twitch above your left eye when you feel out of control," he answered with a grin.

"I don't have a twitch," he retorted even as he lifted a hand to his twitching brow. He sighed and sat back. "I've found my mate."

"You—hold on," Arrow sputtered as he choked on the sip he had just taken from his drink. He coughed and cleared his throat before gasping out, "You *what*?"

"I said I've found my mate," he growled, sitting forward.

Arrow wiped his hand across his mouth. "I thought that was what you said. It must be a human. You've worked with every woman on board the *Rayon I* before. Who is she? What's she like? What did it feel like? What symptoms did you have? Did you have any sensations of disorientation or nausea? Is she like Emma?" he excitedly questioned, then added, "I like Emma."

Adalard shook his head and grimaced. "I said I found my mate, not some unknown disease! She is—different from Emma, but similar in some ways," he reluctantly shared.

"What are the similarities and differences? Are they physical or mental? Are you able to connect with her the way Ha'ven can with Emma? Have you had sex with her yet?" Arrow continued.

"Will you shut up with the questions? No, I haven't had sex with her. I only met her today," he snapped.

Arrow shook his head. "Like that has ever stopped you before. How did she react to you?" he asked.

"Good… I guess," he grudgingly said.

"You don't sound too sure. What happened? I wonder if I would have the same reaction to her. You know, like the Twin Dragons. It could be possible that she is also my mate," Arrow mused.

"Never!" Adalard snarled.

He wasn't even aware of lashing out at his brother until his fist passed through the vidcom's holographic image and struck the wall, leaving an impression in the wood paneling. He pulled his hand back and shook it.

Arrow stared at him with a thoughtful, excited expression. "Interesting, very interesting," he murmured.

Adalard shook his head. "I'm not one of your experiments, Arrow. Enough about Samara for now, I have another issue that I need your devious brain for," he grumbled, rubbing his bruised knuckles.

"Samara... I like that name," Arrow said with a nod.

"Will you please focus? There is a device on my transport that is sucking the energy from me. What kind of device can do that, and how can I stop it from draining me so I can find the damn thing?" he snapped.

Arrow's eyes widened with shock, and he leaned forward. "When did that happen? What were you doing when it first started? Damn, I wish I was there," he groaned.

"I need to ask Mother if she dropped you on your head when you were a baby," Adalard muttered.

"Ha-ha. Now give me every detail, and don't leave the smallest thing out," Arrow ordered.

Three hours later, Samara turned onto the gravel driveway in front of the garage. She wiggled her nose when she saw all of her brothers' trucks parked out front. There was only one reason they would all be there at this time of the day—they were planning on ganging up on her.

She had expected that. Her talk with Mason an hour ago went better than she could have hoped. Mason was allowing her to live in the apartment above the barn. Instead of Samara paying rent, he said that her presence would be doing *him* a favor. It would be good to have the space lived in, he said. His only hesitation was her timeline. He wanted her to wait a few weeks. It wasn't hard to deduce what he really meant—wait until Adalard was gone.

She had pressed home the fact that it made sense that she should move in sooner rather than later. Bear needed additional help, and with winter coming, there was a lot of additional preparation that needed to be done. He had reluctantly agreed after she mentioned that she was meeting Bear the next evening for dinner and could discuss everything with him.

Mason was surprisingly cheerful about her upcoming date, asking her questions that she really didn't know how to answer. For some reason, the idea that she and Bear were a couple appeared to put him at ease. Whatever worked was good enough for her. The sooner she was out of this house, the better. If that meant misleading Mason into thinking she and Bear were an item, then so be it.

She pulled into the garage and turned off the ignition. Drawing a deep breath, she held it for a moment before releasing it. She dropped her hand onto the seat beside her and looked down.

The flower Adalard had left for her was still softly glowing. She picked it up and ran her fingertips over the blossom, marveling at how it opened to her touch. She pulled open her coat and slid the flower into the inside pocket before she zipped it up.

"Go in and act like nothing is different. Tomorrow I'll clean up the apartment. By this weekend, I'll be out of here once and for all," she quietly vowed to her reflection in the rearview mirror. "Whatever you do, Samara, don't lose your cool."

Once she felt in control, she pushed open the door, stepped out, and smiled as she slid her fingers over the solid piece of window glass. A hint of mischief filled her as she remembered Jerry's pale, silent retreat to Gary's truck earlier that day. If Adalard really *was* an alien and he could do magic like fix broken glass and create strange glowing flowers, maybe he was also capable of dealing with her brothers if she needed it.

"I wonder if he hires out?" she mused as she slammed the door and locked it.

Her footsteps held a bit more bounce as she thought about Adalard. Her excitement had nothing to do with the kisses they shared and more to do with his chivalry. It felt good to know that maybe she had someone her brothers couldn't intimidate to cover her back. She had nothing against Bear or some of the other guys she knew, but they had all wilted like last week's lettuce at one time or another around her clan.

"It's about time you got home," Rob growled from the porch.

She ignored him. He reached out and gripped her arm. When she didn't react, he squeezed harder. She knew she would be left with an impressive bruise.

"Remove your hand," she ordered in a slow, measured tone.

"Where's the money?" he demanded.

She gripped her captured arm, stepped into Rob, and yanked down and back, breaking his hold at the weakest point where the thumb and fingers met, just like Mason had shown her how to do. She reached out and pulled open the screen door and stepped through the partially opened door. Three sets of eyes followed her as she entered the living room.

Are you in danger?

She barely hid her shock. Pulling her hat off, she partially hid behind it as she crossed the room into the kitchen. Behind her, Gary was anxiously asking Rob about the money. She quickly took the narrow staircase up to her bedroom in the attic.

How can you do this? she demanded.

It… is complicated. Are you in danger? I felt your pain, he demanded.

Samara tripped on the last step going up. Her hand hit her bedroom door, and it swung open. A long string of heated curses swept through her mind when she saw the state of her room. She could almost visualize Adalard's wince at the furious heat behind them.

I gotta go, she growled.

Somehow, she was able to shove Adalard out of her head. She wasn't sure how, but at the moment, it was probably best if he couldn't 'see' what she was thinking. Murder and cheerfully dancing around a bonfire came to mind as she surveyed the wreckage of her normally orderly bedroom. She stepped inside, feeling both angry and violated.

"I'm sorry, Samara. I tried to stop them," Brit quietly said behind her.

CHAPTER TWELVE

*S*amara ignored Jerry the next morning as she placed the last box containing her personal belongings into the back of her truck. The others had either given up on trying to antagonize her into giving in to their demands or had left for work. For some reason, only Jerry seemed determined to continue their futile battle.

"You need to stay away from Paul Grove's ranch," he suddenly stated.

"That's not happening," she replied.

Jerry looked over his shoulder at the closed front door before he jumped off the front porch and stood next to her. She continued to ignore him. Lifting the tailgate, she made sure it was secure. A sharp hiss slipped from her when Jerry grabbed her arm. She yanked it free.

"What do you know about that guy that was with you yesterday?" he demanded.

She shrugged. "It really isn't any of my business," she retorted, walking around the truck to the driver's side.

"Damn it, Samara. You can't fucking lie to me. I know how much money you have, and I know that bastard isn't who he says he is," Jerry snapped.

She opened the driver's door and glared at her brother. "Your sudden concern for my wellbeing is touching," she sarcastically replied with a pseudo sweet smile that didn't reach her eyes, "but I'm just not sensing the sincerity."

Jerry shoved her. She stumbled back against the open door, her eyes widening in wary alarm when he raised his fist. She was already sporting some bruises that she would have to hide. It would be a bit more difficult to pass off a black eye or a busted lip.

Suddenly, Jerry was lifted off his feet and tossed through the air back onto the porch. She gasped, and with her mouth hanging open, stared at the back of a black leather jacket. There was a glowing sword in Adalard Ha'darra's hand. She instinctively reached out and grabbed his wrist in alarm, her attention on the front door.

"Put that thing away," she frantically ordered.

The sound of footsteps against the wood floor warned her that Rob and Gary were coming. She hastily stepped in front of Adalard as the door opened. A quick glance down verified the sword was gone.

"What the hell? What happened to you?" Rob demanded, looking down at Jerry.

"He slipped on an icy patch and fell," Samara said before Jerry could answer.

"Ouch, you okay, man?" Gary asked, holding out his hand to Jerry.

Jerry pursed his lips and nodded. He kept his wary gaze focused on Adalard. Gary lowered his eyes and muttered something incoherently before he turned and retreated into the house. Jerry pushed past a confused Rob.

"Who the hell are you?" Rob demanded.

"He's one of the survival guys from Mr. Grove's ranch. I promised to give him a lift this morning. I've got to go, or we'll be late," she said.

Samara turned and nudged Adalard toward the truck. His focus was still locked on the door where Jerry had disappeared. She swore the temperature dropped another two degrees just from his icy glare.

"We're not finished," Rob called.

She ignored her brother and motioned for Adalard to get in the truck. He turned and strode around the front. Only when he slid in beside her did she release the breath she was holding. She shut her door, started the truck, shifted it into gear, and drove away.

"Damn it," she muttered when the seat belt warning rang out.

She pressed the brake and clipped it in. Adalard did the same. She glanced at his taut face. She chuckled and shook her head when she saw the twitch above his left eye.

"What do you find amusing?" he inquired.

"You've got the Lee-Stephens twitch going," she answered.

"What is that?" he finally asked.

She gave him a sympathetic grin. "It's what happens when anyone is around my brothers for more than a few hours," she informed him with an inelegant snort.

He grimaced and rubbed his temple. "Arrow causes the same thing to happen," he muttered.

"Arrow?" she repeated with a raised eyebrow before she pulled out onto the highway.

"My brother," he answered.

"Oh." Samara didn't know why she never thought that he could have a family. "So, back at the house… where did you come from?"

He was silent long enough to make her curious. She glanced at him. He was moodily staring out of the window. As the silence grew, she wondered if he heard her. She was about to rephrase the question when he spoke.

"I teleported from the ranch," he replied in a low voice.

The truck veered onto the shoulder of the road when she turned and looked at him. She carefully maneuvered it back onto the pavement. She was gripping the steering wheel so tightly that her fingers were beginning to hurt.

"You... teleported. Are you saying you just popped up next to my truck out of thin air?" she demanded in a hoarse voice.

He released a loud sigh. "Yes," he answered in a brusque tone.

Samara warily glanced at Adalard again. "You don't sound happy about that," she observed.

"I've never traveled this far before. My teleportation skills were only recently discovered. My brother, Ha'ven, was the first to conquer the ability. Arrow believes it is a latent ability that we just never explored before. At first, he thought it manifested itself when we met our mate, but we ruled that out when we realized I could do it, too—before I met you. However, Arrow is still working on his theories. The only other way we move from one place to another is through a transporter," he explained.

She silently sorted through each part of his explanation. It wasn't easy since her mind kept going back to the word 'mate.' Was he alluding to her being his mate? Even though she could see the colors swirling around him and hear his voice in her head, it didn't mean she was a bitch in heat.

"Define 'mate,' because I'm not sure your definition and ours is translating correctly," she requested.

He frowned as he turned in his seat and looked at her. "Mate—as in you are the woman for me, and I am the man for you. We are compatible. Our auras have connected in a way that only soul mates can. You are my balance," he quietly explained.

The snort of amusement slipped from her before she could stifle it. She tried to cover it with a cough, but from the scowl of disapproval on his face, he wasn't buying it. At least his definition was more... romantic than her first thought.

"You think that I'm your mate because of some cosmic light show?" she skeptically asked with an amused grin.

"Yes," he tersely replied.

She shook her head. "Well, I'm sorry to disappoint you, lover boy, but I have plans, and they don't include chasing wild colors across the galaxy with an alien—no matter how sexy you think you might be. I've had enough of testosterone driven males for a while," she confessed before giving him an apologetic smile and continuing, "I'm afraid you'll have to find another girl looking for an out-of-this-world-adventure. I'm keeping my size sevens here on Earth."

"Where do you want this?" Adalard asked, holding up a small table.

Samara looked up. She giggled when she saw the cobwebs stuck to his dark hair and a smudge of dirt along his jaw. A surge of warmth swept through her, and she looked away.

"In front of the window. I think adding the two chairs on either side would look nice. Thank you again for helping me with this. It would have taken me days to do half of what we've been able to do in a couple of hours," she said.

"I don't mind," he replied, placing the table in the spot she recommended.

She shook her head. "I'm sure you didn't come halfway across the universe with plans of moving furniture," she teased.

"No. My plan was to bed as many human women as I could," he replied before an expression of dismay crossed his face. "I should probably not have shared that with you."

"Uh... no. You probably shouldn't have told me that," she dryly retorted.

He wiped his hands together and looked at her with a sheepish expression. "I have never had a situation where I found it impossible to lie to someone. It is as if you hold some power over me," he mused.

"I'm not sure how much of a compliment that is," she said before she shook her head and continued, "So, you came all this way to screw human women. Don't you have women where you're from?"

He scoffed. "Of course there are women where I'm from. Some of the most beautiful women in the universe are from Ceran-Pax, Valdier, and Sarafin. There are many other species as well, but I digress. I didn't come just to enjoy the company of human women. We are on a mission. My brother, Ha'ven, and his human mate, Emma, have come to retrieve her mother," he stated.

"You have another brother?" she asked with a frown.

"Yes. Ha'ven is the eldest," he explained.

"And... he's married—I mean mated—to a human named Emma," she clarified.

He nodded. "Yes. Emma saved his life."

Samara gaped at Adalard in surprise, but she didn't ask any more questions. She was still trying to absorb his comment about coming to Earth just to get laid. She was surprised by the intense feeling of disappointment coursing through her.

Why should I think alien guys were any different than human ones? she thought.

"Well, you might find some willing women at Cattleman's Bar and Grill who might be interested in taking you up on your fantasy ride. I can finish setting things up here. Ann Marie gave me some clean linens and towels. I need to wipe everything down, but I have to finish my chores outside first," she said, turning away.

"I've hurt you," he said.

She stiffened when he touched her arm. "No, you haven't hurt me. You just reminded me that all guys are alike—no matter where they come from," she replied before she cleared her throat and continued, "Once I get things finished here, I'll make you a meal as payment."

"Tonight?" he asked.

She shook her head. "Not tonight. I… have a prior engagement. Besides, I don't have any food. Let's plan on tomorrow night. I have tomorrow off and should be able to finish things up," she suggested.

"I will help you," he offered.

"I'm sure you have more important things to do than help me while you're here." She uttered a strained laugh and shook her head. "I can't believe I'm saying this. There are a million and one other questions I should be asking you, but…."

He slid his fingers up her arm and gently turned her to face him. She looked up at him. All the strange feelings she had experienced since she met him came crashing over her again. She absently reached up and pulled the cobweb out of his hair before rubbing at the smudge of dirt on his chin with her thumb.

He gasped at her tender touch. The colors that seemed to be ever present between them swirled from the pad of her thumb. Warmth, and a sense of curiosity, flooded her as her gaze moved to his lips.

Cursing her own impulsiveness, she threw caution to the wind, slid her hand around his nape, and pulled his head down, capturing his lips with hers. She had kissed her share of guys but never with such a physical intensity as this.

A low, muffled moan slipped from her, and she closed her eyes and parted her lips. He wrapped his arms around her and pulled her against his hard body. She tangled her fingers in his hair and gripped his shirt with her other hand.

Samara entwined her tongue with Adalard's, their breaths accelerating as their passion grew until she swore their hearts beat as one. A tingling sensation spread through her body. She didn't know if it was from lack of oxygen or some strange alien mojo, but it was enough to trigger her self-preservation alarm.

She broke the kiss, opened her eyes, and stared up at him with a wary expression. His pupils glowed as did a ring of darker violet around the irises. She could literally see thin bands of energy swirling in the depths.

He opened his mouth to speak, only to close it when a knock at the door drew their attention. She pulled free and smoothed back her hair with shaking hands, wiggling her nose when she realized they were trembling.

"Samara, are you in here?" a deep, familiar voice called out.

"Yeah, I'm here," she answered. She cleared her throat and spoke again, "I'm coming. I'm in the bedroom."

She grimaced when she realized what she'd just said. Adalard's amused snort told her that he had picked up on her twist of words. She gave him a heated glare, took a deep, steadying breath, and straightened her shoulders before she stepped out of the door into the living room.

The loft apartment wasn't huge. The apartment was comprised of two bedrooms, one bathroom, and an open floor plan with the kitchen, dinette, and living room all in one. In the corner, a large pellet stove sat on a platform made of rock. One of the things she loved about the apartment was the huge row of windows that overlooked the forest and mountains beyond.

"Hey, Bear. What are you doing here?" she asked.

Bear's eyes widened when he saw Adalard appear behind her. "Mason said you were moving in, and I had some time, so I thought I'd see if you needed any help," he replied, pulling his attention back to her.

She forced a smile on her lips and shook her head. "I've got this. Adalard gave me a hand. I was going to call it quits for a bit and head up to the barn to check on the horses," she said.

"Oh, okay. I guess if you're staying here now, I'll pick you up here instead of at your old place," Bear replied.

"I... yeah, that would be great," she said with a strained smile.

Bear shifted from one foot to the other, glancing curiously at Adalard. She imagined that Adalard was starting to put two and two together. From the growing pressure she was sensing in her head, he was attempting to talk to her in his strange, alien way.

"Well, I guess if we want to keep our jobs we'd better get to work," she suggested with a wave of her hand at the door.

Bear blinked as if coming out of a daze and nodded. "Yeah, I'll see you later this evening," he replied before nodding at Adalard. "It was a pleasure to meet you."

At the door, Samara gave Bear a wave and watched him descend the stairs. Once he disappeared around the corner, she closed the door and turned around. She gasped when Adalard placed his hands on the door just above her shoulders. His violet eyes were glowing again.

"You are meeting him later?" he asked with a slight growl in his voice.

She pushed against his chest and slipped under his arm. "Yes," she stated, not elaborating.

"It is for work?" he demanded.

"No," she replied, taking her jacket off the hook by the door and pulling it on. "We are going out for dinner and a drink."

"Samara," he began.

She turned and glared at him. "Don't go all testosterone fueled on me, Adalard. I've already had enough to last me a lifetime, so I would advise you to be very careful about what you say or do next. Alien or not, I won't hesitate to kick your ass out of here," she threatened.

He raised one eyebrow at her, and the corners of his lips twitched. Raising his hands in the air, he stepped back, giving her space. She eyed him with suspicion.

"I apologize," he quietly responded.

She warily studied him. He didn't look remorseful. In fact, she would swear he had a calculating gleam in his eyes that reminded her of Wilson. God, she missed him. He was the only one of her brothers who had a decent head on his shoulders.

"Okay. I've got to get my chores done. Do you need anything before I leave?" she asked.

"Only this."

She parted her lips when he stepped forward. He paused, the wicked gleam shining in his eyes, before he slid his hands up her arms. She gave him a bemused look before she slid her hands over his chest, and rose to meet him.

"Don't get used to this," she softly warned, peeping up at him.

"Never," he promised.

She sucked in a breath when he captured her lips in a passionate kiss that made her toes curl.

CHAPTER THIRTEEN

*F*rom the moment Samara climbed into Bear's truck she knew this was a mistake. By the time they reached the restaurant and bar, she had buried her misgivings and forced herself to relax. They had chatted about their high school days, her brothers, the weather, and a dozen other topics to pass time during the drive into town.

She smiled as he helped her out of the truck. As they entered the bar, Bear called out to a few guys as they weaved their way around the tables to their seats. Samara glanced around the dim interior.

"Thank you," she murmured when he pulled a chair out for her.

She removed her jacket and hung it on the back of her chair while Bear ordered a couple of beers and some chips and salsa. Between the band playing, the crack of pool balls, and the noise of everyone talking, it made it difficult to hear. She leaned forward and tried to listen as Bear talked about the newest temporary ranch hands Mason had hired.

"I'm glad you came out with me tonight," Bear said in a loud voice just as the music died.

"Nice, Bear," someone yelled.

"Shut up, Carl," Bear replied with a good-natured grin.

"Well, well, well," a familiar voice sneered, "if it isn't the runaway. Where's your scarred bodyguard?"

Samara covered Bear's hand when he started to rise to his feet. Casper wasn't a huge town, and Cattlemen's was a popular hangout for the locals. Turning in her chair, she looked up at her brother with a raised eyebrow.

"Do you miss him? I'm sure I can arrange another lovely man-to-dipshit chat with him if you'd like," she sweetly retorted.

"You're a real bitch sometimes. Does Bear know that?" Jerry responded.

Bear pulled his hand away and rose to his feet. "You shouldn't talk to your sister that way," he angrily replied.

Jerry smirked. "What are you going to do about it, Teddy Bear?" he inquired.

Samara rose from her chair and angrily turned toward her brother. She wasn't going to let him pull Bear into a fight. The mocking gleam in his eyes told her he was itching for a brawl.

"Back off, Jerry. Don't forget that I won't be there to bail your ass out of jail," she warned.

"I'll back off when you give me the money you promised," he goaded.

She waved her hand. "That deal died when you stole my truck," she snapped.

Jerry's hand shot out, and he wrapped his fingers around her wrist. She winced at the bruising grip. Behind her, Bear muttered a curse and came forward to help her.

Jerry shoved her, and she gave a cry of surprise as her heel caught the edge of her chair, making her fall back against the table. Jerry swung a punch at Bear, who ducked and caught him around the waist.

Samara pushed herself back to her feet in time to watch Bear toss Jerry onto a nearby pool table. Jerry lifted his legs and kicked out at Bear, sending him backwards into her. The force of Bear's momentum sent them against one of the load-bearing wall beams. Her head snapped back, hitting a sharp corner.

Shock ricocheted through her before the pain hit. Dark spots danced in front of her eyes from the impact. Lifting her hand to the back of her head, she winced when she felt blood.

"Samara...," Bear said, twisting around and catching her as she slid down the post.

Her lips parted to let him know that she was alright, but no sound emerged. She tried to blink away the darkness, and turned her head, looking at her fingers through a growing haze. Dark red blood coated her fingertips.

Adalard....

She didn't know why his name slipped through her dazed mind, but it did. Bear's arms wound around her before a different pair lifted her limp body and warmth surrounded her. Her head rolled sideways as her eyes closed.

"You... came," she whispered.

"Always," Adalard vowed.

Moments before:

Adalard stared out at the darkened landscape. He flexed his fingers, forming different items at random. After Samara left her new living quarters, he had returned to his transport.

That was a mistake, he darkly thought.

His fruitless search for whatever was draining him of his energy had left him feeling weak and disoriented. Eventually, he was forced to abandon the search out of fear of being stuck inside the ship, drained of life. As much as he hated to consider the possibility, he might have to abandon and destroy the transport.

Even Arrow was at a loss. Unless Adalard could find the device and show his brother, there was no way to figure out how it worked.

Worst of all his problems, though, was knowing that Samara was with another male. It was driving him insane.

It was then that a silent cry from Samara echoed through his mind. Adalard shimmered, his cells drawn to her through her voice and a brief image of blood on her pale fingers.

The room around him faded and another appeared. Samara's aura reached for him through the crowd of people. He pushed through the bystanders, ignoring the hissed breaths of irritation and low curses that died on their lips when they saw him.

The man he met earlier in Samara's living quarters was lowering her to the ground. He stepped forward and slid his arms around her, pulling her from Bear's grasp.

"Hey! Oh, it's you. Where in the hell did you come from? I… she needs a doctor. She's bleeding," Bear said.

"I will care for her," he replied.

Adalard locked his gaze on Jerry. Two men were holding him by his upper forearms. He noticed with grim satisfaction that Jerry's face paled when he saw him. It wouldn't matter how far the man ran or that he was Samara's brother. His attack on Samara this time would not be forgiven.

"I warned you," Adalard said.

Jerry sagged between the two men.

The crowd parted as Adalard strode toward the door. Before he even reached it, he was fading, all thoughts of protecting his identity dismissed as he focused on Samara.

"What the hell...? Where'd they go?" Carl breathed out as he vanished.

"Ow, that hurts," Samara muttered.

Her voice was muffled against Adalard's shoulder. He held her close, trying not to jostle her. He was surprised when he didn't feel the energy drain as he strode through the storage bay of his transport.

"It will soon be better," he promised.

"What would make me feel better is for my brothers to grow a brain," she groaned.

He chuckled. Despite the fact that her brothers were the lowest form of life, he could still sense her compassion for them. She was a better person than he was. He felt no regret at his half-brother's death and wouldn't think twice about killing her brother, Jerry, the next time the opportunity presented itself.

"I'm afraid that is not likely to happen any time soon," he dryly replied.

He carried her through an open door and gently laid her on the bed. She hissed and lifted her head off the pillow, wincing as she tried to sit up. He placed his hand on her shoulder and scowled at her. She glared back and pushed his hand away.

"Do you have any idea what a bitch it is to get blood out of fabric?" she growled.

He looked at her with an expression of disbelief. "You have a gash in your head, a possible concussion, and you are worried about my bed linens?" he exclaimed.

She closed one eye and winced. "Yes. I'm worried. Where are we?" she asked.

"My transport. I need to get the medical kit. Please remain here until I return," he answered.

"'Kay," she responded, peering around the room with only one eye open.

He hesitated, worried about leaving her. The medical kit was in a cabinet on the bridge. He backed out of the room, casting a wary look at Samara once more before he turned away and started down the corridor.

The moment Adalard left the room, a wave of fatigue hit him. A dark gray film greedily surrounded him, making him feel as if he were trudging through thick sludge. He braced one hand against the wall to keep his balance as he forced his feet to keep moving.

The journey to the bridge seemed to take forever though he knew it was only minutes. The vein at his temple throbbed as he gritted his teeth to keep from groaning. The gray matter felt like it was literally trying to pull him apart.

"Dragon's balls," he muttered as he opened the cabinet.

He pulled out the emergency medical kit, almost falling into the chair from the weight of it. In his peripheral vision, he saw gray strands devouring his aura. What puzzled him was that he didn't feel or sense this draining fatigue when he was with Samara.

Clutching the medical kit to his chest, he focused on returning the short distance to the only sleeping quarters on the transport. By the time he made it to the doorway, he was breathing heavily and shaking from fatigue. He looked at Samara leaning back against the hull with her eyes closed and the sleeve of her dark red blouse pressed against the cut on the side of her head.

He stepped into the room—and was surrounded by a surge of energy. The dramatic difference from mind-numbing weakness to feeling like he could take on a hundred Sarafin and Valdier warriors at once almost knocked him off his feet. The impact was so intense that he needed a few seconds to deal with the excess power flowing through him.

He turned and looked back at the doorway. The gray energy shrank away from the entrance as if terrified. He lifted his arm and studied the patterns of colors swirling around him. Bright white, red, violet, and various shades of blue formed an almost honeycomb barrier. He followed the pattern back to its source.

Samara, he silently breathed.

What? she responded, opening her eyes. "Wow! You're coated in like a colorful bubble wrap. What'd you do—run through a rainbow or find Lucky Charms?"

"It is you," he said, stepping forward and placing the medical kit on the bed beside her.

"Me?" she exclaimed in disbelief. She started to shake her head and winced. "Ow. I hope that box has some serious pain killers in it."

He knelt on the floor in front of her and opened the case. "You will be healed in a few minutes. I need to make sure there was no serious brain damage."

Samara released an inelegant snort. "Wilson would argue that you were too late," she mumbled, closing her eyes again.

"Who is Wilson?" Adalard asked.

He pulled the scanner out and held it next to her head. At the same time, he reached out and connected with her, blocking the pain she was feeling. She sighed with relief. A sense of remorse filled him when he felt the sharp, throbbing pain he had taken from her. He should have blocked her pain sooner.

"Wilson? He's the second oldest out of the motley crew of Lee-Stephens, and was, until I left this morning, the smartest one of the bunch of us," she shared.

Using a combination of technology and his own energy, he healed the wound and cleaned the blood from her hair.

"The spot will be tender for a day or two."

She opened her eyes and stared into his. An uneven smile curved her lips. He breathed a sigh of relief when he noticed that her eyes were clear and her pupils looked normal.

"Thank you," she said.

In one of the few awkward moments of his life, he wasn't sure what to say or do. Clearing his throat, he replaced the scanner into the medical kit and closed it. He rose to his feet and held his hand out. She grasped it, scooted off the bed, and stood next to him, looking around with wide, curious eyes.

"You know I plan to kill your brother for this, don't you?" he said.

He almost winced at his unexpected confession. She laughed and shook her head. He looked down at her hand when she patted him on the chest.

"Trust me, you'll have to stand in line, not to mention he just isn't worth it. Karma will bite him in the ass soon enough without your help. So, is this your broken-down bike?" Samara teased.

Adalard frowned before he understood what she meant. With a sheepish grin, he nodded. He had forgotten about her misconception.

"Can I look around?" she curiously asked.

"What? I... Yes, but...," he said, his voice fading as he looked at the doorway.

She tilted her head and looked in the same direction before looking up at him. He could see the dark gray aura swirling outside of the doorway. He instinctively wrapped a protective arm around Samara, pulling her closer to him.

"Is something wrong?" she asked.

He sighed. "Yes. A very dangerous device was placed on the transport that is causing issues. I haven't located it yet," he grimly admitted.

She looked back at the doorway and frowned. "Does it have something to do with the gray swirling smoke?" she inquired.

He started with surprise and looked at her. "You see it?" he demanded.

She gave him a funny look and nodded. "Yeah. For a moment I was worried your ship was on fire until I noticed there wasn't a smell. Then I thought it was the lighting, some kind of breathing chemical, or just a weird alien thing." She shook her head. "I can't believe I'm even saying that."

He shook his head. "The issue appeared on my journey to your planet," he explained.

"Is it another alien?" she warily asked. "I mean, you know—could it be like a virus or some kind of creature that wants to take over your body?"

"No, the bio-filters would destroy any such thing," he said.

She frowned. "Well, have you followed the gray swirling things?" she asked.

He hesitated. "N-o. Until now, I didn't notice the gray aura attacking me. All I felt was the intense energy drain, as if it was sucking the life out of me. I've been searching the ship, but I grow dangerously weak —except when I was carrying you," he admitted.

She bit her lip and looked out into the corridor. "Well, maybe my superpower is keeping the bad aura away from you. If that's the case, maybe I could help you find it," she suggested.

He caressed her cheek. "I would appreciate your help," he said.

She looked up at him and smiled. "It's the least I can do for helping me out tonight—but, there is *one* condition," she warned.

"And what is your condition?" he inquired.

She patted him on the chest and grinned. "You can't kill Jerry, no matter how tempting it is," she cheekily replied before stepping out into the corridor.

He scowled at her before a calculating gleam appeared in his eyes, and a slight smile curled his lips. She had said he couldn't kill her brother. She didn't say he couldn't make Jerry wish he were dead.

Wishing is okay.

He blinked in surprise at her amused response to his thoughts. She looked at him over her shoulder with a mischievous expression. Desire hit him hard. Wicked thoughts danced through his mind. Her soft gasp told him she caught what he was thinking.

"You are a very dangerous alien, Adalard Ha'darra. You should be focusing on finding your device, not mentally undressing me," she quipped with a shake of her head.

"Undressing you is much more pleasurable," he stated.

She rolled her eyes at him and turned away. "Men! I swear evolution made a mistake giving them two heads and expecting them to use the one with the brain," she retorted.

He burst out laughing. Samara was different from any other woman he had ever met. Of course, the main difference was the way their auras connected, giving him a sense of completion, but it was more than that. Most of the women he met were too busy eyeing him as their next toy or anticipating the prestige that being with him would bring them. Samara wasn't impressed with his status—or his physique.

The last thought doused his amusement somewhat as an unexpected and definitely unusual feeling of uncertainty washed through him. What if she didn't find him attractive? He touched his cheek with the scar on it. Maybe he should erase the mark he received years ago.

Now you're just being ridiculous. I think you're cute.

Her response reminded him that his thoughts were open to her. An uncharacteristic blush rose in his cheeks. Once again, she made him feel like an untried lad on his first outing with a beautiful woman.

He was pulled from his uncomfortable self-reflection by a sense of weakness. While he was lost in thought, Samara had ventured toward the bridge of the ship. Less than ten feet separated them, but the malevolent gray fog attacked him with a vengeance. He bowed his head, swaying at the force of the assault, and braced a hand against the inner wall of the corridor.

Samara turned and looked at him, her eyes widening with horror. He lifted his head and shook it.

"Come toward me slowly. I... need to see what happens so I... can share the information... with my brother," he haltingly instructed through clenched teeth.

She bit her lip, nodded, and began to walk slowly toward him. The gray fog parted as if someone drew a line down the middle of it. He counted the steps before her aura surrounded him in a protective cocoon.

Pulling her into his embrace, he breathed deeply, enjoying that she held him tightly against her body. She caressed his back with soothing strokes as the weakness faded. He leaned back against the wall and watched the gray fog swirling in a semi-circle around them.

How can I protect her when I cannot even protect myself? he silently wondered, making sure he kept a barrier between them so she could not hear his worried thoughts.

CHAPTER FOURTEEN

*S*amara stood still with her eyes closed. There was something very comforting about holding and being held by Adalard. His touch was gentle but strong at the same time.

Opening her eyes, she stared at the gray fog that had encircled him a moment ago. A thin film of bright light surrounded them in a bubble. Whenever the gray film tried to move closer, tiny sparks were ignited. The gray matter hissed. The sound reminded her of water landing on a hot burner. Bits of the fog evaporated when struck.

"Thank you," Adalard murmured.

She reluctantly pulled away and brushed her hair back behind her ear. "No problem. I guess we should stick pretty close together, huh?"

"Yes, that might be good," he said, caressing her cheek.

She tilted her head against his hand and smiled up at him. She lowered her gaze to his lips. He groaned and kissed her. She parted her lips, absorbing his kiss like a sunflower searching for the warmth of the sun.

She slid her hands up his arms to his neck. He lifted her, and she wrapped her legs around his waist. He pressed her back against the corridor wall. This position allowed him to run his hands over her sides, hips, and buttocks.

Their tongues stroking the other's in an ancient dance as old as time, touching, retreating, teasing, and tasting each other. He slipped his hands under her blouse, making her moan at his sensual touch. She had made out a few times in high school out of curiosity, but this was nothing like those clumsy caresses.

She moaned again when he cupped her lace-covered breasts. Her nipples throbbed, straining against the thin material of her bra. She wasn't endowed with large breasts like some of her friends. Still, they felt heavy and fuller than normal when he brushed the pad of his thumb over the taut tips.

Shock-filled pleasure tore through her when he pressed his hips against her. There was no denying his arousal. Visions of their bodies clinging to each other with his cock deeply embedded inside her filled her mind. The images were so vivid and the intensity of the pressure building deep inside her so real that for a moment she wondered if they were really locked together in a passionate embrace.

The unexpected heat tearing through her and settling between her legs caused her to rip her lips from his. She closed her eyes and held onto the sexual vision. The pressure of Adalard rocking his hips, the thick bulge of his arousal pressed against her sensitive mound, and the friction of her clothing sent her spiraling out of control.

Gasping, she clutched his shoulders, rubbing against him as he rocked back and forth. The wave reached the pinnacle and crashed. A cry was ripped from her throat at her unexpected climax. Adalard rolled her straining nipples between his forefingers and thumbs, drawing out the pleasure as he held her pinned between his throbbing cock and the wall. That was the only thing keeping her from melting into a puddle on the floor.

She opened her eyes. Shock held her speechless when she saw the passionate and possessive flame burning in Adalard's violet eyes. The vibrant colors of the Aurora Borealis flared outward from him and wrapped around her. Breathless and stunned by what she had just experienced, she cupped his cheeks and kissed him.

As the afterglow of her orgasm faded and reality set in, a feeling of awkward unease swept through her. She was way in over her head in a situation she had never been in before. Adalard broke their kiss and stepped back with a sigh.

"I…," she mumbled, sliding her legs from around his waist.

"Have given me a great gift. I ask for nothing more," he said.

She looked up at him with an amused expression. "Spoken like a true knight in shining armor," she mused.

"I will probably pay for my chivalry later," he replied with a grimace.

"Yes, well, on a good note, the gray fog appears to have dissipated," she remarked.

He frowned and looked both ways along the corridor. Whatever power surge they had sent out either sent the gray malevolent vapor running for cover or made it evaporate. The corridor was clear in both directions.

"This would be a good time to search for the device," he said.

Her throat tightened, and she nodded. What if their intimate encounter destroyed the gray mass? He would be able to leave. The thought shook her, as did the idea of never seeing him again. She looked up when he tenderly caressed her cheek.

"You do not have to worry. When I leave, you will know," he quietly vowed.

"Hey Samara, how are you feeling?" Bear asked the next morning.

Samara looked up from the back of the trailer attached to the UTV. Remorse swept through her when she saw the concerned expression on Bear's face. She had forgotten all about him.

"Hi Bear. I'm good," she replied, leaning on the pitchfork.

He dismounted from the gelding he was riding and walked over to her. She tightened her grip on the handle of the pitchfork when he silently studied her. His intense scrutiny made her wish she had kept her hat on.

"So, what happened?" he asked.

"What do you mean?" she uneasily countered.

He eyed her with a slightly reproachful glare that made her flush. She released a loud sigh, set the pitchfork down, and sat on the bale of hay she had been working on distributing. What happened last night still seemed unreal.

"How is your head?" he dryly inquired.

She lifted her hand and touched the spot. It was still tender if she pressed on it. Fortunately, she was wearing a bandana to keep her hair out of her eyes and it covered the area where she should have had a wound.

"It's fine—a little tender still," she honestly replied.

"So, did you need stitches? Did the doc at the emergency room clear you to come back so soon? After the amount of blood I saw you lose last night, it seems like they would've suggested some extra time off," he reasoned.

As Bear studied her face, Samara had an uneasy feeling that he knew she hadn't gone to the hospital. Deciding deflection was the best tactic, she countered with a question of her own.

"What happened to Jerry after I left?" she asked.

Bear snorted and shrugged. "He might be needing a dentist," he answered.

She stared at his hands. He was wearing gloves, but she suspected there might be a few bruises on his knuckles. The thought made her grin. A look into Bear's amused eyes confirmed her suspicion.

"How many?" she inquired.

Bear grinned back at her. "Two—a front tooth and a molar," he confessed.

She shook her head. "He should have known better than to call you Teddy Bear. You were the State Junior Heavy Weight Boxing champion three years in a row!"

"Yeah, a few guys reminded him of that as they were hauling his ass out of the bar," he said.

The determined gleam reappeared in Bear's eyes, and panic hit Samara when she saw it. Her hope that he would drop what happened to her faded. She was a lousy liar, so she would have to tread as close to the truth as possible.

"So, are you gonna tell me what happened to you after you and the Rock Star vanished?" he asked.

"That was a funny thing, Adalard showing up, wasn't it? I don't remember a lot with all the excitement and being half knocked out, but it turns out he isn't a Rock Star after all," she said.

"What is he then?" Bear pressed.

"He's a doctor—of sorts. He patched me up, and after making sure I wasn't going to pass out on him, he brought me home," she explained.

Bear looked at Samara with a skeptical expression and folded his arms across his chest. "A doctor, you say? From where?" he dryly asked.

She scowled at him. "I don't know. Some foreign place. What does it matter? I'm better. I'm sorry about last night. It is one of the hazards of being around my family. I shouldn't have gone out with you. It would have saved us both a lot of grief," she muttered.

She rose, turned, and grabbed the pitchfork. She wobbled with surprise when she felt the trailer rock. Twisting, she looked up at Bear with a startled expression. It was one of the few times that she witnessed his anger.

"Last night was not a mistake. It isn't your fault your brothers are dicks. I can handle them. What I can't handle is that you got hurt. You don't get it, do you, Samara? I've had feelings for you since the tenth grade," he gruffly replied.

"I... Bear... I...."

She was at a loss for words. No, she didn't get it. Her feelings of guilt multiplied as she remembered all the times that she cut Bear off short when he had started flirting with her during high school. Hell, she had never had time to think of boys—other than the ones that were pissed off at her brothers and wanting to take it out on her. For that matter, half the girls had been the same way thanks to the long string of broken hearts her siblings liked to leave behind. For some reason that she never understood, being a 'bad boy' made her brothers appealing to the opposite sex.

Bear pulled one of his gloves off and gently caressed her cheek. She remained still when he leaned forward and kissed her cold lips. In response, she felt nothing, and remorse filled her because of it.

It wasn't that she was repulsed, but there was no fire there the way there was when Adalard kissed her. Bear's soft hiss of pain made her blink. He pulled away from her with an apologetic smile.

"Sorry about that. The static electricity must be from the cold and my clothes—unless you want to think of it as a spark of passion," he said, rubbing his chest.

"Spark?" she repeated, looking down at her hands.

Samara had unconsciously pressed them against his chest. A dark red swirl of energy with white sparks that looked like tiny bolts of electricity was emanating from them. She curled her gloved fingers, thankful that Bear couldn't see what she saw. She shoved her hands into the pockets of her coat and shook her head.

"I… it must be the cold—like in the freezer section at the grocery store," she mumbled.

He chuckled and nodded. "So, will you give me another chance? I'll take you someplace where I know your brothers won't show up," he promised.

Adalard flashed through her mind. She swallowed and shook her head. There was no way they could ever be together. They were literally from two different worlds.

"I think I'd rather just be friends for now. I'm trying to get my life sorted out… without my brothers," she awkwardly replied.

Bear nodded in disappointment. "I get that. I can be a patient man," he said with a wink. "How about I help you with this so you can take some time for yourself to recoup? I have a few hours before I'm supposed to meet with some of the guys."

"That would be nice, Bear," she softly responded.

"I'll even share my hot chocolate with you when we finish—as a consolation prize for missing out on dessert last night," he said with a roguish smile.

She mutely watched him jump over the side of the trailer and lift one of the square bales of hay from the back. The gelding softly whinnied and stepped forward to take a mouthful.

Lost in thought, they worked in unison with Bear's casual chatter filling the silence. She was sweeping out the last of the hay when Adalard's quiet voice filled her mind.

What is hot chocolate?

CHAPTER FIFTEEN

*A*dalard glared at his brother's image on the vidcom. "You are *not* going to use Samara like some creature you find interesting and want to study in your lab," he growled.

"Adalard, think about this. If our adversaries have perfected a weapon that uses our powers against us, we have to find a way to combat it. Samara may hold the key to unlocking it," Arrow calmly countered.

Adalard gave his brother a disgruntled look before sitting down heavily on the chair in front of the vidcom. He sat back and contemplated the situation. His brother was right. Whatever the device was, it could be devastating to their people. His first responsibility was to protect them.

It wasn't like he was throwing Samara to the Pactors. He would ensure that she was safe and happy despite the fact that Arrow would probably drive them both crazy with his need-to-know experiments. His intentions to take things slowly were also complicated by Ha'ven and Emma's return in a few days. He couldn't stay on Earth, and his people needed her. There was no way around those two critical facts.

"I will bring her back with me," he begrudgingly agreed.

"In the meantime, I'll see if I can find out more information based on what you've told me so far," Arrow replied.

"I'll contact you once I've found the device. Out." Adalard disconnected their link.

He leaned back in the chair and stared up at the ceiling. His expression softened as he thought about the night before. Last night had been both exquisite and excruciating. His body throbbed with need at the memory of Samara's orgasm.

He cursed under his breath and rose to his feet again. Taking it slow was going to be the death of him. He ran his hand over his crotch with a rueful sigh. He wished now he had paid more attention to his brother and Emma's relationship.

"Arrow has probably written a case study on them for the archives," he muttered.

A movement outside of the window drew his attention. Pleasure swept through him when he saw Samara pulling the small vehicle up to the barn across from the main house. Without thinking, he dematerialized and reappeared next to her.

She stumbled back in surprise and he wrapped his arms around her to steady her. She muttered a muffled curse against his shoulder and glared at him before glancing around with a hint of panic in her eyes. He chuckled and she shook her head at him in admonishment.

"You shouldn't do things like that! Somebody might see you," she hissed with dismay.

"And then you would convince them that they didn't see what they thought they saw. I am fully confident in your ability to 'bullshit'," he teased. "I learned a new human word," he confided with a waggle of his eyebrows.

She snorted and patted his chest. "You're going to need something warmer than a thin shirt if we are going to go check out your spaceship," she said.

He held her hand and pulled her closer. Her swiftly inhaled breath told him that she was aware of his desire for her. He brought his face closer to hers and stopped a breath away from her lips.

"Perhaps you could keep me warm," he suggested.

She curled her fingers around his and gazed up at him with wide eyes. Her pupils were dilated, and he could see his reflection in her eyes. His irises were glowing.

"It's a shame I can't bottle your sexuality. I'd be a billionaire by the end of the week," she breathed out.

Her comment startled a laugh out of him and he pressed a hard, possessive kiss on her lips. He gave her a wink as he pulled back a step. A groan stuck in his throat when she parted her pink lips and swept the tip of her tongue across her upper lip.

"The only one I want is you, Samara," he replied in a thick voice.

A blush rose in her cheeks and her eyes sparkled. Hell, her entire body was glowing. He didn't need a coat. The warmth of her aura was wrapped around him, heating his body, and calling to him.

"I'm off for the rest of the day thanks to Bear. I thought I could help you search for your mysterious device again," she said.

He frowned when she mentioned the other man's name. "What is hot chocolate?" he asked.

She laughed. "It's a yummy treat that's perfect on a cold day. How about I make some to take with us, along with some sandwiches, while you get ready?" she suggested.

"That... would be nice," he replied.

He thought about reminding her that he didn't need to return to the house to get ready, but the shy excitement in her eyes held his tongue. Unable to resist, he stepped forward and pressed another kiss on her upturned lips. She responded, touching the tip of her tongue to his bottom lip before pulling away when the sound of tires crunching on the frozen ground warned them that they were about to have a visitor.

She stepped away from him and turned toward the approaching vehicle. Adalard sighed when he saw Mason's familiar face. The man was really trying his patience.

They waited as Mason pulled the truck up in front of the barn. He swore the human was taking his sweet time getting out of the vehicle just to annoy him. Folding his arms across his chest, he glared at Mason when the man raised an eyebrow at him.

"Good afternoon, Samara," Mason greeted.

"Hey, Mason," Samara greeted with an easy smile.

Mason nodded at him. "Adalard."

"Mason," he responded.

Mason's gaze swept over the UTV, pausing on the trailer attached to the back of it. "Looks like you've been busy this morning," he said, returning his attention to Samara.

"Yeah. I finished distributing hay to the upper pasture," she said.

Mason frowned. "How's your head?" he asked, studying her.

Samara lifted a hand to the bandana. "My head… is fine," she replied with a grimace. "Who told you?"

Mason chuckled. "Half the crew on the ranch go to the Cattleman's Bar. Bobby said you were out with Bear and your brother showed up being an ass. He was worried because he said you were bleeding pretty good when the strange survivor guy from the ranch suddenly appeared and swooped in. He said you both vanished," he dryly relayed.

"Yeah, well, lucky for me, Adalard showed up and *drove* me back to the ranch," she said.

"She knows who and what I am," Adalard suddenly stated.

Mason's eyes widened before he pursed his lips and shook his head. "So much for keeping a low profile. Who else knows?"

"No one," Adalard replied.

"No one," Samara repeated, looking at Adalard with concern.

Mason snorted. "After last night's little performance, you've got more than one tongue wagging like a dog's tail when it sees a bone. What part of keeping a low profile didn't you understand?" he growled.

Samara stepped forward and touched Mason's arm. "I was hurt pretty bad, Mason. Adalard helped me. It isn't his fault that my brothers are idiots."

Mason's expression softened and he nodded. "I'm thankful for his help, but this is bigger than either of us. If the government found out about Adalard... well, things could get complicated very quickly. The world isn't ready to know there are... people like Adalard and the others," he replied.

"The others?" she asked.

Adalard wrapped his arm around Samara's waist, pulling her close, and shook his head at Mason.

Mason returned his warning glare with a frown. Adalard wasn't sure if it was because of the look he gave Mason or because of the possessive hold he had on Samara. He clenched his jaw.

"Let's just say Adalard isn't our first visitor." Mason paused and reached into his pocket when his cellphone vibrated. He looked at the text and sighed before looking back at them. "I've got to go into town. Do you need anything?"

Samara shook her head. "No, thank you."

"Alright. If you think of anything, call me. I'll be back later. Adalard, if you don't mind, I'd like to speak with you privately for a moment," Mason requested.

"Of course," he replied in a stiff tone.

An awkward silence descended between the two men.

"I've got to go drop off the trailer and do a few things," Samara said, breaking through the tense quiet.

"I will see you soon," Adalard murmured.

She nodded at him before giving Mason a smile. Adalard watched her as she slid into the UTV and pulled away. It wasn't until she was out of sight that he returned his attention to Mason. The other man had been observing him with a worried frown.

"You knew the rules," Mason stated.

He lifted an eyebrow at the other man's tone. "Yes," he replied.

"I need you to leave—immediately," Mason added.

"No," he curtly replied.

Mason's frown deepened. "What do you mean 'no'? This isn't open for debate. You were told not to tell anyone, not to show off your... whatever in the hell you call it, alien powers, and to stay away from the staff," he reminded in a hard tone.

A surge of anger swept through Adalard. "Careful how you speak to me, human. The Valdier can be short-tempered, but the Curizan can be worse. I know your rules," he growled.

"It would be best if you left... for everyone," Mason grimly reasserted.

"I will leave as soon as I can safely do so," he bit out.

Mason frowned. "Safely? What does that mean?" he asked.

Adalard hesitated. He understood Mason's concerns. That understanding was the only reason they were still having a conversation. If he hadn't met Samara, he wouldn't have broken any of the rules set forth. He couldn't—wouldn't lie to his mate. That, combined with the fact that she was injured, made it impossible to follow the rules. He didn't give a damn who knew about him if Samara's life was on the line.

"My transport has been... compromised. Once it is repaired, I will leave your world," he announced.

"Is it broken? Do you have the parts to fix it?" Mason asked.

"Yes, and yes," he replied.

He didn't elaborate on the problem or the fact that when he left, he wouldn't be going alone. It was no concern of Mason's, and the less the man knew the better—and safer—it was for everyone. His short reply appeared to satisfy Mason.

"Good, good," Mason replied before he grimaced when his cellphone vibrated again. He looked down at the phone before pressing the button on the side and looked up again. "Keep me posted. If you need anything and I can help, let me know. I've got to go."

"I will," Adalard replied.

He watched as the other man turned and walked away. He waited until Mason was heading back the way he came before he reached out to Samara.

What are you doing? he curiously inquired.

Making hot chocolate and sandwiches. Is Mason gone? she asked with a thread of amusement.

Yes. He is not happy with me, he grudgingly admitted.

I have a feeling you get that a lot, she teased.

More than you know. Do you need help?

No, I'll be there in ten minutes. We can take the UTV. It will be warmer and more comfortable, she said.

Can I drive?

Her snort of laughter caused his blood to heat again. His mind filled with vivid thoughts of her melting in his arms like she had the night before. The thoughts spilled over into her mind. She gave a heated curse that made him smile.

Drive me crazy, you mean, she grumbled. *Be ready or I'm drinking all the hot chocolate.*

The smile on his face grew when she abruptly cut their connection but not before he saw in her mind the vivid image of them locked together. The day suddenly seemed brighter. Striding back to the house, he took the steps two at a time. He would be more than ready by the time she arrived.

CHAPTER SIXTEEN

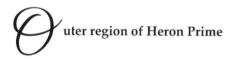 uter region of Heron Prime

Hamade Dos sat at his desk on the modified Marastin Dow warship he had requisitioned and stared at the information flowing across the screen in front of him. The last reported sighting of the *Rayon I* had been months ago, and there was still no contact from the informant on board. He drummed his fingers on the desk in aggravation. A beep drew his attention to the door.

"Enter," he called. The door opened and Lesher entered. "Have you found anything?"

"A transmission was intercepted between the *Rayon I* and the Ha'darra palace," Lesher replied.

Hamade pushed back his chair and stood. "And...?"

Lesher shook his head. "Only that it was an encrypted message from Adalard to his twin brother," he answered.

Hamade clenched his fist. Time and again, he had been thwarted by the Ha'darra family. His eyes glittered with malice. If he could not go to them, then he would bring the brothers to him.

"It is time for a new tactic," he said, walking around the desk.

Lesher bowed his head. "I will command the mission myself, General," Lesher responded.

~

Earth

"Watch your step," Adalard warned as he held out his hand and steadied Samara when she stepped off the trail. There were still patches of snow and ice along the leaf covered path.

Samara absently nodded and placed her hand in his. They had left the UTV at the top of the cliff and followed the path to the bridge before taking the narrow trail on the other side of the cliff down to the bank of the river.

She walked toward Adalard's transport with a sense of awe. This was the first time that she had seen it from the outside. Before, her idea of an alien spaceship was influenced by movies and television. The real ship was a slick, bullet-shape design covered in a shimmering tarp.

"How did you conceal it? I didn't notice anything from above," she breathed out.

"The Goddess's gift to my species is the ability to manipulate energy. Each Curizan possesses a different level and skill, but we are all capable of creating basic items from the energy surrounding us," he explained.

She looked at him with a startled expression. "You can do magic?"

He shrugged and fingered the thin material covering his transport. "I suppose some may call it magic. We Curizans are known more for our technology. For centuries we promoted that idea, but, in actuality, our technology is enhanced by the energy we can harness."

She ran her fingers along the outer hull of the ship. "So, what can you do with the energy besides create a huge bedsheet and teleport—oh, and heal?" she asked as she looked at him and touched the side of her head.

He chuckled. "As a member of the royal family, I have more power than most," he said.

She grinned. "What is one power that you have that you are most proud of?" she curiously asked.

His expression softened as he reached out and caressed her cheek. "Finding you," he confessed.

"What kind of power is that?" she skeptically inquired.

"The most powerful of all," he softly responded before he kissed her. "I want you, Samara."

She tangled her fingers in his long hair, their breaths mingled, heightening the rush of desire inside her. She trailed her fingers down his throat before she pulled away and peered up at him.

Her heart skipped a beat as she slid her hands down the column of his neck to his shoulders. There was something about him. He was literally worlds apart from her brothers and every other man she had ever met. Yet, despite all of that, she was still leery of falling into the trap that had captured her mother and grandmother.

She leaned into him and kissed him again. The raw need reflected in his voice and eyes made her fingers curl against his heated flesh. She wanted more, but fear and caution cooled her longing to say to hell with everything and give in to her desires. Her mother's tired, defeated face flashed through her mind. She took a trembling breath and gave him a shaky smile.

"I'm not ready," she confessed. "I won't lie. I'm very attracted to you, but… well, we are literally from different worlds and… one day you'll go back to yours, and I'll be left alone."

He cupped her cheek. "It doesn't have to be that way, Samara."

She held his hand, squeezing his fingers in response, unsure of what to say. Her heart wanted to say yes, but her brain was telling her to proceed with caution. The very thought of his leaving left a gaping hole in her heart.

"Let's look for that device or your leaving might not be an issue," she finally said.

"You are torturing me," he groaned.

Laughter swelled inside her at his playful pout. She suspected that this was a side of him that few people saw. It was rather empowering in a feminine way.

"Trust me, you'll survive," she teased, pulling him by the arm as she turned away.

"*Tilkmos!*"

Adalard cursed when he hit his head on the cabinet. Lifting a wary hand, he rubbed the tender spot and sent another wave of healing energy over it. This was the third time he had hit his head because of his distracted thoughts.

"Adalard! I found something," Samara called out with excitement.

He gripped the cabinet and carefully stood up, stretching his back to relieve the muscle tension. His gaze swept over Samara. She was lying on her back with her knees up and her feet planted on the floor, with half of her body under a row of coolant piping for the starboard engine.

He moved until he was lying in a similar position next to her. It was a tight fit, but he was able to slide in far enough to see a two-foot glass cylinder attached to the back of the conduit.

Each end of the glass cylinder had metal caps with round holes. From his position, he caught the glow of a green light on a control panel. The control panel must open and close the vents, allowing the matter inside to escape.

He narrowed his eyes when he saw the swirling cloud of matter inside the glass cylinder. The matter was compacted and roiling. Small wisps of the fog seeped through the open vents only to retreat.

As if it is afraid, he mused.

"I was thinking the same thing," Samara said, turning her head and looking at him.

He studied the cylinder. "We need to shut the vents and contain the matter."

"I think I'm small enough to squeeze back there," she replied.

He frowned with displeasure. The idea of Samara being that close to the source of the malevolent fog and not being able to reach her did not sit well with him. Before he could express his unease, she was wiggling under the pipe.

"Be careful," he warned.

She tilted her head and flashed him a grin. "I've got this. When the lift was down at the shop, dad would send me under the low riders. This isn't much different from being under a sports car—only a hell of a lot cleaner," she said.

"I don't believe I would have liked your father any better than I do your brothers," he confessed.

"Yeah, neither did I. I'm almost… there," she grunted.

He silently watched as she pulled herself into a sitting position between the wall and the conduit. She sat still and examined the cylinder while he studied her. After a minute, she looked down at him. A knot formed in his chest when he noticed her expression soften, and she reached down and brushed her fingers across his forehead.

"You've got the tick going again. Did anyone ever tell you that you worry too much?" she teased.

He grinned and shook his head. "No. They tend to say the opposite."

She wiggled her nose at him. "Ah, must be the Lee-Stephens curse then. You might want to move. I don't think it would be a good idea to be stuck under the pipe if this thing blows up," she suggested.

"Son of a *Tiliqua's heads*," he cursed.

She raised an eyebrow at him and motioned for him to scoot back. He grudgingly slid out from under the pipe and rose to his feet. Power surged inside of him as the overwhelming need to protect his mate flooded his body. He flexed his fingers. Energy snapped and popped in the air as the tiny electrical charges danced from his fingertips.

"There are three buttons on the control panel. The top one is green, so I'm going to assume that is the open," she called out to him.

"Is there any writing on the panel?" he asked.

She squatted, and he stepped sideways so he could keep her in his sight. She ran her fingers lightly over the cylinder. His stomach knotted when she paused and frowned.

"What is it?" he demanded as the seconds grew and she didn't respond.

"I think whatever is inside the cylinder is alive," she finally said.

"Why? What is it doing?" he impatiently asked.

"It's swirling around and I swear..." Her voice faded.

He muttered another curse under his breath. "What? What is it doing?" he demanded.

She looked at him with a frown. "Nothing really. It's just wiggling around."

He took a deep breath before he slowly released it. "Can you close the cylinder?" he quietly asked.

She nodded and returned her focus to the device. He tensed when he saw her take a deep breath and bite her bottom lip before she pressed one of the buttons. From this angle, he couldn't see if it was successful or not.

She looked over at him and smiled. "It worked," she said. "I'll see how it's attached and hand it to you."

Several minutes later, he gingerly took the cylinder from her as she held it between the conduits. He stepped back and waited as she dropped to the floor and wiggled out from behind the thick pipes.

Once she was standing next to him again, they both studied the dark, swirling mass inside the container. He touched the cool exterior, and the mass struck out at him, ricocheting against the glass. Intrigued, he pulled his hand away.

"Do you know what this is?" Samara asked.

He shook his head. "No, but I plan to find out."

She nodded and hovered her finger above the container. The gray matter shrank from her touch. Adalard frowned and studied the entity in the glass.

"Well, at least *someone* thinks I'm scarier than you are," she mused.

CHAPTER SEVENTEEN

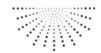

*A*n hour later, Samara sank back against the seat in the narrow galley while Adalard placed their dirty dishes in the alien version of a dishwasher. She absently ran her finger along the smooth surface of the galley table as she watched him. Her thoughts were torn between what they had found and watching Adalard bend over.

Both are dangerous for entirely different reasons. The man definitely fills out a pair of pants in a very nice way, she decided with a tinge of amusement at her chaotic thoughts.

"You are making this very difficult," he said.

She sheepishly grinned at him. "Sorry. I'll try to think quieter."

"I'm not complaining," he teased.

She lowered her gaze to the table and absently continued to make figure eights with her finger. There had only been a handful of times over the years when she mildly considered a more intimate relationship with a guy. The problem with living in the same place her whole life and having five older brothers was that people talked—a lot.

It was bad enough dealing with her brothers' disreputable reputations, she didn't need hers smeared in the mud alongside theirs. Especially when she considered all the guys she knew also hung out with one or more of her siblings.

There was also her personal fear of ending up like her mom. While she had promised herself that she would break the Lee-Stephens's curse, she never intended to become a nun either.

She had blamed her existing virgin status on those two reasons, but now she wondered if it was because she had just never found a guy who interested her enough to want to get hot and naked. After thinking about everything, she realized that her reservations about having a relationship with Adalard were melting away.

Her worries about her family and living in a small community—none of those were a consideration with Adalard. A relationship with him would be different. She didn't have to worry about him gossiping if things went south—and her mom... well, Adalard was nothing like her dad.

Besides, the odds of getting pregnant are probably a million-to-one considering we are from totally different DNA pools, she reasoned.

Of course, that thought made her wonder if they would be anatomically compatible. She dismissed that thought almost as soon as it formed when she remembered Adalard mentioning that his brother's 'mate' was human.

When she added that detail to the way the heat ignited every time they kissed and her reaction to him in his ship, she thought they must be *very* compatible. Just the thought made her want to squirm.

She lifted her somber focus back to Adalard. It was hard to ignore the desire in his eyes. Despite her attempts to hide her thoughts, it was obvious he was still mentally connected to her. He straightened and stared back at her with a look of uncertainty. She rose to her feet and walked over to him. Lifting her hand, she tenderly caressed the scar along his cheek.

"What is it?" she asked.

He covered her hand, his thumb gently caressing her skin. The colors that clung to him reached out and enveloped her. The power behind the colors caught her breath.

"How long is courting supposed to last? It seems rather... long," he confessed.

"Courting? Is that what you've been doing?" she teased. When he frowned in confusion, she softly laughed and kissed him. "I've never been courted before, but I think you've—" She locked gazes with him and continued in a slightly breathless voice, "been doing a very good job." She looked down and bit her lip, fighting a smile.

"Good, because human courting methods are a lot of work," he grumbled.

"Really?" she laughed. "How do you court where you come from?"

"Like this," he said.

He captured her upturned lips in a hard, passionate kiss, unleashing all of his pent-up desire. He slid his arms around her, lifted her up against his body and pressed her against his aroused cock. She parted her lips on a startled gasp, and he took full advantage of her surprise.

He swept his tongue inside her mouth. She tangled her fingers in his hair and held his lips locked to hers. Their tongues brushed against each other, the sensitive tips exploring and challenging. She responded to him with an urgency that reassured him she wanted him as much as he wanted her.

A groan of pleasure slipped from him. She tasted of wine and desire, and he swore he could get drunk on her kisses alone. His blood felt as if it were boiling with the energy building in the air around them. His cock was pressed against the jeans he was wearing, his testicles swollen hard as rocks.

He relaxed his hold on her, and she slid down his body. Once her feet touched the floor, he skimmed his hands over her body and cupped her face, pulling back and gazing down at her. She looked up at him with a passion-dazed expression.

"W-wow. That is... some way to court," she remarked in a hoarse voice.

"I haven't even started," he promised.

She tugged on his hair, pulling his head down. "Do me a favor—keep it up," she breathed before running her tongue along his bottom lip.

Their next kiss was deep and frenzied. Adalard lifted her off her feet again, Samara locked her legs around him, and she felt up every inch of him that she could reach. He returned the favor and they drove each other crazy as they slowly made their way across the galley, often falling against a wall in their passion. When they finally reached the sleeping cabin, they paused, panting, in front of the bed.

Samara unlocked her legs from around his waist and lightly pushed on his chest. He released her, allowing her to stand on her own feet and watched hungrily as she backed away from him and began undressing. He watched the movement of her fingers as she unbuttoned her shirt and let it fall to the floor. She bent over, unzipped her boots, and kicked them off. Her pants, panties, and bra followed until she was standing in front of him as bare as the day she was born.

He swallowed, his violet eyes glowing with desire. The colors swirling around him expanded outward, wrapping around her and caressing her skin with the same gentle stroke as his touch. She moaned softly and walked over to him.

He threaded his fingers through her hair, his gaze intensely connecting with hers. She ran her fingers along the scar on his cheek before skimming over his jaw and down his throat to the top button of his shirt. He closed his eyes for a brief moment, and she began to undress him, pausing to press light kisses to his skin as she released each button.

He remained still as she slid his shirt off of his broad shoulders. She caressed his skin, memorizing every inch of his body as she unveiled it. She followed her fingers with her lips. His breathing grew heavy and uneven as she moved lower.

Her fingers were trembling by the time she released the button on his jeans and slowly pulled his zipper down. She started to kneel in front of him but he reached out and gripped her arms. She glanced up at him as he groaned and shook his head, his throat working up and down as he swallowed.

"I...."

He shook his head again. Her heart melted when she saw the impact her gentle seduction was having on him. This was a man who was used to being in control, and he was on the verge of losing it.

She tugged on his pants, and they slid down his legs. His boots disappeared and she gasped in surprise but soon forgot all about his boots as her eyes swept up to take in him standing before her in his full magnificent arousal. She moaned in pleasure.

"Love me," she gently demanded.

His gaze turned to liquid violet. "Always."

Like magnets moving in accord, she sank down to lie back on the bed, raising her arms above her head, and he followed her, caging her under him. He captured her lips in a deep kiss filled with tenderness and possession. She parted her legs for him when she felt his heavy cock pressing against her thighs.

"Oh, Adalard," she whispered.

He moved down her body, kissing and exploring with the same care that she had given him. She stared up at the ceiling in wonder, focusing completely on the feel of his fingers as they brushed against her skin. She arched upward when he wrapped his lips around her taut nipple. He lavished each rosy bud until they were as hard as pebbles and aching for more.

Liquid fire burned between her legs, and she restlessly moved, brushing against his throbbing cock and drawing a hiss of pleasure-pain from him. Her need grew until she wanted to cry out with frustration.

You are so beautiful.

His soft words flowed through her mind. Mixed with the words was something else… a deeper meaning that she recognized but was afraid to believe. She closed her eyes when he moved down her stomach to her core. Her breathing came in shuddering gasps as he teased her with his lips and fingers. She lowered her hands and cupped her breasts. She pinched her nipples as he slid his fingers inside her.

She spread her legs wider, wanting more, too mindless with need to feel shy. Sparks flew through her mind as she tensed around his fingers. Her low mewing cry grew louder along with the pressure.

He withdrew his fingers, rose, and entered her. She wrapped her arms around him and clung to him as he slowly pushed deeper. There was no pain as he took her, only a fullness that felt wonderful.

She moved with him, wanting to draw out her orgasm. They fit perfectly, moving in a primitive dance. She opened her eyes and watched the expression flitting across his face. It was the most beautiful thing she had ever experienced and she wanted to burn it into her memory.

"Samara…," he gasped.

She parted her lips as he thrust faster and deeper, his body shuddering as his control snapped. She arched her back at the intensity of each thrust. A silver thread wound through the colors surrounding them, brilliant and fragile at the same time. The thread spread outward, winding around them.

It was a cosmic experience, the vision so real that she tried to reach out and touch the thread, but her fingers passed through the sparkling ribbon. A tsunami of intense emotions flooded her. When she realized the emotions were Adalard's as well as hers, tears burned in her eyes.

She dropped her hand to his shoulder, he bowed his head, and she surged up to capture his lips. He parted his lips, and she deepened the kiss, pouring everything she was feeling into it.

I love you, misha la warrior.

CHAPTER EIGHTEEN

"What's put that stupid grin on your face?"

Rob's deep voice drew a low groan from Samara and she wiped the pleased, dreamy smile from her lips. Leave it to one of her brothers to ruin a perfectly fine day. Stiffening her shoulders, she turned and faced him.

"Obviously not seeing you," she retorted.

Rob's pursed his lips in annoyance, and his eyes flashed with a silent warning. She was beyond being intimidated. Now that she was on her own, she didn't know why she had waited as long as she did to leave.

She turned her back to him again and carefully selected the last of the ripe tomatoes that she would need to make homemade spaghetti sauce for dinner tonight. Her hope was that if she ignored her brother, he would magically disappear. That hope died when he stepped closer and stood in her way.

"Excuse me. I need an onion," she said.

"The jerk from Vegas is coming down tonight for the money Gary owes. He'll be at the Cattleman's at nine to collect," Rob said, not moving.

She gritted her teeth, reached around him, and grabbed a large onion before she responded. "It's not my problem."

She tensed when Rob wrapped his hand around her arm. "We don't have the money," he said in a low voice.

Do you need me?

Adalard's soothing voice filtered through her mind. She breathed slowly and focused on keeping her thoughts under control. The last thing she needed was for Adalard to pop up unexpectedly in the middle of the grocery store.

I'm fine. I'm grocery shopping. I think I can handle this all by myself, she responded.

Adalard's soft chuckle echoed through her mind, and she felt him withdraw. She sighed and returned her attention to her brother. He had released her arm and shoved his hands into his pockets.

"It's different this time. This guy isn't one of the local guys that we owe a hundred bucks to and can blow off. This guy is—" Rob shook his head, pulled one of his hands out of his pocket, and ran it through his disheveled hair before he continued. "This is out of our league, Samara. He won't stop at broken bones."

Regret filled her. This was the first time in her life that she had ever seen Rob at a loss—and vulnerable. The problem was this situation was beyond her help. Even if she gave every penny she had, it would only be a band-aid trying to staunch a wound to a major artery.

"I have nothing to give you, Rob," she said, lifting her chin and staring back at him with a look of sad resignation. "Gary will have to get himself out of this one. If he is worried about being physically harmed, then maybe he should contact the police. Annalisa can give him some advice. Or maybe—just maybe—he needs to disappear for a while."

Rob's expression hardened and he dropped his hand down to his side. "When did you become such a cold-hearted bitch? If that bastard kills Gary, it is on your head. Remember, it wasn't just the money that Gary lost. You were part of the pot as well. He'll come looking for you next."

Samara winced when Rob poked a stiff finger against her shoulder before he turned and strode away. It wasn't until he disappeared down an aisle that she realized she was shaking. She looked down at the large onion she was gripping like it was a lifeline.

Samara—

Adalard's questioning voice flashed through her mind again. She looked around the produce section, noticing for the first time that the produce manager was watching her with a look of concern. She gave the older man a strained smile before she placed the onion in her cart, and began pushing it along the rows of fresh produce.

I'm okay. Rob caught up with me, she reluctantly responded.

What did he want? Adalard asked suspiciously.

A shiver ran through her at the dangerous edge in his voice. A wry amusement pierced her cloud of anxiety at dealing with her oldest brother. It honestly didn't take long for her brothers to draw this kind of reaction from people—including aliens!

The same thing he always wants—to drive me crazy and take my money—not necessarily in that order, she sighed.

What did you tell him? I should have come to you, Adalard said in a disgruntled voice.

No, you should not have, and I told him that he and the others were on their own. I can't save them from themselves anymore, she answered with a slightly sharper tone than she intended. *I need to focus on what I'm doing. We can talk later.*

She pulled up the wall in her mind and imagined putting a huge padlock on it for extra measure. Her mind swirled with what Rob had said about the man hurting Gary. She wasn't concerned about the other part of Gary's bargain. It wouldn't be hard to dissuade the man from thinking she was any kind of prize. Besides, if she couldn't convince the man to leave her out of the deal, she was sure Adalard could if push came to shove.

"Damn it all to hell," she muttered as she finished picking up the items she would need for dinner tonight. "This is the last time. I swear this is the absolutely, positively last time I ever help those morons ever again."

～

The Loft Casino and Hotel

Las Vegas, Nevada

Alberto Frank Armeni Campeau looked down along the vibrant avenue from the Penthouse atop one of his recent acquisitions. The Loft would be rebranded over the next six months and absorbed into the Campeau Empire of fine hotels, restaurants, resorts, and casinos around the world. He sipped on the wine delivered by the hotel manager. The 1954 Bordeaux Blend Red from Chateau Mouton Roth-schild, Pauillac, France was excellent but not enough to keep the manager on. The very expensive accountants he used had discovered the man enjoyed the hotel's fine vintage wine as much as he enjoyed gambling at its tables.

A knock at the door drew his attention. A glance at his phone showed that Jack DeSimone, his Head of Security, had arrived. He pressed the buzzer to unlock the door.

"Mr. Campeau, the helicopter is ready when you are," Jack announced.

"Thank you, Jack," he responded.

He finished his wine, placed the empty wine glass on the side table, and strode toward the door. Jack held out a bespoke Canali burgundy ultralight cashmere coat. He slid his arms into it and adjusted the collar.

"How much do you want to bet they don't have the money—only the woman?" he inquired.

"I never bet, sir," Jack replied with a neutral expression.

"That is why you are still with me," he remarked. He pulled a pair of black Salvatore Ferragamo gloves from his pocket and slid them on. "Let us hope they have both. Do you have the information I requested?"

"Yes, sir," Jack replied.

"Excellent. Let's get this over with. I have matters to attend to here," he replied.

Jack bowed his head in acknowledgement and pressed the button for the private elevator door that led to the helipad. Al stepped inside, turned around, and faced the door. He felt no remorse in taking advantage of Gary Lee-Stephens' greed and intoxication. The man and his brothers had been arrogant and crude.

His brief visit to Casper had been unexpected thanks to a flat tire. The parking lot at the Cattleman's Bar and Grill had been relatively empty. A need to relieve himself led him into the establishment—and a local group playing poker.

Normally, he would have dismissed the group. None of the men or women sitting at the table were in his league. The games he played in could be worth millions.

The group's rude remarks, namely from a man called Jerry Lee-Stephens, about his clothing irked him. He seldom responded to such behavior, but the man had stepped into his personal space. Alberto had grabbed the man, drawing a response from his companions. His offer to play a game of poker quickly diffused the situation.

In the first hour he purchased several rounds of drinks, lost a few thousand dollars, and then struck back with a vengeance. In less than half an hour, he had emptied the pockets of all the players except for one, who refused to cave.

Gary Lee-Stephens had raised the bet to ten thousand dollars—on credit, of course. Alberto had started to turn down the offer until Jerry threw in a photo on top of the pile of cash. While the young woman in the photo wasn't remarkably beautiful, there had been something about her eyes and her smile that pulled an almost primitive response from him—something he hadn't felt in a long, long time. He was intrigued by the potential he saw in the young woman, and by his curiosity to see what would happen when she discovered her brothers had offered her up like a broodmare to the highest bidder.

The memory of his amusement that the woman in the photograph wouldn't appreciate her siblings' stupidity made him smile. His unexpected agreement had surprised himself. He was never impulsive. Gary had tried to withdraw the offer of his sister, but it was too late. Alberto accepted the deal—and easily won. His victory did not go over well with the brothers which made his win even sweeter.

Pride goeth before the fall, he thought with amusement as he strode toward the helicopter.

"I have a full crew tonight. They are already in Casper. We'll be ready should there be any incidents like the last time," Jack stated.

"Very good," he responded.

CHAPTER NINETEEN

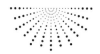

*A*dalard appreciatively sniffed the delicious aroma of the cooking food as he entered Samara's apartment. He could hear her moving around in the small kitchen area. Soft music played in the background.

He removed his jacket and placed it on a hook by the door. A knock beside him caused him to turn in surprise. He opened the door and saw Bear standing outside with a nervous, lopsided grin on his face.

"Hey, Adalard. How are you doing this evening?" Bear greeted.

Adalard frowned when he saw the other man holding a bottle of wine. It took him a moment to realize that Bear was staring in awe at the glowing flowers in his hand. It was too late to hide them.

"What are you doing here?" he demanded.

"Oh, good! You're both here on time," Samara greeted with a warm smile.

"Both…?" he asked with a frown.

Samara wiped her hands on her apron. "Yes. I ran into Bear at the gas station this afternoon and invited him over for dinner."

Be nice! He just found out his grandmother isn't doing well and he is having a rough time, she cautioned.

"It smells delicious," Bear greeted. He belatedly held out the bottle in his hand. "I brought some wine."

Samara took the bottle. "Thank you. Dinner is almost ready. Why don't you two go into the living room? I have some appetizers set out."

"I have some flowers for you," Adalard added, holding them out to her. He had changed them to look like the bouquet Ann Marie had set out at the main house.

Samara smiled up at him while Bear stared at the new bouquet with a perplexed frown.

"They are beautiful. Thank you," she murmured.

"Weren't those different a moment ago?" Bear mumbled in a confused voice.

"A play of light on them," he casually responded as Bear continued to stare at the blooms with a bewildered expression.

"I'll put them in a vase. You two enjoy the snacks I left out," she instructed.

Adalard watched her return to the narrow kitchen. Several pots simmered on the stove, and the makings of a salad were on the counter near the sink. He returned his attention to Bear when the other man spoke.

"She has really made this place look nice," Bear commented.

"Yes," he agreed.

Bear cleared his throat. "So... how are you enjoying your stay here? Has Mason taken you out on the course yet?"

Adalard frowned, trying to follow the other man's question. It took a second for him to remember that Bear believed he was here to do the survival training. His expression cleared and he shook his head.

"I am not here to complete the training," he replied.

"If you're not here for the training, what are you here for?" Bear asked.

"I am simply visiting your world," he replied.

"My world? That definitely confirms that you aren't from around here," Bear chuckled, picking up one of the bruschetta appetizers that Samara had placed on the small table near the window.

"Bear, could you pour the wine?" Samara called.

"Sure," Bear responded, stuffing the small piece of garlic, tomato, and mozzarella topped bread into his mouth.

Adalard silently cursed his slip of the tongue. His irritation and jealousy were making him sloppy. He held out his hand and took the wine glass from Bear when the man returned. He noticed the slight, puzzled crease on Bear's forehead and knew the man was thinking about his reply.

"You know, I don't think Samara ever said exactly where you were from," Bear began.

Samara eyed the clock. It was already eight-thirty. The past two hours had flown by so fast that she wasn't sure if it was the wine making her head spin or the speed with which the evening progressed. She feigned a yawn.

"I guess it is getting late. Let me help clean up," Bear offered, seeing her cover her mouth.

She shook her head. "I've got this. Thankfully there's a small dishwasher and most of the dishes and food have already been put up. All that's left is the dessert plates," she said, rising to her feet.

"You should have left the dishes for us to clean," Adalard said.

She laughed. "If the kitchen was bigger, I would have taken you up on it. It was easier to wash everything as I went so I had more room. I'm used to it."

"Dinner was fantastic. I haven't had homemade spaghetti sauce—ever! Mom always bought the stuff in the jar," Bear replied.

"My mom loved to cook. She would make her own sauce and can it. We had jars of it in the pantry growing up," Samara reminisced.

"Well, if you ever have any extra, you could always send some my way. The guys in the bunkhouse would love it," Bear stated with a cute, hopeful gleam in his eye. "That reminds me, tomorrow we are gathering the last of the yearlings to move south. Mason decided that with the early snows, it might be wise to move the schedule ahead a couple of weeks this year."

"I'll be there," she promised, taking the last of the dishes from the men.

"I'm heading out. Do you want me to drop you by the main house?" Bear asked, looking at Adalard.

"That would be great!" she interjected before Adalard could respond.

She bit her bottom lip when Adalard gave her a surprised glare. Guilt tugged at her, and she turned her back to him and finished loading the dishwasher.

"Yes, I would appreciate a lift," he answered.

She straightened and looked at him with a combination of surprise and relief. Wiping her hands along the sides of her jeans, she cast a covert glance at the clock again. She would be cutting it close. Hopefully whoever the guy from Vegas was, he would either show up late, or better yet, not at all.

"I'm really tired tonight. I had an early morning, grocery shopping, and dinner—especially dinner and the lovely wine. Wine always makes me sleepy. I need a good night's sleep so I can be up early and fresh tomorrow to help," she babbled before internally wincing.

She was a horrible liar. Forcing an apologetic smile on her lips, she waved for both men to head for the door. It might be better to just usher them out and keep her mouth shut before she had a meltdown and confessed the stupid stunt she was about to pull. She could already sense the pressure of Adalard trying to penetrate the wall she was struggling to keep between them.

"Thank you both for coming tonight," she cheerfully said.

Bear pulled on his coat and awkwardly bent to kiss her. She turned her cheek to him at the last second. Her eyes connected with Adalard's. He was studying her with an intense expression.

"Goodnight, Bear. I hope your grandma gets better," she said.

"Yeah, so do I," Bear replied, pulling on his hat. "I'm going to go warm up the truck. I'll meet you downstairs," he added with a touch to his hat.

Samara remained silent as Bear pulled open the door and departed down the stairs. She returned her attention to Adalard and waited as he pulled on his long jacket. She didn't give him time to say goodbye. Instead, she rose on her toes and captured his lips.

"You're not going to tell me what you are up to, are you?" he asked when she pulled away.

She gave him a shaky smile and shook her head. "Good night," she murmured.

She stepped back and held onto the door. She swallowed when she saw the flare of emotion in his eyes. It was impossible to ignore that he wasn't happy about leaving. She didn't like it either, but she needed to handle this alone. It would be far too dangerous to pull Adalard into the mess that her brothers had created.

He stepped onto the landing, turned and faced her. "I'll see you tomorrow?" he asked.

"You bet your ass you will," she promised.

She slowly closed the door after he started down the steps. Closing her eyes, she breathed deeply to calm her nerves. Once she felt in control again, she hurried to her bedroom where she had hidden her cashbox. She retrieved the box, her coat, hat, gloves, and truck keys before pulling open the door and stepping out.

"Just get this over with, Samara, and never, ever look back again," she muttered to herself as she pulled the door closed behind her.

The two men in the truck silently watched as Samara pulled away from her loft apartment and headed toward the main driveway. Bear turned on the truck lights and grinned at Adalard who was sitting beside him in stony silence.

"Samara never could lie," he shared.

"This has something to do with her brothers," Adalard grimly responded.

Bear slowly pulled out, keeping enough distance between his truck and Samara's so that she wouldn't get suspicious. He tightened his fingers around the steering column and nodded in agreement.

"Yeah. There was talk today about something going down tonight at the Cattleman's. That was the reason I made up the story about my grandmother," Bear confessed.

Adalard shot him a surprised look. "Your grandmother is not ill?"

Bear chuckled and shook his head. "Hell no! She's on a cruise in the Caribbean at the moment with some of her lady friends," he answered.

CHAPTER TWENTY

*S*amara groaned when she saw the two identical black SUVs in the parking lot that screamed out-of-towners. So much for her dream that the Lee-Stephens' run of bad luck would magically disappear. She pursed her lips when she saw Brit step out of the darkness.

She pulled into an empty spot on the outer edge of the overflow parking lot. It looked like the whole frigging town knew about what was going down tonight and wanted front seat admission. She shifted the truck into park and turned it off. Before she could unlatch her seatbelt, her brother was pulling open the door.

"You came! I knew you would," Brit breathed with relief.

She gave him a dirty glare. "If you were so confident, then why were you waiting outside?" she snapped.

Brit stood back, giving her room to slide out of the truck. She slammed the door and locked the truck but kept the keys firmly in her hand with the metal tips protruding between her fingers. With the wad of cash she had stuffed in her pockets, she wasn't taking any chances—including with her own siblings.

Desperate times make even the sanest people do stupid shit, she thought.

"Rob thought it would be best if I stayed outside. He knows I'm not good at fighting and didn't want me to get hurt," Brit grumbled, shoving his hands in his front pockets.

"Rob always was a dick. If he really cared about you, he wouldn't drag you into shit like this in the first place," she retorted.

Brit uttered a strained laugh. "Yeah, I didn't think of that," he replied with a shrug.

She fought the impulse to roll her eyes at him but gave up. "Of course you didn't. You're as stupid as the rest of them. If you were smart, you'd leave like Wilson did and never look back," she growled.

Brit gave her a confused look. "Where would I go?"

She stopped, took a deep breath, and counted to ten before she reached out and gripped Brit's arm. He stopped and faced her. Her anger softened when she saw the vulnerability in her brother's eyes. He might be older than she was in years, but in maturation and self-reliance he still had a long way to go before he grew up.

"There's a whole world out there, Brit. Don't be like Dad or the rest of them. You're young, strong, and not afraid to work. Get out of here while you still can," she softly advised.

"I don't know how. This place... Rob... I don't know nothin' else, Samara," he said with a shake of his head.

"You know logging. Go to Alaska. You know how to work on engines. If nothing else, join the military! Grow a pair of balls that Rob and the others don't have a leash attached to! Just get the hell out of here before it is too late!" she raged.

"Geez, Samara," Brit grumbled.

She threw her hands up in the air. "I've done what I can for you. Tonight, I'll do what I can to help the others, but this is it, Brit. After tonight... after tonight I don't ever want to see any of you again. I'm

going to take my own advice and get the hell out of here. I have to—
otherwise I won't be able to survive."

The realization that she needed to take her own advice suddenly hit
her like a punch in the gut. It was true. If she didn't leave her home-
town, then one way or another, her brothers or just the reputation of
her name would keep dragging her down.

"Where would you go, though? You don't know no other place either,"
Brit said.

Her face tilted up to the sky. She could see a few stars shining despite
the light pollution. A soft laugh burst from her and she turned to grin
at her brother.

"Who knows? There's a whole universe out there to explore. Maybe
it's time to check it out," she replied.

"Brit, have you— Samara! I hope you brought some money," Rob said.

Samara sighed and began walking toward the door of the bar. "I see
you're the same prick you were a few hours ago," she observed,
pulling open the door.

Rob grabbed her arm in a fierce grip. "Campeau brought along some
serious backup. They look like fucking military types," he warned.

"I suggest you be nice to me then—if you don't want me leaving your
ass to deal with him," she snapped, giving a pointed look at his hand
on her arm.

Rob released her and stepped back. "Come on. I don't want to leave
Gary and Jerry alone with that bastard for too long. Jerry is already
being an ass. We'll be lucky to get out of this place alive tonight," he
muttered.

Samara stepped into the bar and scanned the room. The regular crowd
was there plus a few who normally only came by on the weekends.
Most people were sitting at the tables drinking but a few were playing
pool. It didn't take her long to deduce where the meeting was being
held. The two men standing on each side of the doorway to a back

room normally reserved for special functions were drawing a lot of curious looks.

"Did everyone in town come to see what a huge idiot Gary is?" she dryly inquired.

"They've always known that, Samara. They just want to see what the guy from Vegas is going to do," Brit replied to her rhetorical question.

Rob glared at Brit. "Shut up and go wait in the truck," he ordered.

"But I want to see what happens," Brit complained.

Samara placed her hand on Brit's arm. "Listen, one of us needs to be outside in case things turn ugly. Who knows, I may need you to bail my ass out of jail this time," she said.

Brit's mouth dropped open before he nodded and retreated back outside. She shrugged when she saw Rob's surprised expression. At this point, she imagined anything was possible.

"Let's get this over with," she said.

She crossed the room to the two men standing guard at the door. Irritation flared inside her when one of the men blocked the doorway. Lifting her chin, she glared back at the man with an unblinking stare.

"Move it or lose it. I need to speak with your dickhead of a boss," she coolly stated.

The man's eyes narrowed for a moment before he stood aside. She didn't miss the mic in the man's ear nor the lascivious appraisal of the elegantly dressed man seated at a large round table. This was going to be more difficult than she first thought. Tactfulness was not her middle name. She really should have just called Annalisa and spilled the beans about the whole sordid mess to the police.

"Watch your mouth," the guard warned as she stepped past him.

"Good luck with that," Rob muttered behind her.

"You are not helping," she retorted under her breath.

She walked over to the table and stopped. Her scornful scrutiny moved over the smug man sitting across from her. He seemed to be in his late thirties or early forties. The man's clothing screamed money.

"You must be the charming sister that your brother was so gracious to add to the pot," the man said.

She gave him a disgusted glare. "I can assure you that the word charming and any member of my family do not *ever* belong in the same sentence," she said.

The man chuckled and motioned to the chair. "Please sit. My name is Alberto Campeau," he greeted.

Samara remained standing. She wasn't about to sit and put herself at a disadvantage. She hoped the guy liked to cut through the bullshit because she wasn't in the mood to play games tonight.

"My brothers are asses. I'm sure it didn't take you long to figure that out—and to take advantage of it. So, here is the deal. I give you five thousand dollars and you go back to your penthouse and forget you ever met these morons. I'm offering this one time, at this moment. It is a take-it-or-leave-it proposition," she stated.

Campeau's eyes narrowed. "The debt was for ten thousand—and you. Why should I take less?" he softly inquired.

"The clock is ticking. You took a gamble that you could con a bunch of ignorant dumb-fucks. I'm giving you an out which is more than you deserve. I'm telling you to take the money and walk away," she said, reaching into her pocket and pulling out her cash.

Campeau pushed his chair back and rose to his feet. Samara lifted her chin and kept her eyes locked on his. The shrewd gleam in them told her he was weighing what she was saying and wondering if she was bluffing. She wasn't, and she didn't bother hiding her thoughts either.

"As intriguing as your offer sounds, Ms. Lee-Stephens, I never walk away from a winning hand. I will only accept what I was promised—

with interest," he coolly replied. "If you don't have it now, I'll collect what I'm owed another way."

"Human trafficking is against the law. I'm sure you are aware of that. So is blackmail. I figure you can get a few years—or at least it will cost you more in bad publicity and attorney's fees than the bet with my brothers to stay out of jail. Are you really sure you want to play this hand, Mr. Campeau?" she said, sliding the money back into her pocket.

He laughed. "How about we play another game of poker? If you win, I will agree to release your brother from the money he owes me—and you still come with me. If I win, you agree to come with me and your brother need only pay the ten thousand dollars. I'll waive the interest that is accruing," he said.

"I don't gamble. Even if I did, that is a lousy offer," she snapped.

"Then, perhaps I can offer a little bonus to help persuade you," Campeau suggested.

"There is nothing you can say that would persuade me," she retorted.

"Not even the chance to keep all of your brothers out of prison?" Campeau inquired.

"What are you talking about?" she demanded.

Campeau held out his hand. The man behind him gave him a manila folder which he then slid across the table to her. She gave him a suspicious glare before she opened it.

She scanned the contents of what appeared to be a very detailed report. The more she read, the deeper the feeling that she was drowning grew. Any hope that the report was fabricated evaporated when she turned the page and saw the photos.

Jerry's muttered curses mingled with Rob's. Gary, who had been sitting silently, closed his eyes and bowed his head. It wasn't until she saw the picture of Brit that the angry tears burning in her eyes turned to sorrow. Drugs, guns, and worse—scared young migrants—her brothers were involved in all of it.

"Was Wilson a part of this?" she quietly asked.

Jerry grabbed the report and pictures and jammed them back into the folder. "Fuck no. Why do you think he left?"

She looked at Jerry. Her anger exploded, breaking through the dam inside her. She turned on Jerry, pushing him back against the wall.

"I always knew you were a piece of shit, but I never thought even you would go this low. Drugs? Weapons? Taking advantage of innocent people searching for a better life?!" Stepping back, she shook her head in horror as the vivid images replayed in her head. "I hope you all rot in hell."

She twisted, knowing she needed to get out of there before she was sick. Rob reached for her, but she recoiled from his touch. As the eldest, he bore the brunt of the responsibility—including recruiting Brit into this mess.

Out of the corner of her eye, she saw Campeau nod to one of the men at the door. She turned and looked, surprised to see that the bar had emptied out. Shock held her still.

"Your brothers are into human trafficking, Ms... Samara—and you were one of the ones caught in their web. It would be difficult to prove you knew nothing of what was happening. After all, you lived in the same house until recently, if I'm not mistaken," Campeau said.

She faced her family's enemy. "I won't be dragged into this," she declared.

"Ah, but you already have been," he said, sliding another photo across the table.

With trembling fingers, she picked up the photo. It was a picture of her talking with a woman who was a few years younger than she was outside of the garage. She vaguely remembered the day. Brit had been really nervous when he found her chatting with the girl.

"Where did you get this?" she asked in a strained voice.

"I think that is a question you should ask your brother—Jerry, isn't it?" Campeau stated.

She stared at Jerry. He returned her stare with a devil-may-care expression. The sickness churning in her stomach started again with a vengeance.

"We needed some guarantee that you wouldn't get all self-righteous and start spouting off at the mouth," he said with a shrug.

Disbelief ricocheted through her like a pinball machine going spastic. She clenched her fist and pressed it against her stomach. Closing her eyes, she tried to focus on what to do. The sound of scuffling forced her eyes back open. Rob had Jerry pinned to the wall.

"I told you not to involve her," Rob snapped.

Jerry sneered at Rob. "It was security, man. Do you think because she is our sister she wouldn't throw our asses under the bus when she figured out what we are doing? I'm not as naïve as you, bro," he retorted.

She shook her head in denial. "It won't matter. I can't let you do this. I can't... I just can't," she whispered.

"One game and all of this can go away," Gary promised, placing his hand on her shoulder. "I swear if you give us a chance, Samara, we'll come clean. I swear there will be no more smuggling or dealing of any kind."

She shrugged off his hand and faced him. "Why should I believe you? All of you have always lied to me—even Brit," she said in a broken voice.

"I don't want to spend the rest of my life looking over my shoulder— or turn up dead. I was hoping that night was going to be a changer for me. I wanted to propose to Pat and start fresh," Gary replied in a low urgent tone.

Her attention moved to Campeau. Every cell in her body wanted to punch the smug expression off of the bastard's face. She couldn't blame him for destroying her family. Her brothers had completed that job a long time ago. She hated that he had ripped the scab off and shown all the putrid infection festering underneath.

"One game, winner takes all the evidence," Campeau said with a sweep of his hand in the direction of the file.

"How can we trust you?" she asked.

"I am many things, Samara, but one thing I never compromise is my word when it comes to a bet," he replied.

"I don't play poker on your scale and you know it. It wouldn't be a fair game. It would be a slaughter," she said.

"Then I will allow you to choose my opponent," Campeau compromised with a wave of his hand toward her brothers.

She contemplated the occupants around the room. She studied each of her brothers. Jerry was too hot tempered. Rob was too impatient. Out of the three, Gary was the best, but even he wasn't great—his loss to Campeau was a testament to that.

"I will play you," a deep voice said from the doorway.

A gasp slipped from her, and Samara twisted around. Adalard stood in the center, one hand wrapped around the throat of one of the guards. The other guard lay unmoving on the floor. Bear stood next to the unconscious man with a look of awe on his face.

"He did it," Bear replied with a nod toward Adalard.

"Adalard... how did you know?" she said.

We are connected in ways you have yet to learn, he silently replied.

My brothers... this... I have to talk to Annalisa. This is bigger than a gambling debt, she said.

I don't think that is an option at the moment, he replied as he nodded his head toward Campeau.

She looked in the direction he indicated. The man silently standing behind Campeau held a gun pointed directly at Adalard's chest. He wasn't the only one in the room armed either. Three men who had been standing in the shadows emerged, weapons aimed. Two more moved into position behind Adalard and Bear in the other room.

"Shall we play?" Campeau inquired.

CHAPTER TWENTY-ONE

$\mathcal{A}$dalard walked toward the table. He paused when Samara stared up at him with a worried expression.

Do you even know how to play poker? she asked in his mind.

Yes. Carmen taught us, he replied.

Carmen? Walker? she demanded.

Yes. She is exceptionally good at this game, he reassured her.

You are going to need to be more than just good, she warned.

As you would say—I've got this, he assured her.

"Are we going to play, or are you going to stare into each other's eyes all night?" Campeau snapped.

Adalard scowled at the other man. "We are going to play," he drawled.

He didn't conceal the slight difference in his appearance. His violet eyes glowed eerily with his power, and the irritation on Campeau's face changed to unease. Adalard pulled out the chair across from the man and sat down.

"I suggest a warm up game before we proceed," Campeau offered.

"Perhaps we should start with a bid," Adalard replied.

Campeau glanced over him and then Samara. "Five thousand dollars."

Samara moved to get the cash from her pocket, and Adalard touched her hand, shaking his head. Lifting her hand to his lips, he kissed the back of it.

"Instead of money, I suggest something personal," he said.

He reached into his pocket and pulled out a Trivarian diamond the size of a walnut. He had brought mostly precious stones instead of money, though Mason assured him that the thin piece of plastic he had given him would act as currency. He placed the large faceted stone on the table in front of him.

"Do you expect me to believe that is a real diamond?" Campeau demanded.

Adalard sat back in his seat and waved a hand toward it. "I can promise that you will never find a diamond as pure as this anywhere else on this planet," he said.

Campeau reached out and picked up the diamond. Adalard watched as the man breathed on it before studying the pure perfection of the stone. Campeau waved his fingers, and the man behind him stepped forward, leaning close to him attentively.

"Bring me a glass of water," Campeau instructed.

Less than a minute later, a tall glass of water was placed in front of Campeau who proceeded to drop the diamond into the glass. The gem immediately sank to the bottom. Adalard watched with amusement as Campeau poured the water onto the floor and plucked the diamond out of the glass. Then he scored the glass and hissed when a deep cut appeared.

"Is it real?" Gary asked.

Campeau didn't answer Gary, instead he looked across the table at Adalard. "Where did you get this?" he demanded.

Adalard knew he had Campeau's complete attention now. "From a small mine that I own," he replied with a shrug. "Are you ready to play?"

Campeau paused and rolled the diamond against his palm. He nodded and placed the diamond back on the table. Pushing back his sleeve, he removed his Patek Philippe watch. He placed the watch next to the diamond.

"Something personal," Campeau replied.

"Let the game begin," Adalard said.

Al fingered the deck of cards in his hands and studied the man across from him. The strange man's sudden appearance—and the ease with which he could incapacitate two of his guards—was perturbing, but if the diamond was real, and he suspected that it was, then the evening had just become much more interesting.

"If we are going to play, we should introduce ourselves. I am Alberto Campeau and you are...?" he soothingly coaxed.

"Adalard Ha'darra," Adalard replied.

He nodded in acknowledgement. "Where are you from Mr. Ha'darra?" he inquired.

"You could say that I'm not from around here. Does this game come with a drink?" Adalard replied.

"I'll get it. What would you like?" Gary anxiously asked.

"Jack will provide our drinks," Al stated.

One lesson Al had learned was never to take a drink from anyone he didn't trust, or who wasn't being paid handsomely to make sure he stayed alive. He continued shuffling the cards. There was something soothing in the feel and sound of the cards as they flowed through his fingers. The delay also gave him more opportunity to size up his opponent.

Adalard Ha'darra was leaning back, relaxed in his seat. One of his arms rested on the table and the other was on his lap. His long hair was pulled back, revealing a thin scar on his cheek. It wasn't only the man's rugged appearance or the fact that he was obviously well versed in violence, but it was Adalard's eyes that made him extremely wary. There was an unnatural glow around the irises—and a color that could only be achieved with contacts. What bothered him was that Adalard Ha'darra didn't strike him as the type of man who would bother to enhance his appearance for appearance's sake.

Jack returned with two glasses and a large bottle of liquor. Al casually watched Jack opened the still sealed bottle at the table and fill his glass before stepping around the table to pour one for his unexpected guest. Lifting his glass into the air, Al paused and smiled.

"A toast to a good game," he said.

Adalard lifted his glass, drained it, and placed it aside for Jack to refill. Al smiled with satisfaction as he took a sip from his glass. The fine Blanton's Straight from the Barrel Whiskey was perfect for an intimate game of poker among like-minded enthusiasts. The whiskey's discerning palate was impressive even to the pickiest drinker with the delicate blend of vanilla and tobacco, a flavor palate rich with citrus, spice, honey, and butter, along with a lengthy finish fueled with notes of peach and smooth chocolate. The savory liquor was also a good way to relax an unknown opponent.

Al leaned forward and placed the deck in the center of the table. The room became unnaturally quiet. The large man who had accompanied Ha'darra into the room gently pulled Samara away from the table.

Behind them, the two guards that Ha'darra had incapacitated a short while ago were now sullenly glaring at Ha'darra's back. Annoyance filled Al at the distraction. He raised his hand to Jack.

"Yes, sir?" Jack replied.

"Have those two wait outside," he said in a dismissive tone.

"Yes, sir," Jack responded.

Ha'darra divided the cards and shuffled them with the ease of a Master Dealer from the Strip. It seemed the man was no stranger to the gambling table and cards, yet despite Al's vast experience in the elite group of high-stakes gamblers, they had never crossed paths.

"Where are you from, Mr. Ha'darra?" he persisted.

Adalard gave him an icy smile that sent a shiver down his spine. "It is Prince Ha'darra, Mr. Campeau," he coolly responded.

"Prince.... My apologies, Your Royal Highness," he stiffly corrected.

"Apology accepted," Adalard replied, replacing the deck on the table.

Samara watched from the back of the room. She started when Bear gripped her hand. He slightly jerked his head toward the door, and she shook her head.

Please, go with Bear, Adalard requested.

But... why? she protested.

His soft laughter sent a wave of warmth through her. It didn't come off as nervous. At the moment, Gary looked like he was about to dissolve into a boneless blob on the floor, Rob seemed to be wishing he was anywhere else in the world, and Jerry—well, Jerry's greedy eyes were glued to the diamond in the center of the table.

I would rather you not be here when Campeau realizes how well I can play this game, Adalard explained.

As much as she would love to stay and watch, she realized that Adalard was right. She could be a distraction, or worse, used as leverage against him. There were times when retreat was the best option, and it wasn't as if Adalard couldn't handle himself if things got heated. Her brothers on the other hand... well, they deserved whatever happened to them.

Just make sure you tell me what happens. I don't want to miss my brothers getting a good ass-kicking, she answered.

What, no concern for me? he teased.

Nah. Something tells me a situation like this is a garden party for you, she retorted.

Silent laughter met her remark. Campeau paused and scrutinized the humor dancing in Adalard's eyes, but he didn't ask and Adalard didn't offer an explanation.

Samara breathed in deeply and squeezed Bear's hand to let him know that she had changed her mind. Releasing Bear's hand, she stepped sideways to exit the room.

Her path was immediately blocked by one of Campeau's men. She looked the guard up and down. The man looked like he was dressed for a Mission Impossible Cosplay event.

"I would like you to stay, Samara," Campeau called from behind her.

She looked over her shoulder at him. "All the excitement makes me need to pee. Unless you want me trying to piss in a glass, I suggest your man move out of my way," she crudely stated.

Campeau chuckled. "That will not be necessary. My man will escort you to the Ladies' Room," he instructed.

"And I'll escort your man," Bear growled, glaring back and forth between the guard and Campeau.

Campeau's smile faded, replaced with a hard glare. "Jack, escort all of our other guests out of the room and shut the doors," he ordered.

"Yes, sir," Jack replied.

Samara pursed her lips to keep from grinning when she felt an unexpected bulge and weight in the pocket of her jacket. She slid her hand into her pocket and wrapped her hand around the device that had suddenly appeared. She widened her eyes when she felt the familiar shape of a gun.

I hope you don't expect me to fight my way out of here. I'd be better off staying with you if that's the case, considering it's like eight-to-one odds out here now, she dryly thought.

Bear has one as well. We had a talk on the way here. He knows who I am. I trust your aim—but the blasters are set to stun should you miss and hit Bear, he assured her in a teasing tone before she felt him pull away.

He trusts my aim, she thought with a mental roll of her eyes.

Samara followed Bear and her brothers out into the main room. She turned when Jack closed the doors to the private room behind him. The sound of hurried footsteps pulled her attention away just in time to see her brothers making a beeline for the exit in the back.

Nothing like a little concern for their sister, she bitterly thought.

Their exit meant that she and Bear would be left to deal with Jack and the rest of the security team. Bear smiled and flashed her five fingers before nodding at Jack. She lifted an eyebrow. She really hoped he was a good shot.

"I thought you needed to use the bathroom," Jack said, pulling her attention to him.

She slipped the weapon out of her pocket and gave him a smile that didn't reach her eyes. "I lied," she said, pointing the alien gun at him and pulling the trigger.

CHAPTER TWENTY-TWO

"*I*s there anything else you can remember?" Annalisa asked.

Samara shook her head and wrapped her arms around her waist. Annalisa reached out and touched her arm in a compassionate gesture of support. Tears burned Samara's eyes, and she shook her head in annoyance.

"So... what... what's going to happen to them?" she asked in a voice thick with emotion.

Annalisa closed the notebook she had been writing in and sighed. "A lot depends on how much evidence there is against them and how much they are willing to cooperate. They all have lengthy records. I won't lie to you. It isn't going to be pretty," she replied.

Samara nodded and brushed a tear from her cheek. "What about me?"

Annalisa squeezed her arm. "Your brothers confirmed that you knew nothing about what was going on. I would be surprised if the prosecutor even called you in to testify. I know turning in your own family was difficult for you, but you did the right thing. Who knows? It might straighten them out."

Samara released a strained laugh and brushed at the dampness on her cheek again. "Yeah, well, according to two of them, I'm no longer family," she grudgingly shared.

"Rob and Jerry don't deserve to have you as their sister, both Gary and Brit know that. Hopefully, those two will use this as a chance to break away from Rob and Jerry's influence," Annalisa replied.

"I really hope they do," she murmured with a tired sigh.

Annalisa grimaced when her cellphone buzzed. "Listen, if you need anything, don't hesitate to call me," Annalisa stated before she answered the call. "This is Hollins."

Samara stood outside of the barn and watched as Annalisa returned to her truck. She lifted her hand in a brief wave as Annalisa pulled away. Pressing her uplifted hand to her chest, she absently rubbed the aching spot over her heart and wondered for the millionth time if she had done the right thing by turning in her brothers. Feeling depressed, she slowly went back up the stairs to her apartment.

The last three days had passed in a blur. After using the device that Adalard had given to her and Bear to knock out the guards, the two of them had escaped out the back where Bear's truck was parked.

She didn't know what happened during the poker game between Adalard and Campeau except that Adalard had won. Bear had been strangely silent since that night. Adalard had disappeared three days ago, and she hadn't seen him since. She wiped another tear away before pushing open the door to her apartment.

A pair of strong arms circled her waist, lifting her up off the ground, and she gasped when a pair of warm lips caressed her neck. She laid her hands over Adalard's and laughed at his playful affection. Tilting her head back against his shoulder, she smiled at him.

"I thought you left," she confessed.

He lowered her to her feet and turned her in his arms so that she faced him. She held onto his forearms when he bent his head and kissed her.

Several breathless minutes later, she clung to him to keep from melting into a puddle on the floor.

"I think you missed me," she teased.

"Very much," he acknowledged with a crooked smile.

She shivered when a draft of cold air blew in from the open door. He reached behind him and closed it. Clearing her throat, she removed her coat and hung it by the door before she turned and walked into the living room.

"Where have you been the last three days?" she asked.

"Ha'ven and Emma have returned. I had to return to my ship," he explained, following her.

"I guess this means you'll be leaving soon," she replied.

"Yes."

Adalard's simple response was like a hot poker through her heart. She kept her back to him and held her hands out toward the hot air blowing from the pellet stove. The brief feeling of joy she'd experienced was quickly replaced with a sharp, aching pain in her chest again. This time the ache was far worse than it had been minutes before when she was talking with Annalisa.

She'd known this time was coming, but it still felt like it had happened too soon. She closed her eyes when he slid his arms around her waist and pulled her back against his body.

Why do bad things always seem to come in series? she silently wondered.

"Wh-when will you be leaving?" she asked in a voice husky with emotion.

"Tonight. It is imperative that we return as soon as possible," he explained.

"Tonight!" she breathed out in a shocked whisper.

"Samara—" He paused and gently cupped her face between his palms.

She looked up at him. Her harsh denial froze on the tip of her tongue as she gazed into his violet eyes. He looked down at her, his softly glowing eyes filled with warmth—and love.

"Samara, I want you to come with me to my world."

She started to shake her head before she stopped. What did she have left here? There was no telling what would happen to her brothers. The only one who might still have anything to do with her was Wilson, and she had no idea where he was. News of what the rest of them had done would already be all over town—the last shred of any honor in her family name destroyed by her brothers' actions. The only one who meant anything to her was Adalard, but—

"What happens if things don't work out between us? What if something were to happen to you? How would I survive in an alien world?" she asked, trying to voice all of the reasons she shouldn't go.

He pulled her closer and kissed her hard. She immediately responded. She groaned as their tongues tangled. He pulled away and rested his forehead against hers.

"You tie me up in knots. I've never understood what it would mean to feel something like this. Our bond is not something that will fade. I need you, Samara. You bring harmony to my energy—a balance—that only a true mate can bring. Look at it. Look at us," he commanded in a rough voice filled with need.

He held his hand up, palm out to her. She lifted her hand and placed it against his. Her smaller hand looked dainty and pale against his darker skin. Swirling colors of vivid reds, blues, and violets mixed with a sparkling white that danced through the mixture.

"You are the white energy. Your energy is the purest I've ever seen," he said.

A surprised laugh slipped from her. "Pure… me? I'm not sure I've ever heard anyone say that about me before," she confided.

"I want you to come with me, Samara. I… my feelings for you will not change. You will be loved and protected by my family. You also won't be alone. Emma will be there. If you ever wish to visit here, I will bring you back. I need you. My people need you," he quietly said.

"Your people—the thing on your ship," she replied.

He nodded. "Yes. Whoever created that has the power to do great harm to my people. With your help, we may find a way to protect ourselves."

Her heart thumped heavily in her chest. She pulled away from him and walked over to the window. Below her, she could see her dad's old truck that she had restored and Mason and Ann Marie's house. She pressed her hand over her heart.

"I've never been anywhere really except for a trip to Seattle in high school. You're asking me to-to—" She couldn't continue.

He walked up behind her, stopping before he touched her, but she could feel the heat from his body. The colors that always surrounded him washed over her and she breathed in.

She parted her lips at the intimate sensation of his mental caress. As she closed her eyes and embraced the sensation, she was unaware that she was sending her own energy out to surround him. She arched her back as the force of their combined energy surged through her. Behind her, she heard Adalard take a deep breath.

"Yes, I'll go. I'll need to tell Mason," she murmured, opening her eyes and staring out the window again with a sense of renewed determination. She turned around and looked at him with a shaky smile. "I'll go." She beamed with a laugh.

He swept her against him and captured her lips in a passionate kiss that seared a path straight to her heart. She wrapped her arms around his neck and returned his kiss with the same passion. They both moaned when he scooped her up in his arms. She pulled away and gazed up at him with a raised eyebrow.

"I could get very used to this," she teased.

"I wanted to do this the first day I met you," he confessed.

She laughed. "That would have definitely gotten you shot," she giggled.

"It would have been worth it," he admitted.

Her throat tightened at the emotion in his eyes. "I love you," she said, caressing the scar on his cheek.

Samara's quietly spoken words washed through him, and he tightened his hold on her as he walked down the hall to her bedroom. His return to the ship would have to wait for a little longer. He wanted to embrace the last few hours that they would have alone. He knew once he returned to his warship, his duties would take away a lot of the time he would rather spend with Samara.

By the time he made it to her bedroom, he was on fire. She was nipping at his earlobe and pressing hot kisses anywhere she could reach. When he laid her on the bed, she dragged him down on top of her and captured his lips. A groan slipped from him and with a thought, he envisioned them both naked.

She pulled back in surprise when she felt the cool air against her naked skin and stared up at him. He gave her a crooked, devilish grin. She giggled, tangled her hands in his hair, and kissed him again.

He responded, opening his mouth and tangling his tongue with hers. She wrapped one leg around his thigh and applied pressure to his shoulder. He realized she wanted him to roll over so that she was on top. He did, without breaking their kiss.

I've always wanted to do this, she silently confessed.

Do wha-at... ah...

His breath huffed out when she wrapped her hand around his full cock and rose up on her knees. He kept his eyes locked on her face as she rubbed the tip against her soft mound, then slowly impaled herself on his throbbing shaft.

Oh yesssss....

"Goddess, Samara, you are beautiful!" he murmured as he captured her breasts in the palms of his hands.

She rose up, sliding along his cock before pressing down until he was buried so deep he felt the tip of his cock brushing her womb. Her eyes were closed, her pink lips slightly parted, and she had a dreamy expression on her face as she rode him.

He uttered a hoarse inaudible curse when she found his nipples and pinched them. Pressing his feet into the bed, he rocked his hips in motion with hers. A sly smile curved his lips when she gasped.

Adalard breathed as he pulled almost out of her. It was pure torture feeling her soft, slick walls stroking the entire length of his cock. Rolling her pebbled nipples between his fingers, he pinched them, applying a tiny spark to give it a little sting. She popped her eyes open, and her channel walls tightened around him.

She splayed her hands across his chest. "Do that again," she requested.

He pinched her nipples again, sending a little more spark to them. She cried out, her body clenching him again as she moved up and down. She wrapped her hands around his as she began moving more frantically. He continued rolling her nipples and sending the tiny shocks to them.

Her sheath turned to molten liquid, slick with their combined desire, as the friction between their bodies heated from the force of their joining. He gritted his teeth, determined to hold on long enough for her to come. When the tingling spread, he knew he wouldn't last much longer.

"Now it is my turn," he grunted.

She opened her mouth to protest when he lifted her off him, but still started to roll so he could be on top. He shook his head. Understanding dawned when he rolled to his knees behind her and held her hips. She bent forward when he entered her swollen folds. His breath hissed out as he watched his cock slide into her.

"Goddess, but you have no idea how sexy this looks," he muttered.

He pulled out to the tip of his cock and thrust his hips forward, impaling his shaft as deep as he could go. Bending over her, he slid his hand across her stomach to her mound and parted her soft lips. He found the hidden nub and gently stroked it, sending the same tiny sparks to it that he had to her nipples, while rocking his hips.

"Adalard!"

Samara's hoarse cry filled the room as she wrapped her hands in the bedcovers and pushed back against him. Her body shuddered as she came. He slid his hand back to her hip and increased the pace of his thrusts to match the pulse of her orgasm. Fire spread through every nerve ending in his body before pooling in his cock. A cry tore from his throat as his orgasm erupted from him, washing her womb with his hot seed.

He shivered in extreme pleasure when she squeezed his overly sensitive cock. He drew in shuddering breaths, waiting for the intensity of their joining to fade enough for him to move. Samara moaned, wilting from the aftermath of their lovemaking. He wrapped his arm around her waist, holding her to him as they rolled until they were both lying on their sides.

"I never knew what the big hoopla was about sex until now. I could definitely get addicted to this," she murmured.

He chuckled, kissed her shoulder, and rocked his hips enough to remind her that he was still buried deep inside her.

"I'll be happy to fill your need anytime you like," he replied.

She laughed, caught his hand, and pulled it to her breast. "How long before your battery recharges?" she teased.

His cock twitched, swelling again, and he sent a slight charge through his fingertips to her nipple. "What makes you think I ever run down?"

Her gasp turned to a moan. *I told you I couldn't lie to you.*

CHAPTER TWENTY-THREE

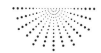

*A*dalard hugged Samara when she swayed. His curse echoed with the hum of machinery in the transporter room and the cheerful banter of his crew. He had forgotten the disorientation that often happened the first time someone transported.

Samara gripped his arm, breathed deeply, and looked around the room with wide, wary eyes. She pressed against him when one of the transporter room techs walked up to the edge of the platform. He murmured for the man to take Samara's luggage to his quarters.

"I was beginning to wonder if you were going to return," Ha'ven drawled.

Adalard grinned. "Samara needed help packing."

Ha'ven lifted an eyebrow as the tech walked by him carrying a suitcase in each hand. "Yes, I can see how that would take a while," he dryly remarked.

Adalard ignored his brother and focused on Samara. "Are you feeling alright?" he murmured.

She swallowed and nodded. "Yeah, I'm okay. That was a bit of a head rush," she shakily responded.

"So, this is the human who has captured you," Ha'ven murmured.

Irritation flashed through Adalard. Ha'ven was looking Samara up and down like she was a Subervi steak. He flushed when his brother gave him a pointed look, and he remembered his own reaction to Emma the first time he met her.

"Be nice," he cautioned.

"Since when have I ever been that?" Ha'ven dryly replied.

He frowned and shook his head. "Where's Emma?"

The humor on Ha'ven's face disappeared. "She is in our quarters. The death of her mother has been difficult for her."

"I understand. I was hoping she and Samara could meet," Adalard said.

Samara squeezed his arm. "It's okay. I know what it's like to lose someone you love. If I can be of help, please let me know."

Ha'ven's expression softened. "Thank you, Samara. I will let Emma know that you are here," he said. "After Samara is settled, I would like to meet with you," he continued.

"Of course," Adalard replied.

"I will see you in an hour in the Command Room. Samara, it has been a pleasure to meet you," Ha'ven said, stepping aside so they could all exit the room.

Adalard guided Samara out of the room and turned to the right. He fought a grin as they navigated the corridors. Between the gawking of his crew members and Samara's fascination, he was rather enjoying the novelty of the experience. Her sudden inhalation of breath made him look up.

"Who is that?" she whispered with wide eyes.

Adalard scowled. "His name is Crom. He is a Moniker. He has assigned himself as Emma's personal guard," he replied.

Crom stopped and stared at Samara with a curious expression. She stared back at the Moniker for a few seconds before she grinned. Adalard gritted his teeth when the Moniker straightened to his full height and rubbed his belly.

"She is off limits, Crom," he growled.

"I might be able to charm her away from you. I know you don't have any," Crom replied.

Samara giggled. "I like him."

He groaned. "Don't encourage him. Ha'ven has enough trouble trying to keep from tripping over this walking rug," he muttered.

Crom grinned. "You and your brother are jealous you don't look this good. All you have is a lot of hair on your heads," he retorted.

"Oh, Adalard's got hair in other places," Samara remarked without thinking.

"Pshaw! I hope you aren't impressed by the tiny patches he has on his —" Crom scoffed.

"It's time to go," Adalard interjected before Crom could finish his graphic anatomy description.

"Bye, Crom," Samara said with an amused smile and a wave.

"Another human woman after my heart," Crom answered as they passed him.

Adalard groaned. "Be careful or we'll never get rid of him," he warned.

Samara's delighted laughter filled the corridor. Crew members paused and smiled before continuing on their way. Adalard wrapped his arm around Samara and hugged her close to his side.

I am going to be fighting off more than Crom if I'm not careful, he mused.

Outer Region of Heron Prime

"Incoming communication DQ187," the computer announced.

Hamade looked up from the report he was reading and accepted the communication. He pursed his lips in annoyance as he scanned the message. The spy on the *Rayon I* finally reported in—if the cryptic message could be interpreted as a report.

Experiment failed. Returning.

The message told him nothing about why the experiment had failed or where the two Ha'darra Princes had mysteriously disappeared to. Frustration swelled inside him as he rose from his desk and walked over to the long rectangular viewport that looked out into deep space. The Empress would not be pleased when she discovered that her experiment was a failure.

There is no use sharing the information with her until I know what happened, he thought, justifying the delay.

The chime of the communicator pulled him back from his morbid thoughts. He returned to his desk and scanned the code on the screen, accepting the communication.

"General, I have the cargo you requested," Lesher announced.

"Excellent. Deliver the cargo as soon as possible," he replied.

"Yes, sir," Lesher responded.

Finally! he thought with satisfaction.

The bait had been caught and they would now set the trap. This would be the end of the Ha'darra family after centuries of failure. It was imperative that nothing go wrong now.

"To the future of a new world," he murmured.

~

Onboard the Rayon I:

Earth's orbit

"I've been doing some research, and I think I may have found some information that will help with the entity that was placed on your transport, Adalard. I won't know for certain until you return," Arrow said.

"Whatever you do, don't release it," Ha'ven warned.

Arrow glared at his eldest brother. "I'm not stupid. I take these things much more seriously than either of you. Did you bring Samara?" Arrow asked.

"Yes, but remember what I said—she is not one of your test subjects," he replied.

Arrow's face distorted on the vidcom for a second before it cleared. Adalard wasn't sure if it was caused by a cosmic interference or Arrow didn't want them to see the obscene gesture that he'd learned from Cara Truman, Trelon Reykill's mate. The extension of a middle finger had a universally crude meaning on Earth that Arrow had embraced.

"I know she is not a test subject, but I will need to study the entity and her together," Arrow insisted.

"What have you discovered?" Ha'ven asked.

Arrow opened his mouth to reply just as a violent shudder disrupted the connection. Adalard helplessly watched as Arrow was thrown sideways out of view. Sitting forward in his seat, Adalard peered at the distorted video feed. All he could see was the collapsed wall behind his twin.

"Arrow!" Ha'ven yelled.

The men sitting around the table watched in grim helplessness at the scene unfolding before their eyes. Adalard unconsciously flexed his fingers and counted as he waited for Arrow to reappear. The seconds stretched to minutes as he and the others listened to alarms, the cracking of mortar, and the sizzling of electronic equipment. He swiftly inhaled when the connection flickered at the same time as he noticed a movement at the bottom of the screen.

"Crimatus deathdealers!" Arrow cursed as he stiffly rose to his feet.

"Are you hurt?" Adalard demanded.

Arrow covered his mouth, smothering his cough. Smoke and debris floated in the air. A fast-acting foam sprayed down from the ceiling, dissipating the dust particles. Arrow scowled and scanned the ruined area behind him.

"I'm fine. I'll get back with you when I know what happened," Arrow grimly replied.

The screen flickered again and went dark. Ha'ven's fist connected with the table. Adalard met his brother's furious expression and grimly nodded. Either one of Arrow's experiments went wrong or the traitors were growing bolder.

"I'll contact Melek. I have a bad feeling about this," he stated, rising to his feet.

Ha'ven nodded. "I agree. This is too much of a coincidence. Between the device Quill found and the creature that was on your ship, I fear we may not have rooted out all the traitors on Ceran-Pax," he added.

Adalard grimly nodded in agreement. "I'd like to speak with Salvin as well. Arrow mentioned he found something. If he did, he most likely discovered the information in the Archives. Salvin is sure to know about it as well," he said.

"I want to speak with Quill again," Ha'ven said, rising to his feet.

Adalard paused as he turned toward the door. "What is it?" he asked.

Ha'ven frowned and shook his head. "I don't know—just a feeling," he replied.

Adalard immediately thought of Samara. He had taken her away from Earth to protect her and brought her into something potentially far more dangerous. Needing assurance that she was alright, he reached out to her. Panic gripped him when she didn't immediately respond.

This ship is amazing! she finally answered. *Emma and I are exploring.*

Adalard relaxed when he heard Samara's excited response. Ha'ven noticed his relief and smirked. He scowled back at Ha'ven, ignoring the glimmer of knowing amusement in his brother's eyes.

I will see you later, he responded.

Take your time. There are loads of stuff for me to check out, she said.

Be careful, he cautioned.

I will. Crom is with us, she cheekily replied.

He groaned at the thought of the Moniker. The other man was probably pouring on the charm even as they were speaking. Ha'ven really should have left the man back on the Red Planet's moon where he belonged.

"Crom is with them," Ha'ven stated.

He rolled his eyes. "So Samara said. Let me know if you find out anything new from Quill," he said before turning and exiting the room.

Quill frowned when the door to the secondary Communications Access room didn't automatically open when he pressed his palm to the entry panel. He pulled his hand away and tried it again. Unease began to fill him and he hesitatingly reached up to tap the communicator he was wearing. He paused over the button as he debated whether to notify Adalard. Deciding to proceed with caution, he tapped his communicator.

"What is it?" Adalard answered.

"I'm not sure, sir. I'm on Sublevel 3 at the Secondary Communications Access room. I ran diagnostics on all the systems before we departed the planet's orbit, and I noticed an unusual signal that was transmitted from the ship. I traced it to this room, but the access door won't open. I-I thought since you asked me to keep things quiet that I should inform you," he responded.

"Wait for me. I'm on my way," Adalard replied.

"Yes, sir," he answered.

Quill studied the door. They would need to gain access to it. He placed his tool bag on the floor and retrieved the small computer module he used to run diagnostics as well as the tools he would need to open the access panel. In seconds, he had opened the panel and plugged the ribbon cable into the computer module. He scanned the code, searching for any changes.

A flash of unfamiliar code caught his attention and he scrolled back to it. Each coder had a specific writing style. He was fairly certain he knew all the onboard technicians' styles. After finding the burnt module, he had taken the time to study them. This one was different. He didn't recognize it. That meant one of two things—either he had missed one or the person who did this wasn't assigned to the engineering department.

He started in surprise when he sensed someone standing behind him. He sighed in relief when he realized it was Adalard. The man moved with incredible stealth.

"Can you open it?" Adalard asked.

"Yes. I wanted to see if I could recognize the code. It is like a fingerprint. Whoever did it was good, not great, but good," he replied. He grimaced when Adalard raised his eyebrow at him. "Give me a minute."

"Who else has access to this room?" Adalard impatiently asked.

"The Officers, Engineering, Software Managers, Maintenance, Electrical...," Quill absently muttered.

"Is there anyone who *doesn't* have access?" Adalard dryly asked.

Quill looked up with a frown. "Not really. It isn't like anyone really uses this access and if they do...," he said.

"They have to use their access ID or the biometric readers," Adalard finished.

"Yes, sir," he replied just as the door silently slid open.

He opened his mouth only to close it when Adalard shook his head at him to remain silent. He warily watched as Adalard stepped past him into the room. He glanced at the laser pistol in Adalard's hand. A frantic scan of his tool bag revealed only a few limited options as a weapon. He grabbed the long handle of a welding torch.

Swallowing, he cautiously followed Adalard into the room. While he was trained to be a warrior, his specialty was in—well, everything but being a warrior. He could read code at a phenomenal rate, understand just about any diagram placed in front of him, and could create an engine with a few wires and the welding tool. Okay, the last part about the engine was a bit of a stretch, but he was pretty good at building things.

He twisted and pressed his back against a power wall designed to keep the secondary communication systems running in the event of a power failure. Sweat beaded on his brow as Adalard motioned for him to move around to the other side. He nodded and squeezed the torch handle to keep from dropping it.

Adalard slid between the wall and a bank of computer equipment. He peered over the edge. A person's shadowy silhouette reflected on the wall.

"Step out now with your hands raised," he ordered.

Whoever the person was, they ignored his command. He looked over at Quill and motioned for him to remain where he was standing. Quill gave him a brief nod.

He peered around the corner of the cabinet again before focusing on the spot where he last saw movement. In seconds, he appeared in the space next to the crouching figure. He gripped the slender shoulder and realized it was a woman.

The woman struck him in the chest with the palm of her hand. He stumbled back and she took off around the corner of the cabinet before he could get a good look at her. A flashing light against the cabinet caught his attention as he regained his balance.

"Explosive! Take cover!" he shouted, diverting his gaze from the brilliant flash of light as he raised his hands to form a protective shield. Fire engulfed the room.

Projectile debris shot out from the mangled computer cabinet. The explosion rippled through the room. The rows of communication equipment were torn from their foundations, falling like dominos. The intense heat and raining debris flowed around his shield.

In the smoke-filled room, the glow from the red emergency lights cast an eerie radiance. Fire retardant rained down from the ceiling and flooded the area. It would be difficult to see until the exhaust fans activated.

Adalard kept the bubble-shaped shield around himself as he picked his way through the destroyed room, searching between the debris for the traitor. A large cabinet lay across a section of the corridor leading to the door and he was forced to lower his energy shield. Covering his mouth and nose in the curve of his elbow, he lowered his eyelids as the acrid smoke burned his eyes. A low moan from behind caused him to twist around. He cursed when he saw that Quill was trapped under one of the tall server cabinets.

"Adalard!" Ha'ven yelled from the entrance to the room.

He looked at the doorway through the red haze. "Quill is injured," he shouted.

"My legs are trapped. I think they may be broken," Quill said through gritted teeth.

"Hold on. We'll get you out of here," Adalard promised.

He worked his way closer to the top of the cabinet. It would be difficult to move. Another cabinet was hovering precariously from a tangle of computer wires above Quill. A live power cable, torn from a conduit overhead, was sending down a rain of sparks. It snaked back and forth.

He would have to be extremely careful. If he moved the cabinet on top of Quill too far, it could dislodge the cabinet hanging from the cables and wires, causing a domino effect that could crush them both—unless the live wires contacted the metal, then they would face electrocution. Neither mode of death sounded pleasant.

"Ha'ven, I'll lift the cabinet off his legs and you get him out of here," Adalard said.

Ha'ven eyed the crackling wires above their heads and grimly nodded. He knelt near Quill and waited for Adalard to get into position.

"Ready," Ha'ven stated with a sharp nod.

Adalard took a deep breath, released it, and focused on the energy pulsing inside him. The cabinet and the one laying on top of it rose a few inches. Sweat beaded on his brow from a combination of the heat and the intense concentration of his focus. Ha'ven gripped Quill under his arms and pulled. The younger man smothered a cry of pain as Ha'ven shifted him clear of the cabinets. Adalard quickly released his grip on the large metal frame, and it dropped to the floor with a loud thump.

"How bad is it?" Adalard asked, climbing over the cabinet and kneeling next to Quill.

Quill looked up at him with pain-glazed eyes and a touch of satisfaction. "I may need to visit medical, but I'm not the only one who will need to go," he said with a grimace.

"What do you mean?" Ha'ven asked.

Quill held up the torch he was still gripping. "I caught a glimpse of them. It was a Changeling. It flashed past me close enough that I was able to leave a nice, deep burn mark across their left arm that has to be hurting as much as I am right now," he replied with a wry, pain-filled grin.

Adalard smiled at the young technician and squeezed his shoulder in comfort. "You did good, Quill," he said, looking up when the emergency response team entered.

He stood up and stepped aside for the medics. Ha'ven walked over and stood next to him. He gave his brother a short nod and they exited the destroyed room.

"We need to find out who did this," Ha'ven stated the moment they were alone in the lift.

He nodded in agreement. "Thanks to Quill, it shouldn't be that difficult. I want to know if there is anyone else on board my ship who doesn't belong."

"Emma is expecting a child," Ha'ven quietly shared.

Adalard started in surprise and studied Ha'ven's worried expression. Adalard's thoughts immediately moved to Samara.

"Crom," he growled into his communicator.

"I'm behaving," the Moniker immediately replied.

He shook his head at Ha'ven. "There is a traitor on board the ship. It is a Changeling. Stay close to the women and keep them in the common areas," he instructed.

He winced when Crom's deep snarl rang in his ear. "I'll rip them apart if they try to harm the women," he vowed.

"Well, keep whoever it is alive long enough that we can interrogate them," Ha'ven replied.

"No guarantees," Crom retorted.

Adalard ended the link when the lift slowed. "I'll warn medical to be on the lookout for anyone coming in with a burn on their arm and have them closely monitor their medical supplies. Have you heard back from Melek or Salvin yet?"

"No. I'll contact Melek again and meet up with you on the bridge," Ha'ven answered.

Adalard nodded and stepped out of the lift. He strode down the corridor and headed for the medical unit as his thoughts raced with a mixture of anger and fear. The thought that he had brought Samara into danger was weighing heavily on his mind.

CHAPTER TWENTY-FOUR

*S*amara gave Emma a questioning look when Crom stopped another warrior from entering the small café-type lounge they had entered a few minutes earlier. She didn't know what was going on, but something had clearly upset the man.

"Do you have any idea what has his fur in a wad?" she murmured to Emma.

Emma shook her head and glanced under her eyelashes at Crom. "No. Something is wrong. I can feel Ha'ven checking on me every few minutes."

Samara picked up the tray with the meal she had programmed in the replicator, sniffed it, and shrugged. It looked like a grilled cheese sandwich and fries. She wasn't up to trying any alien replicated meat yet.

"How do you know it is a bad sign?" she inquired.

She followed Emma to a table near a window that looked out into space. It still felt surreal to be on an alien spaceship hurdling through space at an unbelievable speed. She placed the tray on the table and slid onto the bench seat.

Emma smiled. "Because while Ha'ven may not be saying anything to me, I can sense he is troubled. It is the same sensation I felt when..."

Samara paused, the sandwich halfway to her mouth, and shook it at Emma. "You are not going to leave me hanging, I hope."

Emma shook her head and smiled. "I guess that *would* be rude. I... was not well when I first met Ha'ven," she began.

Samara listened with fascination as Emma quietly shared the details of when she met Ha'ven. By the time Emma was finished, Samara had forgotten about her meal. Lifting a hand to her cheek, she brushed away a tear.

Samara, you are well? Adalard's deep voice echoed through her mind.

Yeah. I think I'm going to like your brother, she replied.

Adalard's chuckle sent a flush of warmth through her. She looked out the window into deep space. Her nagging fear about whether she had made the right decision to give up everything she knew was slightly diminishing.

"Adalard, meet me in the command office," Ha'ven growled.

"On my way," Adalard replied.

He exited the medical unit and strode down the corridor. In the hours since the explosion in the communications room, he had poured through the personnel data bank. There were a hundred and eighty personnel onboard, and he was no closer to finding the Changeling. No one had come to medical for burns, and the biometric scans were still showing all rostered personnel.

He entered the bridge a few minutes later and crossed to the command room. He paused when he saw the holographic view of Arrow's lab. One end was heavily damaged. Ha'ven turned when he entered and gave him a grim nod.

"Have you heard from Arrow?" Adalard demanded.

Ha'ven shook his head. "No, but I spoke with Melek. Mother has been taken," he grimly replied.

"What!" he hissed out in shock. "How? When? What happened?" he demanded.

Ha'ven waved at the hologram. "Melek—Father—said he and Arrow believe the explosion was a diversion. Mother was in the garden with Salvin when it happened. Salvin said a group of men dressed as royal guards appeared seconds after the explosion. They said Melek had sent them to escort Mother back to the palace. She hasn't been seen since."

Adalard ran his hand along his scarred cheek. "Did Salvin recognize any of the men?" he asked.

Ha'ven shook his head. "No, but Salvin hasn't been as involved with the new recruits. They all wore the guard's color, and he stated their auras reflected their positions," he replied.

"How is that possible?" he demanded.

"I don't know. Either they *were* members of the royal guard, or they have discovered another way to camouflage their identity," Ha'ven replied.

"Camouflage...," he repeated thoughtfully.

"What is it?" Ha'ven asked.

He shook his head. "I've had no luck with the biometric scans. What if they were able to create a filter of some kind that could distort their aura?" he mused.

Ha'ven frowned. "They would need a portable device as well," he said.

"Yes. When is the last time someone spoke with Arrow?" he asked.

"Arrow disappeared into the archive with Salvin. Melek said that Arrow had mumbled something about phantoms and vanished a short time later," Ha'ven responded.

"Phantoms… that sounds an awful lot like our missing Changeling," he commented.

Ha'ven's eyes widened at the thought. "We need to find out who it is. If they are using a device, it could lead us to whoever kidnapped Mother," he said.

"My thoughts exactly," Adalard replied.

"What's the matter?" Emma asked.

Samara gave Emma a rueful smile and shook her head. "Nothing," she replied.

"Do you want to check out the hologram deck?" Emma asked.

"Hologram deck? You mean, like when you wear one of those virtual reality masks and feel like you are really there?" she asked with a raised eyebrow.

Emma laughed and threaded her arm through Samara's. "Something like that, only much better," Emma enticed.

"I'll wait outside," Crom groused, walking past them.

Samara looked at Emma with a curious expression. "What's wrong with him? He's been glued to us like a fly stuck to flypaper and now he doesn't want to go," she murmured.

Emma glanced under her lashes at Crom and leaned close. "He did a random program once and ended up in the middle of the desert. He swears it took him a month to get the sand out of the crack of his ass," she replied with a giggle.

Samara couldn't help looking at the big guy's tight ass as he walked ahead of them. The guy may have a light coating of fur over his body, and he definitely looked like an alien, but damn if he didn't nicely fill out a pair of pants. His snort of disdain told her and Emma that he was listening to their conversation.

"That would be cool," she said.

"Where would you like to go?" Emma asked.

Samara frowned. "What do you mean?"

Emma waved a hand at the computer screen. "You just say a place and the computer will generate it," she said.

"A place? Like any place in the world?" she repeated.

Emma laughed and nodded. "Well, any place that has been programmed into the computer," she amended.

"Don't pick Zanzibar or the Wastelands," Crom warned. "They are hideous planets with nothing but endless mounds of sand."

"Is Earth programmed in it?" Samara asked.

Emma nodded. "Yes. Ha'ven had it added so that I could visit whenever I felt homesick," she said.

Samara bit her lip. "I always wanted to go to Paris," she confessed.

Emma grinned. "Then Paris it will be," she announced.

"Along the river where the used book stalls are," Samara added. Emma gave her an inquiring look. She grinned and shrugged. "It's a scene from one of my favorite movies."

"Paris, France, Earth simulation," Emma asked of the computer.

"Generation complete," the computer replied.

The door to the hologram room opened. Through the opening, Samara gaped at the tree-lined sidewalk. Pedestrians strolled around, stopping at the displays of used books and artists lining the Seine River. Behind them, she could see boats traveling along the waterway. In awe, she stepped through the entrance after Emma. The door behind her closed and disappeared.

They stood on the sidewalk, taking in the surrounding sights. Curious, she walked over and ran the tips of her fingers along a row of books. She could feel the textures of the printed cloth covers against her fingertips. A pedestrian walking by bumped into her and murmured a quick apology.

"How is this possible?" she breathed, watching the distracted woman hurry away as she tried to catch up with her child.

Emma shook her head. "Don't ask me. Ha'ven tried to explain the science behind it, and it went over my head. I think it's something like the replicators, only it's a temporary thing," she confessed with a laugh.

"Who cares about the science. This is cool," she laughed, twirling in a circle. "I want to see it all."

∾

Four hours later, Emma ruefully said, "I'm afraid I'm going to have to sit this part out. I... I don't do well in confined areas and I have to admit I need a nap."

"I'm so sorry. I've been dragging you all over the place and never thought about how exhausting it must be," Samara said with an apologetic look.

Emma shook her head. "I've had a wonderful time. I just need to lay down for a bit. The last few months have been pretty exhausting for me," she confessed.

"I'll walk with you back to your cabin. I can always visit again," she said.

"No, you really wanted to go through the catacombs. Why don't you stay here?" Emma suggested.

Samara bit her lip and gazed longingly at the phonebooth-sized entrance to the catacombs. The underground tunnels had been at the top of her must-see list for Paris sites. She looked back at Emma when the other woman touched her arm.

"Stay and have fun," Emma encouraged.

"What about Crom?" she asked with an uncertain expression.

Emma chuckled. "If he hasn't died from boredom or been arrested for beating someone up, I'm sure he'll be alright with you staying a bit longer. I'll check to see if he would like to join you. Something tells me he might enjoy learning more about humans," she replied.

"That would be fun," Samara agreed.

"I'll meet up with you later," Emma promised.

"I'll see you then and tell you if I learn anything new," Samara replied with a grateful smile.

She watched as Emma ordered the computer simulation to reveal the exit. It was shocking to see that they were only a few dozen feet from it. It felt like they had walked miles!

"Whoa, that is so cool," she breathed.

Emma laughed. "Enjoy. I'm off for a nap," she said with a wave of her hand.

"Tell Crom I'll be in the catacombs," she called behind Emma.

She waited a few minutes before turning and heading for the entrance to the catacombs. She stepped through the door and smiled at the attendant. Another advantage of the simulator was that there were no lines and no money was necessary for anything.

"Please be careful. There are 131 steps leading down to the catacombs and 112 steps leading back up," the attendant said, handing her a headset.

"Thank you," Samara replied with a happy grin.

She adjusted the headset over her ears before she stepped through the doorway and descended the curving steps. She ran her hand along the stone wall, marveling at the realistic feel against her fingertips. Shaking her head in amazement, she tried to think of other places she would like to visit.

"It's a good thing they didn't have one of these things at the high school I went to. No one would have ever left," she mused.

The temperature dropped several degrees by the time she reached the bottom, and she shivered. A wide, arched, dimly lit corridor angled downward. She followed the path deeper into the catacombs, listening to the virtual tour guide.

In the late eighteenth century, when major public health problems associated with the city's above ground cemeteries led to a decision to transfer their contents to an underground site...

CHAPTER TWENTY-FIVE

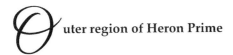

Outer region of Heron Prime

Narissa Ha'darra shivered as cold air swirled around her in the unheated glass prison cell. Through the transparent barrier, she noticed dark, uneven walls. The layers of iron-ore and silicates indicated that the prison cell was in an abandoned Antrox mine.

She winced with pain and gently touched her swollen lip. She sent a wave of healing energy to the damaged area. Lifting her hands higher, she did the same to the cut on her forehead and the bruises on her cheek. The bruises on her arms and wrists would have to wait until her hands were free before she could heal them.

She turned when she heard the sound of an outer door opening. A tall, broad shouldered man strode through the doorway. Behind him, she noticed a vast room filled with electronic equipment. The man paused outside of her cell and studied her.

Trying to intimidate me, she thought.

She lifted her chin and returned the man's glacial scrutiny with a haughty glare of her own. She would never bow to the evil she saw lurking in his eyes. He pressed on the locking mechanism. They were both silent as the door slid open, and he stepped inside.

"Narissa," the man greeted.

"Queen Ha'darra to you," Narissa coolly replied.

The man's eyes narrowed. She swallowed but remained still when he took a threatening step closer. She flexed her fingers, drew on the energy surrounding her, and enveloped herself with an invisible shield.

"Queen Ha'darra," he repeated before reaching out and stroking her cheek. "I am General Hamade Dos."

She turned her head away from his touch. He chuckled at her disdain. An electrical charge shot out from her shield and zapped the tips of his fingers. She knew the charge must have been painful, but Hamade gave no indication that he felt it.

"A General of what? Deceit? You are nothing but a traitor to your people, Dos. You have made a grave mistake kidnapping me. Do you really believe that my sons will not find you?" she scoffed.

Hamade chuckled again. A shiver of unease ran through her at the menacing sound. It was not the sound of someone who was worried about the consequences of his actions.

"I would be very disappointed if they didn't," he coolly replied, lowering his hand from her cheek.

"What do you want?" she demanded.

"To see for myself if our little experiment works," he replied.

"What... experiment?" Narissa warily asked.

Narissa stepped back when two people entered the small cell carrying a cylinder. A dark shape agitatedly moved inside it. She flinched when Hamade reached for it.

"Welcome to the beginning of the end for the Ha'darra family," he maliciously chuckled.

"No...," Narissa hissed in horror and recoiled.

Hologram deck:

Samara was studying the intricately carved castle created by one of the excavators when an unexpected sense of unease filled her. She rose to her feet and scanned the surrounding area. Holographic tourists moved past her like ghosts.

She pulled the tour-guide headphones from her head and switched off the audio player. A young couple walked by her followed by a single woman in her fifties and an old man with a cane. They continued along the passage.

A movement in the shadows drew her attention. The young woman who had been standing on the other side of the old man was now partially blurred. There was a haze of swirling blood-red with green dots surrounding the woman.

"The castle is beautiful," the woman reflected, stepping closer to her.

Samara nodded and glanced at the stone carving. "It is. It must have been agonizing and therapeutic for the man who carved it," she said.

"Why do you say that?" the woman inquired.

Samara indicated her headphones. "This said the man who carved this was imprisoned for years and the castle was the only thing he could see. I imagine the conditions of the prison were horrible and seeing such a beautiful castle was like salt in a wound," she reflected.

"The imprisonment could be no worse than confinement in an Antrox mine or a Curizan prison," the woman replied.

Samara started when she noticed that the woman had stepped closer while she was distracted. She tried to step aside, but the woman blocked her path. Samara's eyes widened as it dawned on her that none of the other holograms had the swirling aura around them.

"Computer, end simulation," she called out.

The area around her faded. The woman did not. Samara backed up. She looked around wildly, scanning for the exit. The woman stood between her and the door.

"What happened on Ha'darra's shuttle? How did he survive?" the woman demanded.

Samara frowned. "What in the hell are you talking about?" she demanded.

"The entity I placed on his ship—how did he survive it?" the woman persisted.

The woman gripped Samara's arm in a bruising hold and Samara hissed with shock when the woman's hand and arm rippled and changed. Gone was the pale skin of a young French woman. In its place were dark green scales.

"What the hell are you?" Samara demanded in a shaky voice.

The woman's grip tightened and her claws dug into Samara's arm. Samara instinctively reacted. She swung, punching the woman in her forearm. Her assailant gasped and yanked her hand back, cradling her arm.

"Computer, simulate Paul Grove's Ranch—Earth," Samara frantically ordered.

The landscape surrounding her rippled and changed. The familiar buildings and wooded area appeared. The woman snarled at her and struck out. Samara ducked and rushed the woman. She gripped her assailant's arms and the woman shrieked with fury.

"Never start a fight with a woman who has five older brothers, bitch," Samara snapped as she drove her knee into the woman's groin.

"I'll kill you," the woman hissed, falling on her side.

"Good luck trying," Samara retorted.

The woman reached for a weapon at her waist and Samara kicked out, her foot connecting with her assailant's injured arm. The impact sent the small device sliding across the ground. Samara dove after the device, falling when the lizard woman wrapped a clawed hand around her ankle.

"Samara, where are you?" Crom's booming deep voice called.

"Crom! Help!" she cried out.

She rolled onto her back and kicked out at the woman. The illusion of the woman evaporated. In her place was Adalard. Samara gaped, the moment of disorientation paralyzing her.

"Adalard?" she whispered.

"Samara, it's okay. Tell me how you were able to see who the woman was," he ordered.

She scrambled back, shaking her head. "You're not Adalard. You're... you're some kind of chameleon," she said.

"How did you escape the entity?" Adalard's deep voice demanded.

"Fuck off," Samara growled, kicking at the pseudo-Adalard figure.

She rolled, scrambling to reach the device. She wrapped her fingers around it and twisted back around, but the chameleon had disappeared.

"Lady Samara," Crom said, hurrying forward.

Samara turned the weapon on Crom. He stopped and held his hands up. She released a trembling breath when she noticed that his aura was normal. Lowering the device to her lap, she reached out for his hand when he held it out.

"What happened?" he asked.

Samara rubbed her bruised arm. "Some lizard-shifter attacked me," she said.

Crom uttered a low, rumbling growl and scanned the area. "Computer, end simulation," he ordered.

The familiar landscape faded, leaving Samara with a deep sense of loss. The room was empty save for them. She would have thought she had imagined the whole incident if not for the ache in her arm and the weapon in her hand. Her stomach clenched at the memory of the alien creature in Adalard's form.

"Did the Changeling hurt you?" Crom asked.

She swallowed and shook her head. "No... no, I'm fine. It just shook me up a little. I'll be alright," she quietly replied. She looked down at her hand before offering the weapon to Crom. "I knocked this out of her—its—hand. I'm not sure if it will help you locate the perp," she added.

"Come, let me escort you back to your quarters," Crom replied.

Samara nodded. She followed him to the door, pausing in the doorway to look back into the empty room. A sigh slipped from her before she turned and followed Crom.

"I'm fine," Samara said for the dozenth time. Her voice echoed in the narrow confines of their bathroom.

"You have bruises," Adalard retorted in a gruff tone.

She laughed and shook her head. "Trust me when I tell you these are nothing. I've had a lot worse," she replied.

He gently ran his fingers over the bruises and sent a burst of healing energy into the damaged tissue. She hissed in surprise when she felt the tingle.

"This should never have happened. You were supposed to be protected," he said.

She looked up at him with a tender smile. "Crom couldn't be in two places at once. I wanted to stay, and Emma was exhausted. The choice was simple. None of us could have anticipated that some lizard bitch would attack me. Crom was only gone for a few minutes. Heck, you even said there was no record of who this chameleon is or that they even entered the hologram deck through the main door. Now that I know what to look out for, I'll be more careful," she said.

"I should have told you there was a danger. I didn't want...," he said before he shook his head.

"You didn't want what?" she asked, leaning back against the doorframe of the bathroom.

His tired sigh was deep as he wound his arms around her and pulled her close. When Crom had informed him of what happened, he was shaken to his core. The thought of something happening to Samara terrified him. It was a foreign emotion to him. He closed his eyes and rested his chin against the top of her head.

"I wanted to take you away from the danger of your brothers and protect you. Instead, I have brought you into a world far more dangerous," he said.

"You asked me to come. I made the decision on my own. It doesn't matter where you go in the universe, I guess. There will always be good guys like you and bad ones like my brothers somewhere in the mix. I can't live my life in fear. I have to hope that everything will work out and fight like hell when it doesn't. That is part of the adventure," she said.

He opened his eyes and kissed the top of her head before leaning back and looking at her face. He gave her a tender smile, kissed her again, and cupped her cheeks.

"You are good at fighting," he acknowledged.

She laughed. "You bet your ass I am. That lizard lady didn't know what hit her," she said with a wiggle of her nose.

"You are sure it was a female?" he asked.

She frowned and shook her head. "Not really. One minute she looked like one of the women you have on board and the next... the next she looked like you," she confessed as she played with the fastenings on the front of his shirt.

Concern gripped him. Changelings were adept at mimicking, but their auras gave them away. If they had an ability to camouflage that as well as their biometrics, it would make them virtually invisible.

"What was really weird was the color surrounding her. That was what alerted me that something strange was going on," she murmured.

He held her hands. "You saw something different?" he asked.

She looked up at him and nodded. "It was like this hazy swirl of red with green dots."

Hope flared inside him. "Get dressed," he suddenly replied.

"Where are we going?" she asked.

Grim determination filled him. "With any luck, to catch a Changeling."

"Anything yet?" Ha'ven asked.

Samara shook her head. "No, they all look like people on a monitor," she replied.

Adalard shrugged his shoulders when Ha'ven glanced at him. Samara leaned against him and he slid his arm around her waist, pulling her close. He gently squeezed her waist when he noticed that she was worrying her bottom lip.

"Let's move to the next level," Ha'ven suggested.

The technician nodded and pulled up the next set of images on the screens. Samara studied each person as they went about their daily activities. There would be two shifts. This was the first one. Over the past hour, the four of them had been scanning each level.

"Maybe this won't work using a screen. Maybe it will only work if I see them in person," she said.

"Let's try this first," Adalard suggested.

She sighed and shook her head. "This isn't going to work. Don't ask me why, I just know it isn't. I need to see the person," she said after they finished another level.

"I fear she is right, Adalard. The shifts will be changing soon," Ha'ven added.

"It was worth a try. I'll have each division chief schedule a time for all members to gather. We will go level by level. We need to find the person before they do more harm," Adalard growled in frustration.

The door to the security room pinged and slid open, revealing Crom holding on to a woman who had a flare of blood-red color with green dots swirling around her. Crom had his hand wrapped around the woman's nape and was holding one of the woman's arms behind her back. The woman lifted her head and glared at them.

"That's her," Samara blurted out.

Crom grimly nodded. "I caught her in the flight bay," he said.

"How did you find her?" Adalard asked.

"I followed the stench," Crom replied.

"Filthy Moniker. Your people will be among the first to die," the Changeling promised.

Crom grinned and squeezed the woman's neck. The woman bit back a groan and struggled against the pressure. Samara watched in silence.

"We will take it from here, Crom. Can you escort Samara to our quarters?" Adalard asked.

Samara wanted to protest, but something told her she didn't want to see or know what was about to happen to the woman. Fear flashed through the woman's eyes before they hardened. Samara stepped aside when Crom released the woman and pushed her into the room.

"You are all going to die," the woman scoffed.

Samara paused in the doorway and looked over her shoulder at Adalard. She swallowed at the emotion—or lack of it—in his eyes. This was a side to him that she had never seen before, not even when he was dealing with her brothers.

"Lady Samara," Crom said.

She nodded and turned away. As she walked away, her surroundings took on a new meaning. The glamour of being here, on an alien spaceship heading for an alien world, faded, and the reality hit her hard. That nagging fear in the back of her mind raised its ugly head, and she stopped in the middle of the corridor, suddenly feeling nauseated. Crom turned and looked at her.

"Are you feeling unwell?" he asked.

She swallowed and looked back at him. "Can you take me to the hologram deck, please?" she asked in a low, slightly unsteady voice.

"If that is your wish," Crom stated.

She tried to smile before giving up. "It is."

He nodded and resumed walking. Samara followed him in silence, trying to quell the growing anxiety threatening to overwhelm her. She stepped into the hologram room, turned, and held out her hand to stop Crom from following her.

"I'd like to be alone, if you don't mind," she said.

A deep frown furrowed Crom's brow, and he looked hesitant. "Adalard said I was to stay with you," he reminded her.

"And I am telling you I need my space," she stubbornly replied.

Crom released an unhappy grunt and stepped back. "I'm not moving from the door, and if I sense anything wrong, I'm coming in," he warned.

"That's fine," she acknowledged with a curt nod.

"Human women are—" he muttered.

The closed door cut off the rest of his sentence. She turned and leaned against the door, running her trembling hands over her cheeks.

"Com-computer, simulate Paul Grove's ranch on Earth," she requested in an unsteady voice.

The walls, ceiling, and floor rippled around her and in seconds, she was standing outside the barn. She slowly walked over to the door and pushed it open. The soft neighs of horses and the fresh smell of hay hit her hard. She parted her lips, pulling in deep, gulping breaths as a wave of homesickness and uncertainty threatened to send her to her knees.

She stumbled forward, gripping the door of a stall. A mare lifted her head and stared back at her. Pieces of hay stuck out from the sides of the mare's mouth and she slowly chewed. Samara reached a hand out, craving the touch of the soft muzzle. Tears coursed down her cheeks as she picked up the brush next to the stall, opened the door, and stepped inside.

"Hey, there. Did you miss me?" she softly asked.

It didn't matter to her that none of this was real. For a short time, she would lose herself in her preferred surroundings, doing a familiar chore. She ignored the tears coursing down her cheeks, blinding her. Leaning her forehead against the mare's neck, she sniffed.

"What was I thinking? I should never have left. This world—it isn't for me. I'm not like Emma. Back home I knew how to fight. I still had a family. They may have been rotten to the core, but they… they were mine," she whispered, closing her eyes and curling her fingers in the mare's mane.

She sniffed again and rubbed her cheek against the mare's coarse mane. There was no doubt in her mind about what Adalard and Ha'ven would do to the Changeling. The stories Emma had shared were enough to alert her to the fact that justice was very different here in space. These were powerful beings capable of doing horrible things. In this world, Adalard wouldn't threaten Jerry with a 'man talk'. He would kill him without a second thought.

She opened her eyes and straightened. As much as she wanted only to see the gentler side of Adalard, she had to acknowledge there was a darker side as well—and as much as she loved him, she knew she wasn't ready to be a part of it. She wanted... needed to go home.

"We're still close enough to Earth, surely he can take me," she said, wincing at the desperate sound in her voice. She stroked the brush along the mare's side. "Tomorrow... I'll talk with him tomorrow. When I feel calmer."

CHAPTER TWENTY-SIX

*S*amara kept her eyes closed early the next morning, listening as Adalard quietly moved around their quarters. He retrieved a change of clothing and entered the bathroom. Only when the door closed behind him did she drop her ruse of sleeping. She rolled onto her back and stared up at the ceiling through gritty eyes.

"I didn't mean to wake you," Adalard said, standing in the doorway of the bathroom.

She had been so lost in thought that she didn't realize he was finished. She blinked and sat up. She studied him and noticed that he hadn't shaved. The dark shadow of facial hair gave him an edgy appearance. She also noted faint shadows of fatigue under his eyes.

"Are you going out again? Shouldn't you get some rest?" she asked.

He walked over to the bed and sat on the edge. She curled her fingers when he reached for her hand. Under his sudden, intense scrutiny, she bowed her head and forced herself to relax when he cupped her hand in his.

"There are… things that I must take care of," he said, caressing the back of her hand with his thumb. "You were very restless last night."

She lifted her head and frowned at him. "How did you...?" she asked before shaking her head and looking down at their joined hands again.

"Samara," he murmured, caressing her cheek.

She turned her head away. "What is going to happen to the woman?" she asked in a soft voice.

He didn't immediately reply. Samara looked up at him, noticing his averted eyes. Deep down she already knew the answer to her question. Still, there was a masochistic part of her that needed to know.

"It is best if you do not know," he finally replied.

She shook her head. "Don't you have laws, courts, ways of dealing with people, Changelings, whoever it is?" she insisted.

He pulled away from her and stood up. "There's much that you'll need to learn about life in my world. I must go. We can talk later."

She drew her knees up, wrapped her arms around them, and nodded. "Okay."

He groaned as he leaned over and cupped her face between his palms. When he gave her a brief, hard kiss, she instinctively responded, wanting more, but he was already pulling away. She curled her fingers in the bedspread as she watched him turn and exit their quarters. Only when the door closed behind him did she fall back against the pillows. She squeezed her eyes closed and breathed deeply, fighting for control.

"I will not cry," she muttered.

Throwing back the covers, she stood and made the bed. She grabbed some fresh clothing and headed for the bathroom. A hot shower and a little time alone were just what she needed at the moment.

She stepped into the shower, trying to push away the vivid mental images she had glimpsed last night. Adalard had erected a wall between them to protect her, but a couple of times disjointed fragments of information had slipped through. The images had been disturbing. The Changeling was dead.

She stepped out of the shower, dried, and dressed. The sound of a muted ding caused her to frown in puzzlement. The ding came again and her frown deepened as she searched for the source. Under a discarded towel on the counter, she found the source—Adalard must have forgotten his communicator device. Her thumb swiped over the screen, and she blinked when a woman's face suddenly appeared.

"Uh... hello," she greeted.

A flash of annoyance swept across the woman's features before it shifted to curiosity. Samara waited for the woman to respond. She wondered if the woman could maybe see her but not hear her.

"Hello, can I help you?" she asked.

"Where's Adalard?" the woman demanded.

Samara instinctively looked toward the door before she returned her attention to the woman. "He isn't here. Can I give him a message?" she politely asked.

The woman laughed. "Yes, you can tell him Niria, Traya, and Doray are impatiently waiting for his return. You can also tell him that he will need a bigger bed if he keeps bringing women back with him," Niria said.

Samara gaped in surprise when two other women waved back at her. They were scantily dressed and draped across a bed. She held the screen a little farther away when the first woman reappeared.

"Make sure you tell him that we miss him," Niria instructed.

"I'll be sure to do that," Samara replied in a tight voice.

She stared at the blank screen with a sense of detachment—as if her mind and body were disconnected from each other. She wrapped her fingers around the device, her initial sense of despair changing to a slow burning rage.

"*Three? He has three fucking bitches in his bed!*" she growled. "He's nothing but an alien man-whore!"

She turned when the outer door opened. Stepping into the doorway, she pursed her lips when Adalard entered the room. He stopped and warily studied her.

"I... forgot my communicator," he said.

"Yes... you did," she replied with a bite in her tone.

She held the communicator up and slowly walked over to him. She thrust the device against his chest. He caught the communicator when she released it and stepped back.

"Samara...," he warily said.

"This was a mistake. I shouldn't have come. You said that if I wanted to return to Earth, you could make it happen. I'm holding you to your promise," she gritted out.

The wariness on his face changed to shock. "What happened? If you are upset about the Changeling—there are things you are not aware of."

She shook her head and wrapped her arms around her waist as pain gripped her. It wasn't his fault. They were too different. Hell, they were literally galaxies apart. If anyone was to blame, she was for being young and naïve. Despite having shit-heads for brothers, her inexperience with men should have been enough to make her more cautious.

"It's more than the Changeling, Adalard. I was stupid to think this could ever work. I... I want to go home," she said, looking away from him.

"Samara...." He paused when she shrank away from his touch. He dropped his hands to his sides. "Samara, talk to me. You have shut your mind to me, so I cannot see what has happened. Please... talk to me," he encouraged.

"Who the hell are Niria, Traya, and Doray?" she suddenly blurted. "If I had known you were planning on adding me to the notches on your bedpost I could have saved you the trouble! If you won't take me home, I'll find someone else who will," she finished, angrily wiping a tear from her cheek.

He opened his mouth to reply only to close it when the communicator in his hand pinged. She winced as a shaft of pain swept through her at the thought of the woman calling again. She didn't bother to hide the vivid images of the three women that flashed through her mind. Adalard's low curse told her that this time he did receive the full visual of her thoughts.

"Adalard, I need you on the bridge," Ha'ven said.

"I'll be there shortly," Adalard replied.

He pocketed the communicator and reached for her. She backed away, shaking her head, and bit her lip. She needed time alone to get her emotions back under control.

"The women mean nothing to me," he said.

She released a bitter laugh. "Yeah, I've heard that line about a million times. It doesn't look like they got your memo." She released a long, shaky breath. "Let's just chalk this up to a lesson learned. Impulsive decisions are never a good idea, especially when based on emotions. I want—need—to return to Earth, Adalard," she reiterated.

He muttered a hoarse curse when his communicator pinged again. She remained still while he answered. Lifting her chin, she didn't quite meet his intense scrutiny when he finished.

"You are my life now, Samara. I would do anything for you," he stated.

She looked back at him. "Then let me go," she softly replied.

"This conversation is not finished. I need to take care of some urgent matters, but I will return as soon as possible," he said in a tone edged with frustration.

"Take care of whatever needs to be done. It's not like I have anywhere else to go," she said with a shrug, looking away from him again.

He caressed her cheek before turning and exiting their quarters. Samara bit her bottom lip to muffle the sound of her sobs. She sank down onto the edge of their bed and buried her face in her hands. Rocking back and forth, she waited for the worst of the waves of pain to subside. Only when she felt more in control did she rise, return to the bathroom, and wash her face. As she did, she made the decision to find a place where she could think—in private.

She stepped back into the bedroom, gathered a jean jacket, and exited the room. She turned left, wanting to avoid the main corridors. Crom had shown her and Emma a few lesser used maintenance corridors. At first, she thought about going to the lounge where she and Emma had lunch, but she soon found herself outside the Hologram room. The first two were in use but the smaller, third room was free. She entered and requested the door be locked behind her.

Shoving her hands into her jacket pocket, she stood, lost in her thoughts. After a few minutes, she walked to the center of the room. A lone tear coursed down her cheek and she quickly wiped it away.

"Computer, show me a meadow on Ceran-Pax," she requested in a soft voice.

The wall panels rippled as if being turned by a roulette croupier, and the white walls changed to an alien landscape. She stood in a meadow of knee-high, purplish grass. Wildflowers of every color imaginable dotted the landscape. Twin mountain ranges, the peaks covered with snow, rose up on each side of the meadow. A winding river, three-car-lengths wide, meandered through the center.

She walked along an animal trail, holding her right hand out at her side, gently brushing the flowers. She stopped when she startled a large deer-like creature that had been lying in the grass. The animal had thick blue hair with brown strips running along its side and spiraling green antlers. The creature stared at her with startled bright-green eyes before it twirled and bounded away. She followed the graceful animal as it crossed the river and disappeared into a stand of trees on the other side.

The world was beautiful—but alien. The grass, the animal, and the twin moons gave the world a surreal feeling. She stopped and studied the meadow around her.

The deer-like creature stepped out of the woods, followed by several more, and began to graze. She walked over to a nearby rock under a lone tree near the river and sat down. The scenery around her calmed the emotional rollercoaster inside her, and she reflected on the decisions she had made.

As much as she loved Adalard, she recognized that coming here with him was a mistake. She was nineteen, what did she really know about the things she wanted in life? Ever since she could remember, she had been taking care of someone else—first her mom, then her brothers. She didn't count her dad much, though she did all the cooking and cleaning.

She never had much time for doing what she really wanted to do. Just as she was making plans, all hell broke loose and Adalard showed up. Now, she questioned if what she was feeling was really love or a flight response and a need to escape. She felt like a frog in a pot of water coming to a boil.

"You're supposed to wait for me to escort you," Crom growled.

She turned on the rock and gave the huge man a crooked grin. "How did you find me?"

He shrugged. "If I tell you, you might find a way to prevent me from doing it again," he replied as he stepped forward and sat down beside her on the rock.

"Shouldn't you be with Emma?" she asked.

"The child in her womb has made her very tired. She wished to rest today," he said.

She nodded and fell silent. Neither one of them spoke, and a comfortable sense of companionship fell between them. She focused on the calm movement of Crom caressing the gold wristband wrapped around his arm. There was something soothing in the unconscious act. After a few minutes, she chuckled as a random thought flashed through her mind, and she shook her head at it. Crom looked at her with a raised eyebrow of inquiry.

"You remind me of someone back home—a friend. His name is Bear. I've known him forever… and yet, it's like I never really saw him," she murmured.

"You care for this male?" Crom asked.

She smiled. "Yes, I care about him as a friend," she softly answered.

"Adalard did not kill him?" he asked.

She laughed and shook her head. "No, Adalard didn't kill him," she responded with an unexpected break in her voice.

Crom compassionately reached for her, and she turned into him. Low sobs shook her shoulders. She was powerless to stop the grief after it burst through the dam she had built.

Samara knew she was crying for more than the last twenty-four hours. She was crying for the loss of her mother, the lack of a relationship with a father who only saw a daughter as a tool, not a person. She cried for her brothers and the way they had thrown their lives away for a fast buck, alcohol, and women who would never care about them. She cried for her inability to see Bear as more than a friend. But most of all, she cried because she knew that at this moment in time, she was not ready to accept what Adalard was offering. She needed to find out who she was before she could be something that someone else needed.

"I hear the sound of heartbreak in your sobs. If you cry for the Changeling, she is not worth your tears. She made her path and lived with the consequences of her actions. She would have killed you without remorse," Crom said.

"It… it isn't just her. I… this is a mistake. I shou-shouldn't have come here," she sniffed.

Crom lifted her hands in his. She looked up at him. His face might be different from a human's, but his eyes weren't. In them, she saw compassion and resolve.

"Tell me, and I will do what I can to help you," he vowed.

She opened her mouth to reassure him that she would be alright, but instead, she began sharing the story of her life back on Earth. He asked a question every once in a while. The question invariably led to more sharing on her part until she realized that she wasn't holding anything back. A deep sadness filled her when she drew to the shuddering end of her story: the heartbreaking introduction to Adalard's lovers.

"I should be telling Adalard all of this, not you," she confessed.

"He may already know," Crom kindly responded.

"Adalard, what is it?" Ha'ven asked.

Adalard shook his head and looked away from his brother's concerned gaze. He closed off the pain coursing through him at Samara's haunting words. As much as he wanted to go to her, his duties to his people and his family had to be his first priority.

"Nothing. Arrow, what have you found out?" he replied.

"There is—or I should say was—a hidden base on the outer region of Heron Prime. I think they may have taken Mother there. Melek has gone after her," Arrow replied.

Adalard and Ha'ven both cursed at the thought of Melek going alone. Whoever they were up against held an arsenal of deadly weapons they knew little-to-nothing about. Melek was experienced, but he was also older—not to mention that Ha'ven had only recently discovered the man was his father and not his uncle.

"Arrow, do you think if Ha'ven and I combined our energies, we could make a jump that far?" Adalard asked.

Arrow's eyes widened, and he whistled under his breath. "Honestly? I don't know. That much energy expenditure could tear the ship apart... or both of you. It would definitely drain you both. A quick calculation in my head... I'd have to go with the first of the two options. You might be able to do short bursts, like skipping a rock across the water. The momentum of the hops could theoretically cause a wave of energy that could propel the ship forward without depleting you or causing a temporal anomaly that would rip apart the time-space continuum, or...," he mumbled in a distracted voice.

"Can we cover the distance if we do shorter bursts?" Ha'ven impatiently inquired.

Arrow slowly nodded. "Theoretically, yes. In reality, no one has ever tried. You aren't even sure how you were able to do it before, Ha'ven. I mean, we are talking about not just you two, but an entire ship with hundreds of crew members on board. Ha'ven did it when Emma was in danger, but we've never replicated it. Adalard, you've never transported—have you?" he asked.

"No, at least not the distance we are talking about," he ruefully acknowledged.

"You should be able to increase the power to the engines by point three percent without any chance of damage. That increase will get you to the base in seventy-two hours give or take two added jump gates. I'll have those in place by the time you get there. I'll send you the coordinates," Arrow added.

"Will you have the jump gates operational in time?" Adalard asked with a frown.

"Yes," Arrow answered with a grim smile.

"Make it happen, Arrow," Ha'ven ordered.

Arrow nodded and the screen went black. Adalard turned to leave, but stopped when Ha'ven reached out and gripped his upper arm. He impatiently shrugged his brother's hand away.

"Are you sure everything is alright? You seem distracted," Ha'ven said.

"Everything is fine. I'll check in with the chief engineer," he tersely replied before exiting the room.

He strode across the bridge, his mind on Samara. She had shut him out again. There was one thing he needed to do before he met with her again. Something he should have done a long time ago.

Stepping into the lift, he waited until the doors closed before he retrieved his communicator. Anger burned deep inside him—not at Niria, Traya, and Doray but at himself. Initiating the connection, he waited until one of his former lovers answered.

"Adalard! Who's the new woman and does she like having a bit of fun?" Niria purred in greeting.

CHAPTER TWENTY-SEVEN

Three days later, Adalard silently entered the hologram deck. Samara had taken over the smallest room for the most part, only vacating the room out of guilt at depriving other crew members of their access to it. She wandered the ship most of the time, seldom sleeping. He knew she was avoiding him.

She was sitting on a rock near a wide river. He recognized the area. It was just south of the palace. Hope filled him that she was giving his world a second chance and trying to acclimate.

"This is one of my favorite areas back home," he commented.

She glanced at him before returning her attention to some far-off spot. He sat beside her and sighed when she didn't look at him again. He ran his hand tiredly over his face.

"Emma said we should be on your world in a couple of days," she finally said.

"Technically, we will be in Curizan space. There is a matter that we need to take care of before we return to Ceran-Pax," he replied.

"The kidnapping of your mom?" she asked.

He blinked with surprise. "Yes… how did you know?" he asked with a frown.

She looked down at her hands. "You've been distracted. It wasn't hard to see what was going on. Besides, the whole ship is talking about the explosion in the communication's room, the attack on me, and the connection to your mom's kidnapping. I'm sorry about your mother. I hope you can find her in time," she added.

He reached for her hand. She pulled away from him and stood up. She tucked her hands into her front pockets and walked a short distance away. He rose and walked over to her.

"I should have told you what was going on. I should also have ended my previous relationships much sooner. For both, I apologize," he said.

She shifted from one foot to the other. "I would be lying if I said it didn't bother me, but it is more than that. I hate feeling or acting wishy-washy. It was naïve of me to think—" She stopped and shook her head. "Well, I know you're a good-looking man and a Prince to boot. Why wouldn't you have a legion of fawning women waiting for you back home? Hell, it happens on Earth, why not on some alien world," she replied with a shrug.

"You said it was more than that. What else?" he asked.

She sighed. "Emma," she said.

He frowned. "Emma? I don't understand. Emma is very happy with Ha'ven," he inquired.

"Yes, she is very happy with Ha'ven," she replied.

"Samara, I don't understand," he repeated.

She turned to him. "What do Emma and the others who have come to your world have in common?" she quietly asked.

"The others…. Do you mean the other humans?"

"Yes, the other humans," she said with a wave of her hand.

His frown deepened. "They are human," he replied with an uncertain expression.

"They didn't have family, or if they did, they brought them with them," she retorted in a voice laced with frustration.

Confusion darkened his eyes. "You want to bring your brothers to my world? After all they have done to you?" he asked with an incredulous expression.

She blew out a breath and shook her head. "No, I don't want you to bring my brothers to outer space—though it might help them realize they aren't the center of the universe. If nothing else, it would scare the shit out of them. That might not be a bad thing to help them get their heads straightened out. As crazy as it may sound, not all of them are bad. You never met Wilson, and despite what has happened, Brit and Gary aren't bad. They are just weak. Gary has Pat. She's been through worse with him, but Brit doesn't have anyone."

"Your brothers are grown men. You said Wilson left. He obviously did not care what happened to you if he left you without protection. Brit needs to stand on his own feet. You have a life," he growled.

She jerked away from him. "What life? I traded being under the control of my brothers to being under your control!" she retorted. She regretted her words the moment she said them. Closing her eyes, she breathed deeply before opening them. "That came out wrong."

"Perhaps it did," he replied.

She shook her head. "I promised I would help you and your brother figure out what that glob is and hopefully how to stop it. I know it's important."

"Your happiness is what is important to me, Samara," Adalard said.

She closed her eyes when he caressed her cheek. She didn't want to respond to his touch, but it would have been easier to stop breathing. Regret filled her at her conflicting emotions. How could she feel this torn between wanting to be with him and wanting to go home?

"Give me time to adjust… and deal with… things," she said in a hesitant voice as she opened her eyes and looked at him again.

"I will give you all the time you need," he promised.

She gave him a rueful smile. "Did you really tell the three bimbos to take a hike?" she asked.

A confused frown furrowed his brow before understanding dawned, and he nodded. "Yes. It would appear they have already moved on to new territory," he wryly replied.

She wiggled her nose with distaste. "I hope your alien ass can't catch any STDs," she muttered.

"STDs?" he inquired with a puzzled expression.

"Sexually Transmitted Diseases, Einstein. If you gave me anything, a Changeling and black slime will be the least of your worries," she threatened.

"You are fine. You do not have any signs of sexually transmitted diseases or injuries," Orin, the healer on duty, reassured him with a faint smile.

Adalard grunted as he finished dressing. "Good."

"Is there anything else I can help you with?" Orin asked.

"No, that is all," he distractedly replied.

The ping of his communicator pulled his attention back to the present. He glanced at it. They were entering the outer region of Heron Prime.

"I finished the autopsy scans on the Changeling. A small, explosive capsule was injected into her brain," Orin said.

"An explosive capsule? How was it activated?" he asked.

"The only way is if she had a trigger on her... or someone else realized she was captured and wanted to silence her. I searched her and found nothing," Orin said.

"Thank you. Send your completed report to Ha'ven and me," he ordered.

"Yes, sir," Orin answered.

He finished fastening his shirt as he exited the medical unit. He strode down the corridor toward the lift. Stepping inside, he requested the bridge.

What's wrong? Samara's soft voice filtered through his thoughts.

He hesitated a moment before he replied. *Stay close to Crom. There may be another spy on board.*

I'll stay close to Crom. Thank you for telling me, she said.

I also do not have any STD. I will send you the healer's report, he added.

Her soft chuckle warmed his blood. *I look forward to reading it,* she dryly stated.

He still had a grin on his face when he stepped out of the lift onto the bridge. Ha'ven raised an eyebrow in inquiry. Adalard shook his head.

"Are you and Samara doing better?" Ha'ven asked.

He frowned. "Why do you say that?"

"Emma might have mentioned that Samara has been very withdrawn. She also may have mentioned that Samara was homesick and wished to return to Earth," Ha'ven commented.

He scowled. "My relationship is fine. If I remember, you had problems with Emma when you first met her," he retorted.

The amusement on Ha'ven's face faded, and he nodded. "Yes, and it scared the shit out of me."

"Not to mention being painful when she kneed you in the groin." He sighed deeply. "Niria decided to contact me... and she wasn't alone."

"Ah, yes, I can see where Samara might find that offensive," Ha'ven reflected.

"Enough about my relationship, we need to find Mother and Melek," he said.

"Arrow triangulated the coordinates of the base where he suspects they are holding Mother. It will be dangerous. Until we know how to fight the creature that you brought back, it will leave us vulnerable," Ha'ven warned.

"We don't have a choice," Adalard pointed out.

"Agreed," Ha'ven said.

"I'm going," Samara said with a wave of her hand.

"No, you are not!" Adalard growled for the fifth time.

Samara gave him a pointed look. "I'm not one of those too-stupid-to-live women who has a death wish. I'll follow your directions. You say duck, and I'll kiss the floor so hard the ground will shake," she dryly replied.

"This is far too dangerous. We have no idea what we will encounter," he snapped.

"Exactly. If they have released that energy glob, you and the rest of your guys will be defenseless. Out of everyone tested onboard so far, only Emma and I can repel it. None of your shields have worked; it still sucks you dry. Emma can't go because she's pregnant, so I'm the logical choice. Whatever mojo I have, that thing can't stand it," she countered in a calm voice.

He stepped forward and gripped her arms. "I can't lose you," he stated in a hoarse voice.

She shook her head and caressed his scarred cheek. "You won't. Trust me, Adalard. You need my help. I wouldn't insist if I thought there was any other way. You've seen the tests Arrow insisted on having Quill do the last two days. I've learned a lot. One of the things we learned is that I can hold off the creature from more than just you. Without it, the blob almost killed Quill," she said.

"I don't like this," he muttered.

She took a long, deep breath and shrugged. "I don't like it either, but the idea of you guys going down there with your pants around your ankles in grizzly country is just plain stupid," she remarked.

He raised an eyebrow and shook his head. "I don't even want to know what that reference might mean," he retorted.

"Forget it. I'm going and that is the end of this discussion," she said.

"May I speak now?" Ha'ven dryly interjected.

Samara bit her lip to keep from grinning when Adalard shot his brother a dark scowl. "No, because you'll agree with her," he replied.

Ha'ven nodded. "Only because she is right. I've reviewed the tapes. She *is* correct, Adalard. If we hope to save Mother and Melek, we need to have every advantage at our disposal."

Samara sensed the moment Adalard relented. She squeezed his hand. Ha'ven's deep sigh showed that he wasn't happy about the decision either.

"Let's go find your family," she quietly said.

CHAPTER TWENTY-EIGHT

*A*dalard held his hand out and Samara pressed her back against the wall. She took several deep, calming breaths in an effort to quiet her rapidly beating heart. She kept her focus glued on Adalard.

I don't know how people do this kind of work. I could barely make it through a game of hide-n-seek back home. These guys put the Navy Seals that used to train at the ranch to shame, she thought.

"Clear. Move out," Adalard ordered in a low voice.

Half a dozen men moved in units of two, each sweeping the area with their weapons raised. She took a step forward only to pause when Quill put a hand on her arm, holding her back.

"Careful, my scanner is picking up a disturbance at the end of the corridor," Quill murmured into his commlink.

The men slowed, scanning the area. Ha'ven peered into a nearby room and shook his head. Samara frowned. The entire base was eerily silent.

A shadowy mass surged out of the dark end of the corridor.

"Look out!" Ha'ven warned.

The four men in front tried to retreat, but the mass split and surrounded them. Guttural gasps came from the men as dark bands wrapped around their throats. The dark blob lifted the men off the ground.

Horror filled Samara when she saw the men struggling in vain to escape. Their legs twitched as they frantically clawed at their throats. Without a second thought, she pulled away from Quill's restraining hand and stepped into the corridor.

"Release them, you sorry-ass-son-of-an-alien-blob," she growled, raising her hands.

She drew even with Adalard, and a burst of blinding white energy flowed outward from her hands. The blob recoiled from the white energy. Sections of it sparkled like flashes of light from a welder's torch before falling to the ground and disappearing in a golden fog. The reaction emboldened her, and she strode forward with determination.

"How are you feeling?" Adalard asked.

"I've got this," she said through gritted teeth.

"Get the men out of here as soon as they are free," Adalard ordered.

The wave of energy that she was projecting surrounded the men. They were released and fell to the ground. Their low groans and gasping breaths sounded loud to her ears.

Ha'ven motioned to two men to help their downed comrades. In seconds, the injured men disappeared—having been transported back to the warship. Adalard stayed on her right side while Quill was on her left. The remaining mass hissed and retreated down the corridor.

"What are you seeing?" Quill asked.

"A hazy, swirling dark mass," she replied in a tight voice.

"Anything else?" he asked.

She frowned. "It... it was like the other mass, only it's larger. When my light burst hits it, it's like bright white sparkles and then it turns to a gold-colored fog and disappears," she said.

"Gold fog?" Quill repeated.

She glanced at him and nodded. "Yeah, didn't you see it?" she asked.

"No," he replied, looking over her head at Adalard.

"Does it look any different to you from the mass back on the ship?" Adalard asked.

She frowned and thought about the mass on board. "It's less dense and turns into gold fog after I zap it. It... It's weird, but the one back on the ship felt like it was alive and scared of me. This doesn't have that reaction. It feels... cold, lifeless. Almost like it's a copy, but something that didn't quite replicate in every detail."

"Adalard, Quill, we've found the lab," Ha'ven called.

Samara lowered her hands and shivered. She followed the two men into a large room. Overturned chairs, still smoldering computer equipment, broken glass cylinders, and an array of strange equipment littered the area.

"What were they doing here?" she asked, walking over to one of the broken cylinders.

"If I had to guess, I would say replicating the negative energy mass," Quill answered.

She silently counted the number of cylinders. There were eight. Seven were intact but empty. One of the cylinders was shattered. She swallowed and looked around.

"They left in a rush. Someone must have warned them of our arrival," Ha'ven commented.

"The traitor who killed the Changeling," Adalard guessed, looking around. "Quill, see if you can find anything that will help us figure out how to kill these things. The rest of you spread out and search the area."

"I should go with them. That mass is still out there," Samara reminded him.

"Ha'ven, I will go with Samara and the other men," Adalard called.

Ha'ven nodded in acknowledgment. Adalard and two men stayed ahead of Samara while one guard followed behind her. She scanned the surrounding area, trying to quell the nervous roiling of her stomach. The sound of something falling behind them in the lab caused her to jump.

"We'll protect you, Lady Samara," the guard behind her quietly reassured her.

She gave him a nervous smile. "Thanks," she murmured.

The lights overhead flickered. Memories of horror-film scenes flashed through her mind—specifically the ones from Alien and Predator. She cursed the day she decided to watch the damn things.

They neared the end of the corridor where the mass had disappeared. She rubbed her hands on her jeans before lifting them in preparation.

There was an open door ahead. When they were almost to it, Adalard shouted "Take cover!" just before laser fire erupted from a side room. She gasped when the guard behind her abruptly stepped in front of her.

Adalard and two guards entered the room. Flashes of light nearly blinded her, and she lowered her head. She touched the wall behind her, running her hand along its uneven surface until she felt the edge of an open doorway. The guard motioned for her to stay down as Ha'ven and Quill came out of the lab at a run.

"Quill, get her to safety," Ha'ven yelled as he grabbed Samara's guard and they ran into the room where the battle was taking place.

Quill grabbed her arm to guide her back to the lab. As she backed away, a movement out of the corner of her eye drew her attention back to the end of the corridor.

"Quill, the blob!" she cried out in warning.

The mass surged out of the room at the end of the corridor, heading straight for them. She lifted her hands and projected the white energy.

She poured everything inside her into stopping the creature. The force of the white energy drove the mass back. Samara followed it.

"Lady Samara, it may be a trap!" Quill warned.

"I can't let it get into the room with the others," she replied.

She followed it through the doorway at the end of the corridor. The mass swirled around her, hissing and shrieking. She was vaguely aware of the door behind her slamming shut. She was unaware that her body was beginning to glow with the same white energy she was projecting. The mass, unable to retreat, now attacked her in a vicious wave.

"You can't harm me, and I won't let you hurt anyone else," she snarled with determination.

Huge drops of the mass fell around her, littering the floor before dissolving into a plume of golden smoke. Her energy expanded outward, overwhelming the mass until every square inch of the room was saturated with the bright light.

A guttural cry of triumph ripped from her throat when the last of the blob disintegrated. The cry faded when she caught sight of two people slumped in an embrace on a bunk attached to the far wall. She began to tremble uncontrollably.

"Oh, God, no! Please, no!" she whispered.

Samara forced her legs to move. She slowly approached Melek and Narissa Ha'darra. Sinking down in front of them, she reached out and tentatively touched the pale hand of Adalard's mother. She yanked her hand back when she felt the icy flesh.

"Samara!" Adalard's harsh, frantic voice called.

The door behind her swung open, crashing against the wall behind it. She couldn't reply. Her eyes remained locked on the still faces of the man and woman. Strong hands wrapped around her and drew her up and back against a warm body. Samara couldn't stop shaking. She didn't think she would ever be warm again.

"Adalard, get her out of here," Ha'ven ordered in a deep, grief-filled voice.

Spots began to dance before her eyes, and she tried to shake her head to clear them. There was a loud, irritating clicking sound. She realized it was her teeth chattering. She tried to clench them, but it didn't help.

One second, she was in the horror-filled room and in the next she was on the warship. Her stomach churned, and she frantically searched for a bathroom or trash can. She pulled away from Adalard, rushed to a trash receptacle, and lost the contents of her stomach. She continued to dry-heave between the ravaging sobs rocking her body.

"I've called for medical," a tech in the transporter room murmured.

"Thank you," Adalard replied.

Samara whimpered when Adalard tried to touch her. She shook her head. Even with the tight control he was holding over his own emotions, she could feel the waves of grief crashing through him.

The door behind her swished open. A draft of cool air hit her, sending her stomach churning again, and she clung to the side of the trash receptacle as her stomach revolted once more. A low groan of protest slipped from her when she felt cold hands against her brow.

"She is in shock," Adalard murmured to the man with cold hands.

"Pl-please… just leave me al-alone," she begged.

The words had no sooner left her lips than she felt a slight pressure, and the world turned hazy. Adalard caught her in his arms when her knees gave out. Her head wobbled from side-to-side before she rested her cheek against his shoulder.

"Adalard," she murmured in a barely audible voice.

"What is it, *misha petite lawarrior*?" he asked.

"I'm so sor-sorry," she choked out.

"So am I, *misha petite lawarrior*."

Samara closed her eyes. Tears welled and coursed down her cheeks. She wished they could wash away the pain and grief she had witnessed. She would never forget the haunting sight of Melek Ha'darra lovingly holding Narissa, his Queen and only love, in his arms.

"I'm so cold. I don't-don't think I'll ever be-be warm again," she forced through chattering teeth.

"I'll keep you warm, my beautiful warrior," he murmured.

She turned her face into his shoulder and began to sob. The healer murmured something, but she didn't hear what he said. The man pressed his hand to her neck and the haze turned to darkness as the world slid away. She wanted to scream that she didn't want to fall asleep in case the monster that attacked Melek and Narissa came after them, but it was too late.

CHAPTER TWENTY-NINE

*T*wo days later, Adalard stared out at the palace garden through the office window. The flowers didn't seem as vibrant. It was as if they struggled to thrive without his mother's energy.

He didn't bother to turn when the door opened behind him. He sensed his twin the moment Arrow entered the room. Arrow crossed the room and stood next to him.

"How is Samara doing?" Arrow asked.

"Better. Jaron wanted to keep her another day, but she refused," he said.

They both turned when Ha'ven entered the room. Adalard studied his older brother's face. From the irritated expression on it, he suspected that at least one of Jaron's other patients was being as difficult as Samara.

"How are they doing this morning?" he asked.

"Mother is still unconscious. She is in serious but stable condition. Jaron felt it best to keep her sedated until she is stronger. He's threatening—with respect he assures me—to knock Melek out if he tries to get up again," Ha'ven growled.

"He and Mother were barely alive when we brought them back to the ship. I am amazed they survived. Was Melek able to tell you anything?" Adalard asked.

Ha'ven nodded. "He recognized Hamade Dos."

Arrow cursed under his breath. "I knew it! The information I've been able to obtain has that bastard's mark all over it. I was also able to pull some research off of one of the less damaged servers. I'm still piecing things together."

Adalard stared out over the garden again, not seeing it. "Have you made any progress with the creature we brought back?"

"Not yet. I'm hoping the information found in the base's lab will allow the experiments with Samara to evolve and give us a better under-standing of how Samara repelled it," Arrow replied.

Adalard turned and faced his brothers. He wanted to argue that Arrow needed to find a solution that didn't involve Samara. As much as he hated the idea, he knew that if they were going to defeat Hamade and stop the mass production of those deadly creatures, Arrow would need Samara's help.

"You have until the end of the week," he calmly replied.

"The end of the week! What happens then?" Arrow asked in confusion.

He took a deep breath before he replied. "I leave to find Hamade. I should never have stopped until I killed him. This time I won't."

"Adalard… this isn't your fight alone," Ha'ven said.

He studied both of his brothers' faces. "Arrow is needed here. If anyone can understand what these creatures are and how to stop them, he can. You have Emma… and a kingdom to protect. Out of the three of us, I have the most experience out in the field. I know Hamade. I'll find him and this time, he won't escape."

Arrow looked at him with an expression of concern. "What about Samara?"

Adalard stiffened as pain radiated through him. "She wants to return to her world. She... has family there. Besides, she will be safer there while I'm gone."

"What? When did she say that?" Ha'ven demanded.

He shook his head. "It doesn't matter."

"Adalard.... We can protect her here," Arrow said.

"Can we? We still haven't located the traitor aboard the ship. Mother was taken from these very gardens—right under our noses! Your lab was bombed. How can I hope to protect her when I won't be here?" he tersely replied.

"Emma...," Ha'ven began.

He turned on Ha'ven. "Emma has no family back on her planet, but she has you here. Samara... it is different. I have to take into considera- tion that I may not come back," he reluctantly admitted.

"Adalard," Ha'ven protested.

"Samara and I have discussed this. We both agree that it is for the best. It will give her... time for closure. You understand how important that was for Emma. Samara deserves nothing less. I will return for her after I've dealt with Hamade. In the meantime, you and Arrow can find out who else is involved," he said, looking at both of his brothers.

Ha'ven gave him a critical, assessing look before he finally nodded. "Let us hope it does not take you long to find Hamade. I will person- ally interview every member of the crew. No one has been allowed to depart the ship."

Adalard nodded. "Once you finish, Quill and I will scan the ship and ready it for departure. I've asked Bahadur to escort Samara back to Earth," he said.

"I guess I'd better get busy finding out how to stop whatever in the hell Hamade created," Arrow muttered.

"I'll notify you when I'm finished with the crew," Ha'ven said before he turned and exited the room.

Adalard paused when Arrow put a hand on his arm. He looked at his twin with a shuttered expression. Arrow's fingers tightened when he started to turn away.

"You can lie to Ha'ven, but you can't lie to me. Samara has no knowledge that you are sending her back to her world, does she?" he asked.

"Stay out of this, Arrow," he replied before pulling his arm free and walking away.

Samara stood on the balcony in the dark, enjoying the light breeze. She had spent the morning with Emma and the afternoon with Arrow and a man named Salvin. She unconsciously smiled at the thought of the older scholarly man. He reminded her a lot of an older version of Mason with his quiet disposition.

Between Arrow's constant teasing and Salvin's calming influence, she felt steady again—or at least as steady as she could feel on an alien world. She wrapped her arms around her waist when she sensed Adalard's approach more than heard it. A moment later, his warm hands wrapped around her, and he drew her back against his body.

"How are you feeling?" he murmured.

She relaxed and released a deep sigh. "Better. I'm sorry… about the meltdown I had."

He tenderly turned her in his arms until she faced him, and brushed her hair back from her cheek. She tilted her head, enjoying the feel of his skin against hers.

"You never have to apologize. You saved our lives yesterday. Without you—" He stopped, shook his head, and kissed her before continuing, "... you saved Melek and my mother's life. They would have perished if you had not stopped that... creature from attacking them again."

She could feel tears burning in her eyes. The memory of the couple, wrapped in each other's arms, was seared into her brain.

"Samara," Adalard murmured, stroking her cheek with his thumb.

"I'm glad they will be alright. Arrow told me that they... that they survived," she said, her voice trembling on the last words.

"Yes. There is something I need to discuss with you," he said.

She pulled away and stepped back an arm's length from him. Dread filled her, and her stomach knotted as she studied his expression. The way he said that brought up old memories. She had heard that tone before—way too often.

Samara, there is something I need to discuss with you... the memory of the sound of the doctor's voice telling her that her mother's treatments would end and hospice would be brought in.

Samara, there is something I need to discuss with you.... Chad's deep gravelly voice as he explained her father's Last Will and Testament to her and how to navigate her way through probate since none of her brothers had bothered to show up.

Samara... Her mind shut down the soft, pleading voice of her mother.

"Every time anyone has ever said that to me, it's bad news," she said, wrapping her arms around her waist again.

He sighed and lowered his eyes. "I fear this will be another one of those times."

She stiffened her shoulders and lifted her chin. "Don't sugarcoat it," she stated.

He stepped closer to her. She didn't pull away when he rubbed her forearms. She wasn't sure if her legs would hold her if she tried to move.

"I have to go away. There is something that needs to be done," he began.

"You're going after the people who created that creature—the ones who hurt... who hurt your family, aren't you? How... how long will you be gone?" she asked in a slightly unsteady voice.

"Yes, I am. I have the best chance of finding them... and stopping them," he explained.

She looked up at him. "You didn't say how long you'd be gone," she pointed out.

He shook his head with regret. "That's because I don't know. The longer it takes me to leave, the colder their trail will be."

"I can go with you. Now... now that I know what I'm up against, I'm less likely to have a meltdown," she replied, thinking out loud.

"No, my little warrior. This is a journey I must take alone," he said.

"You can't take all of them on by yourself! Surely, you've got an army. I mean, you have a warship. There's Ha'ven and Arrow and Crom and... and... Quill," she argued.

He cupped her face between his palms and kissed her. She parted her lips under the pressure and returned his kiss, sliding her arms around his waist and holding him tight. She wanted to protest when he pulled back and rested his forehead against hers.

Instead, she closed her eyes and breathed deeply. In the few unguarded moments before their kiss, she had seen his anguish—and his unwavering resolve—at doing what needed to be done to protect not only his people but her. As much as he tried to shield his emotions, she could sense his despair at his decision. She didn't want to add to it.

I'll wait for you, she silently promised.

"You are an incredible woman and I am one unbelievably lucky man," he said.

She opened her eyes and gave him a slightly crooked smile. "You bet your ass you are," she teased before she wrapped her arms around his neck and captured his lips again.

Three days later, Samara decided she wasn't as brave as she thought. She had spent the last couple of days working with Arrow. From early morning until well into the evening they had worked on perfecting the new defense system in his makeshift lab. By the time they finished each day, she was in awe of Arrow's analytical mind and trembling with fatigue from their trials.

"Hi Samara, how are you feeling?" Arrow asked.

She smiled and shrugged. "Like I've been run over by a very large semi which then backed up on me a few times," she joked.

He gave her a sympathetic look. "You have expended a lot of energy these last few days. That isn't easy if you aren't used to it," he said.

She chuckled and shook her head. "Until a few months ago, your definition of energy and mine would have been vastly different. I still don't understand how all this aura-mojo-energy-transference stuff works. We would call it magic back home," she ruefully replied as she descended the last few steps.

He laughed. "I guess I can understand that. I really wish you were staying longer. I'd love to figure out how Adalard unlocked your abilities," he said with an exaggerated sigh.

She threaded her arm through his and squeezed it in sympathy. "Hopefully I won't be gone long. Besides, you still have Emma. Maybe she will help you."

Arrow's face twisted with an expression of disgust. "Are you kidding? Between Ha'ven and Crom, I'll be lucky if I can get within shouting distance of her—especially now that she is with child. You'd think from the way they act I'm about to abscond with Emma to my evil laboratory," he muttered.

"Well, isn't that exactly what you want to do?" she teased.

He grinned. "Yes, but my lab isn't evil, though," he defended.

"I think Ha'ven is more concerned with you trying to sweet-talk Emma away," Adalard dryly commented, appearing behind them.

"Holy crap! You scare me when you sneak up like that," Samara grumbled.

Arrow chuckled, wrapped his arm around her waist, and swung her around to face Adalard. "Fear not, my beautiful lady, I shall protect you," he teased.

"You're about to remember why I'm the one who goes out on missions. Let her go, brother," Adalard growled.

"You may be the twin with the savage brawn, but never forget I'm the one with the superior brains—and the better looks. I could defeat you in a fight without even breaking a sweat," Arrow retorted.

"If we didn't need your 'superior brains', I'd be happy to remind you of the last time we met in the training room," Adalard dryly responded.

"Ah, yes. If I remember correctly that was after I'd spent the night with three very beautiful— I was tired," Arrow awkwardly finished.

It didn't take much of an imagination to understand why Arrow had been tired. It would appear the two brothers enjoyed many of the same adventures. Samara rolled her eyes as she pulled away from Arrow and stepped over to Adalard. They both ignored Arrow's playful groan of disgust.

She glanced back and forth between the two. As far as she was concerned, they were evenly matched in brawn, brains, and good looks. The only difference she could see was they were like day and night in personality traits. Where Arrow was cheerful, teasing, and brash, Adalard was reserved, quiet, and observant.

"Have you made any headway with a device to repel the creature?" Adalard asked.

Arrow's playful expression changed to a serious one, and he nodded. "Yes, thanks to Samara and Salvin."

"We discovered that I was using a certain energy band that not only repels, but can penetrate the creature," she said with a triumphant smile.

Arrow nodded. "Salvin was the one who suggested it. He found information in the archives that talked about the power behind certain energy bands. Between what he found, what Samara explained happened when she faced the creature, and the information I recovered from Hamade's lab, I managed to identify the effective energy band. It is incredible! It is actually a combination of fifty different wavelengths woven into one," he enthusiastically shared.

Adalard waved his hand. "Can you replicate what she does?" he growled.

"Yes, but only by using an Energy infuser. I've created a prototype, but I don't know if it works yet. It isn't like I've had time to work out the issues. You only gave me a few days. I planned on testing the device this morning," Arrow replied.

"Let's test it then. The longer it takes for you to finish, the farther away Hamade has a chance to hide," Adalard said.

Samara bowed her head and breathed. They had talked about the best possible plans, and she hated them all. With each one, he would go after some sociopath and the man's cult followers, and she would either stay here or return to Earth. There was no timeline, no assurances, nothing but the understanding that if he didn't stop the man, his people and the galaxy would be in grave danger.

I am very good at what I do, he silently reminded her.

She looked up and gave him a slight smile. "Let's go see if Arrow's latest invention works," she said with a wink at Arrow.

Adalard looked back and forth between the two of them. Samara fought to hide her grin at Arrow's pained expression and Adalard's suspicious one. She stepped away from Adalard, gripped his hand and pulled him behind her.

"This isn't the first prototype you've made, is it?" Adalard warily guessed.

Arrow chuckled and slapped Adalard on the shoulder. "No," he replied with a wry grin.

Adalard gazed down at Samara. "What happened to the last one?" he asked.

She pulled her hand free and lifted both of them in the air, simulating an explosion. Adalard groaned and shot a pained expression over his shoulder at Arrow.

"Hey, don't blame me if things don't work perfectly! You were the one who wanted a miracle in less than a week," Arrow defended with a shrug.

CHAPTER THIRTY

*A*dalard eased the tension in his shoulders and nodded. He was ready. He would send his energy through the devices attached to his wrists, which would convert the energy to the precise levels he needed to protect himself against the creature. He studied the mass attacking the glass.

"We only allow a small amount of the mass to be released in the experiments. The creature from your shuttle was created using organic material and there is something in Samara's energy composition that reverts the creature back to its natural state. I haven't figured out what it is yet, but I will. The issue we may have is that the entities found at the lab were all replicated. Their composition is only slightly different, so the energy blast from the devices should—in theory—cause them to disintegrate as well. Without an actual lab specimen, we don't know for sure. What we do know is that Samara's energy worked on both of them," Arrow explained.

"Thanks for the warning," he dryly replied.

Samara stood behind the glass partition, ready to enter if the device failed. Adalard rolled his shoulders, lifted his hands, and nodded. The lights changed on the panel, turning from red to green. Arrow opened a narrow slit in the cylinder.

The entire entity exploded outward in a long thin stream like an arrow heading for the center of a target. A vision overcame Adalard's senses, and he shoved the distraction aside. A split second before the tip of the mass reached him, Adalard sent his energy through the device on each wrist.

A glowing shield formed in front of him. The entity shrieked when it collided with the shield. Small explosions lit the energy field at contact and the dark mass dissolved and fell to the floor of the lab, revealing golden flakes within. The gold glimmered for a moment before dissolving too. Adalard kept the shield active until the last wisp of the mass was gone.

"Adalard, are you alright?" Arrow asked with concern.

He nodded as he allowed his energy to fade and lowered his arms to his side. Silence filled the enclosure. He traced the spot where the last vestige of the entity had disappeared.

What is it? Samara asked.

I... sensed something, he replied.

A frown furrowed his brow as he tried to recapture the fragile connection between himself and the entity for that split second. Closing his eyes, he focused on the vision. It was an implanted idea that bloomed in his mind the longer he focused on it. It contained far more than the brief onslaught of that first impression; it was a knowledge sent in its entirety.

Take my blood. It contains the power you need to defeat the creatures created by the others. Only when they are defeated will I be free.

Shaken and confused, he somehow came to understand that a shadowy figure had handed a vial of golden liquid to someone. Adalard focused on the scene that was unfolding in his mind, categorizing each movement. The shadowy figure reached out with the vial—

A hand made of gold, he noted.

The cloaked figure reached for it. The person's features were covered from head to toe: gloves, slender wrists, long fingers, small feet, graceful—

A woman, he suspected.

They were in a dark cave, someplace he had seen before. He focused on identifying the exact location, but a hand on his shoulder interrupted him.

"Adalard, what is it?" Arrow asked.

He stood and looked at his twin. "I need to speak to Morian Reykill," he said.

"Morian? Why? What happened?" Arrow demanded.

He turned his troubled gaze to his brother before looking back at Samara. "This is larger than just Hamade Dos," he finally replied.

Ceran-Pax Orbit

***Ion* Command Room: Curizan Scout Ship**

Adalard held Samara tightly against his body. He stared through the window down at the planet. Lights from the larger cities could be seen twinkling like scattered fires. He had moved up her departure to Earth. He wanted her far from this galaxy before he began his mission. They had attacked his family once. If they knew about Samara, he had no doubt that they would focus on her.

Ha'ven had the same concern for Emma. They would stay at the Valdier palace, surrounded by the Dragon Lords and their human mates. At first, Adalard had considered sending Samara there, but they had both agreed that returning to Earth would be the best for her in the long run.

Emotion threatened to overwhelm him. He'd never dreamed that saying goodbye to someone could feel as though his heart was being ripped out. He tightened his hold on her, never wanting to let her go.

"It isn't goodbye," she murmured as she clung to him.

"If there was another way," he said.

She kissed his neck. The briefest touch of warmth seared his flesh, and he bowed his head. Closing his eyes, he breathed deeply. She caressed his back with a loving, tender touch.

"We talked about this. It is the only way you can focus on what you need to do without worrying about me. It will also give me time to get closure back home. I want to find Wilson… and I'd like to make sure that Brit and Gary will be alright. I—Bear also deserves to know… that I'm alright," she added in an uneven voice.

He straightened and cupped her cheeks between his palms. "It shouldn't be more than a few months," he promised.

"I'll wait for you, no matter how long it takes," she vowed.

"I love you, Samara," he said.

She covered his hand with hers. "I know you do," she murmured.

"Adalard, we are ready for departure," Bahadur said from the doorway.

"Please… be safe. Kick their asses, but first and foremost, come back to me," she pleaded, clutching his hands tightly.

"I will. I promise," he replied.

Their lips met in a passionate kiss filled with love and longing before he stepped back. Energy swirled around her in the beautiful, vivid colors that he remembered from the first time he saw her. Memories flooded his mind of that day. Her wary smile, the soft curve of her lips, the sound of her laughter, the first time they made love—

"Keep her safe, Bahadur," he ordered, turning and exiting the room before he changed his mind.

～

Samara watched Adalard disappear through the doorway. She rubbed her chest, just over her heart. A sense of surrealism filled her, and she knew it was a form of shock. She looked at the man standing a few feet from her.

"Unless you want to see what ugly-crying looks like on a woman, I think it would be best if I had a few minutes alone," she warned in a voice thick with emotion.

An expression that almost resembled panic flashed across the man's face before he bowed his head. "I'll leave you to—" He waved his hand in a circular motion. "If you need anything you can ask any of the crew members," he said before exiting the room.

Samara took a long, shaky breath and looked out the window. She stepped closer, watching as a shuttle returned to the planet. Beneath her feet, she could feel the powerful engines engage as the warship pulled away from Ceran-Pax.

She gripped the windowsill and leaned forward as deep, anguished-filled sobs shook her body. Tears streamed down her face, snot dripped from her nose, and she was sobbing so hard that she could barely breathe.

Several minutes later, she reached into the pocket of her jacket and pulled out the washcloth that she had taken from their living quarters on the planet. She'd suspected she would need it, and she had been right. Breathing heavily, she turned and slid down along the wall until she was sitting on the floor. She pulled her knees up and leaned her head back as she gulped in deep breaths of chilled air.

She looked at the door when it opened again. Bahadur had returned with a tray. He glanced around the room before he narrowed in on where she was sitting. A wry, watery smile curved her lips when he raised an eyebrow. She could imagine how she must look with her hair messy, her eyes, nose, and cheeks red from crying, and sitting like a discarded sack of potatoes on the floor.

"I thought some strong tea would be of assistance," he said, holding up the tray.

"Looks like you have experience with this," she commented, waving a finger in a circle at her face.

He gave her a mysterious smile and placed the tray on the table. "Would you like to sit in a chair or stay where you are?" he asked.

She leaned her head back against the wall, wiped her running nose again, and looked at the tray. She lowered her hand and patted the floor. He smiled and nodded.

"The floor it is," he said.

He poured two cups of tea and brought them over. She accepted the one he held out and watched as he gracefully lowered himself to the floor beside her. She grunted her appreciation as she took a sip of the hot, soothing beverage.

"I'm impressed. Hot tea and being able to sit down without spilling it," she murmured.

He chuckled. "You were right. I've had a little experience. I have two sisters—one older and one younger. They trained me well," he said.

She laughed weakly. "You had to learn in order to survive?" she countered.

He sipped his tea. "That as well," he replied with a slight grin. He relaxed against the wall and rested one arm on a bent knee while holding his cup. "If it is Adalard that you are concerned about, you needn't be. There are few in the galaxy who could defeat him, and I assure you, none that can hide from him for long."

"What if—what if the person isn't—isn't like what he's chased before?" she asked.

"You can trust me when I say whoever is behind the entity and the attack on the Royal family will wish they had never crossed the path of Adalard Ha'darra," he replied with a confident smile.

She lifted her tea cup and tapped it against his. "I hope you are right," she said before drinking the rest of her tea. She wiped a hand across her mouth and frowned at the cup when she felt a slight buzz. "What kind of tea is this?" she asked, looking at him.

He chuckled. "The kind with a little Tiliqua liquor mixed in it," he replied.

∾

Gardens of the Royal Palace:

Valdier

"Adalard, what a wonderful surprise. I heard that Ha'ven and Emma had come for a visit, but didn't realize that you were joining them," Morian greeted in a pleasant tone.

Her golden symbiot watched Adalard intensely. The massive beast was in the form of a Werecat. A thick golden mane flowed down around the beast's head. Rippling lines creased its prominent brow. Twin fangs, half the length of Adalard's arm, glistened in the sunlight. Its paws were the size of a serving plate with long, sharp claws just peeking out between the golden fur coating its toes. It yawned, revealing rows of razor-sharp teeth.

If the beast can't tear someone apart with its teeth and claws, it can change to any number of shapes and kill in a thousand other ways, he thought. He pictured the golden flakes from the entity on his ship.

"I won't be staying," he replied, looking around the garden. "Your gardens are beautiful. They remind me of Mother's gardens back home."

"Zoran told me about the attack on Narissa and Melek," she responded.

"Thank you for your kind invitation for them to stay at your mountain residence," he said.

Morian smiled compassionately and patted his arm. "The healing springs there will help them both recover more quickly, as will having some time alone. Your mother and I have a lot more in common besides having very hard-headed sons. But, I suspect you did not visit just to thank me," she said as she continued caring for the various plants near the path.

"I need information," he confessed.

Morian looked at him with a shrewd expression. "Information that only a Hive Priestess can supply," she inquired.

"Yes," he replied.

She turned away and was silent. When he didn't continue, she glanced at him with an inquiring expression. Adalard knew there was a fine balance between saying too much and not enough. Memories of the war between their species briefly flared to the forefront of his mind before he pushed them away.

"Raffvin was able to convert his symbiot into a different type of matter. Do you know how he accomplished that?" he asked.

She nodded. "His soul was filled with hatred and insanity. Our symbiots live off our essence, the energy we give out, much like your own. When that energy is tainted with rage and hatred, it pulls from a source as dark and empty as a black hole. Raffvin learned how to harness that darkness and magnified it until the pureness within the symbiot was suffocated, tortured... and deformed into an anomaly that went against everything that the Goddesses created," she said.

"Would it be possible to replicate that symbiot?" he asked.

She turned and faced him again. Concern darkened her golden eyes and she stared at the symbiot lying near them. She appeared to be communicating with it. He silently waited until she refocused on him.

"It might be possible… if whoever has a connection to the symbiot can harness that type of darkness. It would be extremely difficult. Even with Raffvin's connection to his symbiot, it fought against his tainted essence. Raffvin's imprisonment of the creature was slowly destroying it—and his dragon. Have you… seen another such creature?" she asked.

He nodded. "The first one was more of a mist. It was placed on my transport. Once it was released, it drained my energy. It grew stronger as it devoured the energy from my body. It was only a matter of time before it would kill me," he explained.

She frowned with concern. "How did you contain it?" she inquired.

"I didn't. My mate, Samara, was able to repel it. It was terrified of her," he said.

"Samara? She wouldn't be the young girl that Paul has told me about, would she? A human woman?" she asked.

Adalard nodded and looked away. "Yes. I've sent her back to Earth until I can find and stop those behind the attacks," he replied.

"I am so sorry, Adalard. I know that had to have been a difficult decision for both of you," she said. She stepped closer and placed her hand on his arm in comfort.

He shifted from one foot to the other in discomfort. He wasn't used to someone showing compassion. He cleared his throat and gave her a nod of appreciation.

"Do you have it with you? Perhaps I can connect with it," Morian said.

He shook his head. "There is nothing left now. We found a lab where the rebels were trying to replicate the original. The replicated mass was different, more violent and draining. My brother, Arrow, was able to use the recovered data and Samara's assistance to create a device that would protect us from the creature. In the process of testing it, the original entity was destroyed," he explained.

Morian frowned. "If it was destroyed and you have protection, then I don't understand how I can help you."

Adalard breathed out a long sigh. "I... saw something—a vision—a split second before the entity dissolved."

"What did you see?" she asked.

"A shadowy figure with a hand made of gold giving a woman a vial of liquid that reminded me of your symbiot. It was a male voice. He said —" Adalard paused a moment, his gaze turning back to her symbiot, "... he said... Take my blood. It contains the power you need to defeat the creatures created by the others. Only when they are defeated will I be free," he replied.

Morian's dismayed gasp seemed to hang in the air. She looked at him with a troubled expression. He waited for her response. She dusted her hands off and lifted her chin.

"Remain on the planet until I return," she requested in a quiet but firm voice.

He bowed his head in agreement. She motioned to her symbiot and gracefully strode down the path several yards before she shifted into a stunning white dragon with flakes of gold rimming each scale. Her symbiot companion split in half. The first half transformed around her, shielding her head, neck, and chest with gold armor while the second part shifted into a large bird-like creature.

With a powerful flap of her wings, she took off. He braced himself against the blast of air that hit him from her departure. A sense of awe and admiration struck him. He was seeing the power behind not just Morian Reykill's dragon, but the woman who was connected to the Goddesses. He turned away, troubled by her concern and her swift departure. He shared a worried glance with Paul Grove.

"Paul," he greeted.

"Adalard," Paul responded with a nod.

He noted Paul's grim expression. "Something tells me that your sudden appearance is about more than just my visit with your mate," he warily guessed.

Paul bowed his head in agreement. "Yes."

Adalard sighed. "Samara has returned to Earth," he said before Paul could ask.

Paul's expression hardened with disapproval and concern. "Why?"

"Because it was the only way I knew to keep her safe," he quietly replied.

He held Paul's gaze as the seconds lengthened. Paul's expression softened, and he relaxed his stiff stance. A feeling of discomfort swept through him at the expression of compassion in Paul's eyes.

"Morian does not usually go to The Hive with such urgency," Paul stated.

He looked at Paul with a grave expression and gave a sharp nod. "I fear what I have discovered is something every species in the known galaxy should be worried about."

CHAPTER THIRTY-ONE

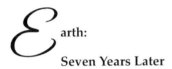arth:

Seven Years Later

"Is this where you grew up?" an excited voice asked.

Samara glanced at her six-and-a-half-year-old daughter and nodded. "Yes, this is where I grew up," she replied.

"Cool," Adaline replied with a grin.

Samara's throat tightened when she noticed the curious expression on her daughter's face. Adaline reminded her so much of Adalard. She had his dark hair and stunning violet eyes framed by thick black lashes. Even as a baby, it had been impossible to take Adaline anywhere without someone commenting on her unusual appearance. Many people commented Adaline reminded them of a young Elizabeth Taylor.

"This is where the house and garage used to be," she commented, pulling off the highway and into a parking lot.

"It's a Dollar General store," Adaline replied in a disappointed voice.

"Yes, your uncles sold it a few years back," she absently replied as she made a loop through the parking lot and turned onto the highway again.

Adaline wiggled her nose. "Will I get to meet them now?" she asked.

Samara silently groaned. This was a topic that she had hoped Adaline had forgotten. Since her return almost seven years ago, there had been only minimal communications between her, Brit, and Gary. Rob and Jerry had written her off. Wilson was still MIA, though she had heard rumors he was working overseas for some billionaire.

"Probably not, love," she finally answered.

"Awwww," Adaline drawled in disappointment.

"Trust me when I say you aren't missing much," she chuckled.

"It's just weird having family but not having family," Adaline muttered.

"You'd better not tell Bear that," she teased.

Adaline giggled. "Bear *is* pretty awesome."

"Yes, he is," she agreed.

Samara's stomach knotted with anxiety. She had moved away shortly after her return to Earth partly because of Bear. Now, she had no choice but to return. It was the only place where she felt she could protect Adaline.

"Will I have to be careful about using my gifts once we get to Mr. Grove's ranch?" Adaline anxiously asked.

Samara glanced at her daughter again. "We already talked about this, honey. Only Bear, Mr. Chad, Mr. Mason, and Ms. Ann Marie know about your gifts. You can't let anyone else see them," she warned.

"If my daddy comes, will he know to come to Mr. Grove's ranch?" Adaline asked.

Samara ignored the sharp pain that lanced through her at Adaline's innocent question. She had been honest with her daughter about her origins. It was impossible not to be. Her connection with Adaline had formed while her daughter was still in the womb. It had been a shock… and a treasured connection to Adalard.

"Yes, he would come to Mr. Grove's ranch," she replied in a thick voice.

Adaline nodded, turned her head, and stared out the window of the old truck. Samara made sure that her thoughts were shielded before she pulled up her long-suppressed memories of the first two years after her return. There were some things Adaline didn't need to know yet… including the very real possibility that Adalard was either dead or had decided he didn't want to return.

Why should he? He has no idea about Adaline, she thought.

The first couple of years without him had been the most difficult. Adalard's promise that he would return once his mission was over had kept her going. There had been a communication device left at the main homestead in case she needed to reach him. She thought about using the device the moment she discovered that she was pregnant with Adaline. Logic battled with emotion before she decided it would be best to wait. After all, Adalard was on a dangerous mission, and the last thing he needed at the time was to worry about her.

Her moment of hesitancy would prove unfortunate. The communication device was destroyed when a tree close to the house fell during a severe thunderstorm. The tree tore through the office in the house, taking out the power lines, and causing a fire that destroyed nearly a quarter of the house.

Her joy and excitement slowly changed to despair as the weeks turned into years, and Adalard didn't return. Mason, Ann Marie, and Bear had been her rock. Deep down, she knew that if she remained at the ranch, she would always be searching for Adalard in the shadows. In the end, she made the decision to move on with her life.

"Are we there?" Adaline asked with excitement as she sat forward.

Samara blinked and nodded. Lost in her thoughts, she hadn't realized that she had turned on the blinker to turn onto the long driveway. Sudden doubts swamped her, and she wondered if she was making a mistake coming back.

"Yes, we're here. Remember what I said about—" she began.

"I know. I know. Don't use my gifts in front of anyone," Adaline interrupted with an impatient wave of her hand. "Do you think Bear will take me riding?"

Samara laughed. "Yes. Bear would love to take you riding."

"I missed him. He's funny, and he really likes us," she said.

"I know, honey," she murmured.

"He knows about me, too, so I don't have to pretend to be normal around him," Adaline continued.

"That's true, but you still have to be careful," she insisted.

"He would make a great dad," Adaline commented.

"Adaline," she rebuked, slowing the truck to a crawl.

Brilliant violet eyes turned toward her with an expression far older than her six years. Samara shook her head and pulled to a stop on the road. She twisted as far as she could with the seat belt on and looked back at Adaline. She opened her mouth, closed it, shook her head, and tried again.

"I love Bear just as much as you do, just not in the way... well, just not in the same way two people who get married do. I love him more like a brother," she tried to explain.

Adaline's nose wrinkled. "Your brothers aren't good," she bluntly stated.

"Some of them are. Your Uncles Brit, Gary, and Wilson aren't so bad," Samara defended.

Adaline pursed her lips and folded her arms across her chest. "I've never met Uncle Wilson. Brit and Gary are cage-rats," she stubbornly retorted.

Samara frowned. "Cage-rats? Where did you hear that?" she demanded.

"It was on the television and it fits. They were in jail and they were bad, otherwise they wouldn't have been put in jail," Adaline pointed out.

"Well, they got out and they have been doing the right thing ever since. It isn't like people don't make mistakes. They made a bad one and they paid for it," she defended.

"Bear's never been in jail. Neither have Mason or Chad," Adaline replied.

"I'm not going to argue with you about your uncles' bad life choices— or about Bear. We are friends, that's all," she said.

Adaline sat back and stared out the front window of the truck. Samara didn't miss the glisten of tears in Adaline's eyes. It was frustrating because she knew all Adaline wanted was to be normal.

"He's not coming back, you know. If he was, he would have come already," Adaline muttered.

"Who's not coming back?" she asked.

"My real dad," Adaline responded.

Samara's heart hurt at the resignation in her daughter's voice. She leaned over and kissed Adaline's temple. She didn't know what to say. All she could do was love Adaline with everything inside her and hope that it would be enough.

"How about after we get everything unloaded, we see if Bear will take us out for some pizza?" she suggested.

Adaline shrugged and stared out of the window. Samara released a sigh and straightened in her seat. The feeling of diving from the frying pan into the fire swept through her again, and she silently groaned.

Adalard, if you ever come back, you're going to have more than me to answer to, she silently thought.

"Adaline Ha'darra Lee-Stephens!" Samara warned in a low tone from the doorway of her daughter's bedroom nearly three hours later.

Adaline grimaced and shot her an apologetic smile. Samara fought a smile at her precocious daughter's expression. Adaline bit her lip and peered back at her with wide, pleading eyes.

"No one's here," Adaline defended.

"Yeah, but explaining how you did this in less than two hours is going to be difficult," Samara retorted.

"The only ones who'll see it will know," Adaline reasoned.

Samara shook her head. "It does look pretty spectacular. Here are your last boxes. I think the top one is the one you were looking for," she said with a grin.

"Thank you! I love you," Adaline said, her voice muffled as she dug into the box.

Samara shook her head in resignation. She had to admit, the room was amazing. Ann Marie had already gone overboard getting things ready, but Adaline had placed the finishing touches that only a six-year-old with a love for fairy-tales could create. Wispy drapes that looked like a brilliant night sky with twinkling diamond stars hung from the ceiling and floated downward to enclose the full-size bed. A tall dollhouse that hadn't been part of their meager possessions was against the wall near the window. Adaline had already decorated it, added lights and a small yard that looked suspiciously like it had real flowers growing from flower boxes. Adaline's missing box had been the one with her dolls in it.

For a moment, Samara wondered if she should have given Adaline the larger of the two rooms in the loft over the barn. Shaking her head at the thought, she lowered the remaining box to the floor.

"Don't forget that we are having dinner with Bear," she reminded.

"I won't. I'm glad we moved back here," Adaline replied, her voice muffled from the box she was halfway draped in.

Samara smiled and turned away. She stepped out of the room, absently listening to Adaline singing as she finished unpacking. Pausing at the end of the hallway, she caught sight of the pile of boxes in the middle of the living room floor and released a loud, tired sigh. The three-day drive from Texas had been brutal, and she was exhausted. The sound of boots on the stairs warned her that she was about to have company.

"Samara?"

She walked over to the door and peered down the steps at Bear. He had his arms full of grocery bags. She raised an eyebrow at the items. He gave her one of his heart-melting grins and lifted them up a little higher.

"I thought I'd fix dinner here tonight. I figured you'd be pretty exhausted," he said, climbing the stairs.

She stepped back on the landing when he reached the top. Taking a few of the bags, she studied him with an amused expression. A bag of Adaline's favorite Gummy Bear candy was sticking out of the top of one of them.

"Did you leave anything at the store? You know that Ann Marie has already filled the refrigerator," she warned.

"Yeah, I know, but I thought she might have missed a few things," he stated as he walked into the apartment. He paused and looked around with a frown. "I told you that I would help you unload things."

"We don't own that much. Why don't you make yourself at home in the kitchen while I unpack some boxes and get them out of the way?" she suggested.

"Sounds good," he replied.

The slightly gruff tone in his voice caught her attention. He faced her, and she stumbled to a stop. They stood contemplating each other in silence for several seconds before he gave her a crooked grin.

"I'm glad you're back," he said.

She smiled back at him. "So is Adaline… and so am I," she confessed. "I'll put the stuff on the counter. Just put it wherever you think things should go," she added. She cleared her throat, stepped around him, and placed the items she was holding on the counter.

"Sounds like old times," he chuckled.

"You always knew the kitchen wasn't my favorite place to be," she quipped.

"Food poisoning was never on my list of things to experience more than once," he playfully shot back.

"You are such a wuss sometimes," she retorted with a dramatic sigh.

His warm laughter made her smile. It had been a long time since she felt this sense of peace. She turned away and began unpacking the boxes while he put away the groceries and began dinner.

Maybe Adaline is right. Maybe I should think about Bear in a different light, she mused.

CHAPTER THIRTY-TWO

Warship Rayon I:

Heading toward Earth

Adalard rolled his shoulders, ignoring his aches and pains, and waved a hand at Brogan, the man standing across from him in the training room. The huge, dark-haired male sneered as he wiped blood away from his lip. Brilliant green scales with white flakes ran along Brogan's neck as he tried to control his dragon.

Adalard was questioning his sanity for antagonizing the Valdier warrior. Brogan was one of the legendary twin dragons. There were only two sets of twin dragons in all of Valdier history who had learned to control their incredible power without going on a murderous rampage, and while Adalard was familiar with the tactics that Cree and Calo used, Brogan and his twin brother, Barrack, were older and edgier—more like him, he realized.

Brogan's eyes narrowed when Adalard smiled at him—okay, the smile was more of a smirk and the curve of his lips might have held a little too much arrogance. He was glad they had decided on the rules of engagement before the match—more for the sake of the ship than their personal safety. Still, from the way Brogan flexed his muscles, Adalard knew he was going to be sporting even more bruises than he already had.

Brogan charged him. Adalard, anticipating the attack, blocked the man's bone-shattering blow, twisted and struck back. His fist connected with Brogan's shoulder, knocking the man forward. Brogan curled into a roll, rose up, and attacked again. He fell back when Brogan's bare foot caught him in the chest. Grabbing the man's leg, he swung around and planted his elbow in Brogan's stomach. Disgust ran through him when Brogan didn't even grunt from the blow. He stumbled forward when Brogan shoved him away. Twisting, they circled each other, each assessing their next move.

Brogan growled, rubbed his bruised shoulder, and scowled at him. "What's got you so uptight?"

"Nothing," he replied in a curt tone.

He feinted an upper left cut to Brogan's jaw before striking out with his other fist. The dragon-shifter twisted away and Adalard missed. An alarm sounded, bringing an end to their session, and they relaxed their postures. Sweat dripped from their brows. The thin material of Adalard's shirt was soaked with it. Brogan had ripped his shirt off ten minutes into the match.

"Your temper has been getting shorter and you've become increasingly tense the closer we get to the planet. Either there is something we need to be concerned about or you need some stress management," Brogan muttered, wiping his face on his tattered shirt.

He paused and studied Brogan's expression. "Who put you up to this?" he suddenly asked, waving a hand at the room.

Brogan gave him a crooked grin. "Everybody on board. They are all sick of you stomping, moping, and biting everyone's heads off. I volunteered to try beating it out of you," he explained.

He ran his hands through his damp hair before dropping them to his side. With a deep sigh, Adalard studied the other man. Everything Brogan said was true. He just thought he had been able to conceal it a bit better. Turning away, he walked over to a bench against the wall and sat down. Brogan followed him and sat beside him.

"My mate is on the planet. It... has been a long time since I've seen her," he confessed.

Brogan stared at him with an expression of disbelief. Adalard leaned back and rested his head against the wall. He didn't know why he had shared that information with the man.

"Are you daft, Curizan? You have a mate and you have ignored her for years?" Brogan exclaimed.

He glared at the other man and jumped to his feet. "I haven't exactly been ignoring her! I've been trying to save the galaxy," he growled.

Brogan leaned back, folded his arms across his chest, and looked suitably unimpressed. "Nothing is more important than your mate, not even the galaxy," he stated.

Adalard paused in his pacing and glared at Brogan. "Perhaps it is a little too much to get through that thick skull of yours, but without a galaxy, there is no place for my mate. I wasn't going to put her in any more danger than I already had," he snapped.

Brogan grew surprisingly quiet. "I remember my death. I remember the deep despair of my dragon and the craving to find my mate. When... Barrack and I were given a second chance... a chance to find a mate that would accept both of us... we knew that we would do whatever it took and wait however long we must to find her. Now, as we grow closer, I wonder if everything is a dream. I could not imagine finding her, then having the strength to let her go again," he admitted in a quiet voice.

Adalard returned to the bench and sat down with a grunt beside Brogan. He leaned forward and rested his elbows on his knees. A multitude of emotions swept through him—fear, regret, depression, nervousness.

"We both agreed at the time that it would be best. I just… did not expect to be gone for so long," he confessed.

"I'm assuming your mission was successful," Brogan reflected.

Adalard sighed and leaned back again. "No, it wasn't. I think that is what makes the situation even worse," he admitted.

"It isn't like a Curizan, especially one from the royal house, to be defeated," Brogan observed.

"I haven't accepted defeat. I came because I sent my mate to her planet to keep her safe," he snapped.

"And… she is no longer safe," Brogan guessed.

Adalard muttered a curse and rose to his feet again. "No, she is no longer safe. A message was received from an informant planted within the group of traitors warning me that Samara has been targeted," he replied.

"How do you know the information is reliable?" Brogan asked.

He glanced at Brogan before looking around the training room. The information had come from Blaze, Vox's long-lost brother, who was positioned deep within the rebel group. Blaze had risked exposing his own position in order to relay the information.

Hamade Dos had always stayed one step ahead of him. He didn't know how. Ha'ven had ferreted out the second traitor onboard the *Rayon I* not long after their return but obviously not before the second Changeling had shared the information with Hamade that Adalard's new interest was not just another lover—but a mate.

What he didn't understand was why it had taken Hamade so long to act on it. He could only speculate that his constant pursuit had delayed the Curizan's ability to find Samara, but it still didn't make sense. He turned and glared at Brogan.

"It is reliable," he said.

Brogan rose to his feet and placed a hand on Adalard's shoulder. "Then save her—and kill the bastard who is after her," he stated.

"That has always been my plan," he replied.

He stayed where he was for a short time after Brogan left. Walking over to a row of windows, he stared out into space. They would be arriving on Earth tomorrow. He had promised Jaguin and Sara that he would keep an eye on the twin dragons, and he would—from a distance. He had spent enough time during the journey to know that no one could contain Barrack and Brogan if they didn't wish to be contained. Besides, he had more important things to deal with.

For seven long years he had searched every nook and cranny in the galaxy for Hamade. The general had proved a wily adversary. They had clashed a few times, including at their last encounter on Kardosa when he was sure that he had mortally wounded the other man. Hamade had tried to kill him with the black symbiot. Visions of their clash played through his mind as if it had only just happened.

Kardosa six months ago:

The lower level was unusually quiet for the Spaceport. The few open vendors hurriedly closed the doors to their shops. Adalard stood at the far end of the empty corridor while Hamade and two of his men stood at the other. After six-and-a-half long years and a path paved with the dead followers of the New Order Cult, he had finally caught Hamade before he slithered back into the shadows.

"This is the end, Hamade. Your bases are destroyed. There is nowhere else for you to hide," he called out.

Hamade straightened the sleeve of his tattered uniform. The two men behind him stepped aside. Adalard wasn't concerned about them.

"This is a war you cannot win, Adalard. Do you think destroying a handful of bases and my warships will stop what is going to happen? You've only delayed it. This is larger than both of us," Hamade retorted.

"It is over for you," he promised.

He was ready when Hamade pulled out the glass cylinder and tossed it. Adalard shot all three men before the cylinder hit the hard metal floor of the spaceport. He pocketed the laser pistol and lifted his hands when the dark mist spiraled upward from the shattered container. He didn't yet activate the shield that his brother had refined over the years. He needed the creature to come to him. Pulling a compact cylinder from the satchel he was wearing across his chest, he placed the oblong container on the ground in front of him. The container was specially crafted by his brother and Morian Reykill.

He straightened and waited for the creature to attack him. It didn't take long. He triggered the cylinder a split second before the creature reached him. A brilliant arc of energy surrounded the creature. The darkness surrounding the core of the symbiot disintegrated, leaving only the golden entity that had been trapped inside. In seconds, the living metal was contained within the trap.

He picked up the cylinder. If the entity had been a replica, there would have been nothing left. Morian had given him a set of instructions upon her return from the Hive and begged him to do everything in his power to protect the living symbiots trapped inside the entities.

"Please, they cannot resist what they are ordered to do. If you can save them, I can return them to a place where they can heal. Your brother will know what to do," she said.

The instructions had been gibberish to him, but Morian had been correct that Arrow would be able to understand. His brother had been very quiet, which was unusual for Arrow. Within days, Arrow had delivered the trap to him.

He slid the cylinder back into the satchel and looked over in the direction where Hamade and his men had fallen. He cursed when he noticed only two bodies instead of three. Striding forward, he closed the distance between them until he was standing over the two men. Both were dead. He pulled a protective shield around his body and turned in a tight circle, scanning the shadows for any movements.

"They're gone," a high-pitched voice informed him.

Adalard's eyes narrowed on a dirty boy wearing tattered clothing who was partially hidden behind a disposal container. The boy stood up and held his hands in the air. Adalard motioned for the boy to come forward.

"Where did he go?" he asked.

"For twenty credits I'll tell you," the boy countered.

The scar on his cheek pulled when he scowled down at the boy. The scamp didn't bat an eyelash at the dark expression on his face. Adalard didn't know whether to be amused or worried that the boy would get himself killed since it was obvious the kid didn't have a lick of self-preservation in his bones. He withdrew one hundred credits and handed them to the boy. The boy's eyes widened with delight before he quickly pocketed the credits.

"A woman came out of the shadows and took him. He was still moving—barely. You shot him good. I've never seen anyone shoot that fast," the boy said in a breathless voice from talking so fast.

"Where did they go?" he demanded.

The boy shrugged. "She teleported them out. No tellin' where they went."

Adalard frowned and looked around in frustration before he returned his attention to the boy. He blinked when he saw the boy holding out a portable vidcom disk. He took it, stroking it for a moment before he looked back at the boy.

"What is this?" he asked.

The boy shrugged again. "A man paid me to find a Curizan with a scar on his cheek and give it to him. When I asked him how I was supposed to find you, he said look for the bodies. He was smart," the boy said with a grin.

He rolled the vidcom between his fingers. "What did the man look like?"

"I don't know. He kept his face covered, but I think he might have been a Sarafin. He had spots like they do on his neck, and he moved like a cat-shifter. He disappeared real quick," the boy replied.

Adalard pulled another hundred credits out of his pocket and tossed it to the boy. The boy caught the coins with a hiss of delight, nodded at him before he twisted around and disappeared into the shadows.

He activated the device, and a facial scan logged his features while a second scan focused on his eyes, then a grainy image appeared, and he could hear the voice of a woman.

"The planet where Adalard Ha'darra's mate lives has finally been revealed to our Master. His instructions are that you will retrieve her and bring her back to him," the woman ordered.

"What use is a human woman to him?" Hamade questioned.

"It is not your place to question his desires, only to fulfill them," the woman retorted.

"I will leave immediately," Hamade replied with a bow of his head.

"Be careful. My sources have instructed me that Ha'darra has tracked you to Kardosa," the woman cautioned.

"I will travel—" The message cut off before the woman finished what she was saying.

A cold wave of dread washed through Adalard at the memory, and he snapped back to the present when several crew members entered the room. Their laughter died when they saw him, and they bowed their heads in respect. He rose to his feet, nodded to them in return, and exited the training room.

For seven years he had followed Hamade from one end of the star system and back again. Each moment was engraved in his memory because it meant another second he was away from Samara. In the end, he had come full circle—trying to protect Samara from Hamade.

"Adalard, we will be in position on the dark side of the planet's moon in two hours," Jaguin informed him.

"I'll be ready," he replied.

Jaguin's low laugh echoed through the communicator. "You may be, but is the planet ready for Barrack and Brogan? I'm seriously having second thoughts about this," he muttered.

"It is a bit late for that. If it helps, I helped Brogan work out some of his anxiety," he replied.

"And you are still alive? I'm impressed," Jaguin laughed.

"Have you been able to communicate with Mason yet?" he inquired.

"Nothing yet. There must be something wrong with their communicator," Jaguin answered, his tone changing to one of concern.

"Let's hope that is the case. I'll be on the bridge shortly," he replied, ending the communication.

In a little over four hours, he should be on his way to the planet. The inability to communicate with Mason or Chad was troubling. If the main communication module was down, it could explain why they weren't answering. He hoped that was the case and not something more sinister.

CHAPTER THIRTY-THREE

"$\mathscr{H}$ere you go, honey," Samara said, holding out a pair of small wool-lined leather gloves. "Make sure you listen to Bear."

"Thanks, mom. I'll listen," Adaline promised.

"That's a big basket," Bear observed.

Samara laughed and placed the large picnic basket in the backseat of the UTV. "You both have bottomless stomachs and knowing my daughter, you'll be back later than you plan. She'll be starving the entire time you're out," she teased.

"I'll keep a good eye on her," Bear said.

"I know you will," she replied with a smile before turning her attention back to Adaline. "If you start to feel cold at all, you let Bear know. Don't wander off on your own," she instructed.

"I knowwww," Adaline groaned, leaning her head back against the seat.

Samara kissed Adaline's upturned forehead. "And remember, no magic."

"I promise, Momma," Adaline whispered back.

Samara stood back and watched as Bear drove away. He looked up in the mirror and their eyes connected. Her heart was in her throat when she lifted her hand in response.

She dropped her hand when they disappeared down the road. There was a lot to do. There was a bad storm coming in, and they were short-handed. The crew that was here would handle the cattle in the North-west range, but there were still the horses, chickens, and other live-stock close to the house. Feeding the cattle and caring for those that couldn't handle the prolonged cold would be a full-time job alone for those on hand if the weather got as bad as the meteorologists were predicting.

Samara pulled on her gloves and headed for the UTV parked under the carport of the barn. Thanks to Bear, she had finished setting up the loft apartment last night. Of course, it helped that she and Adaline didn't have very much in the way of worldly possessions.

Regret filled her for a moment before she pushed it away. She took a deep breath of the cold mountain air and embraced the familiar tingle as she looked out over the old farmhouse.

"At least we'll be safe here," she comforted herself.

Climbing in the UTV, she pulled away from the yard and headed up the road. She glanced at Paul's old house. Memories of Adalard standing on the steps caused her to linger while she looked at the house. She shook her head and pushed those memories away as well. It was hard to believe now that there had ever been any damage to the house. She pulled in front of the barn and parked the UTV.

"Remember, Samara, you promised yourself you'd let the past go. It's time to start over," she muttered as she turned off the motor and pushed open the door.

Four hours later, Samara helped Mason store the last of the hay he had brought up to the barn. The horses were settled in clean stalls. It would be a full house until after the storm passed. Already she could feel the wind picking up and shivered at the bite in the frigid air. She hoped that Bear didn't keep Adaline out too much longer.

"It looks like we're done," Mason said. "I'm going to leave the truck and trailer here for Bear. He's going to pick it up later when he drops Adaline off."

"Sounds good. Did he give you an update about when they might be back?" she asked.

Mason chuckled. "He said to tell you not to worry. The storm has slowed down, so they are taking advantage of the lull and are doing a few extra chores before they head back. He said he would have Adaline back by six at the latest."

"Six! I didn't realize they would be out so long," she hissed with dismay.

"He had to take some wire and fencing out to Shooter's Pass. Some fence posts were in bad shape and had broken off. The crew wanted to get it fixed before the snow hits. Don't want the damn cattle getting spooked and going over the ravine in the storm. Even so, some of the men are staying in the cabins out there, just in case. It'll be faster and easier for them to get to the herds if something happens. Bear and Adaline are stocking the cabins with enough supplies to last a couple of weeks," Mason added.

"Thanks for the update," she said with a rueful smile.

Mason chuckled. "I take it you aren't used to Adaline being away from you."

Samara shook her head. "No, it… wasn't wise to leave her with anyone else," she softly admitted.

Mason's expression softened, and he nodded. "You have one very special little girl, Samara. It would be best if she was with her own kind. Earth is not a very forgiving place for someone with Adaline's abilities."

"Well, there isn't a lot I can do about that, so the ranch will have to be the next best thing," she responded, trying to keep the tinge of bitterness from her voice.

The gnawing guilt that she had felt since shortly after Adaline's birth flared. It was like the mythical hydra, every time she thought she had cut off the last ugly, guilt-poisoned head, another would take its place. She'd known the minute Adaline first displayed her unusual powers that she had sentenced her beautiful daughter to a life of imprisonment. Mason was right, their world was a very unforgiving place.

"What is it?" Mason asked.

She blinked and shook her head. Mason had already climbed into the UTV, and she realized that she was standing with the door open. She reminded herself that she was safe here at the ranch before she climbed into the driver's seat.

"Nothing. I was just running through my list of chores to make sure I didn't forget anything," she lied.

"Well, now that you mentioned that, I do have one more item for you," Mason said with an apologetic expression.

"What do you need?" she asked.

"Would you mind staying at the big house during the storm? I know you and Adaline are just getting settled in, but I'd feel a lot better if we lose power or get snowed in knowing you were there," he said.

She looked at the house as she turned the UTV around. The last time she had been in there had been with Adalard. She started to shake her head to clear it and realized that Mason would probably take that as a no. She forced her head to move in the opposite direction.

"It's no problem. We haven't exactly settled in yet," she replied.

"I appreciate it. It sounds like it is going to be a bad storm. Ann Marie has some things for you to bring up with you. Last thing I want is for another tree to fall on the house and the damn thing to burn to the ground—or worse, that something happens to the barn with it full of horses," he said.

"Alright. Adaline will love it. Plus, I can't complain. If the storm is as bad as they are saying it is going to be, the big house has a generator and the apartment doesn't," she replied.

"Now why didn't I think of that?" Mason teased.

They both laughed. She parked the UTV near the back door and stepped out. She would grab the items Ann Marie had for her before heading over and packing a suitcase for herself and Adaline. Her mind ran through what she would need to bring.

One good thing about Adaline's gifts, she can entertain herself, she mused.

She pulled open the back door and entered the mud room. The sound of unfamiliar voices in the kitchen made her frown. Apprehension filled her at the thought of strangers at the ranch. She stepped into the room and stopped. A tsunami of feelings crashed over her: shock, disbelief, and dizziness.

Dark spots danced before her eyes, and she gripped the doorframe. It felt like every drop of blood in her body was now pooling around her ankles. A low, hissing curse slipped from her.

"Mason, your house is infested with aliens again," Samara muttered, glancing at the other two people standing in the room with a scrutinizing look. "Well, at least with two. I think you'll only need to exterminate one of them, though," she added.

"Samara."

The husky sound of Adalard speaking her name after so long sent her into a panic. She had to get out of the house, away from everyone where she could think.

"Who is it this time?" Mason asked, stepping up behind her and temporarily blocking her escape route.

She twisted and desperately pushed past him when her stomach threatened to revolt. "Don't ask me. I prefer to keep my distance from the lot of them. I've got horses to bring in. Let me know when they are gone," she said, ignoring the fact that she had already completed that chore.

"Samara," Adalard growled.

Samara raised her right hand and lifted her middle finger as she departed. Adalard stiffened and grimaced when he realized that his shock at seeing her and her cool reception might have caused him to have a little edge to his tone that she could have misconstrued as disapproval. It was just that none of the scenarios that he imagined had prepared him for the reality of seeing her again, nor the impact of his aura greedily seeking her calming touch.

"So, I recognize two of you – you're Jaguin, correct?" Mason was saying.

"Yes. This is my mate, Sara Wilson," Jaguin replied.

"Ah, the mysterious Sara Wilson," Mason murmured.

"You've heard of me?" Sara asked with a startled look.

Adalard distractedly listened as Mason explained about a woman named Delilah who recently visited the ranch looking for Sara. The news was obviously a shock to Sara. Mason's description of Barrack and Brogan visiting earlier explained their disappearance from the ship.

"So, what should we do now?" Adalard absently asked. His companions' plans would affect his own, after all.

Jaguin sighed and shook his head in frustration. "We have to go after them."

Mason frowned. "Yeah, well, I wouldn't be in too big a hurry. The East Coast is about to get slammed with a Nor'easter that they are calling the new hundred-year storm. They are expecting up to fifty inches of snow in some parts with temperatures dropping well below freezing and winds in excess of one hundred miles an hour. We've got our own storm heading this way. It is supposed to hit this afternoon. We've been rounding up all the horses and trying to get the place ready to be snowed in for up to a week," he cautioned.

"Did Barrack and Brogan know about this?" Jaguin asked.

Mason nodded. "I told them, but they didn't care. I'm guessing maybe you aliens can handle this kind of extreme weather better than we can. Whether you can or not, they are still in for a rough journey," he said before his expression changed. "I have to admit, I'm glad you're here. We could use some extra help. We only have a skeleton crew on the ranch at the moment. The few hands we have are working our North-west range. That is where most of the cattle are, but that still leaves this section. With the weather, I can't safely take the helicopter up. There is only Samara, Bear, Ann Marie, and me to handle things on this end of the ranch. We've got five thousand head of livestock that will need to be taken care of. We've already moved them to more sheltered pastures, but they'll have to be fed," Mason said, shoving his hands in his front pockets.

Determination flared inside Adalard and he answered before Jaguin or Sara could.

"We will stay," he stated in a firm tone.

"Thank you. Whatever you do, though, just make sure that you stay away from Samara. I'll let Ann Marie know," Mason ordered.

Adalard didn't answer. He had stayed away for seven years. That might be a blink of an eye in the grand scheme of the universe, but for him it had seemed forever. Samara's warm touch and shimmering eyes had kept him going and he wasn't about to stay away from her a second longer now that they were together again.

CHAPTER THIRTY-FOUR

*S*amara leaned back against the door of her small loft apartment and raised a shaking hand to her throat. Her heart was thundering in her chest. She bowed her head and closed her eyes. Adalard was back.

She drew in deep breaths, trying to calm her shaking body. The shock of seeing him hit her hard. The colors surrounding him and the sudden connection between them had struck her like a blast of super-heated air.

Seven years and twenty-eight days, and he suddenly comes back, she thought.

She jumped when there was a knock on the door behind her. Adalard had found her. She knew it from the way her heart was banging against her chest, the warmth surrounding her, and the nudge of awareness pushing against her mind. She ran her shaking hands down her thighs before lifting them to her tangled hair.

At least I don't have hay in it, she hoped.

Taking another deep breath, she pulled open the door. The breath she had inhaled whooshed out when he wrapped his arms around her waist, pulled her against him, and captured her parted lips. A low groan rumbled between them. She didn't know if it was from her or from him.

She returned his kiss with a fiery passion mingled with a tang of salt. It took her a moment to realize that she was crying. She tangled her hands in his hair and twisted their position around until he was pressed against the wall. Her booted foot caught the door and she slammed it shut.

"You...," she tried to say between kisses.

"I've missed you," he muttered, his hands cupping her buttocks and pressing her against him.

She swept her tongue inside his mouth. He returned the gesture and sucked on it. His deep, throaty groan resonated through her. Cool air touched her overheated skin. She continued kissing his lips, his jaw, his face, as he lifted her into his arms. The cool touch of the bedspread under her naked back and his warm bare chest against her aching breasts made her arch into him.

"I forgot how easily you could do things like make our clothes disappear," she breathed as he dipped his head and captured one of her taut nipples between his lips.

Adalard caressed Samara's hip as she tenderly stroked the hair on his chest. The colors of their auras mixed, flowing in an elegant dance all around them. He kept his eyes on the twirling colors as he bent his head and kissed the top of her head. She ran her bare leg along his.

"If you keep doing that, it will lead to something else," he teased.

"Mm, something that has to do with this?" she murmured, tilting her head back and looking into his eyes as she slid her hand down his chest and wrapped her fingers around his cock.

His cock responded immediately, swelling with need. He chuckled and rolled, keeping her caged within his arms as he settled on top of her. She spread her legs for him so that his cock rested against her love-swollen mound. He watched her face as he pushed past her soft folds and into her wet and ready channel.

Her eyelashes fluttered half closed, and she moaned as he slowly slid into her. He could watch her forever. He rocked with slow, even movements, drawing out and savoring each delicious stroke.

"I plan to do this all night," he murmured.

She groaned, arched against him, and shuddered as she came. "You... we can't," she breathed.

He slid his arms under her, holding her tighter, and began to rock faster. He thrust his hips forward one last time before the familiar tingling in his spine shot outward through his nerve endings, encompassing every inch of his body. The burst of his hot seed filled her womb.

"Goddess, I'll never get enough of you," he mumbled.

The power of his release, the relief of having Samara back in his arms, and the years of living on little sleep swept through him. For the first time in his life, he felt as if he were actually crashing—in a very good way. The exhaustion that he had pushed aside caught up with him as the last of his orgasm spilled into Samara's warm haven. In the last few seconds of consciousness, he rolled until Samara was on top.

"Sleep... I need... sleep. I haven't slept well since the last time I held you," he muttered before a warm and deliciously fuzzy darkness pulled him into a deep slumber.

"Adalard... Adalard?" Samara's warm voice called from the far end of the dark tunnel.

A pleased and contented smile curved his lips. The universe may still be crazy, but for the moment, it was everything he wanted it to be. He couldn't imagine anything that could change that now.

The Loft Casino and Hotel

Las Vegas, Nevada

Alberto Frank Armeni Campeau looked up from his desk when his Head of Security, Jack DeSimone, quietly entered the room. He glanced at Jack's expressionless face before returning his attention to the view outside the penthouse windows of his luxury apartment. Jack walked over to the windows and stared out.

"Such a serious expression, Jack. Has someone tried scamming the tables again?" Alberto inquired.

Jack turned and faced him. "No, sir. You requested that I keep you updated on any developments with Ms. Lee-Stephens and her... daughter."

"And..." he demanded.

"Three days ago, she suddenly vanished. No one at the track knew she was planning on leaving, the people I hired to monitor her didn't suspect anything. Josephine confirmed that her apartment was cleaned out," Jack explained.

"Do you know where she went?" he asked.

"Yes, she has returned to Casper," Jack responded.

Alberto swirled the wine in his glass. "Any sign of the man?" he asked.

"No, sir. There is no indication that he has returned. The private detective states that she was alone with the little girl," Jack said.

"Have a team retrieve the girl," he ordered, looking at Jack.

"Yes, sir. What do you want them to do about the mother?" Jack quietly asked.

Alberto looked down at the red wine in his hand. "Make it look like she met with an untimely accident. I don't want to take any chance that her maternal instincts will kick in. The last thing any of us needs is Adalard Ha'darra discovering that he has a daughter."

"I'll oversee the project myself," Jack replied with a bow of his head.

Alberto waited until Jack exited his suite before he rose to his feet and looked out over the busy streets of the city known as the Entertainment City of the World. He slid his hand into the pocket of his trousers and wrapped his fingers around the unusual jewel he had carried for the last seven and a half years. The renowned gemologist, Johan Kevlar, confirmed that the diamond was exactly as the mysterious Prince Adalard Ha'darra had stated: *he would never find a diamond as pure as this anywhere on this planet.*

At the time, Alberto had waved away the unusual comment. By the end of the most memorable night of poker he had ever played, he was very aware that he was dealing with someone who was as unusual as the diamond that he held in his possession. He had lost every single hand played that night. Memories flooded his mind, and he tightened his grip around the stem of his wine glass until he was amazed it didn't shatter under the pressure.

"Stay away from Samara's brothers. Their debt to you is settled," Ha'darra stated.

"Who are you?" he remembered demanding.

"Someone you don't want to cross," Ha'darra replied, tossing the gem to him.

He had automatically caught the gem and watched as Ha'darra turned and walked out. Alberto stood in shocked disbelief when he saw all of his men, including Jack, unconscious in the other room. Jack remembered very little when he finally roused. He said that Samara Lee-Stephens had stunned him with a strange Taser-like device that looked like something out of a science fiction story.

Curiosity was an interesting thing for a very rich man. In his life, he had seen and done many things. When you could buy anything you wanted, life could get boring. Gambling helped, in some ways, to relieve the boredom. His stop in Casper, while seemingly inconsequential at the time, had ended up changing his life.

After that fateful night, he had researched Prince Adalard Ha'darra, only to discover that there was no evidence that he existed. There were no fingerprints on the glass he had carefully pocketed before leaving the bar either. He was positive Ha'darra had not wiped it clean.

Money gave him opportunities and connections the average person didn't have. A few calls to the right people and the exchange of money could smooth the path to getting what he wanted—and he had wanted information. Out of the four brothers, only Jerry had the information he was seeking.

At first, he questioned whether the man was conning him or doped out. The expression of genuine fear on the man's face finally convinced him that there was some truth to what the man had experienced.

"I'm telling you, the man isn't human! He... he did things, talked to me in my head, and... and... he showed me images of what he would do to me if I said anything."

With Adalard gone, Jerry finally did talk after he was offered a small monetary incentive, and the more he said, the more intrigued Alberto became until finding out additional information about the elusive prince became an obsession. All leads dried up when both Ha'darra and Samara Lee-Stephens disappeared. Finally, after nearly a year of silence, Jerry notified him that his sister had returned—alone.

He had immediately set up surveillance on her. As the days grew into months with no appearance of Ha'darra, he was about to give up when a report came in that Samara was pregnant. It didn't take much to put two and two together. The question wasn't who the father was, no, the question that needed to be answered was what would the child be—and which parent would she take after more?

This intriguing question compelled him to make certain arrangements, but tracking and monitoring Samara and her newborn was challenging on the Grove Ranch. Samara unexpectedly made the situation easier when she started applying for positions as far away as Florida and Texas. A few calls and the offer of a lucrative position at Manor Downs in Austin had set the wheels in motion.

Initially, he wondered if he was wasting his time. Samara was very protective of her young daughter, but he chalked it up to being a new mother and her past experience with her brothers. Then, the reports began to come in of strange occurrences. A series of small events that could easily be shrugged away with an excuse, but together created a pattern. The incidents were like pieces to a large puzzle. Most intriguing of all was a thirty second video from two weeks ago.

He placed his wine glass on the table and reached for his phone. After unlocking it, he pulled up the video the detective had sent him. It was a video of a little girl talking to a horse. Nothing unusual there, until she suddenly appeared on the back of the horse that seconds before wasn't wearing a saddle or bridle and now was wearing everything the little girl needed to ride.

"Shush, don't tell mommy what I did. She doesn't like it when I use my gifts," the little girl said into the horse's turned back ear.

"Adaline! Oh, honey, you know you can't do things like this. Someone might see you," Samara cautioned when she appeared.

"I just wanted to ride him, mommy," Adaline pleaded.

This video was the only one to survive whatever device Samara used to destroy the numerous sound and video recording devices they had installed over the years in her apartment. The private detective had immediately sent him the video before whatever Samara used to jam the signal affected it.

"It is time to discover what other gifts you have, Adaline, especially since I don't have to worry about your father any longer," he mused, watching the video again and again.

CHAPTER THIRTY-FIVE

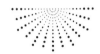

*A*dalard reached out to pull Samara into his arms, only to find the spot next to him empty. He sat up with a curse and scanned the room. Swinging his legs over the side of the bed, he stood up and ran an impatient hand through his tangled hair. The muted sound of voices filtered through the closed door.

He frowned when he recognized Bear's deep voice. A shaft of jealousy swept through him. Bear had enjoyed seven years with Samara, and the thought of the two of them— He couldn't help but look at the messy sheets.

"Tilkmos!"

The Curizan curse word slipped from him even as he waved an impatient hand and dressed himself. He opened the door to the bedroom and strode down the hallway. A wall of guilty silence struck him the moment he stepped into the living room.

He immediately noticed Samara's distressed expression before he glanced over at Bear, who had a hard, displeased look in his eyes. Adalard lifted an eyebrow in inquiry. Bear stared back at him with an expression of barely concealed animosity.

"So, it's true," Bear said.

"If you mean that I have returned, then yes," Adalard coolly replied.

Bear's lips pursed in a line of displeasure, his fingers curling into a fist. Adalard stepped closer to Samara when Bear turned his attention to her.

"I've got to finish getting things ready before the storm hits. If you or Adaline need anything I'll be here for you like I've always been," he said in a gruff tone.

Bear turned away, grabbed his hat and coat off the hook next to the door, and pulled it open. From the other side of the door, Adalard heard a young girl's excited voice.

"Hey, Bear. Are you coming back for dinner? Ann Marie has the entire collection of..." The young girl's voice trailed off when Bear stepped aside and her unusual violet eyes locked with Adalard's.

He stiffened in a moment of immediate recognition even though they had never met before. Her aura swirled, closing around her like a protective blanket. Bear added to the protective stance by placing one of his large hands on her shoulder and stepping behind her.

The little girl's long, dark hair was pulled back into a ponytail. Her cheeks were rosy from her excitement and the cold weather, but it was her eyes that held him captivated. She stared back at him with a curious and cautious expression.

"Adaline, I..." Samara said in a hesitant voice. "This is Adalard... your father."

Adaline covered Bear's hand with her own. "Are you staying for dinner?" she asked, keeping her eyes locked on him even though she was speaking to Bear.

Bear gently turned Adaline to face him and kneeled. He brushed a tender hand across her flushed cheek and shook his head. Adalard had to give the other man credit for keeping his true emotions concealed.

"Not tonight, sweetheart. I need to finish getting things done before the storm. I'll stop by tomorrow and check on you and your mom," he promised.

"Ann Marie said we would be at the big house. You'll come by there?" Adaline asked.

Bear glanced at him before focusing his attention on Adaline. "I'll find you no matter where you are, I promise," he reassured her.

Adaline threw her arms around Bear's neck and hugged him. "I love you. I'll see you tomorrow," she said.

Bear nodded and stood. Adalard could see the conflict on Bear's face when he looked first at Adaline, then Samara, before his gaze locked with his again. Foreign emotions ricocheted through him—disbelief, awareness, awe, shock, jealousy, grief—and remorse.

"I'll see you tomorrow," Bear murmured to Samara before he nodded to him and exited the apartment.

Adalard studied the little girl who stared up at him. His heart melted when her lower lip trembled and tears glistened in her eyes. He stepped forward and knelt on one knee in front of her. He lifted his hand to wipe a tear from her cheek and she jerked back from him.

"I wanted *Bear* and my mom to be together. He loves me and he loves mommy. He won't leave us—ever. Why did you have to come back?" Adaline tearfully demanded.

"Adaline," Samara murmured.

Adaline shook her head, pushed him until he nearly toppled, and rushed down the hallway. He rose to his feet and watched his daughter disappear into her bedroom. A shuddering breath slipped from him when Samara touched his arm.

"She didn't... Give her time, she is just shocked to see you," Samara murmured.

He turned to her with a dazed expression. "How... why didn't... I have a daughter?" he muttered.

She released a strained laugh and nodded. "Yes, you have a daughter —who is a lot like her father, I might add," she said. "Come sit down before you fall down."

He looked down the hallway as she pulled him toward the couch. He sank down on the edge of it and leaned forward, resting his elbows on his knees, and breathed deeply. There were so many questions he wanted—no needed—to know.

"Her name is Adaline Narissa Ha'darra Lee-Stephens and she is six years old," Samara said, sitting in the chair across from him with her hands folded.

"Narissa.... You named her after my mother?" he asked, searching her face.

Samara smiled and nodded. "And you... well, as close as I could. It felt right, though, Adaline may hate having a name a mile long when she gets older," she said with a wry smile.

"How... why didn't you notify me?" he asked.

"I was going to, but things happened. I knew what you were doing was important, and I didn't want to distract you from your mission. I thought I had time. There was always a chance that... that I might miscarry. Once I felt confident that everything would be alright, the communication device was destroyed in a fire. There was no way to contact you," she explained.

He watched as she nervously rubbed her hands together and stared down at them. Regret coursed through him that he hadn't been here for her—or Adaline—when they needed him. His thoughts turned to Bear, and he instinctively looked toward the front door.

"Adaline appears to think that you and Bear—" he began, unable to put his fear into words.

"She loves him, and he has been there since her birth—literally. It hurt him when I moved away. Now that we are back, I think she imagined that...." She stopped and shook her head. "After all this time, I guess none of us expected you would return."

She rose to her feet, wrapped her arms around her waist, and walked over to the window. Snow was beginning to fall. Adalard stood, mesmerized by her silhouette. The glow of the late afternoon light cast shadows around her, but he could see the colors of her aura. Peace washed over him as it swirled outward and connected with his.

"You love him," he stated.

In the reflection of the glass, he could see her sad smile. Jealousy raised its ugly head again—along with a taste of fear. He braced himself for her response.

Yes, but not the way or as much as I love you. I told you that I would wait as long as it would take, she replied.

Samara had dropped the wall between them, and he swayed as a torrent of emotions and memories flowed through him. In the space of a few minutes, he traveled back in time over the last seven years of her and Adaline's life. He stepped behind her and wrapped his arms around her waist, bending his head and pressing his lips against the top of her head.

Tears burned his eyes when she shared the pain and joy of giving birth and her yearning for him to be there. Her elation swept through him when she held Adaline in her arms for the first time. A husky laugh of joy slipped from him at the almost-real sensation of holding Adaline that came through their connection.

He tightened his hold on her when she shared her sense of peace as she breastfed Adaline. He lived through each of his tiny daughter's accomplishments and milestones—the first time Adaline rolled over, the moment she learned to scoot, Samara's sense of wonder when Adaline giggled and made the mobile above her bed swirl with colors, and the joy and worry at their daughter's abilities.

"She got her first tooth at seven-and-a-half months, walked before she was a year old, and was potty trained by eighteen months. She loves broccoli, hates beets, and her favorite meals are chocolate chip pancakes and macaroni and cheese," Samara murmured.

"Why did you move away from the ranch? If I had returned... if someone found out about Adaline," he said.

She turned, wrapped her arms around his waist, and laid her head against his chest. "It's complicated. If you returned, Mason, Bear, and Ann-Marie knew where to find me—us. I had to leave. My brothers—" She stopped, shook her head, and looked up at him. "Somehow, my brothers had a top-notch lawyer. Rob and Jerry were given a five-year prison sentence, but released after two, followed by probation. Brit and Gary were given time served, probation, and community service. I was happy about Gary and Brit, but something didn't feel right considering the severity of the crime. I didn't want any of them near Adaline— especially Rob and Jerry," she confessed.

"And Bear?" he asked.

"And then there was Bear. He was protective of me when I came back, but it was nothing like after Adaline was born. I knew he wanted a deeper relationship than I could give him. I couldn't lead him on by letting him think that anything would change between us. When the job in Texas came up, it was too good to turn down. I could set my own schedule, keep Adaline with me, and I made enough to support us. The owners were fabulous and very understanding. I worked with the horses that needed one-on-one care," she said.

"If it was so good, why did you come back?" he wondered.

She pulled out of his arms and looked around the room. "I felt something—danger. I was afraid. It sounds crazy, but my gut was telling me to grab Adaline and run. Since she was born, I've been careful about where I go, who I talk to, and who saw Adaline. I took her to the same doctor, but never let him draw her blood. As soon as Adaline could understand, I made sure she knew she mustn't let anyone see her gifts.

Last week… last week I was working with a horse that Adaline really loved. There was a bond between them that I didn't understand. I had stepped out of the barn to grab some fresh bandages for another horse I was working with when I saw a woman. She had her camera out. She took off the moment she saw me, and there was something in her eyes —triumph… and secrets. When I entered the barn, Adaline was sitting on the horse that was known to be unmanageable. He was so uncontrollable that he was going to be euthanized. I knew the woman had seen Adaline, and I knew in my gut that I had to get our daughter away from there and somewhere safe as quickly as possible," she said with a wave of her hand.

"So you came back home," he said.

She gave him a rueful smile and nodded. "I came back home, told Mason what happened—he bought Chester, that's the horse, by the way. He purchased it through a friend of a friend of a friend and is having him shipped here after the storm passes," she said with a rueful smile.

"I assume Chester is aware of the arrangements and will be on his best behavior," he chuckled.

"Yes. Adaline made sure of that," she softly replied.

"Once we leave here, I swear I will do everything within my power and the power of the Ha'darra family to protect you and Adaline," he vowed.

The smile on her face changed to concern. "Did you catch the people responsible for the creature in the lab? How is your mom and Melek?" she asked.

"No—at least not all of them. That is something I must discuss with you. To answer your other question, Mother and Melek have recovered, though it took time and the help of Morian Reykill's symbiot," he said.

"Are you talking about my grandma and grandpa?" a small voice inquired.

Adalard turned and looked at Adaline. She was standing just inside the living room, watching them, and holding several dolls against her chest, almost as if they were a shield. Her eyes were still red from her recent tears, and her cheeks were flushed. She looked back at him with wide, curious eyes.

He smiled at her and nodded. "Yes, would you like to see them?" he asked.

"In person or in pictures?" Adaline replied.

"In video now and in person soon," he responded.

Adaline glanced at Samara for guidance before she shrugged. "I guess so," she mumbled.

He pulled the portable vidcom player from his waist, placed it on the coffee table, and sat down on the couch. With a wave of his hand, he connected with the *Rayon I* through his personal link. The relays set between his world and this one would take a few minutes to respond since he didn't have the main communication console at the big house to connect through. He smiled when his mother's surprised face appeared on the screen.

"Adalard! Is everything alright? Do you need me to get Melek or Ha'ven?" she asked with concern.

He grinned back at her. "No, at least, not yet. I have someone who would like to speak with you."

"With me? Who could possibly want to talk to me?" she asked with a frown.

He motioned for Adaline to come sit next to him. She slowly walked over and leaned against his knee. Adaline studied his mother with a curious expression before reaching out to touch her grandmother's face. She ran her fingers through the hologram. Adalard smiled when Adaline pulled her hand back and studied her fingers before tilting her head to look at his mother with wonder.

"Are you my Grandma Narissa?" Adaline asked in a shy, uncertain voice.

Narissa lifted a hand to her throat and gazed back at Adaline with a tearful expression. "Oh, Adalard," she whispered.

CHAPTER THIRTY-SIX

"**C**an you do *this*?" Adaline asked

Samara peered over the kitchen counter. Adaline was running her hands over her long, wavy hair. Flowers appeared between the thick strands. She pulled back and grinned when Adalard was silent for a moment. Adalard had been their daughter's captive audience for the past hour, and Adaline was relishing being able to show off her talents.

Her worry about Adaline accepting Adalard's return slowly dissolved as Adaline's natural curiosity overcame her fear. It was also a brilliant move on Adalard's part to introduce their daughter to her grandmother. Narissa's immediate acceptance of Adaline soothed not only Adaline, but Samara's worries as well.

"Instead of decorating my hair, I prefer to give flowers to your mother," Adalard said, creating a bouquet.

"Oh! Mommy, these are so pretty. They glow! Can you teach me how to make glowing flowers?" Adaline asked.

"Yes. Your Grandma Narissa grows these in her garden," he replied.

Samara's heart melted at the low, husky sound in Adalard's voice. This was one of the things she loved about him. He had a tender, loving heart under his tough exterior.

"I've almost got all the stuff I want to bring to the big house ready," Samara said, stepping into the living room. "Adaline, can you go get your bag and put it by the door?"

"Can Adalard... Daddy... help me?" Adaline asked.

Tears burned her eyes as Adalard's unconscious reaction to Adaline calling him Daddy for the first time hit her.

"I'm sure he will if you ask him," she replied with a tender smile.

"Will you?" Adaline requested, looking back at him.

"Of course," he quietly replied.

Adaline slipped her small hand into his when he stood. Samara's gaze followed them as they walked down the hallway. She started when her cellphone vibrated. Pulling it from the back pocket of her jeans, she glanced at the screen. A sad smile curved her lips when she saw the text from Bear.

Is everything okay? How is Adaline? How are you doing?

Everything is fine. Adaline is adjusting and getting to know Adalard. I'm okay. I...

She paused and bit her lip. Tears burned her eyes again and her stomach knotted. She didn't want to hurt Bear. She also wouldn't lie to him. He deserved better than that.

I... hope you understand. I'm happy that he is back, she typed.

There was a pause as she waited for his reply. Her chest felt tight when she saw the dots showing he was responding. She lifted her hand to smother the sob as she read his response.

Adaline is a very special little girl, just like her mother. I love you both. I'll be here if you need me—always.

She wiped the tear from her cheeks and typed the only response she could think.

We love you too. Thank you.

She turned back toward the kitchen and closed her eyes. It felt like she was saying goodbye and leaving a piece of her heart. Another sob escaped, and she knew she needed a few minutes alone.

I'll watch Adaline, Adalard's compassionate voice filled her head.

Thank you, she responded.

She twisted around, grabbed her coat and hat off the hook by the door, and quietly exited the apartment. She placed her hat on her head, pulled her coat on, and pulled her gloves out of her coat pockets as she descended the stairs. The frigid air cooled her heated cheeks and helped to clear her mind.

The sky had darkened, and the snowflakes were beginning to thicken. It wasn't nearly as bad as it was predicted to get. Shoving her hands in her pockets, she stepped off the stairs and headed for the UTV parked behind her truck. They would be taking it to the big house.

She had only taken a few steps when a sharp prick on the back of her thigh caused her to wince and stumble. The sensation of a wasp sting caused her to mutter a muted curse. Reaching down, she started to rub the aching spot. Her hand bumped against something attached to her jeans and she looked down to see what it was. A wave of dizziness washed over her when she bent over and picked up a thin dart.

"What the…?" she hissed in a slurred voice.

She sank down to her knees as the world tilted to the side. Her fingers tightened around the cylinder before relaxing as darkness surrounded her, and she fell onto her side. She didn't see the man standing in the shadows under the staircase nor the grim smile of satisfaction on his face.

Adalard carefully accepted the doll clothes and dolls that Adaline handed him and packed them in the bright pink bag with a glittery unicorn on the front. He still couldn't get over the fact that he had a daughter. A soft laugh slipped from him when he thought of his brothers' reactions when they found out. His mother said she would share the news with Melek, but she thought it best if he told Ha'ven and Arrow—mostly because she wanted to see his brothers' reactions.

The memory of her delighted laugh made him smile. It suddenly dawned on him that Ha'ven's daughter, Alice, and Adaline were almost the same age. The realization that Adaline wouldn't be alone filled him with joy.

"Do you love my mommy?" Adaline suddenly asked.

Adalard blinked with surprise at the question. She waited for his response in silence, her violet eyes were serious and held an expression of awareness that was much more mature than he expected from a six-year-old. He sat down on the bed so that he wasn't towering over her.

"Yes, I love your mommy very much," he said.

Adaline frowned. "If you love her, then why did you leave us? Bear loves mommy, and he never left."

He reached out and cupped her hands, but was surprised when she climbed up on his lap. Sliding his arm around her, he brushed her hair back from her face. He marveled at how soft her cheek was against the tips of his fingers.

"What did your mommy tell you about me?" he asked.

Adaline held his hand and played with his fingers while she answered. "She said that you lived far away. She said if I looked up at the stars, that is where you were. I thought that meant you were dead. Bear told me when his daddy died that he went to the stars," she said.

"My world *is* very far away. I live on a planet called Ceran-Pax," he explained.

She looked up at him. "Can you use your gifts there without being afraid?"

He smiled and nodded. "Yes, you can use your gifts all you want and no one will care. You have a cousin your age there. Her name is Alice. She is very gifted and loves to drive your uncle crazy," he chuckled.

"Are you… are you taking me and mommy with you?" she asked, looking back down at his hand.

He hugged her close and kissed the top of her head. "Yes, Adaline. I'm taking you and your mommy with me this time. I should never have sent your mommy away. If I had suspected… if I had known that you were coming, I would have made it work," he murmured.

"I wanted my mommy and Bear to be together. I didn't know you. I'm sorry," she said with a sniff.

"It isn't your fault, *toneewa*. I'm glad Bear was here for you and your mommy when I wasn't," he reassured her.

She looked up at him again with a hopeful expression. "Can Bear go with us? And Uncle Mason and Aunty Ann Marie and Chester?"

"Chester? Aw, yes, the horse. I don't think a horse on a spaceship would be a good idea," he said, not answering the question about Bear or the others.

"He would be very good. He could stay in my room," she pleaded.

"I think he would be much happier here with other horses and plenty of room to run, don't you?" he suggested.

A disappointed expression appeared on her face before she nodded. "I guess so," she conceded.

"Let's go put your stuff by the door like your mommy asked," he said.

He slid her off his lap and stood. Adaline grabbed her pink backpack and zipped it closed while he picked up her suitcase. He absently responded to Adaline's questions about Alice as they walked down the hallway to the living room.

Samara? he silently reached out, testing to see if she was ready for them.

A deep, unnatural silence greeted him at the same time as the familiar sensation of danger struck him. He released his grip on the suitcase, twisted, and picked Adaline up in his arms. She wound her arms tightly around his neck.

"My mommy... she can't wake up," she whispered near his ear.

"Don't be afraid," he responded.

"I'm not," she answered before burying her face against his neck.

Adalard held her tight before he focused inward on the image of Mason and Ann Marie's kitchen. In the blink of an eye, he was standing next to the large table. Ann Marie squeaked in alarm and dropped the ladle in her hand back into the pot while Sara gasped and rose from where she was sitting at the table.

"Land sakes! Mason!" Ann Marie hollered.

Jaguin reached the kitchen first with a harried-looking Mason skidding to a stop behind him. Jaguin and Mason's dark frowns of disapproval turned to worry when they noticed the expression on his face. Adalard tried to school it so that he wouldn't alarm Ann Marie or Sara any more than he already had.

"I need you to protect Adaline," he said.

"What's wrong?" Jaguin and Mason demanded at the same time.

"I'm not sure. I... need to find Samara," he glanced at the huge Valdier before turning his gaze to Mason.

"Sara and I will take care of Adaline. You men go find Samara," Ann Marie instructed, reaching for Adaline.

"Give me a second to get some things together," Mason said.

"Adalard, what is it?" Jaguin asked.

"I'm not sure yet. Samara went outside for a few minutes. Neither Adaline nor I can communicate with her. I... sensed something is wrong," he replied.

Mason stepped back into the room as he was explaining. He carried a handgun in one hand and a rifle in the other. Jaguin gave Mason a sharp-toothed grin and shook his head when Mason held out the handgun to him.

"How often are you wrong when you get this feeling?" Mason asked.

"Never," he replied in a low voice.

"Can you tell us what we're walking into? Human? Alien? A little intel helps before going into a mission," Mason continued.

"It could be either," he admitted.

Jaguin gave him a sharp glance. "Hamade?" he asked.

"Possibly. I had a warning that he might attempt to come here. I didn't think it was possible for him to reach the planet this quickly," he confessed.

Mason pursed his lips and nodded. "Since you aren't sure, we'll go on the assumption that any stranger is hostile. The element of surprise could be in our favor if they think you are either still in the apartment, or they don't know you're here. I suggest that I exit and head that way as if everything is normal. The snow will give me some cover. If you can do your popping thing and come up behind the building, we'll start our search there. Jaguin, you go out through the basement door. I'm assuming that if you are in your other form, you'll be able to handle the weather. A little air recon and coverage would be nice."

"Mason... if this is an alien, he will be extremely dangerous. Whatever you do, don't confront him on your own," Adalard warned.

"I think you both have some explaining to do after we find Samara," Mason muttered.

Adalard nodded. He would have preferred that it was just he and Jaguin going. He knew the dragon-shifter could take care of himself, but Mason knew the area better than he did, especially with the worsening weather. He shook his head when Mason held out the gun.

"I won't need it," he assured him.

Mason lifted an eyebrow but nodded. "I didn't think you would, but figured it wouldn't hurt to offer it, just in case. Ann Marie, you and Sara make sure the house is locked up," he urged as he leaned the gun against the wall by the door and pulled on his jacket.

"We will. Jaguin take Honey with you," Sara suggested, motioning to the golden symbiot standing in the doorway.

"Keep a portion with you," Jaguin replied, kissing Sara before he motioned to his symbiot to divide.

"You men be careful," Ann Marie instructed with a stern look.

Mason picked up the rifle and winked at her. "I'll be hungry when I get back."

"Daddy, you'll find mommy?" Adaline asked in a soft voice.

Adalard stepped up to Ann Marie and Adaline and tenderly touched his daughter's cheek. "Yes, *toneewa*. I'll find mommy," he promised before he kissed her on her forehead.

He turned away, pulled the door open, and stepped out into the mudroom with Mason right behind him. The other man reached out and touched his arm before he opened the backdoor on the mud porch. He looked over his shoulder at Mason.

Mason gave him a sharp nod. "We'll find her," he said.

He nodded, his throat thick with emotion as he remembered the look in Adaline's eyes when she asked him if he would find Samara. Focusing, he disappeared.

CHAPTER THIRTY-SEVEN

*H*amade cursed as he carried the human female over his shoulder. He had been forced to limit the use of his powers for fear of alerting Adalard and any warriors in the area of his presence. He cursed when he stumbled in the deepening layer of snow.

He dropped the woman on her back in the snow and rested against a tree. He touched the aching wound on his stomach, looking down and scowling at the bloodstain on his hand. He rubbed the alloy cuff attached to his wrist that contained a series of vials.

Curse the traitorous bitch, he thought as he pushed away from the tree.

The Empress might have saved his life, but it had come with a high price. His body, and thus his powers, were now connected with the entity she had created. The more energy he drew from the surrounding area, the more he fed the entity—and the more it fed on his life essence. Until he could find a way to remove the device from his arm, he had to be careful about using his powers if he didn't want to lose complete control.

A movement out of the corner of his eye made him pause, and he crouched behind the tree. He followed a group of men with a narrowed-eyed focus. They were dressed all in white and moving slowly through the wooded area. Each man held a weapon, and they were moving toward the buildings he had left minutes before.

It was obvious they were not searching for him, and from their lack of auras and the way they moved, he knew they were human. Something was going down—and he wanted to know what it was. He fought between the need to get his target to the concealed shuttle he had arrived in and finding out what was happening. In the end, he decided to follow the group. He targeted a man who had moved out of formation from the others.

He glanced at the woman. She would be unconscious for a while longer. The restraining cuffs on her wrists and ankles would hold her. He checked the gag he had covered her mouth with to make sure it was secure in case she woke. Satisfied that she wouldn't be going anywhere, he rose to his feet in search of his target.

From the van parked on the service road two miles away, Jack oversaw and directed the assembled team. He looked at the weather forecast before focusing on the heat signatures on the scanner screen. He reached out and activated the body cam and communicator on the team leader's vest.

"T1, you have approximately forty-five minutes before white-out conditions begin," he cautioned.

"T1, Oorah!" T1 responded quietly.

He looked at the screen again and frowned. There were ten men on the team, but only nine of the heat signatures were still in formation. He pressed the communication button again.

"T1, check your flank. T7 is out of formation," he advised.

"T1, Oorah!" T1 confirmed.

He drummed his fingers on the console before he released a curse. Something was wrong. He could feel it in his gut. He stared at the video streams before turning back to the lone heat signature.

"Take over," he ordered to the woman sitting beside him.

"Yes, sir," she replied.

He stood, opened the door to the van, and stepped out. Reaching inside the door, he retrieved a M40A5 sniper rifle before he pressed the button to close the door. He pulled on a pair of goggles and adjusted the hood of his white jacket over his head.

The snow swirled around him, covering the terrain in a white blanket. He pulled out the portable tracker from his pocket and checked his bearings. Turning toward the west, he followed the position of the missing man.

Light, powdery snow crunched under his feet as he moved in an indirect line toward T7's last position. The wind was picking up and hid the sound of his approach. He paused to check his course and the positions of the other men. The rest of the team was near the buildings where their target was located. T7's position had remained unchanged.

He pocketed the tracker and gripped the rifle. When he was within fifty yards of his target, he slowed his pace and dropped to the ground. He extended the bipod, looked through the scope, and slowly swept the area for any signs of life.

Jack paused when he saw a crumpled form barely visible in the snow. He cautiously scanned the area one more time before advancing. T7 was lying face down in the snow. He reached down and rolled the man over. He jerked back, almost falling over when he saw the man's shriveled gray face, wide empty eyes, and open mouth.

"*What the fuck?*" he hissed, stepping closer to examine the man.

T7 looked as if he had been mummified. Jack used the end of his gun to tilt the dead man's head from side to side before he scanned the body. The front video cam had been ripped off.

He glanced around through the white haze and touched the micro-phone in his right ear. "L-zebra to base," he murmured.

"L-zebra, this is base," the woman replied.

"Review T7 video and report," he ordered.

"Oorah…. Negative video on T7. Nothing but snow visible, sir," the woman answered.

"Rewind and search last ten minutes," he ordered.

"Oorah," the woman responded.

He studied the ground. The barely visible indentations in the snow indicated footprints. He followed them, noting that they came from the side. Whoever—whatever—attacked T7 had come from the direction of the buildings.

"L-Zebra, negative enemy contact. Snow only," the woman finally responded.

Ahead was another crumpled figure. He lifted the rifle and took slow, measured steps toward the person. This person was a ranch hand by the looks of the snow-covered clothing that was visible. A hat covered the face. Using the end of the rifle, he lifted the hat high enough so that he could see their face. He knocked it aside, staring in astonishment when he saw who it was.

He crouched and tugged off his glove with his teeth. He held his hand over Samara's nose. Warm air caressed his chilled flesh. She was alive!

He pulled his glove back on, removed the gag from her mouth, and tapped her cold cheek. Her eyelashes fluttered, and she moaned. He wrapped his arm around her and lifted her into a sitting position.

She moaned again and leaned heavily against him. He noticed when she lifted her arms that her wrists were restrained by an unusual locking device. Her head rolled back, and her eyes closed again.

He looked at her legs and noticed they were restrained as well. There was a light flashing on them, and he didn't know if there was an explosive that would detonate if he tried to remove them. He couldn't leave her here. His assignment was to eliminate her, but until he had some answers, he needed her alive.

Slinging the rifle strap over his shoulder, he picked her up, fireman style, and retraced his steps back to the van. He kept a wary eye on his surroundings as he trudged back the way he came. He needed to warn his team that there was something far more dangerous out in the blizzard.

Adalard reappeared behind the building that contained Samara's apartment. He reached out to her again, searching for some thread. Silence greeted him.

He scanned the snow-covered ground, searching for any signs of intrusion. There was a line of depressions leading from behind the structure to the covered area where Samara parked her vehicle. He stepped forward just as Mason called out to him.

"I found something," Mason said.

He stepped under the covered area and walked over to Mason. Mason stood and held out his hand. A small metal dart lay in the center of his palm. Adalard picked up the dart and examined the casing before he lifted it to his nose and sniffed. A rush of burning rage filled him when he recognized the scent.

"Pi'nae. It is a strong sedative derived from a plant on my world," he snarled, squeezing the dart in his fist.

Mason breathed out a deep sigh. "Well, I guess that answers the question of whether the culprit is human or alien," he muttered.

"The answer is actually both," Jaguin said, stepping under the covered area.

Adalard frowned. "Both?"

Jaguin grimly nodded and looked at Mason. "Unless you have a patrol of camouflaged humans carrying weapons and heading this way through the woods, it is more than just one person," he said.

Mason shook his head. "We quit doing trainings after you guys decided to keep popping in. The crew doesn't even come up here—well, besides Bear and Chad," he amended.

"What did you see?" Adalard asked.

"Nine humans moving in this direction from the northwest. They are moving in a military formation, so I would classify them as hostiles. I wanted to warn you before I searched farther out. The weather is making it difficult, but I thought I saw parallel tracks, only moving away from the building," Jaguin replied.

"What the hell is going on?" Mason grumbled.

Adalard stared out at the growing white-out. "They want Samara—and Adaline," he guessed. "If I were to guess, the alien is Hamade Dos. I don't know who the humans are, but I know Samara was worried that someone may have seen Adaline using her powers."

"What do you want us to do, Adalard?" Jaguin quietly asked.

He was torn between his need to protect Adaline and his need to protect Samara. Out of the two, Hamade was the most dangerous. Mason and Jaguin could handle the human team with no problem.

"I have to go after Hamade and finish this once and for all," he finally said.

"We'll take care of the others," Jaguin replied with a nod.

"Don't you worry about that little girl of yours. She'll be safe. You go find Samara and bring her back," Mason added.

"Thank you, my friends," Adalard replied.

"Jaguin, if the weather still permits, you take to the air and we'll show these sons-of-bitches what happens when they mess with this family," Mason muttered.

Confident that the two men would take care of the threat heading in their direction, Adalard turned and disappeared into the blinding snowfall.

CHAPTER THIRTY-EIGHT

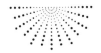

*a*dalard followed the tracks until they disappeared. The weather condition was rapidly deteriorating. Pulling on the power of his connection with Samara, he breathed and lifted his hand, allowing the power inside him to flow outward.

"Show me," he murmured.

A thin ribbon of his aura reached out, searching for a connection to Samara. He grunted with satisfaction when the beam of violet energy shot forward. He clung to it, following the faint thread through the blinding, wind-driven snow.

He slowed in his progress as the snow on the ground became thicker. He ducked when a tree branch snapped in the high wind. The distraction broke the fragile connection between him and Samara. He gritted his teeth, lifted his hand, and focused again. The thin strand of energy flickered like a whip in the wind before fading.

"No!" he hissed.

Ice clung to his jacket and coated his eyelashes and cheeks. There was no way Samara could survive for long out in the dropping temperatures—and there was no way he would be able to find her in time if Hamade made it to his transport. He swallowed his fear and held his hand out again.

"Show me where my mate is," he commanded with clenched teeth.

This time, the energy thread burst out and greedily cut through the blizzard. He watched in amazement as the band expanded and glowed. The white veil in front of him radiated with color, expanding and engulfing the hunched form struggling to walk.

He rushed forward when the form staggered and dropped to one knee. As he came closer, he noticed the person was cradling another in his arms. Anger coursed through him, melting the ice that had settled in his veins, and a sword formed in the palm of his hand.

Surging forward, he lifted the sword to strike before Hamade realized he wasn't alone, but when he got close enough to recognize the man's familiar attire, he stopped in mid-motion. He lowered his arm when Bear looked up at him.

"We need to get her back to the house," Bear breathlessly choked.

"I'll take her," he said, bending and gently lifting Samara's limp body into his arms. "Hold onto my arm."

Bear stiffly rose to his feet. Adalard was thankful that the man didn't question his request. He focused on Mason and Ann Marie's house. In seconds, they stood next to the table. Bear groaned and sank down onto a chair while Ann Marie uttered a startled shriek that drew Sara and her symbiot into the room.

"Land sakes! You have got to quit doing that!" Ann Marie snapped in an angry voice before she saw Samara. "Oh my, follow me. Sara, please get Bear a cup of winter coffee. The whiskey is in the small cabinet in the corner," she instructed.

Adalard followed Ann Marie out of the kitchen and down the hallway to a guest bedroom. Ann Marie pulled back the covers, and he lowered

Samara onto the crisp, powder-blue sheets. Ann Marie reached down to remove Samara's boots. Her low hiss of dismay pulled his attention away from Samara's pale face.

"The bastard who took her tied her legs up," she said.

"I'll take care of her. You might want to check on Bear. Transporting for the first time can cause a bit of disorientation," he said.

"I'll get a kettle going and make some tea. Samara will need to be warmed up from the inside out," she replied.

"Thank you," he distractedly murmured.

His attention was already back on Samara. He focused on the restraints, removing the ones around her legs first, and then those on her wrists. With a wave of his hands, he also removed her boots, gloves, and jacket. A soft knock on the door behind him caused him to look over his shoulder. Sara stood in the doorway with her symbiot by her side.

"I don't know exactly what abilities the Curizan have when it comes to healing, but I thought Honey might be able to help," Sara offered.

Adalard held Samara's icy hand in his. He looked at the symbiot. It was in the shape of a large dog. He knew the power of the symbiot's healing ability—it came from the Goddesses and was not something they, nor the dragon-shifter they were attached to, would casually lend to another.

"I would like that very much," he replied.

The words had only just left his lips when the symbiot surged forward. He was about to protest when he saw it leap into the air, but before he could admonish it, the symbiot transformed into a golden fleece, settling over Samara's body.

He tucked Samara's cold hand under the golden blanket. Behind him, Sara was pulling up a chair for him to sit down. He looked at her with a surprised expression.

"I know how I would feel if that were Jaguin. I wouldn't want to be away from him. I'll bring some winter coffee for you and some tea for Samara," Sara said.

"Thank you, Sara," he murmured.

She gave him a brief smile before quietly leaving the bedroom. He pulled the chair closer to the bed and sat down. Sliding his hand under the symbiot blanket, he breathed a sigh of relief when he felt that Samara's skin was already warm. He bowed his head and closed his eyes.

I am so sorry. I should have protected you. I have done so many things wrong but loving you is not one of them, he silently said, unsure if she could hear him. *Letting you go seven years ago was the hardest thing I've ever done. My biggest fear was that something would happen to you, and today, that fear came true.*

"I knew... why. It-It wasn't... just you. I-I wasn't... ready," Samara murmured.

He looked up and studied her. A contrite smile curved his lips when she gave him a crooked smile. Reaching out, he caressed her cheek. The color was returning to it.

"Hello," he said softly.

"Hi, yourself," she replied before uttering a soft groan.

"Are you in pain?" he asked.

She started to shake her head before she grimaced. "Just the normal tingling when your fingers and toes defrost."

"You are supposed to heal her without pain," he growled at the symbiot.

She frowned, lifted her head as far as she could, and looked around the room. "Who are you being so grumpy at?"

"Honey, Sara and Jaguin's symbiot. It is healing you," he said.

She raised her hand, lifting the golden blanket up, and released a long hissing breath. The symbiot shimmered in response, and a corner lifted and waved at her. She looked back at him, her wide eyes filled with wonder.

"My blanket just waved at me," she whispered.

"Symbiots tend to have a mind of their own," he replied with a chuckle.

"Thank you for saving me," she said, reaching for his hand.

He looked down at their joined hands and gently caressed the back of her hand with his thumb.

"I wish I could take credit for that. Bear saved you. Do you know what happened?" he asked.

She shook her head. "No. One minute I was on the verge of having a meltdown and, the next, everything went dark. I honestly don't even remember being cold except for a brief moment."

"It's good to see you awake."

He turned on the chair and rose to his feet when Bear spoke from the doorway. Bear gave him a smile and held up two cups, stepping into the room and handing him one of the cups.

"You'll want to sip on that. Ann Marie got a little heavy-handed with the whiskey," he murmured.

Adalard placed his cup on the nightstand when Samara struggled to sit up. Sliding his arm behind her back, he propped her up against the headboard, cushioning her back with a plump pillow. Bear handed her the second cup he was carrying.

"I might have added a little whiskey to your tea," he said with a wink.

"Thank you. Where's Adaline?" she asked in an anxious voice.

"She's in the kitchen with Ann Marie and Sara. They are making after-the-battle chocolate chip cookies," he said.

She laughed with relief and relaxed against the headboard. "Thank goodness," she murmured.

"How did you find Samara?" Adalard asked.

"I was heading back to the ranch from town when I saw a white cargo van and a box truck on the service road that led to the cell tower substation. I thought it was weird that they would be doing anything with the storm coming. Hell, Casper looks like a ghost town. The only places open are the bar and the Chinese restaurant—which, let me tell you, were packed. Anyway, it seemed off, so I pulled over and decided to see what was going on. After about ten minutes, this guy climbs out of the van all dressed in white and carrying a military-grade weapon. He takes off heading south toward the houses. My first thought was that the government finally figured out what the hell was going on here and decided to use the storm as cover to attack. Anyway, I cut through to the old logging road just west of him and parked at the top near Copper's bridge so I could follow him. That's when I saw the spaceship down near the river. I tried calling to warn you guys, but my cellphone is crap, and I didn't bring the satellite phone with me." Bear paused and took a deep breath.

"You saw a spaceship?" Adalard asked.

"Yeah, down in the canyon near the river," Bear replied.

"That sounds like where you landed before," Samara murmured.

"What happened next?" Adalard impatiently demanded.

Bear rubbed his neck. "I wasn't about to get between the government and an alien shoot out, so I hung back a bit. The storm was picking up which gave me some cover. I followed behind him, and that's when I saw him stop. There was another man dressed like him lying in the snow—and Samara. I saw him pick Samara up and toss her over his shoulder. He seemed real spooked. I thought it strange he would just leave his man down until I saw why," Bear said with a shudder.

"What do you mean?" Samara asked.

Bear looked at them both with a haunted expression. "Whatever happened to the dead man wasn't natural. His skin was all sunk in as if he had been drained dry. Anyway, it scared the shit out of me, and I knew I needed to get Samara out of there. I had the advantage because he was carrying Samara, and I knew the terrain. I caught up with him and pulled a gun on him. That's when I realized I knew him, and he wasn't from the government."

"Who was he?" Adalard asked.

"The guy from Vegas—Campeo's or whatever he was called—security guy. You know, the one from the bar," Bear said.

"Alberto Campeau? Why would he kidnap me?" she asked with a frown.

"I don't know," Bear said with a shrug. "All I know is he dropped you in the snow and disappeared."

Adalard had heard enough. He had warned Campeau to stay away from Samara. If his security guard was working on his own, then he would deal with the man. If he was working under orders from Campeau, Adalard had promised the man a visit he would never forget. He needed to keep his priorities straight, though. Hamade was still out there. It didn't make sense for Hamade to discard Samara unless he had discovered a bigger prize from the deceased man.

"Where are you going?" Samara asked, reaching for his hand when he moved.

"There is only one reason I can think of for Hamade to leave you, and only one that I can think of that would motivate Campeau to send his men here," he said.

She watched him with a worried expression. "Adaline."

"Yes."

"Mommy, do you want a cookie?" Adaline asked.

Samara turned from the window and smiled wanly at her daughter who was carrying a small plate of hot cookies.

"That would be lovely," she responded.

Adaline placed the plate on the coffee table. "I saved some cookies for Daddy, Uncle Mason, and Uncle Jaguin," she said.

"They'll be back soon," she replied.

Adaline sat down on the couch and swung her feet back and forth. Love filled her when Adaline clasped her hands and looked up at her. She walked over, sat down, and wrapped her arm around her daughter.

"How would you feel about going on a spaceship to Daddy's world when the storm blows over?" she asked.

"Daddy says I have a cousin there my age, and I have a grandma and grandpa, and the flowers he likes to give you grow there," Adaline said.

"It seems like you and your daddy did a lot of talking," she mused.

"I like him," Adaline said.

"Me too."

"He says Bear and Uncle Mason and Aunt Ann Marie and Chester can't go with us," Adaline replied with a droopy lower lip.

"Chester? You asked him if you could bring Chester into outer space?" she exclaimed.

Adaline nodded and sighed. "He said Chester would be happier here."

"Yes, I think Chester would be happier here than on a spaceship," she agreed.

"Samara," Sara softly called.

Samara looked up. The expression on Sara's face made her pick Adaline up and rise to her feet. Honey paced back and forth in front of Sara in agitation.

"What is it?" she asked.

"My dragon is sensing danger, and so is Honey. I think it would be best if you and Adaline find a place to hide. I've warned Jaguin," she said.

"I've got the perfect place," Ann Marie said.

Samara nodded, hugging Adaline to her. She followed Ann Marie down the hallway. They crossed the large master bedroom to a floor-to-ceiling bookcase. Ann Marie pulled the third book on the bottom shelf and the bookcase popped open. Behind the bookcase was a thick metal door with a manual lock. Ann Marie spun the dial, unlocking the massive safe, and pulled it open.

"This is a fireproof walk-in gun safe and shelter. Mason went a little overboard when he left the military and wanted to make sure none of these weapons fell into the wrong hands," Ann Marie explained. The lights turned on automatically when she stepped inside. "There is a battery backup. You can open the safe at any time from inside by pulling this lever. Check the video cam to make sure it is clear before you do. It has its own environmental system."

"What about the rest of you?" Samara asked with surprise when Ann Marie started to step back out of the room.

"Those men are after you and Adaline. Trust me when I say that is never going to happen. Mason isn't the only one that is good in a fight," Ann Marie said with a surprisingly ominous smile.

Samara watched in disbelief as Ann Marie closed the door, sealing her and Adaline inside the safe. She turned in a slow circle as she took in the weapons lining the walls behind clear glass panels. Never in her life had she seen so many advanced weapons in one place except in the movies.

"Boy, Uncle Mason sure has a lot of guns," Adaline murmured in awe.

"Yes, he does, sweetheart," Samara quietly agreed.

CHAPTER THIRTY-NINE

*A*dalard squinted upward through the driving blizzard, watching as the silver and green dragon dropped two men on the ground beside him before landing with a menacing growl when they tried to bolt. The men dropped to their knees, whimpering and cowering. Adalard formed a metal cage around them as Jaguin shifted.

"Mason said he saw the last two humans 'running like two bitches in heat being chased by a pack of horny wolves'—his words, not mine," Jaguin dryly replied when Adalard lifted his eyebrow in confusion.

They turned when Mason appeared out of the snow. He was gripping his hat with one hand, his head bowed against the wind, and carrying his rifle in the other. He looked up at them and shook his head.

"I don't think the others will be an issue. The storm is only going to get worse. If they don't make it back where they came from, the storm will kill them," Mason said, speaking as loudly as he could through the muffler he was wearing to protect his lower face from the wind and cold.

"It would serve them right," Jaguin retorted before he suddenly stiffened.

"What is it?" Adalard asked.

"Sara... her dragon senses danger," he growled.

"Hamade!" Adalard hissed.

"You two go take care of the alien. I'll deal with these guys," Mason said.

Jaguin shifted back into his dragon with a terrifying roar and took off, causing the cowering men in the cage to shriek with terror. Irritated with the humans, Adalard waved his hand and dissolved the cage so Mason could deal with them before he turned back, heading in the direction of the farmhouse, and disappeared. In seconds, he was back at the house.

"Adalard, where is Jaguin?" Sara asked.

"He will be here in a moment. What is it? Where are Samara and Adaline?" he demanded.

"They are safe, but something has that golden creature really upset," Ann Marie said.

"My dragon feels the same way," Sara confessed.

Honey was pacing back and forth in the living room, pausing to peer out the window. A shadow flickered outside of it, and the symbiot actually cowered and backed up. Adalard looked at Bear when the man came and stood next to him.

"Do you think its reaction has anything to do with what happened to the man I saw in the woods?" Bear murmured.

He thought about what Morian had told him about the entity being a corrupted symbiot. His gut was warning him that whatever new weapon Hamade had developed, it could be deadly not only to the humans, but to the Valdier and their symbiots. He knew deep down that he would have to face Hamade alone.

Not alone, warrior, a soft unknown voice whispered through his mind.

"What...?" he exclaimed, twisting in a circle.

He froze when a vision appeared in front of him as surely as if he were watching a vidcom. Hamade's distorted, grotesque body, twisted and covered in a dark liquid, advanced in the direction of the farmhouse. Adalard could sense the malice, danger, and power emanating from the other man.

In that moment, he knew that there was only one power strong enough to combat it. What he didn't know was if that combined power would be enough to destroy the creature that Hamade had become. He swallowed as the vision faded, and he found himself staring into three pairs of concerned eyes.

"I... Sara, tell Jaguin to stay with Mason and for both of them to stay away from the house. I want you all to find a safe place," he instructed in a resolute tone.

"Adalard...," Bear protested.

He shook his head. "He will kill you—all of you. Hamade has... changed," he said.

Ann Marie reached out to him. "Is there anything we can do to help?"

"I need you to watch over Adaline," he said.

"I've warned Jaguin. He'll stay with Mason. We'll protect Adaline," Sara promised.

"Whatever happens, do not try to help," he replied.

Samara, I need your help, he called.

"I'm here," she said from the entrance to the living room. She gave him a weak smile. "I saw."

He gave her a tender smile before returning his attention to the others. Sara's symbiot was pressed against her side. He could tell from the way it was shimmering that time was running out.

"Take your symbiot with you, Sara. Hamade will use it against me if you don't," he instructed.

Sara nodded and murmured to the symbiot. He reached out a hand to Samara, needing her touch as the others hurried down the hallway. She wrapped her arms around him and held him.

"I fear for you," he murmured.

"Welcome to the club. I guess this is going to be some scary shit. I don't know how you've done this over and over for the past seven years. One thing I do know is that it is time to kick this guy's butt once and for all," she said with a strained smile.

He threaded his fingers through her hair before he kissed her. "If Hamade...," he began.

She rested her fingers against his lips and shook her head. "He won't."

The door in the kitchen burst open. They both turned, and Adalard instinctively stepped in front of Samara. Doubt filled his mind. She rested her hand on the center of his back, and he felt some of his tension ease.

We've got this. Good versus evil, right? Good always wins in every great book and movie I've ever read and watched. This time we're the superheroes, she silently joked.

A chuckle slipped from him. They were facing possible death, and she made him feel like it was an evening out at the bar. The smile on his lips faded when the first chill of the entity with Hamade entered the living room.

Stay behind me, he murmured.

Her hiss of shock and horror mixed with his when Hamade stepped into the room. The Curizan general looked nothing like his former self. The entity flowed throughout his body like a cancerous parasite, creating a dark gray mist around him. His flesh was distorted, his veins were thick and bulging where the dark matter of the entity flowed instead of blood. Hamade's eyes were solid black and lifeless.

"I see time hasn't improved your taste in company," he commented.

"You mock me, Curizan, but I now have a power that not even you can defeat. You have saved me time by bringing your mate here. By the time I am finished with her, she will wish she had died in the storm," Hamade stated.

Adalard stiffened. "You have defiled the Goddesses' blood for your own greed, Hamade, and you are paying the price. This will not end well for you," he coolly replied.

Hamade's unnatural laugh sent a chill through him. The entity reached out for him and Adalard swiftly lifted his hand, triggering the protective shield of energy that his brother and Samara had developed and Morian Reykill had helped them improve. The wisps of gray matter retreated, but quickly returned. He narrowed his eyes in contemplation when he noticed the wisps were searching the shield.

Hamade's hollow laugh drew his attention back to the man. Reaching down with his free hand, he laid his palm against Samara's leg, and they stepped in unison when Hamade advanced a few steps. Unease rose inside him at the smug expression on the other man's face.

"You have the power of the Goddesses protecting you," Hamade observed as he continued to advance. "But I have the power of a God flowing through me."

Hamade lifted his hands, Adalard wrapped his arm around Samara, twisting them sideways, and dark energy daggers flowed out of Hamade's hands just as they tumbled over the back of the long couch and onto the floor.

"Son of a bit—" Samara muttered.

Adalard lifted his hand, his focus on the massive wooden coffee table. He sent it back in the direction they fell, and rolled to his feet, crouching as Samara did the same. The coffee table exploded, sending a million deadly slivers of wood in all directions. They lifted their hands in unison, creating an energy shield. The fragments of wood harmlessly bounced off the shimmering barrier protecting them.

"Where is the child?" Hamade demanded.

Fury rose inside Adalard. "You'll never touch her," he vowed.

Hamade chuckled. "The great and powerful Curizan prince's love for his offspring. The Empress and our Creator wanted me to bring her back. They knew that such a prize was too much to ignore. I thought they meant to kill her, but their plans are much more complex than I understood," he said, lifting one hand and watching as the mist swirled around it.

Hamade closed his fist, and the mist became a roiling mass of powerful energy that sparked like an intense lightning storm. Currents of red, orange, and yellow flashed through the dark cloud. Adalard could feel the hair on his arms and head lifting with the static electricity building in the air.

"What plans are those?" he growled.

Hamade smiled again, his lips curved in a menacing but satisfied smirk. "To recruit and use her to bring down her own family."

"You will not use our daughter," Samara snapped, stepping out from behind Adalard.

Fear for Adaline surged through Samara. A protective surge of power rose inside of her, and she embraced it. There was only one thing more powerful than fear, and that was love. Gripping Adalard's hand, she connected with him and focused. Their energies combined, creating a brilliant beam of energy as pure as the power of a newborn star. It was born from their love for each other and their need to protect their daughter.

We are more powerful together, she thought as hope built inside her that they could defeat whatever force was standing in front of them.

Hamade snarled and attacked them as the energy surrounding them expanded, threatening to engulf him. He countered by releasing more of the entity. Powerful bands whipped against their combined shield. Samara focused on projecting a wave of white-hot energy outward just like Arrow had shown her in the lab. Pain lanced through her when it connected with the dark energy Hamade was projecting. It almost sent her to her knees.

To add to the chaos, Hamade was using the articles in the room against them. The furniture exploded, creating sharp daggers. The room looked like an angry poltergeist had appeared. She barely managed to duck when the iron shovel and poker from the fireplace set shot through the air like a missile. The forged-iron handles vibrated when they embedded themselves in the wall across from them.

She trembled and gasped when a stabbing pain suddenly radiated through her. An intense agony swamped her senses for a moment before it was gone. Confusion, followed quickly by understanding, cascaded through her when she realized the pain was coming from Adalard. A long spear of the dark matter was protruding from his chest.

Samara realized that when the room exploded, Adalard instinctively began feeding his energy into hers. He was trying to protect her from the onslaught of Hamade's attack. In doing so, he left himself vulnerable for a brief moment, and Hamade had taken advantage of his lowered defenses.

"Adalard!" she cried, losing her own focus.

She wrapped her arm around his waist and held onto him when he slumped forward. Hamade's harsh laughter broke through her panic. The entity was pouring into Adalard's body. If she didn't stop it, he would become a replica of Hamade.

She tried wrapping her hands around it. Blistering pain, as if she had placed her hands on a hot burner, scorched her. She bit her lip to keep from crying out, but then gasped when a thick band wound around her arms, capturing her in its embrace. She clung to Adalard as the band wrapped around her throat and slipped under her skin.

Ice filled her veins as the entity slid through her body. She tried to focus on the lessons Adalard and Arrow had given her, but fear held her in its ugly grasp, and she couldn't think. The dark symbiot's menacing intent was clear—if successful here, it would spread and take over the Royal Houses of the Curizan, Valdier, and Sarafin through their children.

"This is the end. Now, there will be nothing that can hold back the power of the Empress and our Creator. We will finally bring down the houses of the Curizan, Valdier, and Sarafin—and the Goddesses themselves who protect you. Your child will be the first of many," Hamade vowed.

"No!" Samara fervently denied.

Samara, there is a way to stop him, Adalard's soft words whispered through her mind.

A vision of his intentions filled her. If they abandoned their defenses and unleashed their power into Hamade, they could destroy him and the dark symbiot. It was suicide, but it would protect Adaline. A calm acceptance filled her, and she closed her eyes. Grasping his hand, she breathed deeply and released her fear. Instead, she focused on her love for Adalard and their beautiful daughter.

She drew on the memories of the first time she saw Adalard—the colors swirling around him, snow falling and dotting his jet-black hair with crystals of white, and the color of his violet eyes. Tears poured down her cheeks when those eyes changed to Adaline's. She remembered the first time she held their tiny daughter in her arms, and how she felt a sense of longing and peace as Adaline's tiny fingers wrapped around hers.

Power flowed through her, chasing away the cold. Love filled her heart, and she shared it with Adalard. He wrapped his arms around her and their heat grew. The dark energy retreated, but they didn't release it. This time, it was their captive. They surrounded it with the power born of their love. They were willing to make the ultimate sacrifice—give their lives for their daughter.

"Stop!" Hamade hissed.

Samara opened her eyes. Adalard was staring down at her. The love in his eyes took her breath away. For seven years, he had fought alone to keep this evil away from them. She finally understood exactly what those years had cost him. He opened himself to her, revealing the intense loneliness he had endured and how much he had longed to reach out to her. He played a vidcom of her that she hadn't known he had taken so he could see her and hear her voice.

"You'll never be alone again. I promise," she whispered as she gently caressed his cheek.

He turned his head and kissed her fingers. "We will watch over her from the stars," he murmured.

Tears burned her eyes when she saw the acceptance of their deaths in his. Closing her eyes, she wound her arms around his neck and held him as tightly as she could. She parted her lips on a gasp when the energy within and around them swelled and exploded outward with the force of the brightest super nova.

A sense of peace flowed through Adalard. He felt as if he were floating. The mist of the dark symbiot had been replaced with the hues of the universe. Nebulas glimmered among the billions of celestial bodies floating in a sea of black, lit by the brilliant light of newborn stars and reflecting the colorful gases that had formed them.

He looked down when Samara moved. He gently caressed her cheek only to pause when his hand passed through her translucent flesh. Her lips parted with wonder and dismay.

"Is this what it's like to die?" she whispered, gazing up at him with wide, wonder-filled eyes.

"I... don't know," he admitted.

"Adalard...," Samara breathed, her eyes focused over his shoulder.

He turned, his arms still protectively wrapped around her waist, and stared in awe as a golden figure approached them. He knew in that moment, he was in the presence of a power far greater than any he had ever encountered—including the dark symbiot that Hamade had wielded.

"Goddess," he murmured.

The woman smiled at them. "Greetings, warrior. Samara," she replied.

"You know who I am?" Samara squeaked in surprise.

The woman laughed. "Yes, thanks to a very special little girl who loves her mommy and daddy very much."

"Adaline," Adalard murmured.

The woman bowed her head. "She asked me to watch over you."

"What… happened? Is Adaline… is she okay?" Samara asked.

"She and the others are fine. Unfortunately, Hamade… and my brother's creation made a poor choice," the woman explained.

Adalard took a deep breath when the scene around them changed, and he saw the last few seconds of their lives.

"I will control them. You have made them weak," Hamade Dos growled.

Adalard and Samara watched themselves.

They were locked in each other's arms with their eyes closed. The house expanded outward as they absorbed the energy surrounding them, and they glowed with a brilliant white light.

They lifted their hands to shield their eyes.

A golden woman appeared and a shimmering gold protective bubble encased Adalard and Samara.

"You have chosen poorly, Pallas. Aikaterina, I, and the others will fight you," the woman said.

"Aikaterina has grown weak," Pallas retorted from within Hamade, "and you and the others are no match for me, Arilla."

"Feeding on the darkness of others has contaminated you, Pallas. You cannot sustain yourself on the negative energy. The ancients will not tolerate it, and neither will I. The small amount of blood you gave to this creature is no match for the power of love and the willingness to sacrifice for the protection of others. You have failed once again, brother, and you will fail again and again until you are no more," Arilla stated.

"Then I will take this planet with me," Pallas threatened.

The dark symbiot contracted before bursting outward. The first thing to crumble and dissolve was Hamade. The Curizan's horrified scream was frozen on his lips as his body twisted and turned into stardust.

Samara released a small, distressed cry of denial and Adalard tightened his grip around her.

The powerful white energy emitting from the couple swelled and encased the dark energy. Around the glow of white, a thin layer of gold appeared, trapping the expanding energy within the orb. Without anywhere to go, the dark energy struggled to expand and began to feed on itself until nothing of it was left.

"What happened?" Samara asked.

"For now, balance has been restored in the universe," Arilla said.

"But it is not over," Adalard murmured. It was a statement, not a question.

Arilla shook her head. "There will always be a battle between the light and the dark forces."

"What will happen to us?" he asked in a low voice.

Arilla studied them with a playful smile. "I guess you'll have to be superheroes," she teased.

Before he could ask what Arilla meant, the world around them shifted. He opened his eyes, surprised that they had been closed, and looked

THE DARK PRINCE'S PRIZE

around the living room. Samara moved in his arms. He caressed her cheek, marveling at her soft, warm skin under the tips of his fingers. They both rose to their feet and studied the room with awe. Everything looked normal. It was hard to believe that a battle for the planet had ever taken place there.

"Mommy," Adaline called.

"Adaline," Samara cried with delight.

Adaline ran across the living room and threw her arms around Samara's waist. Adalard bent down and picked her up, holding her against him while Samara clung to them both. He looked across the room where Ann Marie, Sara, Bear, and Sara's symbiot stood. His expression softened when he saw the look in Bear's eyes.

"We saw everything on the cameras," Sara explained.

"I made a wish, Mommy. I wished that you and Daddy would be alright," Adaline said.

"I know you did, sweetheart. Thank you so much," Samara murmured, brushing Adaline's hair back and kissing her temple.

"Is it over?" Ann Marie asked.

Adalard smiled at Ann Marie before he looked at Samara. "Yes, it is over—for now," he said.

"Thank goodness for that. Sara, if you can tell Jaguin that it is safe for him and Mason to come home, I'll get some food on. I don't know about you, but all this supernatural stuff has me wanting a stiff drink," Ann Marie said in a gruff tone.

"I'll second that," Bear muttered.

EPILOGUE

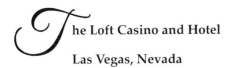

he Loft Casino and Hotel
Las Vegas, Nevada

Al looked up when Jack entered the suite. There had been nothing but silence for the last couple of days, and he had begun to wonder if the man was dead. He raised an eyebrow when his normally calm security chief walked over to the bar, poured himself a drink, downed it, and poured himself another. Jack didn't turn around until he had finished the second round of expensive bourbon.

"From your behavior, I take it the mission did not go as planned," he stated, rising from his seat.

Jack shuddered and stared down at his empty glass before he turned. Al studied Jack's haggard appearance. Jack straightened, walked across the room, and stood in front of him.

"The men are dead," Jack said, his voice devoid of emotion.

Al frowned. "All of them? I thought they were professionals. What happened?"

From behind them, a deep voice announced, "I will tell you what happened: you took a gamble and you lost. You both lost."

Al jerked and turned. He could actually feel the blood drain from his face. He stumbled back several steps. Glancing at Jack, he saw the look of resignation in his bodyguard's eyes.

"You led him here," he accused, pointing a shaking finger at Jack.

Jack released a sharp, bitter laugh and shook his head. "He's a fucking alien. He already knew where you were. He was just taking care of loose ends before he came for you."

"Loose ends? What the hell are you talking about?" he demanded.

"I gave Jack a choice. He could surrender and live the rest of his life on my world or...." Adalard didn't finish his sentence. He just shrugged his shoulders.

Al turned his attention to Jack. "You son-of-a-bitch."

Jack suddenly disappeared and Al staggered back further. Turning frightened and furious eyes back on Adalard, he swallowed.

"What are you going to do to me?" he choked out.

The scar on Adalard's face stood out when he smiled menacingly back at him. "I suggest a game of poker. Winner takes all—and the loser dies."

~

Grove Ranch:

"I guess this is goodbye," Bear said, shifting awkwardly from one foot to the other.

Samara nodded and bowed her head, unable to look into his hurt-filled eyes. "Yes."

"Have you talked to any of your brothers?" he asked.

Samara nodded. "Brit and Gary. Brit is in Canada, hauling logs for a lumber company up there. Gary and Pat are doing okay. They hear from Rob on occasion, but Jerry has dropped out of sight. Gary thinks he's in Arizona or Florida. I finally found an address that might work for Wilson, thanks to Chad. I've sent him a letter."

Bear looked at her in surprise. "Did you tell him about… you know—" he waved his hand in the air.

She laughed and shook her head. "No, I just told him not to worry about me, that I was going away and wouldn't be able to stay in touch much but that if he ever really needed to get in touch with me he could contact Mason or Chad."

Bear grimaced and shoved his hands in his pockets. "Will you keep me posted on how you and Adaline are doing? You know that I'm really going to miss you both, but I also want you to know that I'm really happy for you."

The sincerity in his voice made the tears she was holding overflow. She sniffed loudly and nodded her head. She wiped them away with the back of her hand.

"Jaguin and Adalard installed a new communication system in both the main house and in Mason's office. Hopefully if disaster strikes again like it did with that fire, only one of the systems will be taken down," she said.

"Speaking of aliens—those two big ones aren't planning on staying, are they? They kind of creep me out," he muttered.

Samara laughed and shook her head, looking out the door where Barrack and Brogan, two huge men who were practically mirror images of each other, were laughing with Jaguin and Adalard. Adaline had taken a shine to them as well, especially after one of them—she wasn't sure if it was Barrack or Brogan—put her on his shoulders, turned into a dragon, and acted like an oversized pony.

"Delilah seems happy. I couldn't imagine dealing with two horny Adalards," she mused.

Bear's chuckle made her blush. She hadn't meant to say that out loud. Outside the window, the men suddenly all froze and looked toward the road. Barrack and Brogan disappeared into the woods while Adalard motioned for Adaline. An SUV bearing law enforcement colors was rounding the bend with Annalisa behind the wheel.

"I'll let Mason know that Annalisa is here," Bear muttered.

She nodded. Shoving her hands into the pockets of her jacket, she descended the steps off the porch and crossed over to Adalard. Thanks to Jaguin and the twin dragons, the entire area was clear of snow and ice. It might be a little difficult to explain, especially after the thick snowfall less than a week before.

She waited as Annalisa parked the SUV and climbed out. From the direction of the house the sound of the front door opening and closing carried, informing her that Mason and Bear were coming out as well. She forced a smile when Annalisa raised her eyebrow at Adalard holding Adaline. There was no way the detective could miss the resemblance between the two.

"Hi Samara. Hi Bear, Mason," Annalisa greeted.

Samara kept the smile on her lips. "Hey, Annalisa. How are things in town?" she asked.

Annalisa shrugged. "Same ol', same ol'. A few crazy out-of-towners thinking it would be fun to party in a blizzard," she dryly replied with a sigh before turning her attention to Adalard. "I don't think we've ever met. I'm Annalisa Hollins."

Samara bit her lip when Annalisa held out her hand. Adalard grasped Annalisa's hand and shook it. There was a moment of silence as they assessed each other before Mason broke the tension.

"What brings you out here, Annalisa? The roads are still pretty bad to be coming all this way," Mason observed.

Annalisa glanced around before she sighed. "I need to ask you a favor, Mason. Is there someplace where we can talk?"

Mason looked surprised and nodded. "Of course, come on in the house."

Annalisa looked back at her vehicle and lifted her hand. The small group watched as the back-passenger door opened and a woman slid out. Jaguin's low curse surprised her.

"Do you know her?" Samara asked.

The woman's eyes were locked on Jaguin. Annalisa looked back and forth between Jaguin and the woman with a frown.

The woman stopped in front of them. "You are El Dragon. You rescued two women many years ago. I… I need your help," she said.

"What women did you save and where?" Annalisa demanded in a suspicious tone.

Ceran-Pax:

Samara lost track of how much time had passed. The last few months had been filled with one adventure—and surprise—after another. Sitting back in the chair under the shade tree, she sipped the cool drink Adalard had brought her, and laid her hand on her stomach.

What is wrong? Adalard asked.

I think I felt a flutter, she replied.

Already? Do you need me? he asked.

No, Adaline and I are enjoying visiting with your mom and Alice. Don't you and Arrow have something to blow up? she inquired with amusement.

Adalard grunted. *He had something else to do.*

Maybe I can ask your mom to keep an eye on Adaline, and I can come help you, she suggested.

"I already asked and she said yes," he murmured as he placed a kiss on her lips.

Samara started with surprise and looked up at him, laughing. She grasped his hand, chuckling and wrapping her arms around his neck.

"How are things going?" she asked.

He sighed. "We have a lead on another possible base from the informant within the rebel group. Arrow is going to meet him."

She frowned, leaned back, and stared up at him. "Arrow? I thought you normally handled things like that."

"My face is a bit too well known for the mission," he replied ruefully.

She lifted an eyebrow. "Uh, Arrow is your identical twin. You think his face isn't recognizable?" she retorted.

"He assures me that not even I would recognize him once he is done," he said.

"You still plan on going, though, don't you?" she murmured.

He shook his head. "No, not this time. My place is here. After the attack on you and Adaline, Ha'ven, Melek, Arrow, and I decided it would be best that I remain here to help protect our family. There are others who can do the field work."

"I thought no one could do that but you," she said with a suspicious look.

She studied the calm expression on his face as he looked out over the garden to where Adaline was playing with Alice. He shifted his focus to meet her gaze and smiled.

"Not anymore. I have something much more precious here that needs my full attention," he said.

She threaded her fingers through his hair and leaned into him. "Yes, yes, you do," she agreed before capturing his lips.

More stories to come....

ADDITIONAL BOOKS

If you loved this story by me (S.E. Smith) please leave a review! You can discover additional books at: http://sesmithfl.com and http://sesmithya.com or find your favorite way to keep in touch here: https://sesmithfl.com/contact-me/ Be sure to sign up for my newsletter to hear about new releases!

Recommended Reading Order Lists:

http://sesmithfl.com/reading-list-by-events/

http://sesmithfl.com/reading-list-by-series/

The Series

Science Fiction / Romance

Dragon Lords of Valdier Series

It all started with a king who crashed on Earth, desperately hurt. He inadvertently discovered a species that would save his own.

Curizan Warrior Series

The Curizans have a secret, kept even from their closest allies, but even they are not immune to the draw of a little known species from an isolated planet called Earth.

Marastin Dow Warriors Series

The Marastin Dow are reviled and feared for their ruthlessness, but not all want to live a life of murder. Some wait for just the right time to escape....

Sarafin Warriors Series

A hilariously ridiculous human family who happen to be quite formidable... and a secret hidden on Earth. The origin of the Sarafin species is more than it seems. Those cat-shifting aliens won't know what hit them!

Dragonlings of Valdier Novellas

The Valdier, Sarafin, and Curizan Lords had children who just cannot stop getting into trouble! There is nothing as cute or funny as magical, shapeshifting kids, and nothing as heartwarming as family.

Cosmos' Gateway Series

Cosmos created a portal between his lab and the warriors of Prime. Discover new worlds, new species, and outrageous adventures as secrets are unravelled and bridges are crossed.

The Alliance Series

When Earth received its first visitors from space, the planet was thrown into a panicked chaos. The Trivators came to bring Earth into the Alliance of Star Systems, but now they must take control to prevent the humans from destroying themselves. No one was prepared for how the humans will affect the Trivators, though, starting with a family of three sisters....

Lords of Kassis Series

It began with a random abduction and a stowaway, and yet, somehow, the Kassisans knew the humans were coming long before now. The fate of more than one world hangs in the balance, and time is not always linear....

Zion Warriors Series

Time travel, epic heroics, and love beyond measure. Sci-fi adventures with heart and soul, laughter, and awe-inspiring discovery...

Paranormal / Fantasy / Romance

Magic, New Mexico Series

Within New Mexico is a small town named Magic, an... unusual town, to say the least. With no beginning and no end, spanning genres, authors, and universes, hilarity and drama combine to keep you on the edge of your seat!

Spirit Pass Series

There is a physical connection between two times. Follow the stories of those who travel back and forth. These westerns are as wild as they come!

Second Chance Series

Stand-alone worlds featuring a woman who remembers her own death. Fiery and mysterious, these books will steal your heart.

More Than Human Series

Long ago there was a war on Earth between shifters and humans. Humans lost, and today they know they will become extinct if something is not done....

The Fairy Tale Series

A twist on your favorite fairy tales!

A Seven Kingdoms Tale

Long ago, a strange entity came to the Seven Kingdoms to conquer and feed on their life force. It found a host, and she battled it within her body for centuries while destruction and devastation surrounded her. Our story begins when the end is near, and a portal is opened....

Epic Science Fiction / Action Adventure

Project Gliese 581G Series

An international team leave Earth to investigate a mysterious object in our solar system that was clearly made by someone, someone who isn't from Earth. Discover new worlds and conflicts in a sci-fi adventure sure to become your favorite!

New Adult / Young Adult

Breaking Free Series

A journey that will challenge everything she has ever believed about herself as danger reveals itself in sudden, heart-stopping moments.

The Dust Series

Fragments of a comet hit Earth, and Dust wakes to discover the world as he knew it is gone. It isn't the only thing that has changed, though, so has Dust...

ABOUT THE AUTHOR

S.E. Smith is an *internationally acclaimed, New York Times* **and** **USA** *TODAY Bestselling* author of science fiction, romance, fantasy, paranormal, and contemporary works for adults, young adults, and children. She enjoys writing a wide variety of genres that pull her readers into worlds that take them away.